DISGUISED for LOVE
THE STRICKLAND SISTERS

J. B. LIFFLANDER

Disguised for Love – The Strickland Sisters
Copyright © 2011 J.B. Lifflander
Published by AsGold Media
Ridgefield, Washington 98642
www.asgoldmedia.com
Artwork by Duncan Long

ISBN 978-0-9711339-6-9
LCCN 2011945138

Printed in the United States of America

1

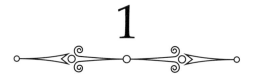

Alice Jamison rang the doorbell of the Strickland mansion over and over again, but no one answered. Crying, she began pounding on the door so hard that she hurt her knuckles and they began to bleed. She was dressed in a long chartreuse and white print dress, which had gotten soiled from the long run she had taken from her parents' house to the Stricklands'. She was tall and willowy with soft brown hair, green eyes, and a delicate, pretty face. But now that face was contorted and her eyes were bloodshot from crying as she sank down at the front door, sobbing. "They probably aren't home," she said to herself in frustration. But just as she finished speaking, the front door opened, and Mr. Standish, the Stricklands' butler, an Englishman of about fifty with snow white hair, looked down on her with curiosity. Suddenly she felt very embarrassed and even disgusted with herself as she realized what she must look like to him—a momentary picture of herself flashed through her mind as she noticed how impeccably he was dressed in his well-tailored butler's suit.

"May I help you, Mrs. Jamison?" he inquired, smiling professionally, but with warmth, and acting so much as if he had not noticed her unusual circumstances that it made her wonder if perhaps he had not. With his eyes stayed on hers rather than on her clothing, nothing in his gaze betrayed the fact that she was crumpled on the doorstep, her soft brown hair in disarray and sticking to her face because of the tears. Trying to compose herself, she wiped her tears away and pushed her hair back as she slowly stood up. He reached out and offered his hand, and she took it as she arose.

"You are ever the gentleman, sir," she said as she steadied herself. "Are any of the sisters home?"

"Yes, madam, they are all home. May I announce your presence?"

"Yes, please," she answered, as Esther Strickland entered the foyer and noticed her at the door. Mr. Standish moved out of the way to let Esther walk out to her friend. The oldest of the Strickland sisters at twenty-six years of age, she was also the tallest, at about five foot seven inches in height. She had dark brown hair, brown eyes, and her face was attractive and strikingly elegant. It was not that Esther was exceptionally pretty, but her face was distinguished, almost regal, as if she were born cast for the part of being the elder sister of one of the wealthiest families on the East Coast. Her posture added to her prominent features—she walked very uprightly, with an air of self confidence but not haughtiness. Of all the Strickland sisters, she had been the closest to Alice, as they were only one year apart in age. Alice lived close by in the same exclusive Larchmont neighborhood and had met Esther when they were children—their mothers had also been friends for many years. And when Esther's mother died, seven years ago, Alice's mother had helped Mr. Strickland and the girls work through their grief.

Since the two friends had shared their most intimate secrets as they grew up together, Esther knew how particular Alice was about her appearance. She was normally quite well coiffed and always dressed in clean and pressed clothing. This made her wonder all the more what could have happened to make Alice come over unannounced and looking as she did. Alice had recently married and was living several miles away, so she must have walked from her parents' house, Esther thought. Something devastating must have happened, and Esther wondered if Alice's mother might be sick.

"Alice, is Mrs. Sherrill well?" she asked.

"Yes...yes. Mother is quite well," Alice said as she walked through the door, wobbling a little. "I'll tell you what happened in a minute. Can I sit down for a moment?"

"Of course." Esther guided her friend to the largest couch in the living room—a tufted emerald green sofa that stood out for its finely carved wooden legs and trim. The exquisite carvings were of angels, and Alice remembered how Mrs. Strickland, when she was alive, had told them it was made in Italy in the 1700s. Mr. Standish helped Alice to her seat, and she sat, her fingers outlining the carving of an angel as she looked around the large, sumptuous room, which was graced with a beautiful painting by Claude Monet that hung across from her on the west wall. The room made her feel secure and stable—it was just like the Strickland family, she thought, and it brought back memories of better days. She hadn't appreciated it when she was younger, but now as she looked at the beautiful imported furniture, some of it antique and some modern, and how it blended together so nicely, she realized how much it was a testimony to the taste and talent of Mrs. Strickland.

Remembering how sad the family had been when Mrs. Strickland had died of cancer, Alice was happy to have a reprieve for her thoughts, but then her present situation weighed heavily on her again as Mr. Standish stood over her, waiting for a request. Esther looked over at him, which he instantly took as a cue to leave, and he disappeared in the direction of the kitchen. Esther took Alice's hand and held it, and as they sat silently together, Esther's two sisters walked into the room, a little surprised to see Alice, and at first not realizing that she was upset.

"Did he finally give the little woman a day off?" Priscilla asked jokingly, but there was no answer. And as she and the youngest and prettiest sister, Anna, got closer, and sensed Alice's distress, they stopped for a moment, their faces sobering. Priscilla then walked over to the couch and took Alice's other hand. "Oh, excuse me for my impertinence. Whatever is the trouble, Alice? What has happened?"

Alice looked up at her and forced a smile. "Oh, Prissy, I know you were joking, don't worry about it."

"Priscilla, would you mind asking Mr. Standish or one of the others to make some coffee? Would you like some coffee, Alice? Or some tea?" Esther said.

"Tea would be nice," Alice answered, haltingly.

"But I don't want the help in here right now—just have them make it and we'll serve ourselves," Esther said.

"Yes, of course," Priscilla said, used to taking orders from her older sister and not resenting them. At one time she had resented Esther for telling her what to do after their mother died, but now she realized how much Esther had gone through for her younger sisters by taking on so many responsibilities that would normally have been beyond her age, and she admired her for it. She walked back to the kitchen, then reappeared quickly, not wanting to miss the reason for Alice's unexpected visit. She had never seen Alice looking the way she did today.

Anna was still standing when Priscilla came back, and Alice was gently crying. "It's my marriage—it's terrible," Alice said. "After two years of marriage it's falling apart."

3

"If you've just had an argument…" Esther began, but Alice spoke again, interrupting her.

"I wish that's all it was," she said, trying to catch her breath which had escaped her from the crying. "He doesn't love me."

"Of course he loves you. He courted you for years before you married, and he was always the perfect gentleman. That doesn't change overnight," Esther said.

"No, he doesn't love me," Alice said, this time with a rising voice tinged with anger. "It was all a charade, all an act to marry me for my money—for my family's money, anyway."

"But Roger is from a rich family himself. He doesn't need your money," Priscilla said.

Alice cried a little more and closed her eyes, opening them slowly. "His family used to be rich. They lost most of their money in the 1929 crash, but they kept up the facade for as long as possible. They will lose their mansion soon, and then everyone will know."

"But you are an attractive girl and a sweet person. Just because he lost his money doesn't mean he doesn't love you. You shouldn't jump to that conclusion," Esther said, squeezing her hand.

Alice looked up at her, and then at the other two sisters. "You are my best friends in the world, but I shouldn't have just barged in here. It wasn't proper, and I have to leave now—I've said too much already." She began to stand up.

"It is very proper," Priscilla said. "That's what friends are for, and I know you'd welcome us if we needed your help. Now please don't leave. Tell us the whole story. You are too upset to go now—you need to tell us."

"No, I'm really not that upset," Alice said slowly, trying to smile. But then her face became even sadder, and she started crying uncontrollably. Esther moved closer and hugged her until she settled down, and Anna gave her a large handkerchief to dry her eyes.

"We had an argument—we've had several since we married. But in the last one he told me that he couldn't stand me and he only married me for my money."

"People say lots of mean things when they are angry. I don't think he meant it," Esther said, stroking her hair.

"I appreciate…the sentiment," Alice said, choking back her tears. "But if you had heard the way he said it…"

Esther shook her head, not knowing what to say. Everyone was quiet for a moment, and then Priscilla walked over to her.

"Can you get a divorce?" she asked.

"No, never, it would be a scandal. I would never bring that kind of shame on the family. Besides, I made a vow and I will keep it—richer or poorer, loved or unloved, we are joined in holy matrimony."

Esther gave Priscilla a look showing that she disapproved of her asking such a question.

"Are you staying with your family now?" Anna asked.

"Yes. I walked from there. The grass was wet with dew, and I fear I've ruined my dress…my dress…what does it matter?"

"Did you tell your mother?" Esther asked.

"Yes, and she thought I was making something out of nothing. She said I should just be the best wife I can be and make the best of it. But her generation was different—I can't just pretend…" she trailed off crying again.

"I still don't think he meant it. He was just trying to hurt you because you were arguing. I've said things I didn't mean before."

They were interrupted by a knock on the door that led into the kitchen area. Priscilla walked briskly to the door, opened it, took the tray from the main cook, Betsy, and set it down on a large rosewood table near the sofa, then moved the teacups over to the coffee table in front of it.

"You must stay tonight," Esther said.

"No, I couldn't—I would have to go home for a change of clothes and a nightgown, and I don't want to see Mother right now. She doesn't seem to understand why I'm so upset—it just doesn't register with her."

"Nonsense, you can choose from any of our extra nightgowns, and there are scores of dresses that will fit you. And I'll call her for you. I've missed you ever since you moved away and this is a chance for us to chat, and Father adores you and will be so glad to see you when he comes home for dinner," Esther said, and she walked towards the telephone.

"No, Esther. I'd be imposing, and I'm not good company right now," Alice protested.

Esther ignored her and picked up the telephone.

"Okay, but don't tell your father or your brother—it's too embarrassing."

"Of course I won't. Anyway, Paul is on a dig in the Middle East. He won't be home for a few weeks," Esther said as she began dialing. "Hello, Mrs. Sherrill?" she said into the phone. "This is Esther Strickland. I just wanted you to know that Alice is here and she'll be spending the night…. Yes, everything is fine…. Yes, Father is in good health. Yes… good-bye."

Esther walked back to the couch and sat down next to Alice. "It will be just like when we used to spend the night when we were little girls," she said, smiling.

"Does that mean pillow fights?" Anna asked, also with a smile, but it faded as she watched Alice's face grow somber again.

"You know I must admit I sort of liked being envied by the other girls because we are rich. But now I think it's more of a curse than a blessing."

"Why would you say that, Alice?" Priscilla asked.

"Because you never know if a man likes you for yourself or for your money. There's always that niggling question in the back of your mind: is it me, or is it the money? If he'd met me at a department store where I was a clerk, would he still have been interested? If my family had just lost all their money, would he still have wanted to marry me, or would he have looked for a rich girl?"

"Oh, Alice, it's not a curse. Look at the things our families have. How many girls go to college, and how many travel abroad and get to live in a home like this? I love living at Eagle's Rest," Esther said, using the name for the Strickland Estate. "How many people have a tennis court, and a swimming pool and horses and stables?"

"At what cost? My father was always working late or out of town visiting one of the factories, and when he got home he was grumpy and had no time for us…. Okay, I'll quit complaining. Anyway, yours isn't like that, is he?"

"No, he always made certain he was home for dinner and spent time with us unless something really urgent happened," Esther said and she looked at the clock. "In fact, he'll be here soon, so why don't we find you a clean dress. Priscilla, would you tell Betsy we have a guest for dinner?"

Upstairs they led Alice to Esther's closet first, and she began looking at the dresses. Alice smiled a real smile for the first time since she had entered the house as she looked at the variety of dresses. "Oh, I think you have as many dresses as Bloomingdale's. Have you been to their new store yet on Lexington Avenue?" She held up one dress after another against herself before a large dressing mirror trimmed with cherry wood on a stand next to the closet.

"No, I haven't, but Prissy's been there, haven't you, Prissy?" Esther said, pleased that Alice was getting her mind off her marriage.

"It's incredible—it takes up a whole block, and it's eleven stories!" Priscilla said.

Alice held up a few more dresses and then looked at the sisters and smiled again. "Okay, I'll take them all," she said, laughing now as if she were her old self. As she finished speaking, Mr. Standish stood at the hallway near the open door to Esther's room.

"Dinner will be served in twenty minutes," he said.

"Is Father home?" Esther asked.

"Yes, he's downstairs. He just walked in, and Mrs. Ingersoll is with him."

The sisters exchanged glances, and as they looked back at Mr. Standish, Esther thought his face betrayed his misgivings about this woman who was pursuing their father.

"Well, there goes what might have been a pleasant dinner," Priscilla said. Esther frowned disapprovingly, and hoped that Alice had not heard, but she had, and from her expression, Esther knew her friend wanted to ask what the comment meant but was too polite to pursue it. Esther decided to tell her.

"Mrs. Ingersoll is a very wealthy widow who has developed a keen interest in charities ever since she met Father."

"Oh, she's one of those Ingersolls," Alice said, referring to the fact that the family name was known. "Well, your father has always been generous with charitable giving."

"Yes, and now Mrs. Ingersoll cannot seem to do without his advice on where to give," Anna interjected. "And she's very pretty—especially for being maybe thirty-eight or forty years old."

"I'm afraid that Father likes the attention he's getting from her—she is quite a bit younger than him. But I doubt he really thinks she's after him. As sharp as he is in dealing with most people, he seems kind of naïve about her," Priscilla said.

"Are you sure she's after him?" Alice asked.

"We're all sure. Believe me, we're sure," Priscilla said.

"But if she's rich and attractive, what's the problem?"

"You'll find out when you meet her, I think. We'd better get a move on." Esther turned toward the hallway. "Come down when you've changed, and we'll introduce you."

2

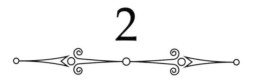

From the time they were children, the Strickland girls had always greeted their father when he came home, and they went downstairs to do so now while Alice changed clothes and fixed her hair. Joseph J. Strickland III was fifty-three years old, about five foot eight inches tall, and had gray and white hair that gave him a distinguished appearance. He exercised regularly swimming and playing tennis, which kept him looking healthy and fit, in spite of the many hours he spent working. His presence in any room was instantly noticed, for he had a subtle charisma that was almost like an aura about him.

Unlike many of the industrial barons of his time who always seemed restless and needed the next business deal to feel complete, he normally had a steady peace about him, an inner strength that had a calming effect on people. However, those who had interpreted his peace as a weakness and attempted to exploit it soon saw another side of Mr. Strickland, for he was not a man to trifle with, and his pleasant demeanor could change remarkably when he was angered. Disloyalty would earn his wrath, and if a man tried to deceive him in a business transaction, he would become a tenacious foe, for he dealt with any dishonesty quickly and often harshly. This was a fact that those who knew him, and especially employees, were careful to keep in mind. His children learned this early on—because punishment had been swift and severe when they were caught lying or cheating.

The girls walked down together into the large living room. Their father was not in the room yet, and Mrs. Ingersoll was sitting down, dressed in what bordered on formal evening attire—a beautiful candy-apple red satin dress with sequins that was tight enough to show off her voluptuous figure. An exquisite ruby and diamond necklace graced her neck, and her matching shoes were ruby red with two-inch heels. Her long auburn hair had been carefully twirled and pinned up with several sparkling diamond clasps, and her makeup was perfect, if a little overdone. Her attire was probably inappropriate for someone visiting just for dinner, but no one could deny that she stood out as a strikingly beautiful woman—especially for one in her early forties. Mr. Standish was standing next to her, and he was listening to her as they entered the room.

"Now please be careful, because if my fur is pressed upon by other clothing, it leaves an indentation. So can you hang it by itself? Preferably in a room with air circulating and not in a small closet?" Mrs. Ingersoll's tone was what one might use when instructing a child.

"Of course, madam," the butler said, taking the fur stole from her and hanging it over his arm. He turned to walk away, but she raised her voice as he began to move.

"Oh, no, that won't do at all—you must not let it lie on your arm. It must be held from the top, as if on a hanger. The fur should not touch your arm."

"Why is she even wearing a fur in the summer?" Anna asked in a low tone.

"Because she's got to show it off—that and the family jewels. Just to discuss a benefit! I'd say she's dressed to kill," Priscilla said. Esther turned to both of them with a cross look, concerned that they might be overheard. Suddenly Mrs. Ingersoll's attention was turned to the girls, and she smiled at them. Alice had since walked down the stairs and was a few feet behind them.

"Hello, girls, it's so good to see you again. And who is this with you?" she asked, looking at Alice. As she did, the girls looked back at Alice and then back to Mrs. Ingersoll.

"This is Alice Jamison," Esther said.

"Are you George Jamison's daughter-in-law?"

"Yes, I am," Alice answered politely.

"Well, then, it is very good to make your acquaintance," Mrs. Ingersoll said, as Mr. Strickland walked back into the room. When he saw Alice, he smiled warmly.

"Alice! What a pleasure it is to see you again. It seems like it's been such a long time. You used to visit regularly before you married, and we miss you," he said kindly.

"And I miss all of you."

Mr. Strickland, who was looking into the girl's eyes, noticed a small grimace. "Is everything well with your family, Alice? Mrs. Sher-

10

rill has not visited for a long time."

"Yes, sir, everything is fine. Mother is in good health," Alice said unconvincingly.

"Well if I can be of assistance in any way…"

He was interrupted by Mrs. Ingersoll, who seemed bothered that she was not the object of his attention. "Shall we go over the plans for the charity gala now, Joseph?"

He turned towards her, slightly disconcerted by the interruption but not wanting to offend her. At that moment, Mr. Standish announced that dinner would be served in five minutes.

"Let's discuss it after dinner, Betty. I take it you've been introduced to Mrs. Jamison already?" he asked.

"Oh, yes—my pleasure. She and all your daughters look so beautiful." Mrs. Ingersoll took his arm, indicating her readiness to walk into the dining room.

The long, teakwood dinner table with inlays of other fine woods and a strip of gold which encircled it in an oblong shape, could seat twenty people, but it was set for six that evening, and everyone sat at one end of the table, with Mr. Strickland sitting at the head of the table. Alice noticed that the dining chairs, which were upholstered in a rich crimson-colored satin, appeared to have a slightly deeper color than the last time she had visited, so she knew they had been recently redone. She looked at the ornate engraving on the legs and arms, which was filled with gold paint, and remembered how Mrs. Strickland had given the girls a history lesson on the table and chairs when they were in elementary school. She normally did not like history, but the way Mrs. Strickland described the historic period in France, it made her appreciate the subject and changed her attitude about it in school.

How thoughtful and caring Mrs. Strickland was, she thought. Her wealth had not gone to her head, and she never put on airs—she was always down to earth, and yet sophisticated. How unlike Mrs. Strickland was the woman now sitting across from her, who she noticed was staring at Mr. Strickland at that very moment, trying to keep his attention—and giving the impression that she did not want to share him with anyone else. Suddenly, almost as if she might have discerned Alice's thoughts, Mrs. Ingersoll turned and looked at her curiously, then she smiled in a way that seemed superficial to Alice.

"Alice, I remember reading in the society page about your wedding several years ago. It sounds like it was a wonderful affair, and, knowing who you married, I think you made a very wise choice. That's a wonderful family you married into—my congratulations."

Esther looked over at Alice sheepishly, and Alice held down her head for a moment, but when she raised it she was smiling. "Thank you so much, Mrs. Ingersoll," she said, and Esther let out a slight sigh of relief.

"Joseph, did you get a chance to look at that list of charities I had sent over last week?" Mrs. Ingersoll asked, but Mr. Strickland looked as if he were taken by surprise at the question.

"Last week…" he said, trying to remember.

"Father, we did receive the list," Priscilla said. "You gave it to me, and I researched some of them, but I haven't finished."

"Oh, very good, dear. Then you must join us after dinner and advise us."

"You gave the list to Priscilla?" Mrs. Ingersoll asked, with surprise in her voice.

"Oh, yes—she is my business gal—can't do much without her. She knows everything about the business, and her advice is always excellent. Last year she went over the books for the steel mill in Pennsylvania and found errors that no one else had caught. She even helped the engineers redesign the flow of materiel in the Syracuse plant, which increased efficiency and saved me thousands."

"My, you have unheard of talents for a woman," Mrs. Ingersoll said, with a tone that seemed subtly envious to Priscilla. She then turned to Joseph again. "I would have thought that your son would be the one to…"

"Take over the business? Yes, he could do it, and he would if I asked, he's got the ability, but his heart would not be in it. He loves archeology—he's getting his doctorate, you know. And he's made some incredible discoveries excavating ancient cities in what used to be Mesopotamia. It's very exciting work."

"So, are all the girls interested in business as you are, Priscilla? What about you, Esther?" Mrs. Ingersoll asked. "Joseph tells me that you are engaged to a Holt—you girls can't miss with all these old-money families."

"Well, we are not actually engaged yet," Esther said.

"And what are you waiting for? Hasn't it been several years?" Mrs. Ingersoll asked.

"Well, first of all, he has not asked me, and I'm also continuing my education. I've gone back to college to get my master's degree."

"Your master's degree! My, how accomplished your children are, Joseph."

"Yes, Esther is majoring in English. She'd like to be a writer, I think. She's written some advertising copy for me that is quite good," Joseph said.

"So, you are a businesswoman also?" Mrs. Ingersoll said, with a bit of irony in her voice.

"No, I just like to write. I'm not involved in the business," Esther said.

"Well, advertising is part of it—it's very important," Mr. Strickland added.

As he finished speaking, the cook and her assistant came in and began serving the main course. Then Mr. Standish entered and walked towards Mr. Strickland but said nothing for a moment. "What is it, Standish?" Mr. Strickland asked, a little irritated to be interrupted.

"A phone call for you, sir."

"You know I don't take them after six, and especially not during dinner."

"Yes, and I would not have interrupted you, but Mr. Calvin insisted. He says there has been a fire in Albany."

"A fire? Well, I must be excused then," he said, looking at Mrs. Ingersoll. "I'll take the call in my study, Standish."

After he left the room, Mrs. Ingersoll looked over at Esther, and Esther looked back, waiting for her to speak, but she hesitated, as if considering whether or not she should.

"Would you be open to advice from me?" she asked.

"Well, of course. What might it be?"

"You are still young, but not that young, and you have a man from a fine family who is interested. But all this education could put him off. That may be why he hasn't proposed yet. Most women don't go to college, and a man wants to feel that he is the one who is wise and worldly. You may lose your catch if you're not careful. There are many young women who would like to snare a man like that."

"Well, anytime my catch wants to swim away, or if he gets snared by a younger, uneducated woman, that's fine with me. I'll just wile away the hours as an old spinster with…" Esther stopped speaking for a moment as the family cat ran in and jumped on her lap, and purred, hoping for some food from the table. Esther gave her a tidbit as she continued, "…with my cats as companions." One of the cooks ran in after the cat and took it off her lap, apologizing for letting the cat in.

Anna and Alice both started laughing, and Mrs. Ingersoll pursed her lips in displeasure. "I was only trying to help."

"Yes, I understand, and I thank you for your concern," Esther said, and then Mr. Strickland walked back into the dining room, and sat down.

"Was it serious?" Priscilla asked.

"No. There was a fire, but it was put out, and one machine is down because of it, but we have a spare. The line should be running again by tomorrow afternoon. Calvin knew we had the spare, but he wasn't sure it was functional, and he wanted to check with me. It really could have waited until tomorrow, and I think the chief engineer could have told him, but he wasn't there, and you know how nervous Mr. Calvin can get."

"Yes, I do. When I visited that plant, he seemed to be scared to death of me. At first I thought he was hiding something because of the way he was acting," Priscilla said.

"Yes, he's always been that way, but he's an excellent manager," Mr. Strickland added.

"Oh, Joseph, I simply don't know how you keep track of all these different factories, making these different products. However can you ever remember all the details?" Mrs. Ingersoll asked in a gushing tone.

"Well, Betty, it's not so hard. Normally our managers don't need me at all. This was an exception. But it's easier with Priscilla helping. Now that she's graduated I have her full time."

"Yes, that's very nice," Mrs. Ingersoll said, but it was obvious to the girls that she was not pleased that her remark resulted in a compliment for Priscilla.

After they were finished eating, Joseph looked over at Priscilla. "We will be in the study in about five minutes. I don't need you very long, because I know all of you want to spend time with Alice."

The girls began to move towards the stairs, as Joseph and Betty walked towards the study. Betty took his arm, but after a few steps she stumbled, and Joseph reached out and took her other arm to keep her from falling. She grabbed his shoulder and her body moved against his as she caught her balance. The girls turned and watched as she slowly disengaged herself from Joseph. "Oh, that was close—thank you so much," she said, smiling at Joseph, but also hesitating as she held both of his arms for a moment. "You are so strong!" she added.

"Are you okay?" Joseph asked with a sincere tone.

"Oh, yes, I am now. Just a little embarrassed for being clumsy."

"Think nothing of it," he said, and the girls turned again to go upstairs. When they got to Esther's room, they burst out laughing.

"You are so strong!" Priscilla said, barely able to get the words out because of her laughter, but mimicking Mrs. Ingersoll's voice with uncanny accuracy.

"I guess she knows how to snare her man," Alice said.

"Doesn't Father see what she's doing?" Anna asked.

"He seems to be blind to it, somehow," Esther said in a quiet voice. "He's so perceptive with most things, but there is something about this woman."

"Yeah, there's something about her, and I don't think he's too blind to see—she's beautiful," Priscilla said.

"So you think she really likes Father? I mean she must be twelve to fifteen years younger than him," Anna said.

"Well, Father looks good for his age, but the fact that he's fifteen hundred times richer than her might be part of the attraction," Priscilla added.

"What do you think, Alice? You're more objective than us."

"I think she's a snob who wants to marry the richest man she can find. But don't get me wrong, your father is quite attractive for his age, and he's a perfect gentleman—he makes a woman feel so at ease. I think many younger women would be attracted to him, and he doesn't need this society climber."

"You took the words out of my mouth. But can he see it?" Esther asked.

"I don't think he even realizes she's after him," Priscilla said. "Maybe I should mention it."

"I think that would be a big mistake," Esther said. "Let's see if it goes anywhere. She can only invite herself over so often to talk about charities."

"Well, you're probably right about not telling him, but I think this hussy will find a dozen ways to waylay Father if she puts her mind to it. I just hope he has enough discernment to see what she's really like," Priscilla said. Then, mimicking her again, she added, "Oh, Joseph, I simply don't know how you keep track of all the factories, you are so strong, handsome, clever, and by the way, I never noticed before—wonderfully rich! And now I'm so clumsy that I just happened to fall into your arms. Are you snared yet, you guppie!" The girls began

15

laughing again, and then Priscilla composed herself and walked out of the room to join her father and Mrs. Ingersoll. When she got there, she was still amused and had to restrain herself from giggling.

3

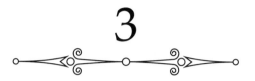

Later, Alice and Esther were alone in Esther's room, and Esther was brushing Alice's long hair. Alice looked at the pale teal-colored velvet curtains that hung from the long floor-to-ceiling windows, and then she looked down at the matching sofa where she was sitting, remembering how Esther had helped decorate the room with her mother when they were teenagers. The large canopy bed was an antique, and she remembered how they had played on it one night until one of the legs broke, almost bringing the canopy down on top of them. Esther's mother scolded them that night, but by morning all was forgotten, and after breakfast they swam in the large swimming pool, then rode in Mr. Strickland's new car, an open-topped Duesenberg touring car. When Mr. Strickland accelerated, they giggled as it threw both of their heads back against the rear seat. She had never ridden in a car with so much power and speed, and although it frightened her at first, it was a thrilling ride, and she always remembered it. Thinking about it, she smiled now, and Esther noticed.

"What is it? Something good, I think?" Esther asked.

"The first ride in the Duesenberg—I'll never forget it."

"Nor will I—I was so scared that I had to go to the bathroom, but I was afraid to ask Father."

"But I loved it after we got going. There were no speed limits in the county then," Alice said. "Does your father still like fast cars?"

"Yes, I'm afraid that is one of his weaknesses. But that was a Duesy A, now he has a J, and it's so fast it scares me now."

Suddenly Alice's mood changed again, and her eyes welled with tears. "Do you think my life will just be miserable from now on?" she asked.

"Of course not. You need to give this time. I've been thinking

17

about this. Roger certainly had other women he could have married, and he chose you, so it couldn't have been just for your money. He was probably angry and frustrated and he lashed out at you—but you shouldn't jump to conclusions," Esther said soothingly.

"You truly are a dear friend. I don't know what I'd do without you," Alice said and she hugged her. "But after this has happened to me, doesn't it make you wonder about what any man's motives are towards you?"

Esther had finished with the brushing, and Alice turned towards her as she spoke. "Of course I have, in general. But I'm not concerned about David, if that is what you're thinking. I know him well enough to know that he would never marry any woman for her money—he's a very genuine person."

Alice nodded in agreement as Esther walked to her dresser to put her brush away. As she moved, some doubt about David suddenly interrupted her thoughts. She had never questioned his motives, and she knew that his family was well off, but would he have considered marrying her if she had not been a Strickland, she wondered for the first time. She knew many wealthy parents wanted their children to marry what they called "equals," which really meant those with similar financial dispositions. Then another thought crossed her mind— would she have been interested in David if he were not wealthy? Was she being a hypocrite with these thoughts about his motives? For a moment she imagined him without his wealth, and she knew that it was him she cared about. For richer or poorer, she thought, as Alice walked up to her. She was sure it would not matter if he were poorer.

"Esther—are you going to hold that brush all night?" Alice asked, smiling at her. Esther looked at the brush in her hand and realized that she had been standing at the dresser for a long time. She put the brush in the drawer and she sat down.

"Your situation has made me do some deep thinking," Esther said as she sat down on the sofa next to Alice. Alice looked at her curiously, in anticipation of what she would say next, when suddenly Priscilla and Anna burst in the room. As they did, Esther and Alice both gave them a startled look.

"Oh, I'm sorry—we should have knocked first," Priscilla said, and Esther nodded in agreement. "Well, should we leave and come back later?" she added, a little irritated at her sister's response.

"No, of course not," Esther said, softening. "It must be important, I presume?"

Anna looked at Alice and noticed her hair was brushed out. "Oh, your hair looks so beautiful," she said, as she walked up and stroked it. "I wish mine looked like that."

"Is that what you two came in here for?" Esther asked, a little sardonically.

Priscilla looked at Esther, then at Alice and back at Anna, with a capricious smile on her face, which seemed to say, just wait until you hear this! "I have the greatest idea. We will become, in some way incognito—at least Anna and I will, I'm not sure about Esther yet. It will be like in those spy books about Mr. Moto! It will be very exciting and then we will find out the truth."

Esther shook her head. "You've lost me—what do you mean?"

"Well, we worried about men liking us for our money but not for ourselves, right? So we will go incognito and see what happens. We can have clandestine meetings later to discuss things."

Esther and Alice continued to look at Priscilla with puzzlement. Priscilla looked over at Anna and smiled before she spoke again. "I'm going to get a job, but I'll use Mother's maiden name—you know, my middle name, Avery. And I've got another plan for Anna. You know she's going to that new resort in Florida, and Father wants her to take our maid Lucy as a companion. So she and Lucy can exchange identities. Then she can experience life as a maid. Lucy knows enough about the family to be able to pass for Anna, and she's only three years older."

"Priscilla, are you serious?" Esther asked with a disapproving tone.

"Of course, I am. It will be so exciting. It's also an intriguing social experiment—you may even write a book about it, Esther."

"Well, at least I won't have any part of it. I've already found my beau," Esther said.

"Well, I also have a way for you to be sure of David..." Priscilla began, but Esther interrupted her.

"Prissy, I am sure of David, so please stop this now. And if you really are going to do this, you must get Father's approval."

"Esther, you can't tell Father. Please don't. Anna and I think this is important for us, we don't want to..."

"End up with my problem," Alice finished her sentence, and Priscilla shook her head. "It's okay—I think you should do this. I wish I had."

Esther looked at Alice for a moment, then back at her sisters. At first she was against the whole idea, but after Alice spoke, she reconsidered. If she stopped them from proceeding, she did not want them blaming her for a bad marriage, she thought. "I'm still concerned about keeping this from Father," she said, with a softer tone.

"I don't think he would go along with it, and we're old enough to make these decisions for ourselves—our lives and our futures are at stake," Anna said pleadingly.

Esther looked at her sisters, then back at Alice, and then at Priscilla. "Do you really think you can get a job these days—do you know how many people are out of work?"

Priscilla's face brightened and she smiled confidently. "Yes, I know, but all I can do is try. Will you keep it quiet then?"

Esther looked at both of them for a moment and reluctantly nodded her head.

"Thank you, Esther. We're off to bed now," Priscilla said, walking with Anna towards the door.

After she and Anna left the bedroom, Esther looked over at Alice. "Well, that will probably last for at least a day before they forget about it."

"I don't know—isn't that what we thought when she started helping your father with his business? She's a pretty determined person."

Esther stood up and walked towards her bed. When she was almost there, she turned around and looked at Alice. "I wonder what she had in mind for David and me."

"You could always ask her."

"No, I don't want to know. It seems—dishonest or sneaky or something."

"Or something—maybe the `something' is prudent," Alice said, and Esther grabbed a pillow from the bed and threw it at Alice.

"Oh, shut up!" she said, and they both started laughing as Alice threw the pillow back and hit Esther in the face.

"Don't forget who the pillow fight champion used to be," Alice bragged.

4

"My that was a delicious repast, and it's so much easier to get a reservation now, since the crash," David said, and touched his mouth with the embroidered linen napkin as he finished his last bite of cherries jubilee. Esther stared at him for a moment, watching his movements, thinking that somehow she might be able to discern something from them. Was he the man she loved, or could he be something else—was he genuine in his affections? She loved him, she knew that, but…she had to admit that there was some doubt in her mind since Alice had visited. "Do you like yours?"

He smiled at her, expecting an answer and she mumbled, "Yes, it was quite good. Thank you for dinner."

He looked at her quizzically, sensing something was wrong. Her dark hair was pulled back that night, making her look more mature, he thought. But that maturity made her more attractive—she looked more like a lady than just a girl. But what was she thinking, what was this about? he wondered. "Is everything all right?"

She looked up at him again, but did not say anything. For a moment she looked at his face. It was as if certain words came into her mind as she examined that face—honesty and integrity. He was not exactly handsome, but he was attractive—especially attractive to her, she thought. And he was very masculine. At five foot nine inches he was not much taller than she was but his presence was…inspiring. Being around him made her feel somehow safe and secure—as if he would always be there. And he was dependable—always on time, always available when she needed him, always steady and consistent. But was there another side? And if there was, how could she tell?

"Dinner was fine, but I was wondering, I wanted to ask you a question," she said.

"Okay, but I want to ask you one first—is that okay?" he asked politely.

"Yes—of course."

"I put something under your plate when you visited the ladies' room. Pick it up."

"Under my plate? What do you mean?" she asked, and slowly picked up her plate to find a diamond engagement ring. "Oh, David— it's beautiful—absolutely gorgeous," she exclaimed so loudly that several other diners looked over at their table. She made a face showing that she was embarrassed and then suddenly he took her hand and put it on her finger.

"This is such a surprise, I just wasn't expecting this."

"I know this is not the most romantic way, but you know the question," he said.

"Yes I do, and you know the answer," she said, tears falling from her eyes, as she clasped his hands from across the table.

"But let me hear it—just to be certain. Will you marry me?"

"Yes, I will—I will."

"Now I haven't come into ownership of the firm yet, but Uncle Henry is retiring, and I'll be taking his position as senior partner in five months, which will greatly increase my share of the profits, and then when Father retires, of course I'll take all of it over, but that may be many years and…"

"Stop, David. I don't care about your income or your position."

"Well, I want you to know that I waited all this time to ask you because I wanted to make certain that I could provide the level of comfort you are used to and deserve. I didn't want your family to think you would be taking a step down when you married me, even if we aren't as rich as the Stricklands."

"David—I don't care about the comfort, I only…"

"So I thought we'd marry then," he interrupted. "In five months. When I get the promotion."

Esther smiled, surprised that he was so worried about providing for her, but also pleased that he had finally asked her to marry him. She had begun to wonder if this day would ever come, and until now, she had not known the reason why he had waited so long, and it had puzzled her. "Five months is fine," she heard herself say as she watched him smile and turn to ask the waiter for the check. How ironic it was that just the other day she knew she would marry him if he was poor, and yet he had been waiting all this time to make certain he was rich enough. Did he really think that the money meant that much to her? Didn't he know that she would be willing to live with so much less just to be with him? The thought that he would not understand this about her bothered her, but she decided not to say anything else. This was one of the best days of her life, and she did not want to spoil it with introspective questions. The big question had been answered; he wanted to marry her.

Anna walked down the street to visit Miles Van Galen, her friend from high school. At nineteen, Miles was one year younger than Anna, and they had grown up together and played together when they were children. They always liked each other—just as friends, and he had helped her with her math homework even though he was a year behind her in school. She remembered the day that Miles, who was sixteen then, dove into a lake and hit the remains of an old pier that was hidden in the water, tearing his spine apart and leaving him crippled from the waist down. She had never cried so hard and for so long for anything except her mother's death. Miles had been so athletic, and he was a handsome boy with striking blond hair and blue eyes. She knew he had a lot of female admirers before that fateful day. But then the girls lost interest and even his male friends stopped visiting.

After that Miles began reading a lot, and her friendship with him grew even stronger, for they shared a love of poetry and literature. He was the only boy she knew who read Jane Austen, and who could quote Keats and Shelley and many of the classic poets. She knew that she was probably his only friend now, but it was no sacrifice to visit him, because they had so much in common. The age difference, which loomed so greatly in school, had faded, and he had matured faster, she thought, since his accident. She shared many things with him that she normally only would have told another girl about, but he was always interested, and always had good insights. However, as she rang the doorbell, she wondered how he could always be in such a cheerful mood when she visited. Was he just pretending for her? How could he be happy tied to that wooden wheelchair, she thought, as the butler answered the door.

The Van Galens' house was huge, but it was also gloomy, she thought as she entered. The long drapes and all the furniture were dark, as was the woodwork, and the drapes were rarely drawn to let in the sunshine. Miles's father was a shipping magnate, and he had always wanted Miles to follow in his footsteps. But perhaps now that dream had faded for him, Anna thought, as the butler led her to Miles, who was in the drawing room. She had always met Miles in the living room until that day, but she liked this other room—it was distinguished from the rest of the house, because the drapes in it were drawn and sunlight filtered through. As Miles turned his chair around, she noticed that there were many newspapers on the table before him, and they appeared to be from different places in the world. She also noticed the Wall Street Journal on his lap, which was easy for her to recognize, since her father always read it.

"Oh, Miles, how are you?" she asked, as she walked over and gave him a friendly hug with her arm.

"All is well," Miles said, smiling.

"Finding any poetry in there?" Anna asked jokingly, pointing at the newspaper.

"Oh, that's Father's. I was just looking for something for him," he answered, obviously a little embarrassed, but she did not know the reason.

"Let's go out to the garden," he suggested, and she moved around to push his chair, but he moved her hand away to push it himself. "I need the exercise," he said as she followed. She was surprised at the strength and muscles in his arms, which he had built up. As he turned in the sunshine she looked at his face, and saw that he looked like a man now—there was little if any boyishness to him anymore, and he looked more handsome than ever. So many girls would have liked him, she thought, if he had not had the accident.

"So what is new in your life, my friend? Are you planning your trip to Florida?"

"Yes, it should be great fun. There's a new hotel there that everyone is raving about, and we'll be staying there."

5

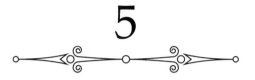

Priscilla walked into the large reception area, which was finished with oak paneling and leather couches and chairs—some of the most expensive contemporary furniture of the 1930s. As she walked towards her father's office door, his secretary, Mrs. Wickland, looked startled and got up to meet her.

"Priscilla, you can't go in there, they are having a special meeting. The mayor and a senator are with your father and they can't be disturbed. They've been in there for hours."

"I wonder what that's about," Priscilla said. "He didn't tell me about it. I'll come back later...."

As she finished speaking the men came out of Mr. Strickland's office. The senator was smoking a cigar, and the fumes from it came out of the office as the man exited.

Neither man was smiling—they in fact looked glum, but Priscilla smiled at both of them as they left and she walked into his office.

"Phew—I thought you didn't let anyone smoke in your office."

"Well, it's hard to tell a senator not to light up," Mr. Strickland said.

"What did they want?"

"Another proposition where I give them money, and they in return make things easier for me so I can make more money."

"Sounds dishonest."

"Yes, absolutely—I would think by now they would know that I don't approve of such things."

"Oh, Father, he used the artifact from Pompeii that Paul gave you for his ashes," Priscilla said, picking up the ancient pot and shaking the ashes out of it.

"Don't worry about that—sit down and bring me up to date on

the factory reports, if you're finished with them."

"I don't have them all ready yet, but I need to talk to you about something else, and please don't be angry with me."

"Why should I be angry?"

"Because I want to work somewhere else."

"What? You can't be serious! You haven't even been here that long since college and you've just gotten a grasp on most of the operations. You can't mean it," Mr. Strickland said, raising his voice.

"Father, please don't be upset—it's just that I need to get out on my own—just for a while," Priscilla said.

Mr. Strickland looked downcast and held his head down for a moment in thought. She had not realized just how upset her decision would make him, and she knew he was hurt and wondered if she could go through with it. She looked away at some of the art on the walls. Amid some of the masterpieces she saw the framed collection of the drawings she and her siblings had made for him when they were children. It seemed so unusual to have those there in this fine office, and they reminded her of how much he cared for all of his children.

"Okay, consider this—I will pay you more, much more. You are worth it, and I should have increased your pay a long time ago," Mr. Strickland said.

"Oh, you're already paying me more money than I know what to do with. It's not that. I just need several months to be my own person."

"I know…I know that sometimes I'm hard to get along with. I can be brusque and aggressive, and I think that's what's bothering you—your mother used to warn me about it and…"

"Father, I don't mind that at all. I like working for you—those things really don't bother me. It has nothing to do with you," Priscilla said, taking her father's hands as she spoke.

"But I need you—I've come to depend on you. What about a compromise?" Mr. Strickland asked.

"What do you mean?"

"If you must work somewhere else, work there part time, and part time for me. I'll still pay you your full wages, and if you want to work there longer than a few months, I'll agree to that. Just don't leave completely."

Priscilla wondered if it would be harder to find a part-time job than a full-time job, but as she looked at her father, and his crestfallen face, she could not turn him down. She felt guilty about leaving at all, and she was also worried about hurting his feelings. She really doubted that he needed her as much as he said, for he had many skillful employees who were much more experienced than she was. But she had noticed that when she was around, she seemed to have a calming effect on him—the same kind of effect her late mother had. He seemed to be wound up in the business more when she was not around, and she was concerned about leaving completely. Yes, this was a compromise that would work, she thought. "Do you want me for part of the day, or for full days part of the week?" she asked.

He exhaled with a sigh of relief. "Either way, I'm just glad you are going to stay. I'll work with your other employer when you get a job."

"Well, in this Depression that may take a long time."

"No it won't—I hire people all of the time, and believe me, you will stand out," he said. "Just don't let them talk you into full time—promise me that."

"I promise. Thank you, Father, for being so understanding."

Miles looked over at Anna as she finished talking about her planned Florida vacation. She wanted to tell him about her scheme to trade places with Lucy, but all of the girls had promised to tell no one, and she would not break her word. She thought his expression looked somewhat sad, but he then began to smile. "Perhaps you'll meet your Darcy," he said, referring to the character in the book Pride and Prejudice.

"Oh, I don't want a Darcy, he was way too arrogant."

"Well, in case you don't meet him in Florida, maybe I can think of someone while you are gone. I could sort of play the Emma role," he said, referring to another Jane Austen book about a woman who was a matchmaker. "I'm going to miss you and…" He trailed off.

"And what, Miles? Tell me."

"And I hope you meet the one who will really love you," he said, and she reached over and put her arm around him for a moment.

"I could not ask for a better friend—I don't have a girlfriend as close as you. Only my sisters are closer. Thank you for being my friend."

"I will always be your friend if you let me."

"Why would I not let you?"

"Well, if you get married, it might be difficult, but we'll see."

"Don't worry; I won't marry anyone who would interfere with our friendship."

"That's nice. Have a blessed trip."

"Thanks, but I'm not leaving yet. I'll see you at church on Sunday, and I'll come by at least once before I leave."

As she left he smiled, but when she closed the door, he looked down at his legs and closed his eyes sadly, and then he jerked his head up, and forced a smile and wheeled over to the newspapers and began reading one of them.

6

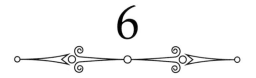

"Did you invite him for a particular reason?" Priscilla said, as she sat in Esther's bedroom, and sniffed the various perfumes and colognes on her dressing table.

"Yes, but I can't divulge that right now—I promised David," Esther answered, smiling.

"Oh, I think I can guess what it is," Priscilla said, as Esther took a pale yellow chiffon dress from her wardrobe and checked to make certain it had no wrinkles. It was a special dress that had been designed for her by Elsa Schiaparelli.

"And now I know what it must be, if you are wearing the dress!"

Esther giggled and began to change into the dress, but Priscilla objected.

"You can't wear that with any old slip—you need the French lace one—the one that you bought for the dress."

"Why? No one will know."

"You will—and now I will."

"I have no idea where it is."

"I'll get it for you," Priscilla said, and she went to an adjacent room where there was a large closet and began going through all the clothing in it. There was a lot to go through, but she found the slip and brought it to her sister. Esther looked at her and smiled.

"Now, won't this make you feel better?" Priscilla asked, as she held the beautiful slip up to her own body and paraded in front of the mirror. The lace was exquisite in its detail and the material was soft silk, and she felt the material as she moved. "It feels so nice, I think I'll wear it tonight since you don't care about it. I mean no one would know if you or I were wearing it."

"Okay, silly, give me that," Esther said, but Priscilla twirled around with it before bringing it over to her.

"So, you do want to wear it," Priscilla said triumphantly, handing it to her.

"Yes, it is beautiful, but I'd forgotten about it. I can wear it on my wedding day."

"Oh, so that is the announcement—that's what I thought."

"No I...I didn't say that it was the announcement, I just said that when I do get married, I will wear it," Esther said unconvincingly. Then she broke into a smile and pointed her finger at Priscilla and Priscilla laughed at her. "Would you get out of here and let me get dressed," she said good-humoredly as she pretended to chase Priscilla to the door.

"Okay, I'm leaving, but you can't wear that on your wedding day—you must wear something new. You can't have a new dress and an old slip. You need something old, something new, something borrowed, something blue. Now, you're old enough to be something old, so..."

"Oh, I'm going to kill you," Esther said, as Priscilla impishly closed the door. Esther laughed to herself and touched the lace on the slip as she recalled the time she spent in Paris as a student when she had bought it. Then she began to change.

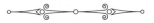

The family and David Holt sat at the dinner table as the cook and her helper brought appetizers.

"Mr. Holt, would you be kind enough to say grace for us?" Mr. Strickland asked.

David Holt seemed a little nervous at the request, but he nodded at Mr. Strickland. "I would be honored, sir." He bowed his head. "Dear God in heaven, thank you for this food and for this wonderful family and may they be eternally blessed. In Christ's name, Amen." Then he looked up and saw Mr. Strickland smile with approval at him, and he felt relieved. He felt intimidated by Mr. Strickland, although he was not sure why—Mr. Strickland had done nothing to make him feel uncomfortable, but perhaps it was because of his immense wealth, he thought as he looked over at Esther, who smiled at him.

"It's so very good to see you again, Mr. Holt," Mr. Strickland said. "I used to see your father quite often, when his office was nearby, but since he built the new building, we rarely cross paths. I must say it's a beautiful structure."

"I'll be certain to pass on the compliment—Father helped the architects design it, so I'm certain he will be pleased to hear that you like it."

"Father, David would like to talk to you about something after dinner, if he may," Esther said.

"Is that so?" Mr. Strickland asked.

"Yes sir."

"Well, whatever could that be?" Mr. Strickland asked with an amused look on his face. "We'd best get dinner served to relieve the suspense," he added.

Anna looked over at Priscilla and giggled, and David smiled at Esther again.

"Mr. Standish, please have dinner served. I fear if we eat any more of these"—he gestured toward the appetizers—"we'll be too full for it," Mr. Strickland said.

After dinner, Mr. Strickland invited David into his study. It was a very refined room with rosewood paneling and was reminiscent of a judge's chambers, David thought. And he definitely felt as if he were walking into a judge's chambers as he entered and waited for Mr. Strickland to sit down at his large desk backed by rows of bookshelves which were filled with a wide variety of books. But Mr. Strickland sat in a chair in front of the desk and offered a seat to David that was separated only by a round mosaic table made up of squares of translucent semiprecious stones. David was impressed by the beautiful table, and could not take his eyes off it for a moment.

"Wherever did this come from? It's beautiful," he commented.

"It was a present from the ambassador from Egypt—we met when our company did some work for them on the Nile. Now what can I do for you, Mr. Holt?"

"Sir, I would like to ask for…for your daughter's hand in marriage," David said.

"Which one?" Mr. Strickland asked, which brought a bewildered look to David's face.

"Well, uh…Esther."

Mr. Strickland couldn't suppress laughter at his little joke, and when David realized the question had been meant for levity, he smiled himself and loosened up a little. He had been sitting bolt upright, but now he relaxed in the chair.

"Mr. Holt, when would this proposed marriage take place?"

"About five months from now. My uncle is retiring and I will take his place as senior partner and also get his income then, so I believe I will be able to support Esther and make her comfortable. I'm also in place to take over the business when father retires—"

"Mr. Holt, I was not asking about your financial situation—I only wanted to get an idea of the timing…although I appreciate your concern about her welfare. But it is about more than just providing money, isn't it?"

"Yes sir. I also love her very much and want to make her happy."

"That's very good. May I ask how many hours a week you work, presently?"

"Hours at work?" David hesitated, trying to figure out how to answer.

"Yes, how many hours do you average every week?"

"Well, it varies. Sometimes I work into the night, and sometimes…I guess about sixty or eighty hours a week, depending on what the business demands."

"And do you work on Sunday?"

"Normally, I don't, but sometimes I do—depending on what I have to do."

"Well, I would ask that if you really want to make her happy, and the children that you might have, that you honor the Lord's day, excepting an emergency, and that you limit your work time so that you are home for dinner every evening. When Esther's mother and I first married, I worked very long hours, and I was gone almost every evening, and it became a point of contention. I was tense when I came home, and I thought of work and little else most of the time. It was controlling me and ruling my life, and Ruth asked me one day, 'Do you love me as much as your job?' I'm sorry to say that I did not answer her right away, although of course I loved her more. 'Do you know,' she added, 'that the Bible says do not overwork to be rich?' I was quite offended by the question and thought it was unfair." Mr. Strickland paused as he looked around the room and then back to David.

"I had inherited a family business and had built it up and increased it one hundred fold and I thought she would be pleased about it. But what she really wanted was a normal life with me home at night. That is when I changed and pledged to her that I would be home for dinner unless an emergency arose. This saved our marriage at a time when we were becoming distant, and I was overwhelmed with my responsibilities. You see, Ruth was not worried about how much money we had, she was worried about how much joy we had."

"Yes sir, I understand. I think that is very good advice and I will take it to heart."

"I like you, Mr. Holt, and have ever since you and Esther met. And I want to trust you. But sometimes when an engagement is made, the man may try to take certain…liberties with his fiancée."

"Oh no, I would never do that, sir. I respect Esther for her purity and would never try to compromise her."

"Good, well, see that you don't—for that is one thing that I would not stand for. And now that we have that out of the way, I welcome you as a future son-in-law, David," Mr. Strickland said as he rose and warmly took David's hand. David was surprised that the talk was over so quickly, and he got up and smiled gratefully.

"Thank you, sir. You made this easier than I thought it would be. I appreciate your kindness and your directness."

"You are welcome, but the hard part is coming—living together. Remember, don't argue over nonessentials. And unless you are willing to make sacrifices for her and her for you, the marriage won't work. Selfishness kills a marriage, but giving and forgiving keeps it alive. She will not meet all of your needs—she is not made for that, so don't expect it. And that is the same thing I will tell her."

"It's very good advice, sir, and I mean that sincerely."

"Okay, David, let's join the others and you can make your announcement."

After the announcement was made and David left, Esther went up to her room and changed into a dressing gown. There was a knock on the door, and she opened it for Anna and Priscilla.

"Oh, Esther, I'm so happy for you," Anna said. "I can't wait for the wedding—it will be glorious. Can I help you pick out the material for your dress? I saw some beautiful material and I'd love to help you."

"That would be nice, Anna. Thank you," Esther said soberly.

"What's wrong? Do you want to pick out your own dress? I'm sorry if I…"

"No, I'd like you to help me—I really would," Esther said, and she looked up at her sister and smiled.

"But there is something wrong, isn't there?" Anna asked.

"No, I just want to rest—it's been a long day."

"Okay, have a good night," Anna said and she walked towards

the door, but Priscilla lingered and when Anna closed the door, she moved closer to Esther and talked softly.

"So you have your doubts, is that it?" she asked.

"Yes, I have my doubts. He could be the most perfect man in the world and I'd have doubts after what happened to Alice. And he is so concerned about being able to support me the way we live here that I wonder what kind of person he thinks I am. Does he think that I would not marry him unless he was rich?"

"Maybe he just does not want to disappoint you—he wants the best for you. That may be all," Priscilla offered.

"Just how do love and wealth get mixed together, anyway? Are they inextricably entwined to the point where no one in our position really knows how much influence they have on each other?"

"I don't know. But I do know a way to test him, if you really want to be sure."

Esther looked over at her sister for a moment, in thought, and then she turned away. "No, I'm not ready for that—not yet, anyway. I'm not sure what I'm going to do yet. This should be the happiest time of my life but now it's wrought with apprehension and anxiety. One part of me is rejoicing and the other is afraid. I trust David and yet I wonder if he even knows why he is marrying me. Maybe he is self-deceived—maybe the Strickland brand has blinded him. It's easy to love a girl who is filthy rich, now, isn't it? It's easy to think you love her when she's loaded."

"I think you're easy to love with or without money—many men would be blessed to have you. Remember, you've turned down many while waiting for David to finally ask."

"Yes, and I always wondered why he was waiting so long and now I find out it's simply because he wants to make certain he's rich enough when we get married, of all things."

"Esther, let not your heart be troubled. A wonderful man has asked you to marry him. Just be thankful for that, because it's a great blessing."

"You're right. I'm sorry to be going on about this."

As Priscilla left Esther's room, she saw her father, who signaled her to come into his study. After they sat down, he pulled out some of the information that she had compiled on the charities.

"It appears from your research that some of these are frauds, and others, although they may be legitimate, are the type of things we don't give to. Like the arts. I'm having dinner with Mrs. Ingersoll tomorrow evening—at a restaurant—and then we will come to the house to discuss this, and I would like you to join us."

"Of course I will, Father," Priscilla said, wanting to ask if the dinner was a date or strictly charity business, but she was afraid to.

"She may have some questions that I can't answer since I didn't do the research."

"Is she still planning the gala?"

"Yes, but if she wants to give money to any of these"—he nodded at the list—" from the proceeds of the gala, I don't want anything to do with it. I won't sponsor the event unless all of the money goes to specifically helping people with food and clothing and jobs."

"Well, you may have a little problem there, because she is on the board of two of the organizations—the museum one and the one that funds young artists."

"If she doesn't acquiesce, I will withdraw my support and we will end it," Mr. Strickland said firmly. "And since we are giving more than the others, I think we have some clout."

"I wholeheartedly agree. What time should I be available?"

"Any time after seven thirty—I will be dining early and will get to the house as soon as possible."

After the discussion with her father, Priscilla ran upstairs and knocked on Anna's door, and they went together to Esther's bedroom.

"What's the big smile about?" Esther asked.

"I think we may be about to see the end of Mrs. Ingersoll!" Priscilla said.

"Why?" Anna asked.

"Because Father won't sponsor the gala if she wants to give the money to her arty charities, and she's on the board of two of them. I'm giving them a report on my research of the charities tomorrow night after they go out for dinner."

"They're going out for dinner? Is Father soft on her, or what?" Anna asked.

"I was hoping it was just business for him," Priscilla said.

"Well, it's definitely business for her, if you know what I mean. But what makes you think she won't give in on the charities? I think she has her eye on the bigger prize, don't you?"

Priscilla's enthusiasm ebbed as she considered Esther's words. "Maybe you're right, but I was hoping.... Maybe I can emphasize the bad points of her charities and provoke her."

"I think you'll only provoke Father. She has her act together, and she won't let the big fish swim away just over a few insults," Esther said.

"I think Esther's right. You could probably call her a brazen hussy and she wouldn't flinch—probably just smile and say 'thank you, dear,'" Anna added.

"Both of you are right. I'll be extremely polite, and I'll only whisper 'brazen hussy' at her when Father is not around," Priscilla said, which made them all laugh. But as their laughter subsided, Anna looked at her sisters for a moment, her countenance becoming more serious.

"What is it, Anna?" Esther asked.

"Is it possible that this woman could become our stepmother? If Father is taking her to dinner, he must like her."

"Oh, the idea of that makes me sick to my stomach," Priscilla said.

"And what if she married him and he died first? She is a lot younger than he is. She would inherit everything," Anna said.

"And if we tried to stop that, if we told him to make an allowance for us in his will, we would probably seem greedy and selfish," Priscilla added.

"Now wait a minute. We've gone from him taking her to dinner to inheriting the Strickland fortune. Let's not get carried away and work ourselves into a tizzy," Esther said.

"Well, it is possible," Anna said quietly.

"Yes, but that works both ways. All things are possible to him that believes. And I for one am going to pray and believe that Father will see the truth about this woman. Will you join me?" Esther asked. The sisters nodded in agreement.

7

"So what kind of research do you do to determine what the charity does?" Mrs. Ingersoll asked Priscilla as they sat in the drawing room with Mr. Strickland.

"Well, I ask for their financial records to begin with, and if they don't give us that information, they fail. But sometimes they give us a general financial statement, but it has no backup information for me to get an understanding of how they are actually spending their money."

"My, you do go into detail, don't you?" Mrs. Ingersoll said, with what seemed like a combination of admiration and distaste.

"For instance, here is one that used thirty percent to maintain their operation and gave away seventy percent, but they don't tell us how the thirty percent was spent. I want to see the salaries as well as other benefits, such as traveling allowances and other things. Often they will inflate the benefits to give themselves a larger slice of the pie, but only release their base salary, which appears modest until you understand the whole picture."

"Well, I never thought of this—this is quite intelligent," Mrs. Ingersoll said.

Priscilla held another paper up. "Now this organization shows that they spent sixty percent of their contributions for maintaining, and only gave away forty percent, which is unacceptable to us because too little is reaching the intended recipients."

"Wherever did you learn such things—and at your young age!" Mrs. Ingersoll exclaimed.

Priscilla thought the compliments were becoming extreme, but she answered anyway. "Father was examining financial statements one day when I was about fourteen years old, and I started asking him questions, and he taught me. I'm just doing what he would be doing."

"So what about my charities—have you found anything wrong about them?" Mrs. Ingersoll asked.

Priscilla looked at her father and then back at Mrs. Ingersoll. "Well, I didn't do too much research on them because they are not the type of charities that we give to."

"They're not?" Mrs. Ingersoll said, with indignation in her voice.

"Ah…Betty, let me try to explain what Priscilla is saying. You see, when we started our foundation for charity, we pledged to help those in need—to feed the hungry, take care of orphans, and help the destitute—people who cannot help themselves. These are the types of needs we are pledged to. It's not that there aren't other good causes, it's just that this is what we are interested in," Mr. Strickland explained.

Mrs. Ingersoll was still facing Priscilla, and she was quiet for what seemed like a long time to her. Her eyes flashed with anger and her expression was sour while looking in her direction, but she took a deep breath, and as she turned to Joseph, her expression changed and she smiled widely. "Oh, Joseph, that is so much more important than the arts—you and your lovely daughter are so righteous in this. My eyes have been opened and I will give to the charities you direct me to. Even though I know that what I give is like the widow's mite, compared to what you give."

Mr. Strickland smiled and sat back in his chair. "Well, Betty, you must know that the amount is not the point, for the widow gave all she had and it was considered more than what the wealthier people gave."

"I am so grateful you have shared your wisdom with me," Mrs. Ingersoll said, and she took Mr. Strickland's hand and squeezed it.

After the meeting, Priscilla went upstairs and her sisters heard her footsteps. They followed her into the bedroom and closed the door and spoke in low voices.

"What happened?" Anna asked.

"She gets the Oscar. She turned the situation into a victory and played it to the hilt. She said her eyes were now opened and it was so much more important to give to our charities and she was grateful for the help and blah, blah, blah. Then she used it as an occasion to grasp and squeeze Father's hand, and he didn't pull away."

"Oh, this is getting more serious," Anna said.

"I've got an idea. Can you research her the way you researched these charities?" Esther asked Priscilla.

"Not really—I mean I just ask for financial information… Oh, you think she might be broke? Is that it?"

"I don't know. Or there might be something in her past. A private investigator might be able to help," Esther said.

"We could never risk that. If father ever found out we hired someone…"

"Yes, you're right," Esther said.

"Anyway, her company is publicly traded and I already checked a little, and it appears to be doing well. I think she just wants to do better," Priscilla added.

"Let's just hope Father's eyes will open," Esther said.

Priscilla rode the subway for about twenty miles and found her way to the manufacturing company that was advertising for a part time secretary. She was dressed in a dark purple suit with cream trim, and a matching hat. The suit was the most businesslike dress she could find, and it took her several days of shopping to get it. Since she wanted to make certain she looked nice for the interview, she also had her nails manicured and her hair done.

The building was older and somewhat decrepit, and there was beige paint peeling on the walls of the room she was directed into to apply for the job. As she entered she saw that there were about fourteen women sitting in folding metal chairs, who she assumed were waiting for interviews. She sighed, wondering if this was a complete waste of time, but she kept walking. The floor was constructed of old wooden planks, and her right high heel got caught between two of them. She pulled with her leg to get it out, but it would not come loose.

Finally, she slipped her foot out of the shoe and leaned over to pull the shoe heel, but she still could not get it out. Looking around and feeling quite embarrassed, she got down on her hands and knees to pull it out, and noticed that as she did, her stocking snagged when it touched the floor, causing a long run. She breathed out forcefully and shook her head in disgust, and tried to loosen the shoe, again to no avail. A man in his mid to late twenties was walking by the hallway that led into the room, and noticing her dilemma, walked in to help her. But she did not see him, because he was in back of her, and when he said hello, she let out a loud gasp, which caught the attention of the other women in the room.

"Yes, what do you want?" she said somewhat brusquely, as she put her hand on her chest to steady herself from the surprise. She was now also upset that he had startled her, but as she turned around and looked up, she realized that he was quite attractive. He had light brown hair, and blue eyes, and he seemed slightly bemused by her predicament, although he was quite subtle about it.

"I only want to help a damsel in distress—if you would permit me," he said with what she thought was a slight British accent.

"Yes, yes, of course I would," she said, and he bent down and grasped the shoe and turned it but could not get it out.

"I'll break the heel if I pull it any harder, and these look like expensive shoes," he said. Then he raised his voice and directed it at the counter where the employees were working. "Helen, find some larger scissors, please." When she heard him speak again, she was certain of the accent and wondered about it.

"Yes, Mr. Blankenship," Helen said, and scurried to find the scissors.

Priscilla was surprised at the authority in his voice, and then noticed that he was wearing a finely tailored three-piece suit. Suddenly Helen was there handing the man the scissors. He bent down and used them to separate the planks and pulled her shoe out. He then proceeded to put it on her foot, but she was uncomfortable with him touching her leg and she pulled away. As she did, her purse dropped from her shoulder. He picked it up and handed it to her.

"Here you are," he said.

"Thank you very much," she said as she took the purse from him. She felt his stare—his eyes seemed very intense, but she resisted looking directly at him. "That was very kind of you."

"My pleasure," he said and quickly walked away. Helen was still standing there, and she bent down and picked up the scissors.

"Who was that?" Priscilla asked.

"That's the owner of the company."

"But he's so young."

"His father had a heart attack, and he had to take over for him," Helen explained. "Are you here about the job?"

"Yes. Yes, I am," Priscilla said as she put her shoe back on.

"Well, there's about a two-hour wait, so get your application at the window."

Priscilla filled out the application, using her mother's maiden name, and leaving out her college education. However, she was careful to document the varied experience she had working for her father's company—under one of Strickland's subsidiaries because she did not want the Strickland name on it, as it might link her to it. The company she chose was Randolph Enterprises, and she had the manager write a reference letter for her in the name of Priscilla Avery. Nevertheless, she knew that if anyone knew much about the company, they would find out it was owned by Strickland. But she had to take that chance.

After sitting for about twenty minutes on the hard metal chair, she got up and walked around a little, careful to avoid the crevices in the floor. More women had walked in for the job, and now about twenty-five were waiting. She sat down again, wishing that she had brought a book to read. Another forty minutes passed, and by then another six women had entered the room and there were not enough chairs. However, she was tired of sitting, so she got up again, and someone quickly took her seat. There was an employment board which had all the available jobs listed, and as she was reading through some of them, which were mostly factory-worker positions such as machinists, Helen walked out to make an announcement. "Please give me your attention. We have many applicants for this position, so I want to tell you what the requirements are now. First, you must have secretarial experience."

Priscilla thought of how she helped her father and had that experience because much of what she did for him fit into that category. "Second," Helen continued, "You must be able to type forty words per minute." Priscilla could type faster than that, and continued listening. "Third, you must be able to take shorthand..." Priscilla did not hear anything else. She was angry that the requirements had changed, but having had experience as an employer working for her father, she understood why. With all the applicants, why not make the requirements more stringent to get the exact experience you want? She did not hear the other things that Helen was saying, but she could hear sighs of unhappiness from the other women, many of whom were getting up to leave. At that moment she was very grateful that although she had spent a lot of time for the interview, at least she did not have to work. She began to have compassion on the other women, because she had never before come this close to understanding the difficulties they faced.

She knew that unemployment was very high getting and worse every day, and she also knew that many of the women would have normally stayed at home and taken care of their families, but because their husbands had lost their jobs, they had no choice but to seek work. She glanced at the employment board one more time as she prepared to leave, and the word bookkeeper caught her eye. She read the paper carefully. It was a temporary position to fill in for the bookkeeper who was ill. They were not certain how long it would last, but it was a full-time job. No, she had given Father her word and she would not break it. She would not work full time. Most of the women had left the room by this time, and as she turned to leave, Mr. Blankenship walked by and he looked at her for a moment, then walked over to her. "Are you leaving already? Were you not qualified?" he asked.

"I was not," she answered.

He looked at her as if he wanted to say something but was not sure what to say. "Well, perhaps something else will come up."

"Actually, I think it has. I can do the bookkeeper job—the temporary one, but I can only work part time. Would that be possible?"

"You are a bookkeeper?" he asked in a doubtful tone.

"Yes, I can do the job," she answered.

"Well, come into my office—it's just down the hall," he said, and she followed him into the room and sat down. As soon as she did, the intercom buzzed and he looked up at her.

"I've got to take this call—it will just be a moment. Please make yourself comfortable on the sofa, if you like." He pointed to a small couch beside a table with several books and magazines on it. She took a seat and picked up one of the magazines, and then noticed that there was a Bible on the table. His conversation went on and on, and she was getting a little impatient. Finally, she picked up the Bible and began reading it. He finally finished talking and hung up, and then looked over at her. "Sorry for that. Do you know the author of that book?"

She looked at him for a moment, surprised by his question, then she smiled. "Yes I know Him—what would I do without Him?"

"Good point. The bookkeeping position has just become vacant—Mr. Willis has taken ill—he has some sort of infection. I have no idea when he will come back to work, but his job is not an easy one. He tracks all our profits and losses, and keeps the checks flowing. Do you think you can handle that?"

"Yes, I think so."

He looked around the room in thought for a moment and then back at her. "Can you start tomorrow?" he asked.

"Tomorrow—why, yes, I could start tomorrow. Am I hired just like that?"

"Just like that—we need someone as soon as possible. But it's just a tryout to see if you can do the job. Are you okay with that?"

"Yes. What time?"

"Eight sharp—don't be late now. And wear some more practical shoes. I know two-inch heels are the newest fashion, but you don't need to look like a Bloomingdale's advertisement to work here. Although it looks nice," he said good-naturedly and smiled.

As he spoke she realized that she was dressed in much more expensive clothing than any of the other women. She had purposely not worn any expensive jewelry, but she was trying to look as good as she could to get the job, and had obviously overdone it. She watched him walk away and wondered if he had hired her on the spot because of her bookkeeping skills or because he was interested in her. Would he have helped any woman who had her heel stuck, or was he also attracted to her?

8

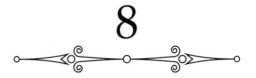

Esther and David were just finishing up their lunch at the country club in New Rochelle. It was a sunny day but not as hot as usual, and they sat outside, watching the boats go by.

"David, that was a wonderful lunch—this has been a very nice day."

"Good, but it's not over yet, I have something I want to show you."

"Okay. What is it?"

David motioned to a nearby waiter for the tab and he signed it and then stood up. "Let's go for a drive and I'll show it to you—it's a surprise." She looked at him, and he grinned with a sort of boyishness. She could tell that he was anticipating her reaction to whatever this might be, and she realized, as they got into his twelve-cylinder Cadillac convertible, she would have to seem enthusiastic to please him. After he drove for a few minutes, she turned to him, questioningly.

"David, where are we going?"

"It's only a few more minutes," he said, as they entered into a new neighborhood in Scarsdale. She looked at the beautiful homes as they drove and noticed that a lot of them were unoccupied.

"Are we visiting someone?" she asked, but he did not answer. After a few more minutes, they pulled into a long driveway of a fairly large estate and continued driving until they came to a lovely, large brick home, about five thousand square feet in size. He parked the Cadillac, and opened the door for her. She looked at him quizzically, but got out and followed him to the front door. He stopped and turned the doormat over and got a key. After opening it, he gestured for her to walk inside. She stepped in and stopped and turned to him. "Why are we here?" she asked.

"This is our new home—I'm making the arrangements now," he said, smiling.

She walked into the living room, which was beautifully finished with marble floors and an eighteen-foot-high ceiling. The walls had wainscoting of exquisitely carved cherry wood which went up five feet from the floor. The carvings were of flowers and vines and they encircled the room. At one end there was a huge fireplace constructed of stones that were sculpted with eagles. They appeared to be flying towards them as they walked into the room, and the effect was stunning.

"Do you like it?" he asked.

She was unable to speak for a moment, and he seemed upset. "I know the Stricklands could buy a hundred of these, but I thought..."

"David, it's beautiful. I love it. But I'm concerned about the cost. Have you made the purchase yet?"

"No, it's not finalized, but it's close. It's a tremendous bargain, and the Federal Reserve cut the prime interest rate from six to four percent last year, so I'm getting the money very cheap." He looked at her face and could tell that she was unhappy about something, but she was quiet, trying to collect her thoughts. "What's wrong? I thought this would make you happy, but you're not."

"David it's a beautiful house, but we're in the middle of such chaos in this country. Over thirteen hundred banks closed last year, and so many are still in trouble. And the drought in the Midwest is causing food prices to go up."

"Yes, I read the news myself," he said quietly.

"We just don't know where or when this is going to end and I don't want you to spend money just for me. I so appreciate the thought behind this, but I would feel guilty taking it."

For a moment David didn't say anything, but he looked at her with anger in his eyes that she had not seen before. He seemed as if he wanted to speak, but was unable. It was obvious he was hurt by her reluctance, but she thought it was an overreaction. He finally got his thoughts together, and when he spoke it was almost as if he were telling her off.

"Our business—the five-and dime-retail business—may not be as rich as all the different Strickland industries, but we have actually seen sales increase or stay the same through these years, because people still need the basic staples to live. And people who were buying things at the expensive stores a few years ago are now shopping at our stores. And our company is out of debt. So I can afford this house, even

46

if I don't have the kind of income that your father has."

"David, you sound like you are in competition with my father. Why would you think like that?"

"Because I think he expects me to do as well for you as he has."

"Now that is ridiculous—he has no such notion. And to try to compete with him is foolish."

"Oh, you don't think I can be as rich as him?"

"Probably not, since he's one of the richest men in the country. But why should that be important to you?"

"Well, I can be—I can make it. I can build our business up the way he built his business up…when I get control of it. He told me how he started when we had our discussion."

"I'm sure he didn't tell you that to lord it over you. I think, from what he told me later, that he told you so you would not chase more money. Wasn't that what he was trying to say?"

"I read between the lines. Anyway, you just threw me for a loop. I wanted you to love this house the way I do."

"I just love you—with all my heart. Isn't that enough?"

He moved towards her and kissed her lightly on the cheek. "Yes, I think it is."

"The house is beautiful and I do like it, but I just don't think this is a good time to spend money. I noticed there are a lot of vacant homes here—are they all foreclosures?"

"Yes, many people left after the crash—some didn't really get hit with it until this year."

"Now don't get angry at me, but we have a large guest house on the estate that Father already said we were welcome to live in." She looked at him, trying to read his face as she made the suggestion, but he didn't react. "Or we could live in your apartment in the city; that's fine for me."

"Wouldn't you rather be near your family?" he asked.

"No, it doesn't matter to me. I just want to be near you and for our marriage to work."

"It will work, because I love you also—and that's all that matters, isn't it? The houses and the money are all irrelevant."

She looked at him, amazed at the change. How had he come to this conclusion so quickly, she wondered, since he was just acting as if making as much money as her father was so important? Whatever the reason, she was grateful for it. He put his arm around her waist as they walked towards the front door, and she leaned into him.

"I'm ever so glad to hear you say that," she said, as she looked back at the living room and noticed that the colors blended beautifully and that they shared the same taste. Perhaps she could redecorate the guest house with his help, she thought.

9

"Father, who is the extra plate set for in the dining room?" Esther asked as she walked by his office and stood at the doorway.

"That would be for Mrs. Ingersoll—she's joining us for dinner."

"Is there more work to do on the charities?"

"Not much, we have the gala planned now, and we're sending out the invitations."

Esther stood at the door but said nothing and her father looked up at her.

"She's just invited as a friend, in case you're wondering."

"Sure, that's fine. I'll tell the others to dress for dinner since we have a guest."

"Esther, please ask Priscilla to come in here when she gets a chance. I understand she got a job today."

"Yes, she did—I'll tell her."

Esther walked upstairs and looked for Priscilla, who was changing her clothes.

"Better dress for dinner—we have a guest," Esther said. "Three guesses."

"Oh, no—not her."

"Yes, and this time it's not business. Father says she has been invited as a friend."

"I thought her only friend was mammon," Priscilla said.

"Well, don't say that to Father—I could tell he was touchy when I asked about why she was coming. There was something in his voice. And he wants to see you, by the way."

"Okay, I'm on my way right now," Priscilla said, as she buttoned up her dress. She then walked to her father's study.

"Did you want me, Father?"

"Yes. Anna told me you got a job today. First interview, and you get a job at a time like this. I'd say that's quite impressive."

"Well, it wasn't all that simple. They turned me down for the secretary job, but this is a fill-in for a bookkeeper."

"Well, you're very good at that—and you told them part time only, right?"

"Yes sir."

"And what company is it?"

"Superior Pump Products."

"Never heard of them. You took the subway, is that correct?"

Priscilla hesitated before answering. "Yes, that's how most people get to work."

"But you're not most people—you are my beloved daughter, and crime has risen about thirty percent in the last two years. There is also much social unrest—the communists are protesting, the workers are protesting, and even Al Capone is out of prison."

"I don't think Capone will be riding the subway, do you? Besides being in Chicago, I think he has the same model of supercharged Duesenberg that you have, doesn't he?"

Mr. Strickland laughed at her comment. "Yes, I guess you're right—Capone shouldn't be a problem. But the street gangs are—there are more murders than ever before, and many kidnappings, and if anyone found out that you were my daughter, you could be a target."

"So are you saying I can't work now? Because before you said it was okay, and I did get the job."

"No, you can keep the job. I just want Ben to drive you to work and pick you up."

"Father, that is impractical—I will stand out like a sore thumb with a chauffeured limousine coming to pick me up. Please don't make me do this."

Mr. Strickland looked down for a moment in thought. "What about this—Ben will let you off around the corner from the company and pick you up there, also. Would that be okay?"

"Yes, I guess so," Priscilla said, somewhat petulantly.

"Darling daughter, I am only concerned for your safety. I know when you are young you feel invincible, but my fears are not unfounded—this is a very dangerous city."

"Yes, I know you mean it for my own good," Priscilla said, her countenance brightening. She then walked over and kissed her father on the cheek. "I'm sorry for having a bad attitude—that's a perfect so-

50

lution and I am blessed that you are concerned about me."

Anna and Priscilla waited upstairs in a hallway area that was open to the living room downstairs until Esther appeared. Together they looked down and could see Mrs. Ingersoll come in the front door and take a seat in the living room.

"What, no mink tonight? She must be slumming," Esther said. They watched as the butler led her in, and Mr. Strickland greeted her. She then reached over and kissed him on the cheek, allowing her body to touch his. He did not return the kiss, but he didn't resist, either.

"This looks bad. Can't we tell Father she's a communist or something?" Anna suggested. Suddenly Mrs. Ingersoll looked up at them, almost as if she could hear what Anna said, which made them feel a little queasy.

"Oh, there are your sweet and talented daughters. Come down and let me see all of you—each a treasure in her own right, I think. And now Esther is engaged!"

As they walked down, Mrs. Ingersoll walked up to each of them and attempted to hug them. At first Esther resisted, but then she realized she would alienate her father, so she acquiesced. This seemed like something their mother might do after a stay away from home, and they all resented Mrs. Ingersoll doing it, but they knew that refusing the hugs would be impolite. She wore strong and pungent perfume, and the sisters could still smell it on their skin after the hugs.

Mr. Standish came in and announced that dinner was ready, so they all moved into the dining room and took their seats. "So, Esther, I suppose my advice was not so bad, after all? Have you set a date yet?" she asked.

Esther was aching to tell her the engagement had nothing to do with her advice, but she bit her tongue. "Not a specific one—but we will be married in about five months."

"Five months! Why, that's hardly time to pick out a dress, let alone plan a wedding. We must get started right away, don't you think, Joseph?" Mr. Strickland nodded in agreement.

"Now I would love to help you plan this, but there is so much to do. I know just the caterer, and there is a decorator that could help with the room. But where will you hold the wedding?"

Esther looked at her sisters and then at her father. There was no way she wanted this woman involved in her wedding plans, and she considered it extremely presumptuous for her to offer her help, but she was afraid if she said no it would upset her father. "We'll have it at our church. But I don't want a big wedding—I just want close friends and family to attend. So there shouldn't be too much preparation needed," she said, hoping that what she said would give Mrs. Ingersoll a hint that she did not want her help without offending her.

"Yes, but dear, you will look back on this as one of the most important days of your life, and many who know your family, if they are not invited, even though they are not close friends, will resent you for snubbing them. So think carefully about how small you want this to be, won't you?"

"Yes, of course. I'll take that into consideration," Esther said quietly.

"Oh, and you know flowers are so important—they must be done just right—by experts..." Mrs. Ingersoll began, but Mr. Strickland finally had enough of it himself and interrupted her, much to Esther's relief.

"Betty, I'm sure Esther appreciates your interest, but I don't know if she needs help at this point," he said.

Mrs. Ingersoll was taken aback by his comment, and the girls could see it in her eyes, but Mr. Strickland, who was sitting next to her, could not. She quickly recovered and found what appeared to be a magnanimous answer. "Of course...of course—I just want you to know that I am available to help in any way I can be of assistance, if you need it. And if not, I will be pleased to simply watch the nuptials, and only hope that I can catch the wedding bouquet!" She then turned and smiled at Mr. Strickland, and he smiled back, and the servers came in with the entrée.

After they had taken a few bites, Mrs. Ingersoll turned to Anna. "I understand that you're going to Florida—to a resort for a month or so?"

"Yes, I'm leaving in a few weeks," Anna said.

"And where is the destination?" Mrs. Ingersoll asked.

"Miami—Roney Plaza."

"Roney Plaza! Why, that's the newest and best resort in Florida. All the celebrities are staying there, and I'm sure you'll have a wonderful time. I'm trying to plan a trip there myself. Now, Joseph, will you join your daughter?"

"No, I don't think so, Betty. This is a critical time for our steel mills. We'll have to cut worker's pay by about ten percent, and the unions are howling. The next few weeks may be quite difficult and I've got to be available. We've also got some antitrust issues with the oil business."

"Oh, but I'd love to get you down there for a vacation when that's over. Does he ever take a vacation, girls?"

Esther looked at Priscilla. "Not too often. There was the trip to Europe but we were children then, and you mixed business with that, didn't you, Father?"

"I'd love to go to Florida, but I want to go in the dead of winter, when everything is freezing up here," Mr. Strickland said.

"Okay, Joseph, all the girls heard you, so I'm going to remind you when it gets cold—so don't forget."

"I won't, Betty."

"So she just wants to catch the bouquet—well, that's quite subtle, isn't it. What about just asking Father to marry her?" Anna said when dinner was over and they were all in her room.

"That's essentially what she did, isn't it? Do you think he understood that?" Priscilla asked.

"It depends if he knows about the tradition that the one who catches it is the next to get married, and I don't think he thinks about these things. You heard what was on his mind—the steel mills, the oil refineries. Would he have even heard the bouquet comment?"

"Well, what about Florida? What's her plan, to travel with him as if she's his wife or something?" Anna said.

"Father would never do that," Esther said.

"I know, but I think she would do it, and that's the problem. What kind of woman says that to a man? Now don't tell me he didn't figure that out," Priscilla said.

"I would tell you that he didn't figure it out, because I don't think he listens to her very much at all, and all he took away from that comment, in my opinion, is that she would like to see him relax on a vacation. I don't think he saw it as a forward move—he doesn't think that way," Esther said.

"Well, maybe he doesn't, but he is a man, and no man would ignore her, especially when she's lovey dovey, holding your hand and just happens to rub up against you," Priscilla said, mimicking her by taking Anna's hand.

"I wonder if her politics…" Anna began, but Priscilla interrupted.

"I know what you're thinking, but you can bet that she's al-

53

ready figured out Father's politics, and hers will line up perfectly with his. One thing, she's no dummy, she's a conniving…"

"Well, I'm just happy I don't have to let her in on my wedding. I was not sure what I could say, but at least Father stopped that one," Esther said.

10

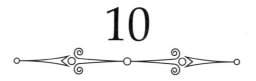

"So you want to see Mr. Blankenship?" The bespectacled secretary, an overbearing woman of about forty-five, asked Priscilla as she stood before her desk. "What is this about?" Her tone was one of superiority, and she clearly relished having the power of deciding whom to admit to Mr. Blankenship's office.

"There are some irregularities with the ledgers—it's quite important," Priscilla said, but the woman did not seem convinced. "It's serious enough to affect the payroll at some point, and I'm certain you would not want to be responsible for such problems, would you?"

She gave Priscilla an acrimonious glance, but got up and walked to Mr. Blankenship's office door and knocked. Priscilla heard him say to come in, and a moment later she opened the door again and ushered Priscilla in.

"So, have a seat, Miss Avery. I understand that you're doing a good job with the books." He smiled at her.

"Yes sir, but there are some problems I need to talk to you about."

"Problems—such as?"

"Well, I think that some money has been…misappropriated."

"Misappropriated? Just what do you mean by that?"

Priscilla moved uncomfortably in her chair for a moment, and he tapped impatiently on the desk with his pencil. "Let's get to the point, shall we. Just tell me what you've found."

"Okay. I believe that Mr. Willis has been embezzling for a number of years. I've only gone back three years but there is a pattern…"

Mr. Blankenship cut her off mid-sentence with a surprising show of anger. "Little lady, Mr. Willis has been the accountant here for over twenty years and is a trusted and loyal employee. He worked for my father, and has never missed a deadline and hardly a day of work until now." Taking a breath, he seemed to calm down a little, but his anger was still flaring. "How dare you accuse him of this! Do you have any evidence?"

"Money has been going to a company which has never sent any products or services to this company," Priscilla said haltingly. She had rarely been talked to in such a harsh way and her voice was quivering as she spoke. Mr. Blankenship realized that he had upset her, and he tried to speak more amiably, but he still seemed angry.

"There must be some mistake. Willis is faithful. Is there anything else?"

"Well, I have his home address here—it was in the payroll records. Do you know where he lives?"

"No, I don't."

"Do you recognize this address?" Priscilla asked, as she handed him a paper with his address on it.

"No, I don't."

"I mean, do you recognize the neighborhood?"

"Yes, of course I do, it's Pelham—an excellent neighborhood."

"Now here is a record—a tax assessment of the value of his home," she said, passing him another piece of paper.

"You did all this research on him—why? Weren't you supposed to be doing the books—that's why you're being paid. Who cares where he lives?"

"I have a record of his salary. You pay him well, but there is no way he could afford a home like this on twenty-five hundred a year."

"I don't know—maybe he inherited some money. Now, I don't like where this is going. I don't like the tone of it," he said, raising his voice as he spoke until he was almost shouting. "You've been here a week, and immediately you're accusing a man who is not even here to defend himself, but he's fighting for his life in the hospital. So, I think we've had enough of your services, Miss Avery. Today will be your last day."

Priscilla stared at him for a moment, not quite believing her ears. She had regained her composure after first losing it with his outburst of anger, and now she was angry herself. She had spent a lot of time to find the bookkeeping problems, and now she was being rebuffed. "That's fine, Mr. Blankenship," she said coolly, and she got up and walked out, slamming the door a little as she left. His secretary was startled when the door slammed and was shocked to see that Priscilla had slammed it.

Priscilla went back to her office and sat down, shaking. Soon she was crying. She didn't want to cry, but the interaction with him was so intense, mixed with being fired, that she could not control herself, although she was trying to. "Be anxious for nothing, let not your heart be troubled," she said over and over again, trying to normalize. What an ingrate, she thought. Here I spend all this time to help him and he fires me.

She had spread ledgers all around the office, and although she was tempted to leave them there and walk out right away, she realized it would be difficult for anyone else to figure out where they should be filed. And he had asked her to finish out the day. Well, she would put everything back where it was when she came, but she was going to leave as soon as that was finished and not stay one moment longer. Perhaps she could call Ben and ask him to come early—and he may as well pick her up in front of the building.

She was still fighting the tears, so she went to the ladies' room and sat in one of the stalls. Then she examined her face and saw how red her eyes were. She washed her face, but her eyes seemed to look worse, and then she decided she didn't care and walked back to her office, determined to leave as soon as possible, no matter what she looked like. But as she opened the door, there he was, sitting in a chair across from her desk. She felt anger coming over her again, and she was also embarrassed knowing how she looked. She turned away to leave, but he shouted out in that unusual accent. "I apologize. Please come back." She hesitated, then found a handkerchief in her purse and dried her eyes, which had started to water again.

"I hope you're very good at apologizing," she said.

"I am—I have to do it a lot because I have a bad temper, you see," he said.

"Where did you get that phony accent—do you adore the British or something? Are you a snobby Anglophile?" she heard herself say. She wasn't sure why she said such a thing, but in her frustration it came out of her mouth seemingly involuntarily.

"I went to boarding school at Eton, and college at Cambridge," he said, not seeming offended. "Father said he wanted me to get the best education possible, although I suspect it was to get me out of his hair at an early age. Please sit down and try to understand. I have always liked Mr. Willis. When I was a child I visited the office and he would bounce me on his knee and give me little presents. He would

57

give me more attention than my father, who would bring me but then get caught up with the business and forget I was here. I instinctively defended him, and I'm not certain that he is guilty even now, but I need to hear everything, and I don't want you to leave. Would you forgive me and give me a second chance?"

"Well, since you put it that way—actually you are pretty good at apologizing, because I was determined to leave as soon as the books were put back."

"That speaks well of you. A lot of people would have left them in disarray after the way I shouted at you—and I couldn't blame them. Now what was the other evidence, please?"

Priscilla took a deep breath. "The company that received funds throughout the years for which I can find no services or products given in return, is a corporation called General Supply Limited, which does not seem to physically exist. So I called the secretary of state's office and traced the incorporation papers to the owners, and one of them appears to be a relative of Mr. Willis's wife. I figured that out by finding her maiden name, which she shares with the treasurer of the corporation. It appears to be her sister, but I'm still working on that."

"My—are you also a private detective? Wherever did you acquire such skills?"

"I appreciate the compliment, but you need to know that it appears that Mr. Willis has embezzled over ninety thousand dollars over the years, and he juggled the books to make it appear that the money is not missing."

"What! Ninety thousand!" Mr. Blankenship exclaimed, jumping out of his chair. "How could he…? When I get my hands on him…! He's lucky he's already in the hospital or I would put him there myself."

"The other problem is that although you have enough for payroll, the money set aside for variable operating costs is actually nonexistent. He has distorted the books to make it appear that the money is there."

"Well, that wouldn't be hard because he's the only one who ever looks at them," Mr. Blankenship said, his anger still rising. "And this when we're having the worst year ever—barely able to make ends meet." He looked over at the ledgers and then at Priscilla, trying to keep his anger from boiling over. "Look, I don't want to offend you, but I need to get some other accountants in here to verify all of this and take it to the police. If you could show them your findings I would appreciate it, and if you would continue to work for us I would even more appreciate it and be forever in your debt. But I really need you full time."

"I will stay—but I can only work part time," Priscilla said.

"Okay, with this as an example of your capabilities, I think that your part time is at least equivalent to anyone else's full time."

"Well, thank you," Priscilla said.

"You know it's funny. All these years I thought of Mr. Willis as the greatest man ever—all because he showed an interest in me when I was a child, but I've thought so much less of my own father. And now I find out it's quite the opposite. My father was gruff and maybe he didn't realize I needed more attention. But he was honest—everyone trusted him, and I saw times when he could have cheated and gotten away with it, but he didn't."

"Yes, I think often we don't appreciate those closest to us. May I put these away then?" Priscilla asked as she picked up some ledgers.

"Of course…of course," Mr. Blankenship said, as he watched her step on a stool and push up on her tiptoes to put the ledgers in the bookshelf. He was showing more interest in her than the ledgers, and she turned around and caught him staring. He quickly turned away and walked out of the office. As he walked down the hallway he muttered to himself, "Just what am I thinking? She's just an employee."

11

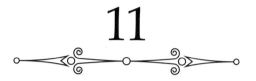

Lucy and Anna were discussing the trip in Anna's bedroom. Lucy was about three years older than Anna, and she was similar in height and measurements, and her looks were mediocre and she was not pretty like Anna, who stood out in a crowd no matter where she was. Lucy had a somewhat coarse look about her. However, she had been working for the Stricklands since she was eighteen, and Anna had been around her so long that she did not realize that Lucy's demeanor was quite the opposite of the typical debutante from a wealthy family.

"But Miss Anna, I don't know if I can do it—I don't know if I can pretend to be you," Lucy protested, as Anna told her the plan for them to switch identities on their trip to Miami.

"It won't be difficult. Just stay in your suite and don't talk to anyone unless you have to. You have enough knowledge of the family that you can answer any questions. And Lucy, you know that gold lamé blouse I have that you like so much? I'm making it a present to you. The only thing I ask is that you don't tell Father about this."

"Oh, that blouse is so expensive! Are you really going to give it to me?"

"Yes," Anna said, and she walked to her closet and brought it out. Lucy took it and stood up in front of the mirror, smiling as she held it up against her chest.

"Oh, it's beautiful—I never thought I'd have a blouse like this. Darryl is going to be so surprised."

"But don't tell your boyfriend about the switch, okay?"

"Okay. But Miss Anna, you've gone to college but I didn't even finish high school. What will I say if someone tries to talk to me about… about college things?"

"Then you just get a headache and excuse yourself."

"Okay—that would work. But I'm so nervous about it."

"It will be all right. Just stay in your room most of the time and no one will be the wiser."

"I hope you're right."

"And start calling me Lucy."

"Okay Miss Anna, I mean Miss Lucy...I mean Lucy."

"We need to start packing. I'll pack both suitcases and you can wear my clothes, and I'll wear some of my older clothes," Anna said as Esther and Priscilla walked in. Lucy walked out and Priscilla lay down on Anna's bed while Esther found a seat on a red velvet sofa in her bedroom.

"Please send me a telegram every day and tell me what is happening, or call long distance if you can get through," Esther said.

"Every day! Esther, I'm twenty years old."

"Okay, every other day—I just want to make certain you are all right."

"How's your job going, Priscilla? Does your boss appreciate you now that you found all those problems?" Anna asked.

"Yes, he appreciates me—I think more and more all the time," Priscilla said with a smile.

"I take it that means he appreciates more than just your genius for business?" Esther asked.

"From the way he looks at me, I would have to agree," she said dreamily.

"Oh...she's in love already," Anna said disparagingly. "Has he asked you to marry him yet? I mean it's been two weeks, hasn't it?"

"No...not yet," Priscilla said, ignoring her sarcasm and still thinking blissfully about Mr. Blankenship.

"What is his first name, anyway?" Anna asked.

"I saw it on the payroll—it's Herbert," Priscilla said.

"You're going to marry a man named Herbert? Are you sure? Could you perhaps get him to change his name or something?" Anna said, laughing.

"Would you quit...it's my dream, let me enjoy it."

"Enough, you two. Anna, I need your complete schedule and the room number at the hotel. When the train gets in, you will have to get a taxi to the hotel, but make certain you ask what the fare is before you get in the cab."

"Esther, I've been taking taxis in New York for years now. I think I know what to do. And if I can deal with a New York cabbie I suppose I can handle one anywhere."

"Okay, I'm just reminding you. You'll be in a strange place, so be careful about who you meet and always take Lucy along if you can."

"What if I meet Mr. Wonderful? Handsome but not proud. Strong but also gentle. Intelligent but not pedantic. Confident but not arrogant. He might want to take me to some nostalgic restaurant for a candlelight dinner, where he tells me how beautiful I am, and how much he adores me. He will tell me I'm the fulfillment of all his dreams, and that he doesn't know what he will do if I turn him down, but he just might do himself in because he is so in love with me. Can I cut Lucy loose then? Because she sure would spoil the evening?"

"No, you really need Lucy then because he's a character that's escaped from some cheesy Hollywood movie," Priscilla said teasingly.

"Oh, I almost forgot, I told Miles I would look in on him before I leave."

"You know I saw him the other day at church, and it's so sad to see him in that wheelchair. But in spite of that he has such a sweet temperament. And he's changed so much—he looks so much older now," Esther said.

"He acts older too—I'm so used to thinking of him as a little kid, but every time I see him, it's like he's reached some new…understanding about life, or something. He's nice to be with and he never complains," Anna said.

"Funny, I don't remember him being that nice before the accident—how much of it do you think is a put-on?" Priscilla asked.

"I don't know—I'm sure he has his bad days, but he seems happier every time I see him. He seems able to accept his situation. It's like he lost one gift, but was given another," Anna answered.

"Miss Anna Strickland is here, Master Miles," the butler announced as Miles was lifting weights from two tables on the right and left of his wheelchair. His muscles were bulging from his dedication to the exercise, and he exhaled and put the weights down. "Shall I wheel you into the living room?"

"No, that's quite all right. I'll do it," Miles said as he grasped the outer metal rails that encircled the wheels of his chair and spun it around to go in the desired direction.

"Hello, Anna. I was looking forward to this last visit before you left," he said, as he made his way to a table where he had been writing.

63

She moved towards him and gave him her customary light, one-armed hug.

"Miles, is there some reason I never seem to see your mother anymore when I come over?"

"Well, she spends a lot of time taking care of her mother in Boston now. She's quite ill, and Mother wants to have some time with her before she passes."

Anna noticed some poetry books on the table. "Are you studying Keats?" she asked as she picked up one of the books. Opening it at random, she read the title of a poem aloud and asked, "What's this one about?"

"Keats loved this woman who was from a rather well off family, and he could not marry her because he was poor. He had already written some great poems, but his genius was not discovered until after his death. Anyway, she loved him, and was trying to work out how to marry him, which would have been diametrically opposed to the wishes of her family. Then he became ill, and died at the age of twenty five—before they could marry. But before he died, he wrote that poem for her."

"What's interesting about her is she was not a woman who normally enjoyed poetry and she did not understand it, but she loved Keats so she asked him to teach her about it. Here she fell in love with this great poet, but didn't really understand poetry—now that's ironic, isn't it?"

Anna read the poem and then looked at Miles.

"So it was his lack of money that stopped true love from taking its course?" she asked.

"Yes, in that day it seems if you had wealth, you were supposed to only marry someone who was also well off."

"I'm not so sure things have changed very much." Anna put the book down and noticed a handwritten poem had been under it. "Is this yours?" she asked, reaching to pick it up. Miles reached for it himself, but she beat him to it.

"Don't read it—it's not very good, really," he protested.

"You wouldn't deprive your friend, would you?" she said, and holding the paper up, she began to read it out loud.

The fleeting glance, the nonchalant word, and the easy pace,
The intense stare, the loud diatribe, and speeding to the race.
What sense have these, from whence do they come?

What makes the difference when it's tallied for the sum?

The rose and petal and fragrance wafting in the breeze.
But what is this, a thorn and bleeding, was it just a tease?
Where do the pain and poetry meet and then get set apart?
How does the loving child become a man without a heart?

Where does this breeze blow, that changes things on earth?
What price must be paid so that life continues with the birth?
How does God measure the varied thoughts of all mankind?
Is it tragic that the face starts smooth and ends up lined?

No, the plan is somewhere between the earth and sky.
It hangs in the balance—in the choices made before we die.
Its intricately woven truth is the only reason why.
And the story can end with a triumph, not a sigh.

"Why, Miles, that's a beautiful poem," Anna said. "I knew you read poetry, but I didn't know you wrote it. May I have it—a copy? I mean, I don't have time now, but I'd like to copy it when I get back from the trip."

"I have plenty of time—I'll make you a copy while you're gone if you really think it's worth it," Miles offered.

"I truly do."

Miles looked at her for a moment—his smile fading.

"What is it?"

"Anna, I want you to have a wonderful vacation, but I must tell you to use caution—be careful, please—I feel I must tell you that for some reason."

"Of course I will, and I'll have Lucy with me the whole time. There's nothing to worry about," Anna said, and she reached over and hugged his arm and kissed him on the cheek. "I'll write to you when I get a chance."

12

The next morning, as Ben drove Priscilla to work in a Pierce Arrow limousine, they were surprised to see an ambulance stop at the factory as they approached. Normally Ben would turn a block before they reached the factory to let Priscilla off, but she asked him to drive around the factory so that she could see what was happening. They saw a man being loaded into the ambulance, and then the ambulance drove away. Ben turned on the block past the factory and let Priscilla out, and she walked towards her office. On her way she walked past Mr. Blankenship's secretary, Mrs. Ross, who had changed her attitude a little towards her after hearing about her bookkeeping discoveries.

"Do you know what happened?" Priscilla asked.

"One of the men in the factory was working on some wiring and he got shocked and fell off a ladder and broke his leg," she said. As she spoke, Mr. Blankenship's door opened, and they could hear him talking to two men, one of which was the shop foreman. "Is he an imbecile?" she heard Mr. Blankenship say in a loud and angry voice. "Anyone knows enough to cut the power before working on a line."

"I think he thought he could do it without touching the hot wire," one of the men said apologetically.

"I could understand better if he forgot, but that's like playing with fire. And now I need to train a new man, because he's bound to be out with that leg injury for a long time," Mr. Blankenship said, still perturbed.

"Jonas is a good man, Mr. Blankenship," the other man said. "He may have made a mistake, but he was trying to save us time by not cutting the power. He's done it before and we've been able to keep the work going."

"He's done this before! Are you just as stupid as he is? Can't anyone follow the rules around here? Just get out of my office now before I really get angry," he said, slamming the door as they left.

"Can he get any angrier?" Priscilla said to Mrs. Ross.

"Oh yes, he can," Mrs. Ross said, rolling her eyes. The men left the office, appearing dejected as they walked back to the factory. As Priscilla walked towards her office, the door opened again, and she heard Mr. Blankenship tell Mrs. Ross that he wanted the injured man fired right away. Priscilla hesitated after hearing this, and then went back to her office. She was only there a few minutes when Mr. Blankenship walked in and sat down, leaving her door open. Mrs. Ross noticed the open door, and walked towards some filing cabinets that were near it so she could hear the conversation.

"Can you write out exactly what Willis did in laymen terms so that our attorney can prepare it for a grand jury indictment?" he asked.

"Yes, of course," she said, without looking up at him and with a curt tone of voice.

"Is there something wrong?" he asked, peering over at her to try to see her face, which he could only see a portion of since she kept it focused on a ledger book.

"No, I'm just busy," she said, still sounding unhappy.

"Well, I'm paying you, so look at me and tell me the truth—you are obviously upset about something."

She finally looked up and took a deep breath. "That man who got hurt is a good employee, and you are being too harsh with him."

"And how would you know what kind of an employee he is, pray tell?"

"Well, I have the attendance records and he stands out as hardly ever missing a day. And he was recommended for a promotion about five months ago, but never got it because profits were down. The foreman, Mr. Palowski, gave me that information because I was trying to project any increase in expenses due to promotions or raises, as you requested."

"Well that shows just how wrong Palowski was about him, doesn't it?"

"It sounds like he was bending the rules, but it was for the benefit of the company—he didn't want to disturb production."

"Yes, I am quite aware of that."

"Do you also know that he has a wife and six children? How do you think they are going to get by when you fire him and he can't work due to the injury? Do you know how hard it is to get a job these days?"

"I guess he should have thought about that before he disobeyed the rules."

"Look, you don't want to really hear anything I have to say, so can I get back to my job…please?" Priscilla asked.

"Of course," he said, and he got up and walked towards the door but before he got there he turned around and faced her, not saying anything for a moment. She felt him looking at her but did not respond, hoping he would leave. He didn't, so finally she looked up at him.

"Yes? Did you want something else, sir?"

"What would you do? Pay him while he's unable to work after he did something so stupid? Would you reward that behavior?"

"No, but I think if he can't work in the factory, maybe he could work in the office doing something?"

"In the office—with the women! Are you kidding?"

"No, I'm not kidding."

"What would he do in the office?"

"He worked in shipping and he knows the product line so maybe he could help taking orders or something."

"He wouldn't get paid as much as in the factory if he did that."

"I think he would rather get paid less and keep his job than have no income. And it would help your relationship with the other workers," she said.

"So you don't think it's good?" he asked.

"Of course it's not. You know that and everyone knows it. You are too harsh with them, and they don't like you."

"Wow—you really don't mince words, do you? I thought employers deserved respect."

"Mr. Blankenship, respect is earned, and you asked me to stay in the position after you apologized. Now please don't ask me a question unless you want a truthful answer."

"You don't need this job very much, do you?"

She waited a moment, considering how she should answer and wanting to make certain she was not lying, but she did not want him to know that she did not need the work. "I don't need it enough to kowtow or lie to you if that's what you mean."

He looked at her for a moment and shook his head in anger. Then he slammed his fist on the desk, making a sound so loud that it shocked her, and got up and walked out briskly and slammed her door as he left.

"That's it," she said to herself, and she opened her desk drawer and began taking some personal things out of it and putting them in her purse. When that was full she got up from her desk and was looking around for a bag to put things in when she heard a barely audible knock on her door. She was hesitant to answer it because she thought it might be him again, but then she heard the knock again and a woman's voice.

"May I come in, Miss Avery?" Mrs. Ross asked very politely, and Priscilla went to the door and opened it.

"Yes, of course Mrs. Ross."

"Can I talk to you for a moment?"

"Yes," Priscilla said, still a little shaken from her encounter with Mr. Blankenship.

Mrs. Ross looked at her purse and the things she had pulled out of her desk drawer, which were now piled on top of the desk. "You're quitting, aren't you?"

"Yes, Mrs. Ross, I'm quitting, and I'm really not in the mood to discuss it...."

"I understand, I heard the whole thing. Mr. Blankenship loses his temper, but he gets over it quickly. Most of the time he is very charming to be around."

"Yes, I'm sure he is, but it seems that I bring out the temper side."

"That's because you tell him the truth. Miss Avery, I know I was not very kind to you when you first came, and I am truly sorry for that—because I really admire you now."

"You admire me?"

"Yes, and I don't want you to quit. Mr. Blankenship is really a decent person; he just had so much rejection and harshness from his father that...well, I don't want to go into that. But he needs you here, and we need you here. The future of this company may depend on you, because no one else will stand up to him."

"Mrs. Ross, you flatter me. I'm just a part-time employee," Priscilla said, as she put some things into a paper bag.

"No, I mean it. Now I don't know if you need this job or not, but being a woman who likes to window shop, I recognize the labels and the quality of your clothing and...well, I don't think you need to be here, so I'm asking if you would stay as a favor to everyone. You already may have saved Jonas's job."

"I don't know about that. He mocked my idea."

"Give him time, dear. He gets angry, but he's not stubborn. He thinks about things, and he is very good at innovation—he's increased efficiency since he's taken over, and he is also very good with clients. And I know he thinks highly of you. I heard him bragging about you the other day."

Priscilla stopped what she was doing and looked at Mrs. Ross for a moment and smiled, but also shook her head. "I don't know, I just don't know how much I can put up with."

"I understand, but please take a little time and think about it—would you do that?"

"Yes, I will. Thank you, Miss Avery."

Mrs. Ross walked from Priscilla's office to Mr. Blankenship's, and waited by the open door while he spoke on the telephone. When he hung up, she knocked and he motioned her in.

"Yes, Mrs. Ross? What is it?"

"It's the girl you hired, Miss Avery."

"Oh, what has she done now? Come in and sit down."

Mrs. Ross gingerly moved towards one of the chairs in front of his desk and slowly sat in it.

"Mr. Blankenship, I've worked here for twenty-three years, and I've never said anything to you or your father before about employees, but I think it's important to speak now. May I speak my mind, sir?"

"Yes, Mrs. Ross, please do."

"Miss Avery is very upset and I think you should apologize to her. I heard what you said and I think it was improper."

Mr. Blankenship took a deep breath and his face began to get red. "What is this, a mutiny—a conspiracy?"

"Not at all. But she's cleaning out her desk right now."

"She is? I need her to testify when we go to court against Willis, and the books are still a mess."

"You also need to take what she says to heart about Jonas."

"What, were you listening in on the whole conversation?"

"Well, the door was open, and your voice is quite loud."

"So you're for this too—you want to put him with the women? Shall we also put him in a dress?"

Mrs. Ross looked at him for a moment, but did not answer. "May I go back to my desk now, sir?"

"Yes," he answered with a dismal tone. "By all means, go back."

Priscilla had stopped packing her things and was filing some accounting papers when Mr. Blankenship looked into her office. "Can I

71

talk to you for a minute?" he asked.

"Well, that depends who you are right now. Is it Jekyll or Hyde?"

"Hmm. I think Hyde. No, Jekyll—that's the good guy, right? Jekyll? Then I'm Jekyll. I must hand it to you, that's pretty clever. Pretty clever, indeed. So are you okay with Jekyll—he's a good deal better than Hyde, isn't he?"

"So what can I do for you?"

"Mrs. Ross said you might be leaving and that I should apologize for my rudeness, and I do."

"Until the next blow-up?"

"Yes, I see your point, and my actions have been inexcusable, but I've been worse than usual because of the pressure I'm under. First there was Willis—whom I've always respected, and then the ninety thousand or so. And I'm trying to sell some real estate to get the company back in the black, and I'm told it's worth about thirty percent of what it was in 1929. I know I look rich to you, and am probably hard to feel sorry for, but these problems are serious and they are weighing on me."

"If I stay, you must promise not to denigrate my suggestions anymore. I'm only trying to do the best job I can."

"I know you are. I'm just not used to someone expressing opinions so freely in areas other than their specialty...."

Priscilla began to frown as he said this, and he tried to rehabilitate.

"I mean I'm not used to it, but I'm...I'm grateful for it. You seem to have a gift for business, and I mean that. And if I say something I shouldn't, please just correct me."

"I will if I can shout that loud," Priscilla said.

"Good, then you'll stay. And I'll give Jonas a chance at the office work—but he can't wear eye shadow."

Priscilla smiled for the first time since he had entered the office.

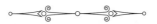

The next morning, Mr. Blankenship knocked again at Priscilla's open door.

"Yes?"

"You know we must get Willis's name off this door," he said, scratching at the W on the glass pane. "Every time I see it I feel money leaving my pocket. But what I came to say was, would you please have lunch with me today?"

"Is this business or pleasure?" she asked, looking up at him. He

72

hesitated before answering.

"Well it's about business, but I hope it's not entirely unpleasur-able—if that's a word."

"What time do you want to leave?"

"I usually go around one o'clock—I'll stop by your office then."

A little before one o'clock, Priscilla went to the ladies' room and freshened up for the lunch. They rode together in Mr. Blankenship's Auburn convertible cabriolet. Priscilla was surprised when they drove up to Stork Club, one of the most expensive restaurants in New York. He noticed her consternation.

"Is everything all right?"

"Yes, but I thought you were on a budget now, and this looks like an expensive place."

"Nothing but the best for my sleuth accountant," he said, as the doorman came up and opened the door for her to get out. Mr. Blanken-ship left the car running, and another man got in to park it.

When they walked in, one of Mr. Strickland's friends, a fat woman of about fifty named Mrs. Reynolds, saw Priscilla. Mrs. Reyn-olds was seated with her husband, but she was walking back from the ladies' room and she came up to her. "Hello, Priscilla—it's so good to see you again. And who's this handsome devil with you?"

Priscilla was embarrassed. She was about to answer when Mr. Blankenship spoke. "I'm Herbert Blankenship, but I'm a lucky devil to be able to take this lady to lunch, am I not?"

"Yes, of course you are," Mrs. Reynolds said and laughed a lit-tle. Then she looked back at her husband who was seated about thirty feet away, and saw that the waiter was there. "Oh, we're being served, I'd better run."

After they were seated, Priscilla saw another old friend of hers from high school, and she tried to avoid her. The girl did see her, but she just waved from her table and Priscilla waved back, relieved that she didn't come over."

"My, you must know a few wealthy people," he said, when she finished waving.

"It's just a coincidence to see them here. It must be a special oc-casion for them. So what did you want to talk about—you said it was business?"

"Yes, I did, didn't I? Well, I wanted to ask you to take Willis's place. But before you answer, let me give you the whole proposition.

He was making twenty-five hundred a year, but I will pay you three thousand. And that's a large salary for that position. I don't think you can get paid more anywhere else."

"Yes, that sounds very generous," she said.

"Then will you accept?"

"No, I'm sorry. It's not the money—I have a commitment that prevents me from working full time and I can't break it."

"Can you tell me what it is?"

"Well, I help my father out—he has his own business and needs my help and I promised him I'd stay."

"Really, what is his business?"

"Well he does a lot of different things."

"Sounds like he's a jack of all trades."

"Sort of."

"Well, sometimes we need a handyman. Do you think he'd help us if we did?"

"I don't know but I could ask."

After lunch they went out to the entrance and saw that it was pouring down rain. The car porter brought the car around and when they got to the office parking lot, which was across the street, the rain was still heavy. "I guess we'd better make a mad dash for the building," he said, and they ran for it, but as they got to the steps of the building, Priscilla slipped backwards and he caught her with both of his arms, and they faced each other for a moment, only inches from each other's face. He held her for a few seconds more, and moved closer to her as if he were going to kiss her, but then he backed away and pulled her up and she stood. "That was…very close, wasn't it?" he said.

"Yes, I guess so," she answered.

"I thought he was going to kiss me," Priscilla said to her two sisters as they sat on the patio in the back of their mansion, which was surrounded with beautifully manicured gardens and a huge swimming pool.

"What would you have done if he had?" Esther asked.

"I would have slapped him across the face. No gentleman would take advantage of a girl in that type of situation. Besides, we were in a public place and my reputation was at stake."

"That sounds like a terrible ordeal, and you seem quite shaken over it," Esther said, and Anna giggled.

"Well, do you still like him?" Anna asked.

"Yes, but he's so hard to get along with, I just think I should quit and get out of there. I think it may be a big mistake. I told you what he can be like—especially with the employees."

"But maybe you are just what he needs," Esther said. "To give him the balance in his life—to tame him."

"I'm afraid that would take a whip and a chair, and it's a bigger job than I can handle. That's what scares me about him. I like him but I wish I didn't."

As she spoke, Mr. Strickland came out to the patio. "Esther, could I speak to you for a minute, please?"

"Yes, Father, I'll be right there." Turning to her sisters, she said, "I'd better see what he wants."

As Esther walked into his study, Mr. Strickland looked up, and passed her a catalog with women's clothing in it. "Mrs. Ingersoll's birthday is coming up, and I'd like to buy her a present and have a little party for her here. Would you mind helping me pick something out for her and plan the party?"

Esther tried to hide her attitude about Mrs. Ingersoll and forced a smile. "Yes, of course, Father," she said, taking the catalog. "How much do you want to spend?"

"Oh, I don't know. Just find her something nice and I'll pay for it."

"And how many people will be coming to the party?"

"I think about twenty-five. I was going to make it a surprise, but I don't know her friends, so I'm just going to tell her to invite who she wants. I'll get the exact number after I tell her about it."

"But what if…what if she wants to invite two hundred and fifty?" Esther said.

"Then I guess we'll have to book it at Hilton ballroom," he said, only half in jest as he looked at Esther's face and noticed that she seemed disturbed. "You know, I realize that none of you like her very much, and I appreciate your helping me with this. I know she is a bit superficial and maybe a bit of a snob. But when I'm with her, I feel good, and I haven't had that since your mother died. She's a lot younger than me, which makes me a little self-conscious, but it also makes me feel young again. It seems like part of me has been dead since Ruth passed on to her reward."

"Father…"

"Yes?"

"Never mind. You know it would be easier for me to go shopping for her than to use the catalog. Can you get her measurements?"

"You were beginning to say something about her, weren't you? Why don't you just say it."

"Okay." Esther took a moment to consider how to answer. She knew if she said everything she thought about Mrs. Ingersoll it would just alienate him. "Do you remember when you gave all of us advice about finding the right person to marry? That was some years ago."

"I remember some of it."

"You said that the person you meet at first is not the real person. It is rather the 'pretend' person in most cases. You told us that only after some time does the real person emerge, and if we didn't give the relationship time to be certain we knew who the real person was, we might have a lifetime of misery."

"Yes, I remember something like that—that's good advice."

"I would ask you then, before making any type of commitment to Mrs. Ingersoll, would you take the time to find out who the real person is? Would you take your own very excellent advice?"

Mr. Strickland looked a little disturbed for a moment, and he looked down at his desk and then back at Esther. "Yes, I will do that. In fact, I think a party for her may be too much right now—and I do find them so tedious. Just find her a nice gift—that would be appropriate."

13

"This is one beautiful hotel," Lucy exclaimed as they drove up to Roney Plaza in Miami. It had only recently been built, and it was seventeen stories high, with a Florentine bell tower that had a copper-capped dome. The building was huge and imposing, and it was a magnificent sight with a backdrop of the Atlantic Ocean.

Lucy was having a hard time containing her excitement as they ascended in the elevator with the bellhop following with their luggage. Anna opened the door and gave him a tip and they walked in. The large, luxurious suite was beautifully decorated in pastel hues, tan leather furniture, and a floor-to-ceiling picture window which faced the ocean. Lucy appeared entranced with the commanding view of the ocean, and then she switched her attention to the room and its furnishings. Next she walked into one of the bedrooms, and Anna followed, watching her as she bounced on the bed like a child, smiling. "Are we really staying here? So this is where rich people stay—what a posh place!"

"Well, you are staying in this room, and mine is adjacent to it," Anna said, and she walked through a connecting door to her own room, leaving Lucy smiling as she stared out the window from the bedroom, which also overlooked the ocean.

After unpacking, Anna went down to the main restaurant and asked to see the manager. He was a chubby, balding man of about forty years old, and he stared at her in what she thought was a lecherous way as he walked out from the kitchen.

"Hi, I'm Lucy Jenkins, I wrote to you about the waitress job. You said you weren't sure if one would be open but to check when I arrived."

He stared at her admiringly. "Oh yes, sister, you have the job.

You can start any time you want to."

She felt uncomfortable, but she smiled. "Can I start tomorrow evening then? What time does the shift start?"

"Four in the evening. Ask for Miss Knapp and she'll get you started."

Later Anna was back in her room, and was trying to get Lucy used to the idea of pretending to be her.

"Are you going to eat or not?" Anna asked Lucy.

"I will...I will, but I'm scared. I just can't pass for you, I know I can't."

"All you have to do is go down and order your food, eat it, and come back up to the room."

"Where will you be?"

"Tomorrow I'll be working as a waitress. I might even wait on you."

"You're going to be a waitress!"

"Yes, I am. And I don't want anyone to know that I'm staying in this hotel, so I will try to come up to the rooms quietly. I booked them both in my name—the Strickland name, that is."

"Since you're upset, let's just order room service tonight," she added. "But you need to go to the door when the bellhop comes up here and give him this as a tip." She handed Lucy some coins. Lucy looked at them and counted them out.

"I guess I should become a bellhop," she said, impressed with the amount of the tip.

The next night, Anna went to the restaurant and asked for Miss Knapp, a thirty-year-old woman who looked more like forty, with bleached orangey red hair and a raspy voice, who explained which tables were Anna's. "Now some of the guests are going to bring in a little extra and slip it into their sodas. It's best that you don't notice that," she said. Anna did not understand what she was talking about, which was obvious by her puzzled expression. "Hooch, booze, moonshine, that's what I mean," she said.

"But isn't that illegal?" Anna asked.

"Yeah, no kidding, honey. That's why I said turn the other way if you want a good tip. What you don't see won't hurt you."

Anna didn't have a chance to think about what she had just heard, because she had to concentrate as Miss Knapp showed her the kitchen and explained more of her duties.

The work was tedious and hard, Anna thought, as she finished preparing the last of the tables. She had sat down for only a moment when another woman, who introduced herself as Jillian, walked out and asked her to work in the kitchen. She dutifully got up and followed her, even though she wanted to take a break. There were several cooks and many helpers in the kitchen, and it looked confusing to her at first. As they walked through the kitchen, it seemed as if all the workers moved away in awe as one man walked through the midst of them, moving in their direction. He was short and fat with balding hair and a round face which at the moment was tense with the anticipation of preparing the evening meal. "This is Mr. Mercier, the head chef," the woman said with a respectful tone. "Here is a helper for you, Lucy Jenkins." The chef looked over at her and smiled as he spoke with a mix of English and French.

"Bon. Vous accueillir, la jeune dame," {Good. Welcome, young lady} "You are…Vous devez être la nouvelle fille—the new girl," {You must be the new girl} he said.

"Oh, Chef Mercier, you must try to speak English so she can understand."

Anna thought for a while, trying to remember her French and then said, "Au contraire, je suis heureux de vous rencontrer, monsieur." {On the contrary, I am pleased to meet you, sir.}

Upon hearing her speak French, Chef Mercier's face seemed to light up and his face beamed at her. "Alors vous connaissez le langage de l'amour!" {So you know the language of love!} "But I must…I must speak only English so the rest will understand, is that not the case, Mrs. Jillian?"

"Yes Mr. Mercier—please do that so we can obey your commands."

"Bon…my commandes…this is very important," he said, chuckling. "Now you all must go back and I will teach mademoiselle."

Anna smiled at him, and they went through the large kitchen, which was lined with tables for the preparation of various foods. As they walked past a table where several workers were making salads, he stopped for a moment.

"Come back on your break, for your free dinner tonight," he said kindly. "Don't forget because it will be délicieux."

"I get a free dinner?" she asked.

"Chef's treat, because you speak Français so extraordinaire. And tonight it will be filet mignon, prepared the way only Chef Mercier can prepare it. Juicy, and so succulent that you can cut it with your fork.... But for now, you can decorate the dessert. You are a special mademoiselle, so I will give you a special job."

They walked to the end of the room to a table where little cakes were on separate plates. Then he picked up a tube with colored frosting in it, and made a circular design with it on the top of the cake. "Now you try it," he said, handing her the tube. She took the tube and began to squeeze it on a cake, but he stopped her. "No, first practice on this." He gave her an empty plate, and she squeezed the tube, sputtering its contents all over the plate. She was embarrassed, but he only laughed and used his finger to wipe off some of the frosting, which he then tasted. "Magnifique!" he said. "Here, watch me and try again."

He took the tube and showed her how to apply pressure and control the stream of frosting, and then handed it to her. The second time, she did a better job, but it still did not look like his. "Oh, I'm sorry...I just can't seem to get it."

"It is no loss, Mademoiselle, because it is still...comestible... how do you say?"

"Edible," Anna said as he tasted the icing again.

"Yes, edible...it is certainly edible. But now, you see, you must apply even pressure until you get to the end, and then you ease off or it will courir, you know...run."

He gave her the tube and she tried again and it was almost like his, but not quite.

"Bon, but you must move your arm in this manner when we squeeze," he said, doing it again and making a perfect design on a cake.

She took a breath and squeezed the tube, and this time it looked like his. He looked at her with new respect. "Aha...now you have it. So you get to sample it," he said, and he took a spoonful of the icing and gave it to her.

"This is a mint flavor—crème de mint. It's delicious, no? And now for the cakes—you are ready."

She wasn't as certain as he was, but she began gingerly, making another swirl and then another. Hers weren't always as good as his, but they were very close.

"Oh, c'est très bon—it is very good—you learn so quickly, not like some of the girls. I need you in the kitchen, but you'll make more money with the tables—there are no tips back here."

"But I'd like to learn," she said, squeezing the frosting again and making a near perfect swirl. "I don't care about the tips."

"I will talk to the boss, then. Maybe we get you back here and fatten you up a little," he added jokingly.

As Anna continued to work, a young man dressed in a tuxedo walked up and watched her as she worked. After a few minutes, it flustered her a little, and she squeezed too much frosting on one of the cakes and then looked at him, questioningly. "Can I help you?" she asked.

"Well, it would help if you could work a little faster, because we'll be serving soon. At this pace, I might mistake you for one of those rich debutantes instead of a waitress. I'm Jeremy Maitland, the maître d'. You'll have the seven tables in the west corner tonight—next to the piano. I'll cover your mistakes," he added and he took the cake she had just attempted to frost and ate part of it. "Shouldn't go to waste, you know."

She stopped and looked at him for a moment. He was brusque, but he also had a charm about him, and, smartly dressed in his tuxedo, she thought he could easily pass for any of the wealthier young men that she knew back home. He had dark hair but pale brown eyes, and his face was quite refined and somewhat handsome, she thought. "Mr. Maitland, I just learned how to do this, that's why I'm a little slow. And I could have wiped the frosting off that cake and used it," she countered.

"Too late now," he answered cheerfully. "And just call me Jeremy. You'll be serving next to the jazz band that's playing, so please walk around the side of the room, not in front of the band and not on the dance floor. Remember, your job is to serve—they are the stars."

"Don't worry, I won't steal the limelight," she said with a slightly sarcastic tone.

"Oh, I think you will, whether you like it or not," he said.

"What is that supposed to mean?" she asked.

"It's a compliment," he said and then turned away. She shook her head, wondering how he could seem insulting at first and then complimentary. As she went back to her work, Miss Knapp walked up.

"We start serving at five o'clock. It will be slow until about seven or eight, so you'll have a chance to get used to it."

"So do I work for you, or Mr. Maitland?"

"You mean Jeremy? You don't work for him. He's just working here for the summer."

"But he acted as if…"

"Yeah, he always acts like he's in charge or something. On a high horse because he's a college boy—going to be an engineer or something so he thinks he's better than us. You can just ignore him."

Anna wondered about him. Evidently he was working his way through college. As she considered his situation, he entered the kitchen again and picked up some glasses, and she watched him. As he turned to take them into the dining room, he looked over at her. She quickly looked the other way, embarrassed that he had caught her looking at him.

She never realized until now, even with all the restaurants she had visited, how stressful it could be waiting on tables. All of her tables were constantly full until the end of the evening, and she kept rushing back and forth, trying to fill orders and not forget any requests. She knew it would be easier once she learned the menu, but there was something else that bothered her. As Miss Knapp had told her to expect, she noticed that some of the patrons had small flasks with them that they spiked their drinks with. Since she knew this was against the law, she wondered if there was something she could do about it. She also noticed that the largest tips seemed to come from the tables of those who had flasks.

As things slowed down a little, she was walking back to the kitchen with this on her mind. Jeremy was in the kitchen on a break eating something and turned around as she walked in. He noticed her grimace. "Do you already hate the job that much?" he asked.

"No, I don't hate it," she said defensively. "Why do you ask?"

"Because of the look of disgust on your face," he countered.

"That's because I've been thinking about the drinkers—some of the people are spiking their drinks and it's against the law."

"Well, some laws are made to be broken, and I think there are more drinkers out there than you think. Some are just sneakier about it, and they have it in perfume bottles or whatever. I wouldn't worry about it. If they weren't drinking here it would be somewhere else."

She looked at him disdainfully for a moment, and then remembered she had to get back to a table. Quickly she poured two cups of coffee and put them on a tray. As she took it from the kitchen, she heard him say whimsically, "Maybe that will sober them up."

It was eleven o'clock and fewer guests were coming in, and several of her tables were vacant. The jazz band was playing slower songs, and she could tell they were tired, and only a couple of people were dancing. Jeremy seated a new couple at one of her tables, and she went to wait on them. As she walked towards the table, she noticed a man walk in with two other male friends, all of whom waited to be seated. The man she noticed was about six foot two inches tall, very strong looking and exceptionally handsome. He had dark brown hair and brown eyes which she felt were gazing at her. He looked sophisticated and was dressed in an expensive silk suit, but his friends looked slightly unsavory. They were also dressed very nicely, but there was something about them that repelled her. As she took the order, she noticed from the corner of her eye that he was definitely looking at her as he spoke to Jeremy.

"Yes sir, there are many seats available," Jeremy said.

The man watched Anna as he said, "Anywhere is okay as long as it's a table that she waits on."

Jeremy looked over at Anna, and seemed displeased, but he knew he had to comply.

"Of course, sir," he said, and he led the three men over to a table next to the one she was waiting on. The man gave Jeremy a quarter, which he took reluctantly, and he walked away. Anna looked over at the new table, and was now certain that the man was staring at her. However, he was so attractive that she felt complimented.

"I'll be with you in a moment," she said.

The man nodded politely and smiled. "Oh, we're in no hurry. We need some time to decide, Gorgeous."

Normally Anna would have been insulted with such a salutation, but instead she felt her heart beating harder and she quickly exited into the kitchen. As she placed the order for the couple, all she could think of was how handsome this man was—and he was evidently interested in her. Or was he? Did he just talk to all of the waitresses like that? Was he just a flirt, she wondered. She prepared the sodas that were ordered and brought them out to the couple. As she did, she noticed him staring at her as she walked. She tried to keep her eyes away from him, and she served the sodas, spilling one of them a little, as she was flustered by his attention. It only fell on the tablecloth, and she wiped it up quickly. "Oh, I'm so sorry," she said to the couple.

"That's quite all right," the man said as she cleaned up.

"Miss," the attractive man said, and she turned around and walked to his table. "We're ready to order now."

"Yes, what would you like?"

"Well, I can't go wrong with filet mignon—especially if Mercier prepared it."

"He did—he said it was his own special recipe," Anna said.

"He is the best. Studied at Cordon Bleu you know," the man said.

"Really, that's quite impressive."

The other men with him indicated that they also wanted that dish and Anna turned to leave. "By the way, I'm Bart Lewis, and you are also quite impressive."

"Why, thank you, Mr. Lewis...."

"Bart...my friends call me Bart."

"Well, Mr. Lewis, if we ever become friends, then I'll call you Bart, also."

"I hope we become more than friends," Bart said, but Anna ignored his comment. She turned away and saw that Miss Knapp was there, listening. She knew she was blushing, and she tried to get into the kitchen as soon as possible. Miss Knapp followed her.

"He likes you," Miss Knapp said. "He's bananas over you."

"Really?"

"Yes, and he's filthy rich. Whenever he comes in here he spends a bundle, and he's a big tipper. But he's quite a playboy, so be careful."

"I will, Miss Knapp." Anna felt her heart sink a little as she realized what kind of person Bart Lewis was. She had thought that might be the case, and Miss Knapp had just confirmed it. She felt foolish for thinking that he might be someone she would be interested in. The man she wanted would be pure and devoted only to her, and he would want a family. The last thing she wanted was a man who chased women, so that was the end of that.

When she walked back out with their food, Bart was smiling widely. Setting the plates down before the men, she wanted to get away quickly, but Bart whispered something in her ear as she set the plate down. She didn't hear what he said, and she didn't want to ask, so she stood up and smiled at him, and then began to walk away. He called out after her, "Could I please get some more sour cream for my baked potato?" She turned back and nodded at him and got some more from the kitchen. As she began to walk through the doors, suddenly Jeremy was there.

"Is he giving you a hard time?"

"No, why would you think that?"

"Because he's been eyeing you all night, and he asked to sit in your section. These rich guys think they own everybody."

"There is no problem," Anna said.

"Do you like him?" Jeremy asked.

Anna looked at him for a moment. He was standing in the way of the double doors which she had to walk through to get to the dining room. "What are you talking about?—he's just a customer. Now I need to get back out there." She waved him away and went through the doors and delivered the sour cream.

"May I ask your name?" Bart asked.

"Well I really don't know why..." Anna began.

"I just want to tell management what a fantastic waitress you are. You're new here and it will help you."

"Okay. My name is Miss Jenkins."

"Do you have a first name? I gave you mine."

Anna hesitated but decided to acquiesce. "It's Lucy."

"Hmm...somehow I wouldn't have taken you for a Lucy—maybe a Mary or a...an Estelle."

"Mr. Lewis, I've got other tables...."

"Yes, of course—but one question. Thank you for the dish. Is there any chance you would like to go out with me tonight?"

"I'm afraid not. I don't even get off until one o'clock."

"Oh, things don't really get going in Miami until then. There are lots of places..."

"Waitress," the man at the table next to them said, and Anna walked over to his table, happy for the interruption.

Anna walked into her room and collapsed on the couch. She was quite tired from the work—not only from being on her feet all day, but from trying to remember all the requests from the patrons throughout the night. She had an apron filled with tips, and she took it off and emptied it on the couch. Bart Lewis had left her a huge tip, and she wanted to give it back, but he had left before she could. She heard a knock on the door that separated her room from Lucy's, and she opened it. Lucy walked in, looking as if she had been sleeping.

"So, how'd it go?" Lucy asked groggily.

"I'm dead tired. That was a nine-hour shift with constant serving."

"Well, so now you know how it feels, huh?" Lucy asked rhetorically, with what Anna thought was a somewhat mocking attitude.

"Yes, I guess so," Anna answered after a bit of hesitation.

"Wow, you hit the jackpot! Is all that dough from tips?" Lucy asked.

"Yes, and I need to get to bed now."

"Tomorrow I think I'll eat downstairs—it sure was lonely here tonight."

"Yes, that's okay," Anna said, and Lucy walked back through the door, which Anna locked after her.

14

David Holt was sitting in his luxurious office—a room with a view of the New York skyline, tastefully decorated with several overstuffed leather chairs and a matching leather sofa, when the intercom buzzed. He picked it up and his father's secretary summoned him to his office. David wondered what he wanted, since his father rarely asked him in the office except when they had meetings scheduled. He had been analyzing sales figures for the company's five-and-dime retail stores and was supposed to prepare a report on his findings, but the meeting for that was scheduled for the afternoon. Thinking there might be some questions about his findings, he grabbed the pages with the sales figures and walked towards the end of the hallway to the office. The secretary nodded and he opened the door and walked into his father's office.

It was a huge office and the view was more commanding than his own. The walls were finished with highly polished teakwood imported from Burma, which he remembered exported more of it than any other place in the world. His father's face, which usually showed no emotion, seemed to him to be depressed as he sat down and looked at him expectantly.

"Are those the sales figures?" Gerald Holt asked.

"Yes. And we're doing all right. Total sales are up, but the things selling are the cheaper items with less markup, so profits have stayed the same."

"That's good."

"Yes, especially with the current problems this country has…I'd say it's very good." David noticed that his father seemed preoccupied. He waited for him to speak, but he said nothing.

"Is that what you wanted to talk about?" he asked, after a long silence.

"Not exactly," Mr. Holt said.

Again there was a long silence, and David began to wonder what was bothering his father. He was normally never one to mince words, and he generally got down to business very quickly. David was used to hearing him mutter, "Time is money."

"I have something I must tell you, David, and it is very bad news. Please brace yourself."

"Yes, Father, what is it?"

"We're bankrupt, and we're losing the company."

"Father, is this some kind of joke?"

"No, David—it is no joke. I wish it was, but I'm deadly serious."

"How could that be? Everything is paid for and we're profitable."

Gerald Holt moved a little in his chair and leaned forward on his desk towards his son. "I never told you, but when the market started going up, I got some great tips on stocks and I borrowed some money to buy them. I made so much on the first investments—much more than we make here—that I continued buying. I had to mortgage the company to get the money, but it seemed like everything I touched turned to gold…"

"I can't believe this. You always taught us to be careful with our money—you always said the market was a gamble…"

"I know what I said, and I can't tell you how sorry I am."

"Well, that's not quite good enough. Part of this company was mine, and I've worked hard to improve it. You said work hard and work late, so I did. You said try until you try so hard that your stomach hurts, and I did. I gave up weekends, I gave up golf and many things I liked to do for you and this company. You had an obligation to ask me before you gambled with it."

"You are right, I did, but I failed you…there's no question that I failed everyone…" his father said as he turned away from David and looked out the window. "PGH Enterprises will be taking over. We've still got about six months to tie out the books and remove ourselves."

"I just can't believe this…it can't be happening. This has got to be a bad dream—a nightmare, and I'm going to wake up. You are a total hypocrite and you've ruined my life. How could you do this to me…how could you!" David said, raising his voice.

"Would you quit reviling me!" his father said, losing his temper. "Don't you think I know what I've done? Don't you think I'm beating myself up every minute over it? But I can't change it now. At least you've got a rich family to marry into—that should help you."

"Do you think I would marry Esther now? There's no way I could marry her when I have nothing. I'd never subject her to that, not to mention the shame you've brought on us. Our name will be mud when this gets out. You think the Stricklands would still want me as part of their family?"

"I don't know. Suit yourself."

"You pulled the rug out from under me, and never said a word. And I used to admire you so much. You told me that if I worked hard someday this company would be mine, and all the time you were wasting it away like a fool! Did you have to spend everything?"

"No, it was incredibly stupid. It's called greed—and once you get that disease you lose all common sense. So be careful."

"You're not lecturing me now, are you? You think I'd ever listen to anything you have to say again?"

"Probably not. But when I said bankrupt—well, it's not quite that bad. We're not declaring bankruptcy—so there won't be that embarrassment. They'll take the company and some other assets, but I still have the house."

"Oh, that's dandy—that is if you can still afford the property taxes."

Gerald Holt looked at his son, anger flashing in his eyes. Then he turned away and shook his head in sorrow. "Will you just rub it in over and over?"

"You just told me. How did you expect I'd feel?"

"I don't know."

"I respected you—I didn't think you would become an old fool."

"That's enough. Get out of my office."

David got up and walked out, slamming the door. His father watched him and then turned away and looked wistfully out the large picture window. David went back into his own office and took a lamp and threw it down on the floor in anger. Then he began to clean out his desk.

Esther sat across from David as they ate dinner at their favorite restaurant. She watched him as he ate. He had been very quiet the whole evening, and she knew there was something wrong, but he would not talk about it. He picked at his food, eating very little.

"Have you lost your appetite?" she asked.

"I told you, nothing is wrong," he answered with irritation in his voice.

"And I know that something is, because you've stopped talking to me. We need to make plans for our marriage—unless you want me to do all of it myself."

He put his fork down and looked up at her. "No, I don't. I'm just not having a good week. It's true—there are a lot of problems at work—things that were unexpected."

"Do you want to tell me about them?"

"No, darling, I just can't right now, and please don't take that as a slight. It's just that I'm trying to work some things out that are quite personal."

She stared at him for a moment, wanting to ask again, but sensing that she shouldn't. He looked up at her and smiled. "I will explain it all…just give me time—because this is not the time."

"I'll wait, dear. I'll be patient. Have you made a decision on where we will live yet?"

"No…I haven't. I haven't had time to think about that much lately."

"But you stopped the transaction on the house—is that right?"

He flashed a somewhat angry look at her and did not answer right away. "Yes, that's over…that is certainly over."

She looked at him quizzically, then finished the last of her meal. "Do you want to take that home?" she asked, pointing to his mostly untouched food.

"Take it home?" he asked, evidently preoccupied with other thoughts. "Oh, the food…yes, well, that would be a good idea."

"Maybe you'll be hungrier later?"

"Yes, later on I probably will be," he concurred. Then he smiled widely and took her hand. "You're a better woman than I deserve," he said.

"I don't think so, David."

"No, it's true…it's really true."

Why would he say such a thing, particularly at this time, she wondered, just as the waiter walked up.

"May we have a container for this?" he asked the waiter.

"Very good, sir," the waiter said.

"It's still early. Shall we do something else tonight?" Esther asked.

"No, I'm quite tired—I'll drive you home now," David answered.

Esther took a breath, and held her peace. She was getting frustrated at the way David was acting—she had never considered him inscrutable, but now he seemed to be so almost all the time. She wondered what the problem was but decided she would pray about it and not ask him any more questions.

15

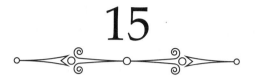

Priscilla heard Mr. Blankenship's voice rise once, and then again. Out of curiosity, she walked out of her office and moved towards his. Mrs. Ross was standing by his door, eavesdropping. She appeared a little embarrassed at being caught by Priscilla, and she backed away from the door and went back to her desk.

"What's this blowup about?" Priscilla asked.

"He's firing James Rafferty—he was drunk on the job," Mrs. Ross said.

"Does the man have a family?"

"Yes…I think seven children," Mrs. Ross said. Suddenly the door opened and Rafferty and two managers walked out. Rafferty had his head down, and he was crying. He stopped and turned around and looked at Mr. Blankenship.

"Please, Mr. Blankenship, give me another chance. I need this job."

Mr. Blankenship looked away from him, then back to one of the managers. "Give him a week's severance pay and send him on his way." The men walked away, and Mr. Blankenship turned to go back into his office, but stopped when he saw Priscilla. He could tell she was unhappy and looked at her questioningly. "Do you want to talk to me?"

"Yes, I would."

"Come in, then. My office is always open to you."

She followed him in his office and closed the door.

"So I've done wrong again, have I?" he asked.

"The man does have seven children," Priscilla said.

"Does it appear to you that I am running a welfare agency here and not a factory?"

"I know what you are running," Priscilla said crisply. "I'll get back to work now."

"Thank you," Mr. Blankenship said, and he looked down at some papers on his desk as she exited.

Mrs. Ross was walking to her desk as Priscilla walked out and she had obviously been listening again at the door. She smiled at Priscilla, and Priscilla went towards her office, but she was stopped by Jonas Mabrey, the man whose job she had previously saved.

"May I have a word with you, Miss?" Mr. Mabrey asked.

"Yes, of course—shall we go into my office?" Priscilla asked, curious as to why he would want to speak to her. He nodded and walked into her office.

"I want to thank you again for saving my job," Mr. Mabrey began.

"Oh, you thanked me so much already…."

"But I need to tell you that Rafferty deserved to be fired. He's been caught drunk more than once, and Mr. Blankenship let him off before. And it may be for his own good."

"How is that? He's got seven children!"

"Well, Miss, he runs a very dangerous machine—it's a heavy press, and he has to pull his hand away from it when it comes down. If a man's not paying attention, he can lose his hand. It'll take it right off at the wrist, and that happened to Ben Smith about…oh, seventeen years ago…and he wasn't even drunk. Yes, Miss, he lost his hand and couldn't work much again after that."

"Thanks for letting me know," Priscilla said, and Mr. Mabrey walked out of her office. Priscilla pulled out a mirror and checked her makeup and hair. Then she walked to Mr. Blankenship's office again. Mrs. Ross buzzed him and soon Priscilla was sitting before his desk.

"There's something I have to say," she said, looking down.

"I'm not hiring him back, so save your breath," he said.

"I don't think you should. I spoke too soon—he should have been fired. Jonas told me more about him, and I've come in to apologize for what I said earlier."

Mr. Blankenship smiled widely. "You mean you're not always right?"

Priscilla looked up, annoyed. "Of course not."

"I'm sorry—I shouldn't have said that. I appreciate your willingness to apologize. By the way, I want you to be my contact and look after the office next week. I'll be in Pennsylvania on a business trip—

it's a very large account if we get it."

"What exactly is the contact person?"

"I don't want everyone calling me if there are problems—they can tell you instead. You're quite articulate, so you can summarize what they have to say if anything comes up. Do you mind?"

"Well, I don't mind, but I don't think I'm qualified. And I don't know if the men will like a woman…"

"If they want to keep working here, they will answer to whomever I tell them to. Anyway, the manufacturing managers will be taking care of their part of the company. Mr. Whittaker, the chief engineer, is the top man there. So, it will mainly be the office part—shipping and sales and all of that. But any issues they have I want them to give to you, and you will give them to me. That will be the chain of command. That way I'm only talking to one person. Will you do it?"

"Yes, but I need to walk through the factory with you—I've got some questions about operations."

"Oh, I'll be training you all week."

The buzzer sounded as he finished speaking, and he picked it up.

"Yes, show him in."

Priscilla got up to leave, but he motioned for her to sit down. "It's the union rep. Stay in here so he can meet you."

A short, plump man came in and said, "Mr. Blankenship, how are you, sir?"

"Very good, and you, Mr. Markowitz?"

"Very well."

"This is Miss Avery."

"Charmed, I'm sure. Would you like a cigar, Mr. Blankenship?"

"No, thank you."

Mr. Markowitz sat down and lit one for himself. After blowing out some smoke, he leaned forward in his chair.

"Let me get to the point because I know you're busy. The workers need another two bathroom breaks—it's only civil to give it to them."

"We've been over this before—there's already too much down time on the lines. I've already considered it and the answer is no," Mr. Blankenship said with firmness in his voice, and a tone that indicated that the discussion was over.

"But, now, you don't want a strike do you—especially when business is so bad? I heard about that embezzlement—must have set you back a bit."

"If this is a threat, it's futile. If they are dumb enough to strike over that in the middle of this economic chaos then they are too stupid to work here. They won't strike, Markowitz, and you know it, so give up the nonsense."

"You might be surprised about that, sir." Mr. Markowitz said huffily. "Good day to you and…Miss Avery."

Mr. Blankenship looked over at Priscilla and raised his eyebrows. "So are you going to tell me that I'm a hard, nasty ogre—like an employer in a Charles Dickens novel?"

"I wasn't going to say a word—I think you just said it," Priscilla said, smiling a little. "But since you asked, older people sometimes do have problems in that area."

"Thank you, Dr. Avery, I will consider your prognosis," Mr. Blankenship said, smiling. "Wear some older clothes tomorrow and we'll go through the factory."

Priscilla toured the factory the next day, and she could tell from the stares of some of the employees that they resented her. Not only was she a woman, but she was also very young, and when Mr. Blankenship would tell his managers to run things by her, some of them grimaced and showed their displeasure. She didn't want to ask, but the way Mr. Blankenship explained it, she wasn't exactly certain how far her authority reached, and she doubted anyone else was either. In fact, she thought herself unqualified for the task. But he had asked her, and she actually relished the challenge.

She came home that evening and waited for her father to come through the door. When he did, she made a special effort to greet him, and then she followed him into his study. He put his briefcase on his desk and looked up at her, questioningly. "What is it, Priscilla? Please don't tell me that you want to work full time—remember, you gave me your word."

"Of course not, Father. I'll be here all day tomorrow and I'll take care of all the things you want me to, but I need to work split days the next week because of something going on at work…. But there was something else."

"What?" he asked, as he proceeded to leave the study to prepare for dinner.

"I just wonder if you would consider buying pumps from the company I work for."

Mr. Strickland stopped moving for a moment. "Of course. Just put their name on the list, and when we've finished with the usual checks and—"

"But Father, that takes a frightfully long time—it would probably be a year before you'd ever get around to giving them an order."

"Well, we do have rules we follow and I don't like showing favoritism—I've tried to treat all the vendors with fairness and to just put one at the top of the list..." he stopped talking, as he noticed that she was sulking. "This is really important to you, isn't it?"

"Yes, but I understand that you have your rules. I'll let you dress for dinner." Priscilla turned away and walked out of the study and down the hallway. He walked out after her and headed the opposite way towards the stairs, but then he turned around. "Priscilla," he said loudly. She stopped quickly and turned around.

"Yes, Father. What is it?"

"This little company you work for. What is the quality like?"

"Oh, Father, it's the best, I promise you. I wouldn't ask if it wasn't the best, and they are also less expensive than your regular suppliers."

"Okay, we'll test them and see, and if they pan out we'll let them fill a small order."

"Oh, thank you so much," Priscilla said, and she ran up and hugged her father.

"It's quite all right. I trust you know what you're doing. Contact Dave Frazier at the Franklin division tomorrow afternoon. My secretary will give you the number. I'll call him and let him know. If they're good, they'll probably have to increase production to keep up."

"I'm sure they would be happy to, and this is wonderful of you."

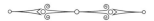

Priscilla was brushing her hair after dinner that evening when Esther knocked on her door. "Come in," Priscilla said. Esther walked in slowly and sat down on the velvet couch next to her bed. "Have you got the whole wedding planned yet?" Priscilla asked.

"No, not yet. How are things at work?"

"Well he's still Jekyll and Hyde at times, but now he's asking me to be his liaison while he's traveling. I'm a little nervous about it, but it's a great compliment."

"I think your gifts are apparent, and he's just fortunate enough to recognize them."

Priscilla stopped brushing and turned from the mirror and looked at her sister. "That's a very nice thing to say. And I think I've been quite selfish. I haven't offered to help you at all with the wedding plans, but I'm ready to do whatever I can."

Esther looked down for a moment and took a breath.

"Is everything okay? What's the matter, Sister?"

Esther looked up, and Priscilla noticed that her eyes were red from crying.

"What is it? Tell me!"

"I don't know…I really don't know. He's just been acting…strange. I don't understand him anymore. He's got some problems, and he won't talk to me about them, and I don't know what to do. I don't even know if he still loves me or not. He seems so…so distant at times."

"Are you ready for the test, then?"

"The test?"

"Yes, you know—what we discussed before. I have a way of testing him to find out if he's genuine."

"What would you do? How could you figure that out?" Esther asked.

"I'll make him think that we're broke—that we lost everything in the crash—and then we'll see if he's still interested in marrying you."

"Well, that's straightforward—so I can figure out if he's a gold digger. Do you think he is?"

"Oh, Esther, I don't think so, but I would never have guessed it would happen to Alice, and I just don't want to see you hurt. If nothing changes, he'll never know about it, so what is there to lose?"

"Well, he is acting funny, and he was very worried about making as much money as Father and—"

"And you aren't sure, are you?"

Esther looked at her for a long time without answering. "No," she finally said, "I'm not completely certain about him. I used to be, but now I'm not." She looked away for a while and then back at her sister. "Isn't it so sad that I would actually consider testing him? Isn't it already a tragedy that I don't have enough confidence to really know?"

"Maybe, but nothing compared to the tragedy if his motives aren't right and you find out after the marriage."

"Okay—do it. Don't tell me the details—just do it and tell me when he thinks we're broke. Oh, Priscilla, I hate doing this." Esther hugged her sister, and tears began to fall from her eyes.

"I know, I know," Priscilla said, and she stroked Esther's hair.

16

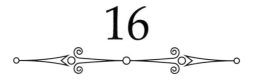

The band was playing the hit song "Dream a Little Dream of Me," and many couples were dancing to it. Anna watched them as the song ended, and Miss Knapp walked up and stood next to her as several new people came in to be seated. One of them was Bart Lewis.

"He's in here every night now because of you," Miss Knapp said.

"I don't think so," Anna said, as she watched and noticed that he was staring at her.

"Oh, yes. He'll ask to be seated at one of your tables, as usual. See, there he goes."

They watched as Jeremy seated Bart. He only had one of his friends with him this time. He looked up and smiled at Anna, but she turned around and went into the kitchen. She was annoyed at the attention he kept showing her, but she knew she had to wait on him. She picked up two orders for another table, and delivered them, and Mr. Lewis signaled her to come to his table.

"Hello again, Beautiful—you look terrific tonight, as usual," he said.

"Thank you. Are you ready to order?"

"Can't you see that I'm hopelessly in love with you? I can't stay away from this place because of you. I'm going to get fat eating here every night if you don't go out with me."

"Mr. Lewis, you are making me uncomfortable. I'm sure there are many young ladies who…I hear there are many you date—and I'm not going to be one of them."

"But you're the only one I want."

Anna put down her pad for a moment and a determined look formed on her face. "And just what interest could I be to you? I am not available for any of your shenanigans. I'm a Christian and I have no interest in playboys, or the stuff you put in your sodas, or speakeasies, or any of the things you do. My life is completely different from that—it's about purity, and I have nothing in common with you and no interest in you."

"My! Well, that's telling me, isn't it?"

"I'm sorry if I offended you Mr. Lewis, but you are offending me with your constant attentions and it's embarrassing me."

"I read you loud and clear. I'll have the steak and shrimp."

"And you, sir?" she said, turning her attention to his friend, who seemed a little shaken up at her rebuke.

"Um…I'll have that too," he said.

"Thank you, gentlemen." Anna turned away and walked back to the kitchen.

"Well, Bart, I guess that's over," his friend said.

"Over? Not at all—I'm still keen on her."

"Come on, there are lots of other girls. She's obviously a virgin and not your style."

"That's what interests me. I won't rest until I get her."

"What? Are you obsessed or something?"

"Yeah, that's a good word for it." Bart watched as Anna walked out of the kitchen and brought food to another table. "And no matter what she said, I'll bet you that deep down she can't resist me.…I won't let her resist me."

As Anna walked towards the kitchen, she saw Lucy come in with a group of people. She watched as Jeremy seated them in her section, and winced at the idea of waiting on Lucy. After she placed Bart's order, she took a deep breath and walked to the table. As she approached she noticed that one of the young men sitting next to Lucy had his arm around her. There were two other couples, and the women they were with were dressed in skimpy clothing and were heavily made up. The young men were expensively dressed, and all of them smiled at her as she approached. She could tell that the women, including Lucy, were jealous as the men diverted their attention towards her. She realized that she was more attractive than any of the girls at the table, but it irritated her that the men showed her so much attention.

"Good evening. Are you ready to order yet?" she asked.

"Well, sweetheart, I'm just feasting my eyes for now," one of the men said, staring at her. She pursed her lips and showed her annoyance.

"Well, call me when you're ready," she said and began to turn away. As she did, Lucy called to her.

"Waitress, I'd like the…the crab Rangoon appetizers to start," she said briskly.

Anna wrote down the order. "Anyone else?" she asked, and the rest of them also ordered appetizers and sodas. When they were finished, Lucy smiled at her.

"No, please change that…I'd like the smoked salmon canapés instead. Thank you, dear," she said sardonically.

"You're very welcome," Anna said and then walked into the kitchen.

When she got there, she let out a breath. Between waiting on Lucy and her group and Bart and his friends, she felt uncomfortable just walking out to the dining room. She didn't like the looks of the people Lucy was with, but she knew there wasn't much she could do about it. The look on her face must have given away her thoughts, because Chef Mercier walked towards her with a concerned expression.

"Is Mademoiselle feeling all right?" he inquired.

"Yes, sir…I just…well, I wonder if I could just work in the kitchen with you. Would you have me? Because I would like to."

"Oh, yes, you would make a fine sous chef. It would be my delight!"

"Oh, thank you," Anna said as Miss Knapp walked hurriedly through the swinging doors and approached her.

"That rowdy bunch is asking to order," she said. "You'd better get out there—one of them is a Strickland."

"Oh, really. How do you know that?"

"She made a point of telling me—proud little…the way she said it, I think she might complain."

"Okay."

As Anna walked towards the table, she could see that one of the men was pouring something into his soda, which he was holding under the table. He stopped pouring and looked up with a guilty smile on his face as she reached the table. The others were laughing, and Lucy's laugh was somewhat raucous.

"We're ready now," the young man with Lucy said, smiling at Anna with a steady gaze while they ordered.

As Lucy started ordering, the man she was with kept touching her under the table and she started giggling and was having a difficult time speaking. Anna looked at her, and her eyes betrayed her annoyance, which the others noticed. "Tony, quit, I've got to order," she said, and the man stopped touching her. "I'll have..." Lucy began, but then she started giggling again, even though she was not being touched, and Anna realized that she had been drinking. She got herself under control again, and slowly ordered. After she finished, the band started playing again and her partner stood up.

"That's my favorite, `Minnie the Moocher,'" the young man said. "We have to dance, Anna."

Lucy got up slowly, obviously impaired from the alcohol, and they began dancing. Anna cringed as she watched her, then turned around and walked back to the kitchen. As she walked she said to herself, "She's going to ruin my reputation."

Anna waited for Lucy in her room, and she was about to fall asleep when Lucy came through the door. "What are you doing here?" Lucy asked.

"Waiting for you, that's what I'm doing," Anna said.

"You don't need to stay up for me, Mommy. I'm a big girl," Lucy said, laughing.

"And you're also a drunk girl," Anna said.

"Drunk? Who, me? I only had some sodas," Lucy said, giggling. "And I had a wonderful time."

"There was obviously liquor in those sodas, and it's illegal."

"Well, I just drank what they put before me."

"Would you drink strychnine if they put it before you?"

Lucy looked at Anna for a moment and she stopped giggling. "It's a stupid law and they say it will be changed soon. The people who got it passed were a bunch of killjoys."

Anna closed her eyes as she sat on the couch. Then she opened her eyes and looked at Lucy, who was now sitting on the bed, propped up against some pillows.

"Lucy, my mother was part of the temperance movement, and she helped pass prohibition, and she wasn't a killjoy. She was concerned about all the damage that alcoholism was doing in this country. Many children were suffering because..." Anna watched as Lucy's head fell back and she started snoring. Shaking her head, Anna walked to her own room.

17

"Miss Avery, Mr. Marcus is here," Mrs. Ross said into the intercom.

"Thank you, I'll be right out," Priscilla said, and she walked out of her office. Mr. Marcus, a tall and chubby man of about forty-five, looked at her questioningly.

"How can I help you, Miss Avery?"

"Well, would you mind following me back to my office?" Priscilla asked.

"Actually, I'm pretty busy today. Can you just tell me here?"

"Okay, we can talk here," Priscilla said, and she sat down in one of the chairs in front of Mrs. Ross's office, but Mr. Marcus continued standing. She looked at him for a moment and sighed, and he finally sat down across from her.

"Since you manage sales, I thought you might want to follow this lead with Strickland—it's a subsidiary, Franklin Oil Field Machinery. They may want to buy some of our pumps."

"Wait a minute, are you telling me to contact someone at Strickland?"

"Yes, Dave Frazier is the name. I wrote the phone number down here," Priscilla said, passing him a notepad with the information on it. "It's all set up."

"Look Missy, I've been working on Strickland for years, without any progress. It's the hardest company to break into, and now you're giving me a phone number and think that suddenly they'll order from us…. Excuse me, Missy, but that's ridiculous."

"Mr. Marcus, my name is Miss Avery, not Missy."

Mr. Marcus hesitated for a moment. "Okay, Miss Avery. I realize that Mr. Blankenship has put you in charge of the office, but I don't think that includes sales, and you can't tell me how to sell the product."

"I'm not telling you—I'm just giving you a lead. But if you don't want to call them, I can do it myself. I just thought you might want the commission."

Mr. Marcus appeared chafed with her words, and he moved around uncomfortably in his chair as he thought about what to say next. "Strickland has very high standards, they don't just…well, I think it's a complete waste of time, but I'll make the call."

"Thank you, Mr. Marcus."

He stood up and left, and Priscilla turned to go back to her office. But as she did, Jonas Mabrey walked in from the inner office area. "Miss Avery, can I talk to you for a second?" he asked.

"Of course, Mr. Mabrey," she answered. "Do you want to sit here?"

He also looked around and appeared uncomfortable to be speaking in front of Mrs. Ross. "Could we go into your office?"

"Yes," Priscilla said, and he followed her in, and she shut the door after he entered and sat down. He seemed hesitant to speak as she sat in her chair.

"I know that Mr. Blankenship thinks that the workers won't strike, but he's wrong, and I'm concerned about the company."

"Would they really strike when things are so bad? How long could they go?"

"Well, I heard the talk, and it won't be a normal strike—it'll be a work slowdown, which is hard to prove. And all they want are the bathroom breaks—they're not looking for more money. They all know about Willis stealing that money, but they're sick and tired of the way Mr. Blankenship is so stubborn. They want to teach him a lesson. But you never heard this from me, mind you. I just thought maybe you could talk to him, seeing as you were able to save my job and all."

"I'll see what I can do."

"But you have to promise you won't tell anyone where you heard it. I'd be in big trouble if it ever got out."

"I promise…."

Priscilla left work and hurried down the street to where the limousine would pick her up. Since the streets were quite busy, often the driver would have to circle around until he saw her. She was in a hurry because she needed to keep her promise to Esther to set up the test to see if David Holt only wanted her for her money. Ben, the Stricklands' chauffeur, smiled when he saw her, and she got in the car. "Please take me to the Yale Club, Ben—I mean, Mr. Salisbury."

"Why, Miss Priscilla, just call me Ben. I've been driving you since you were a little girl—you should just call me Ben. Now, how was your day at work?"

"Oh, it was fine, but I'd like to ask you a special favor."

"Certainly, what can I do for you?"

"I have to drop off a letter for Mr. Holt—David Holt, Esther's fiancé. He uses the Yale athletic club about this time, but I don't want to leave it for him until I know he's there. But I can't go in there—it's for men only. So would you mind asking if he's checked in, and then leave this letter for him if he is? It is very important that he gets it, but I don't want him to know it's coming from me, and I don't want him to see you, either. So if you see him, just turn around and we'll try another time. But if you don't see him, please tell them you are a messenger delivering this. But I need to know that it will definitely reach him and him only."

"Why, of course, Miss Priscilla," Ben said as they drove up to the entrance. The valet came out to park the car, but Ben told him he was there to deliver a letter and would be right out. Priscilla watched as he walked into the building. Ben walked in, and a man at the front counter gave him a frosty look.

"I don't recognize you as a member," the man said, looking at Ben's chauffeur's uniform.

"I'm not; I'm here to deliver a letter to Mr. Holt."

"Very good, just give it to me and I'll see that he gets it," the clerk said.

"The sender says it's important that he gets it. How will it get to him? Does he have a mailbox?" Ben asked.

"Well, there's a slot in his locker, and I'll put it in there right now—is that good enough for you?" the man asked caustically.

"Yes sir. Thank you kindly."

"You're welcome," the clerk said with a curt tone.

Priscilla seemed anxious as Ben walked out and got into the car.

"Everything go all right, Ben?"

"Yes, the man at the counter said he'd put it into Mr. Holt's mail slot right away, and that it will go directly into his locker."

"Thank you, Ben—you are a dear."

As Ben left the building, another clerk walked up to the one who took the letter to take over for the evening shift.

"You ready to go, Harry?" the man asked.

"Yeah, I just have to deliver a letter and then it's home to the little lady," Harry said, and he walked towards the lockers. When he found David Holt's, he put the letter in the slot and then left work, but David had already cleaned out his locker and did not get the letter. In fact, as it was delivered into his locker, he was walking to the counter, and when he got there, he rang the bell. He was carrying a large duffel bag, and he put it down beside him. The new clerk walked out and smiled at him. "Good evening, Mr. Holt, can I help, sir?"

"Well, I'm closing my account and here's the key to my locker," David said, handing it to the man, who seemed surprised.

"Oh, I'm sorry to hear that—you've been a regular for so many years. I hope the club has been satisfactory for you, sir."

"Oh, it's been quite good—no problem there—I just have some changes going on."

"Okay, sir. Should I send the final bill then, and do you need to get anything else?"

"Yes, send the bill. I got everything cleaned out, so all of that is done," David said, holding up his duffel bag.

"Well, Mr. Holt, we will miss you."

18

Anna watched Chef Mercier as he instructed her on how to prepare a chicken. She was fascinated at the way he worked—it was almost like a performance for he moved in a somewhat stylistic manner as he touched the chicken. She considered that it was the way an artist might paint a picture.

"So, Mademoiselle, you will now learn something very few know about—how to keep the bird succulent—how to make it moist and juicy. You see, you separate the skin from the meat, like this…" He pushed two of his short, stubby fingers between the skin and the body of the chicken, and moved them around until the skin was no longer sticking to the body. Then he used the handle of a butter knife and carefully probed deeper where his fingers could not reach. "You must be careful not to break the skin—which is easy to do with the knife. Now try yours." Anna gingerly began the same process, and since her fingers were longer, she was able to go deeper. She then used the knife but broke the skin on her first try.

"Oh, I'm so sorry," she said, almost terrified at what she had done.

"It is quite all right—it is not a problem, so do not concern yourself. Try another one, but put some butter on the end of the knife this time," he said in an encouraging tone and with an understanding smile. She picked up another chicken and carefully separated the skin from the meat, and then coated the knife handle with butter and slowly continued the separation process. When she had finished, he beamed at her and said, "Magnifique! And now I will show you the great secret." He took some olive oil and some melted butter and mixed them together. Then he used a brush and began putting the mixture between the skin and the meat. "This will keep the meat tender and succulent, and make the skin crisp for a beautiful bird," he said triumphantly.

Anna picked up her bird and copied what he did. "But you must keep stirring the oil and butter, so they are mixed," he said as he watched her. So she stirred the mixture as she worked. They worked together in silence. There were about eight chickens left to finish, and Anna was able to work faster with each new one.

While Anna was in the kitchen working, Bart Lewis walked into the restaurant by himself and waited to be seated. Jeremy looked over at him and slowly walked up to the entrance where he stood. "Seat me in Lucy's section," Bart snapped, and Jeremy smiled at him for a moment but said nothing. "I said to seat me in Lucy's section—can't you understand me?"

"I understand quite well, but Lucy is no longer a waitress here," Jeremy said.

"What, where did she go?" Bart asked demandingly.

"Mr. Lewis, we serve fine cuisine here—we do not provide information on employees," Jeremy said.

"Okay, I'll find the manager and ask him," Bart said, but as he began to turn to leave, a waitress walked out of the kitchen, opening the double swinging doors, and Bart saw Anna there. "Oh, you lied to me," he said.

"No, Mr. Lewis, I did not lie. Lucy is no longer a waitress; she is now an assistant chef."

"Yeah, well, the way you made it sound…"

"Do you want a table, Mr. Lewis—I have others to seat if you do not."

Bart looked around, trying to decide what to do. "Yeah, give me a table—one near the kitchen doors."

"Are you certain, Mr. Lewis? You are a prominent customer, and those are the noisiest tables because the servers are constantly walking back and forth…."

"I know they are noisy—now seat me near the kitchen before I call the manager!" Bart said, exasperated.

"Tut, tut—no need for that. Your wish is my command," Jeremy said. "Please follow me to the noisiest table, sir."

"This takes only so much flour. Too much and it won't roll out, too little and it will stick," Chef Mercier said as he expertly used the rolling pin to prepare the dough for a dessert. "You see, it must be just so thin—and cook just so long. Too thick and it will not be delicate, and too long in the oven and it will harden. An exquisite crust is one of the great challenges in baking. It must be prepared with very much care, indeed. You practice rolling while I decorate this special birthday cake. It is the cake for a famous person, I think."

"Who is that?" Anna asked.

"A woman, I think. Strickland. A very rich family, I understand."

"It's not her birthday," Anna said somewhat to herself.

"What was that?"

"Oh, nothing…yes—I'll practice the crust." She began rolling, getting angrier as she thought about Lucy. The restaurant provided a free birthday cake and sang "Happy Birthday," but it was not her birthday. Anna wondered what the damage might be to her reputation, and decided that she had to ground Lucy when she got home that night. As she was thinking about this, the kitchen doors swung open and Bart Lewis walked in. She looked at him, shocked.

"Oh, my dearest Lucy. Forgive me for barging in, but I just had to see you. I came tonight hoping to sit at your table, but you were gone."

"Mr. Lewis, please leave me alone! I told you I want nothing to do with you."

"But Lucy, I am hopelessly in love with you," Bart said, lowering his voice.

Chef Mercier heard the conversation and looked up from his cake decorating and walked over to Bart. As Bart turned around, Chef Mercier squeezed the tube with purple icing in it and sprayed it all over Bart's silk suit.

"Oh, Monsieur, such a tragedy for such a beautiful jacket."

Bart looked at him angrily, and Chef Mercier took a cloth and attempted to wipe it off. "Here, let me help you," he said, and as he wiped it, it smeared more into the fabric and looked worse than before. Anna finally burst out laughing, and then Jeremy walked in, looked around, and, spotting Bart, walked towards him.

"What are you doing in the kitchen? Did you come to get decorated?" he asked.

"Funny. No, I just want to talk to Lucy—I'll be finished in a moment."

"You're finished now. She doesn't want to talk to you, and the kitchen is for employees only."

"Don't worry about it," Bart said.

"Get out of here…now," Jeremy said.

"You can't talk to me that way—I'll have your job!"

"I didn't know you wanted my job. I thought you were a rich guy."

"Oh, a wise guy," Bart said, and then he took a swing at Jeremy, landing a glancing blow on his chin. Jeremy was a few inches shorter than Bart, and a little smaller, and he fell back a few feet, slightly dazed. Then he recovered and grabbed Bart's arm and twisted it in back of him. Bart yelped, and Jeremy guided him towards the swinging doors, then pushed him through the doors out into the restaurant.

Bart looked back at Jeremy. "I'll have your job," he said again.

"You couldn't do my job," Jeremy said, wiping some blood from his mouth, and attempting to straighten his jacket. Anna walked up to him and bade him to sit down. She then got a wet cloth and wiped the blood from his mouth.

"That was very brave…thank you," she said. "And thank you, Chef. Thank you both."

19

"I'm talking as loud as I can," Priscilla shouted into the phone.

"I can barely hear you," Mr. Blankenship said. "Is everything all right?"

"Yes, but there is a union problem," Priscilla said.

"What kind of problem?"

"I think I have a solution," Priscilla said.

"What is it?"

"Well, I think we can—"

"I can't hear you, so we need to hang up. But if you can fix the problem, fix it."

"Okay, I will." Priscilla walked out of her office and over to Mrs. Ross's desk.

"I could hear you in there—I hate trying to talk long distance," Mrs. Ross said.

"Yes, it was a very bad connection this time. Would you mind calling Mr. Markowitz, and Mister…is it Benson? Is he the employee representative?"

"Yes, he is, but what is this about? Are you negotiating for Mr. Blankenship? Was this approved by him?" Mrs. Ross asked, suspiciously.

"Yes, he said to go ahead," Priscilla said.

"Will you also be using Mr. Blankenship's office?"

"No, not at all—they can come into my office when they get here."

After a few hours the men arrived and were waiting for her outside in the reception area where Mrs. Ross sat. Priscilla took a deep breath and told Mrs. Ross to send them in. They looked apprehensive as they walked into her office and sat down.

"How can we help you?" Mr. Markowitz asked.

"I have a proposition for you regarding your request for the additional breaks," Priscilla said.

"You have a proposition?" Mr. Markowitz asked questioningly. "Yes, I've been authorized by Mr. Blankenship."

"You have?"

"Yes."

"Okay, I'm all ears," Mr. Markowitz said, and he smiled at Mr. Benson.

"I want your word that there will be no action against our company of any sort if you agree to my terms. And these are the terms: Each person over forty years of age, and those with a written note from a doctor stating that they need an extra break for medical reasons, can have another one during the day. But if it's going to shut down the line, the worker needs to find a floater to take over. Also, if someone has a medical need for more than another break, that's possible, but they would have to switch to a job which won't shut down the line—maybe be retrained for another job."

"Over forty—this wouldn't be for everyone. Why not?"

"Because younger people generally don't have the same problems older ones have in that area. I know because...where I worked before we had these issues and the doctor told us about it."

"So that's your offer. We want two breaks, and you'll give us one for people over forty?"

"That's it."

"What about allowing..."

"I'm sorry, Mr. Markowitz, the offer is final. This is all I can do. And I can't call Mr. Blankenship back, I can't reach him. So you'll have to take it or leave it."

"Oh, I'd recommend taking it—but I need to talk to the workers. What do you think Mr. Benson?"

"I'm with you. I am just surprised Blankenship would give an inch on this—he never has before," Mr. Benson said.

"Well, maybe he's getting softer, who knows?" Priscilla said.

"Or wiser. This is a good offer and I appreciate it Miss Avery. I think I can get a vote tonight on it, and it should fly."

"Yes, I think the workers will be pleasantly surprised on this one," Mr. Benson said.

As they walked out of the office and Priscilla followed them, she saw Mr. Marcus sitting by Mrs. Ross's desk. His face showed a change of attitude, and he looked up at Priscilla and smiled when he saw her.

"Mrs. Ross, please type up this agreement with the union as soon as possible, so that I can take it to their meeting. I wrote it in longhand, so if you have any trouble reading it, just ask me." Mrs. Ross looked at the contract and her face looked shocked and frightened. She was about to say something, when Mr. Marcus spoke again.

"I owe you an apology, Miss Avery," he said. "I shouldn't have spoken to you the way I did, especially in front of Mrs. Ross."

"Apology accepted, Mr. Marcus. I assume things are working out with the Strickland subsidiary?"

"Beyond my greatest expectations—they are definitely giving us a try, and if they like the products, I think we'll have to increase production. So you really did know what you were talking about. Thank you for the lead. I'm sorry I doubted you."

"I'm just glad it worked out," Priscilla said. He turned and walked out, and Mrs. Ross gave Priscilla a paradoxical look. Priscilla looked back at her, waiting for her to speak.

"Yes? Did you want something, Mrs. Ross?"

"I am just so glad you stayed. But the union people—are you really supposed to be talking to them for Mr. Blankenship? He's never allowed any employee to do that before."

"Well, Mr. Blankenship said on the phone that I should fix a problem if one should come up, and so I fixed the problem, and that's the best I can do. He'll be back tomorrow and he can weigh in then."

"But did he tell you to negotiate for him?"

"Not exactly—the connection was poor and he couldn't hear me very well."

"Yes, that's what I'm afraid of," Mrs. Ross said.

Anna sat down in the kitchen to take a break, and Jeremy walked in and sat next to her. "Is Bart Lewis here tonight?" she asked.

"No—no sign of him."

"You know I appreciate it, but you shouldn't have risked your job for me—it wasn't worth it."

"Yes it was—you're worth it, and so far I don't think he's said anything to anyone. But if he does, I don't care. Now, we're both off tomorrow, so would you go to a movie with me?"

Anna thought for a moment. It was hard to turn him down since he had helped her, and she did find him attractive. However, she also felt a little uneasy around him and so was not sure what to say. Then it occurred to her to ask him a question. "You know that I am a Christian, are you?"

"Of course—yes, of course," Jeremy said. "Now what movie would you like to see? There is Frankenstein and Dracula."

"What are they about?"

"Well, Frankenstein is about a mad scientist who uses different body parts to create a man, Dracula is about...I'm not sure, but I think it's about people who are dead coming back to life by sucking the blood out of live people. What's the matter?"

"I don't like the sound of those, but thanks anyway."

"Wait a minute, Lucy. There's also another one. It's called Monkey Business. It's a Marx Brothers comedy and it might be kind of corny, but..."

"Sounds okay to me."

"Good, we'll see that one. So where do you live?"

Anna did not want to tell him she was staying at the hotel, so she hesitated before answering. "I'll meet you at the theater. Just tell me the time."

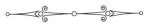

"So when does he come back?" Esther asked Priscilla as they sat together in her bedroom and Esther combed her hair.

"Tomorrow," Priscilla said.

"Do you think you could call in sick?" Esther asked.

"Why should I?"

"Because I think he will be apoplectic when he finds out that you negotiated with the union."

"He told me to fix the problem," Priscilla said airily.

"Well, you certainly have confidence—I could never do something like that. Of course, I wouldn't know the first thing about a union contract, but knowing how angry he'd be..."

"I did it on purpose, Esther. I want to make him angry, to find out how bad it can get. If he's madder than a hornet and he fires me, then that's my answer—he's too hotheaded for me to deal with."

"Yes, I guess what you did would certainly be an extreme test—especially with the way he treats the union."

"Oh, he doesn't have a clue how to get along with anyone. He'll turn every employee against him if he doesn't change."

"I don't think I could ever do that with David. We just don't have that kind of relationship."

"Well, David doesn't have Blankenship's problems. He can obviously manage people, even if he is moody. And by the way, I did it."

"You did what?"

"What you asked me to do."

"You mean the test—for David? You didn't!"

"Yes, I did. Remember, you asked me."

"I know, but I thought better of it, and I sort of feel like a traitor or something...."

"Well, it's too late now—it's done."

As they were talking, the phone rang and Mr. Standish walked down the hallway towards Esther's room. "It's Miss Anna on the telephone," he said.

"Oh, it's Anna," Esther said with excitement. "But don't pick up the extension; it will be too hard to hear. Let's just share this one." Esther picked up the phone and they both listened.

"So what is happening there? We got your letter. Will you be ready to take over the cook's job when you get back?"

"No, but I like working with Chef Mercier—he's so nice, and I'm learning so much. But Lucy's acting strange. Pretending to be me is going to her head, and she has been going out a lot and getting home late."

"Anna, you can't allow this to continue. Your reputation is at stake. You must rein her in and tell her to stay in the hotel room."

"I know, I know. I will."

"Any handsome men down there?" Priscilla asked.

"Yes, a few, but a lot of them are playboys. This isn't the best place to meet another Christian, but I do have a date with one tonight."

"And who is he?"

"Well, he's in college, and he's working here for the summer. I'm not sure about him yet, but I'm going to a movie with him. In fact, I have to get ready, so I'll call back in a few days. And I look forward to your letters."

"Good-bye—have a good time on your date," Priscilla said and hung up the phone.

Esther looked at Priscilla for a moment. "You know, we are both using the same strategy when you think about it. You're pushing Mr. Blankenship to the limit of his weakness, and I am pushing David to see if he's weak in another area. I'm just concerned about our methods. I hope they don't backfire on us."

"Backfire? I don't see how that could happen."

20

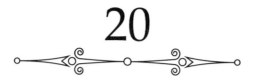

"So, did you like the movie?" Jeremy asked as they sat in a coffee shop frequented by younger people.

"It was pretty funny," Anna said as the waitress approached their table.

"What will it be for you two?" she asked.

"I'll have the chocolate malt," Anna said.

"The same for me, please," Jeremy said. Then he turned to Anna and asked, "So do you like the cooking a lot better?"

"Oh, yes. Chef Mercier is so nice to work with—he's taught me so much that I feel like I'm also in school for free."

"And you don't have to wait on those good-for-nothings who are so rich they don't know what it means to work. I hate to see them wasting so much money."

"But look on the other side—if they didn't waste it, you wouldn't have a job for the summer. And your job pays well, and it's helping you pay for college."

"I don't care about that. The wealth should be taken from them and redistributed—that's the only fair thing to do. Did you see what they spent on the last debutante ball in New York? Here's a clip of it—Barbara Hutton's debutante ball." He took the newspaper clipping from his wallet and showed it to Anna. She looked at it, then was quiet for a moment; she knew the girl who had the ball.

"Her daddy owns Woolworth's," said Jeremy, "which makes its money selling five-and-dime junk to poor people, but you can bet she doesn't shop there, and she couldn't care less about the people who do. Instead, she wastes all this money—lavishes it on herself at a time like this. Doesn't that just burn you up?"

"No—if they earned the money, they should be able to spend it

119

any way they like—it's a free country."

"Didn't you see what was spent? They wasted sixty thousand dollars, which is more money than I may make in thirty years. And most of these coming-out parties cost about fifteen thousand or so, which is also ridiculous, but this takes the cake. And this is while people are in bread lines in this country."

"I think the deb balls are a waste of money and they are foolish—I wouldn't have one," Anna said, thinking about how she and both of her sisters had refused such parties, considering them to be frivolous. Some of their friends had chided them for not having them.

Jeremy laughed. "Of course you wouldn't—you couldn't even afford the flowers for a party like that. That's not the point."

"I know it's not, but I don't see why you are so angry about what someone else is doing. Why does it bother you so much?"

"It bothers me because it's not fair. Rich people get away with all kinds of things we don't."

"Do you think that judgment ends in this life?"

"Oh, a religious question. I don't know about that, but I do know that behind every rich person is a great crime."

"How do you know that?"

"I just know. Wake up, everyone knows that. Do you think justice is the same for the rich as it is for the poor? Do you think that police work as hard for the poor person who is wronged as they do for the rich? And when a rich person gets in trouble, look how often they get off because they have money for the best lawyers and are influential. If the wealth was redistributed, then things would be fair. But as long as people can make as much as they want, it will never change."

"But if it were like you want it, where would the incentive be for people to work hard to start businesses and make money? Who would bother?"

"Do you think rich people work hard? Most of them are lazy."

"I don't think that they are all lazy—many of them work very hard for what they have."

"You're just a poor waitress, but you are sounding like you're a spokesman for the rich."

"Well, you're sounding like a spokesman for socialism."

"Well, I think people shouldn't be able to become so rich that they can tell everyone else what to do, and influence the government. That's just plain wrong, and it's not Christian. Money is the root of all evil, you know."

"No, that's not what the Bible says. It says the love of money is the root of all evil."

"What's the difference?"

"Well you can be rich and not love money—not make it your master. You can use it for good, by providing good jobs for people and giving money to charity."

"I don't think Jesus would approve of rich people having so much."

"Well, Abraham was rich, and King David was rich—even Job was rich. That wasn't a sin."

"Well it's sin now, and our only hope is to redistribute it before the rich people completely take control of our government. That's what Lenin and Marx talk about in their books. That's why things are fair in Russia, and they haven't had to go through this Depression."

"Lenin and Marx? I thought you said you were a Christian."

"I am, and Jesus was the first communist."

"What—are you kidding?"

"Not at all. In the Book of Acts it says they had all things in common. That's where communism started."

"No, it isn't. It says they shared voluntarily, they weren't forced—and Jesus wasn't a communist."

"Well, I think he was. He was a great man just like Lenin and Marx."

"So you rate Jesus with them? Have you read any other parts of the Bible?"

"No, I don't have to—I know enough."

"Well, He was more than a great man, he was God. That puts Him a little higher than Lenin or Marx."

"Yeah, I guess, if you believe that."

"Well, if you don't, you're not a Christian, so don't call yourself one."

"Fair enough, I won't. But don't tell me this Depression would have happened if rich people weren't so greedy."

"And you think in Russia they're not greedy—you think human nature is different there?"

"Yes, I do."

"Then why don't you go there if it's so much better?"

"Because I'm here to change things. I want to do my part."

Anna let out a breath and shook her head. "Well, I think it's time for me to go."

"I've got my car. I'll drive you home," Jeremy said.

"No, that's all right, I'll find my way, thank you," Anna said.

"Look, let's not lose what we have over a little political talk."

"Just what do we have?"

"Well, I don't think that politics and religion are everything, and we were getting along just fine until they came up."

"I'm sorry, Jeremy, but to me religion is important. I don't want to get involved with anyone who does not believe in Jesus the way I do."

"Well, that's close-minded."

"Maybe, but that's what freedom is all about—I can choose because our forefathers shed their blood for it. That's another thing that makes us different from Russia."

"Russia is as free as we are—don't believe our propaganda."

"Have you ever been there?"

"No, but…"

"Then don't believe their propaganda."

Jeremy shook his head and then smiled. "I've got to hand it to you—you can debate. In fact, you sound more like a girl who's gone to the university than a waitress."

"I never said I didn't go to college—you just assumed that."

"Well, have you?"

Anna smiled. "You know, I really need to get going. I'll see you at work."

"Well, let me escort you home," Jeremy said, a little surprised.

"I'm fine on my own, but thank you," Anna said, and she walked away from him and continued down the street, where she waited at a bus stop.

The next morning was a Sunday, and Anna dressed for church and then knocked on the door that separated her room from Lucy's, but there was no answer. Gently she opened the door and saw Lucy sprawled on the bed, sleeping very soundly. The covers were in disarray, and Lucy was lying diagonally on the mattress, and the covers were only over the lower part of her body. Anna walked over to her and muttered to herself, "Well, I guess you're not going to church." Then she pulled the covers up to Lucy's neck and walked out of the room.

The church had about one hundred and fifty people in it, and Anna walked in and sat quietly in one of the back rows as people streamed in for the service. She was pleased that she could finally wear a nice dress, a pale yellow chiffon that was designed for her when she finished her first year of college. The dress was expensive, but she did not expect to see any of the people from work there, nor did she think it would matter if she did. She also wore a matching pale tan hat with a brim that came down almost over her eyes and a white veil. She left the veil down because she did not want to be recognized.

After about ten minutes, most of the people were seated and the choir was preparing to sing. She watched them file into their chairs at the front of the church when suddenly she felt a tap on her shoulder. It startled her, and when she turned around she saw it was Bart Lewis. He was smiling broadly and looked very proper and handsome in a finely tailored three-piece suit. He had a gold watch chain connected to the vest, as was the custom with more mature men. She looked at him a little longer than she meant to, puzzled at his appearance, and then she turned away, not certain what to say.

"Can I sit here—I don't know anyone here," he said, sounding almost boyish. She looked at him suspiciously but did not answer for a moment, and the service began.

"Yes, you can sit anywhere you wish in this building, Mr. Lewis," she said curtly.

"Well, that doesn't exactly sound like a welcome now, does it?" he said, slowly sitting down. The choir sang "A Mighty Fortress Is Our God," and when it was finished, he looked over at her again, but she resisted looking back. "Just why do you dislike me?" he asked.

"I don't dislike you. I just don't know what you are doing here," she said.

"Well, I'm attending church," he answered.

"Between girlfriends and drinks?" she asked.

"That's not fair, Miss Jenkins. As a matter of fact, this is my first time here. I asked Jesus to forgive me and I no longer live that way," Bart said, seeming a little hurt at her rebuff. He then turned towards the front and did not look back at her.

Anna tried to concentrate on the next hymn, "Morning Has Broken," but she was suddenly flooded with thoughts that she tried to reconcile as she thought about what he had said. Had she heard him correctly? Had he really said that his life had changed—that he was now following Jesus? She smiled to herself and glanced over at him, as he sang from his hymnal. It was obvious he did not know the words, but he was trying to sing along, she thought. When it ended, she turned and looked at him for a moment. He noticed her looking from the corner of his eye, and he turned towards her. She quickly turned her face towards the front as he did, embarrassed at being caught.

"I'm a new person in Christ," he said. "When you told me you were a Christian, I started thinking about my life, and I remembered some of the things I was taught as a boy in my grandfather's church. He was a pastor, and I loved him, but I would never take his preaching seriously. Now I have."

Anna looked over at him, and her face softened for the first time. "Your grandfather was a minister?"

"Yes, a true man of the cloth. I only wish he'd lived to see this day—you see, he died probably thinking that his prayers for me were wasted."

Anna smiled at him and then picked up her hymnal again, and turned to the page of the next hymn, "Great Is Thy Faithfulness." After the song ended, the minister stood up and began preaching. Bart appeared to be listening attentively, and Anna smiled to herself this time. He was one of the most attractive men she had ever seen, but she had written him off when she realized what type of life he led. But now he had changed—it was almost like a miracle, she thought. What a wonderful turn of events. But she wondered if he still liked her.

When the sermon ended, she put her Bible back in her purse and stood up. He stood also, and as she turned to leave, he tapped her on the shoulder, and she turned around. "I...I could use your help on this new journey," he said. "I'm just learning about all of this." Anna stopped and looked at him for a moment, not certain what to say. Then it occurred to her that the chances of him coming into the same church that she attended were very slim.

"So, Mr. Lewis, how is it that you happened to come to this church today? Was it a coincidence?"

He seemed at bit taken aback at her question, and his mouth turned down, making him look like a hurt child. "As a matter of fact, I was praying about where to go, and then I got into the car and started driving around. When I saw this church, I felt like God said, "This one." So I walked up to the sign and saw that the service was just beginning. I had no idea that you went here, but after I walked in, I just happened to see you. Actually, I didn't recognize you at first—with the veil and all, I mean. And I wasn't going to walk up to you, because you made it clear last time that you wanted nothing to do with me. So I stopped a few rows back and began praying. Not with my mouth, but in my mind, asking God about where to sit. I wasn't sure if that was a proper way to pray, but then I thought that it would be all right if I walked up to you. I'm sorry if I offended you. Did I?"

"No, Mr. Lewis, you didn't offend me. In fact, I'm quite happy for you."

"Well, then, perhaps we can sit together again—would you mind that?"

"No, not at all—that would be fine," Anna said, and she walked out of the building.

"He's what? I can't hear you very well," Esther said, as Anna raised her voice almost to a shout to be heard on the long-distance call.

"He's a Christian now—Bart Lewis, the dreamboat I told you about. He was a playboy, but now he's changed. I saw him at church, and he was so nice—he's so nice now, Esther. He didn't even know what church to go to, but he happened to walk into the one that I go to. I could never have considered him before, but now I think—I think maybe God has sent him my way." Esther was quiet for a moment, and Anna thought that perhaps the connection had failed. "Are you there… Esther, are you there?"

"Yes, I'm here."

"Well, aren't you happy for me?"

"Yes, of course, but…Anna, I don't want to discourage you, but since this just happened to him, you need to make certain it will last. Just don't anticipate too much. Take a little time to wait and see what his attitude is like."

"Esther, why do you say such things! I told you that he came to church and he's changed. He's like a different man, I promise you. You never seem to trust me—I'm not that young, you know. I have discernment."

"I know you do, and I'm sorry if I spoke out of turn. It sounds very promising," Esther said, trying to patch things up. She knew that Anna was sensitive whenever she questioned anything she did, and she was concerned about this man, but she hoped her apology would make amends with her sister.

"That's okay. I know it's only because you care about me. I know it's hard for you to stop playing mother since you did it for so long."

"So what is he like—I mean besides being handsome? What

does he do?"

"I don't know exactly, but he's very rich—and everyone around here knows it. And he's just—just what any girl would want in a man. But I really don't know him, and I will be careful until I do, so don't worry."

"Well, at least you know he's not after your money," Esther said.

"Yes, that is certain. He thinks I'm poor as a church mouse."

21

Mr. Blankenship frowned as he watched Priscilla walk towards him. He was standing outside his office, about to enter, but he stopped and waited for her. As soon as she reached him he began talking, even though Mrs. Ross was at her desk and could hear him. He knew he should wait, but his temper overcame him. He had been angry at Priscilla ever since he'd received the report about the union negotiations, and when he saw her he lost his restraint.

"You've gone too far this time—you knew I wouldn't agree."

"Agree to what? What terrible thing have I done now?"

"I think you know. You gave in on the union demand, and you already knew I said I'd never do that," he said angrily.

"Now wait a minute—you gave me the authority. I told you there was a problem and you said to fix it. And I did."

"I couldn't hear you—the phone connection was bad, and you know it. Anyway, there was no problem—nothing had changed," he protested.

"Yes, there was a new problem—there was going to be a work slowdown and it would have ruined this company," she said. "It would have been subtle, so you couldn't really pin it on anyone."

"And how would you know that?"

"I was told by a good source, a trustworthy source."

"Who told you that?"

"I can't reveal the name."

"As your employer, I demand that you tell me."

"And as a person who made a promise and keeps her word, I cannot tell you, and I will not tell you."

"So you were pressured into doing something, is that it?"

"Not exactly, I also thought the requests were reasonable—at least my counteroffer was."

"Yes, I read the report. You're a woman, you're soft—you gave in quickly."

"I wasn't soft on Willis—you were soft on him, so keep the woman stuff out of it, please. But maybe being a little softer would help the employees like you better."

"I don't think they all dislike me. And some may respect my firmness."

"You just don't see this clearly do you? You don't know how you seem to them."

Before he could answer, three employees walked into the reception area. Mr. Blankenship looked over at them. They slowly approached Mrs. Ross's desk, and she looked at them questioningly.

"We had something to tell Mr. Blankenship, but we can come back…" the man began.

"Yes? What is it?" Mr. Blankenship said in a slightly irritable voice.

"Well, sir, we just want to say thank you for the extra break. It means a lot to us," the first man said.

"Yes it does," another one said, and the third nodded in agreement.

"Everybody said you wouldn't ever give it to us, and we want you to know that we appreciate it, and we'll work extra hard to prove that."

Mr. Blankenship looked at them and then at Priscilla, and then back at them.

"You're welcome," he said, his tone softening. "So I guess you need to get back to work, then," he added, smiling. They smiled back and left the room somewhat hurriedly. As they left, the intercom on Mrs. Ross's desk beeped, and she answered it.

"Is Mr. Blankenship free yet?" Mr. Marcus asked. Mrs. Ross looked at Mr. Blankenship and he nodded.

"Yes, he'll be waiting in his office," Mrs. Ross said. She then handed Mr. Blankenship some mail, and he paused as he looked through it. Priscilla turned to go back to her office, but as she walked towards it, Mr. Marcus came out of his and stopped her, then he turned to Mr. Blankenship, who was still going through his mail.

"Can she join us?"

Mr. Blankenship looked surprised, but he nodded his approval, and they followed him into his office, where they all sat down.

"So, any sales in my absence?" Mr. Blankenship asked.

"Oh, yes, didn't you get my memo?"

"Marcus, I've got a stack of them and I just got back this morning."

"We got a start with Strickland."

"Strickland—you mean the Strickland?"

"Yes, we're filling a small order for them, and if they like the product they will order more—much more."

"How could that be? That's impossible."

"That's why I asked Miss Avery to join us. She gave me a lead over there and that's how it happened."

"Mr. Marcus, you don't have to—" Priscilla began.

"No, Miss Avery, I wasn't very polite to you—I underestimated you, and I want to give credit where it is due."

Mr. Blankenship looked over at Priscilla, apparently speechless, and when he spoke it was more slowly than his usual pace. "You used to work there—isn't that right? So you still know people there…?" he stopped talking and waited for Priscilla to say something.

"Yes, I know a few people," she said modestly.

"I guess!" Mr. Blankenship said, still awed by the turn of events. "Well, I guess I'd better shut up about the bathroom breaks."

"What?" Marcus said.

"Oh, nothing. Well, very good, Mr. Marcus. I'll read the memo and we'll talk about this later." His tone showed that he was through talking to Mr. Marcus.

"Let me know if you have questions when you read it," Mr. Marcus said and got up and left.

"Well, it seems there's just no end to your blessing for this company. Marcus made a very good point—no one should underestimate you." He stood up and walked around his desk and looked into Priscilla's eyes. "Thank you, Miss Avery."

As they were standing there, the intercom buzzed and he reluctantly went over to it. "Yes, Mrs. Ross?" But before she answered, a tall and very pretty blonde opened his office door. Mrs. Ross followed, and from the look on her face it was obvious that she was powerless to stop this young woman. The woman took off her large sunglasses and stared at Mr. Blankenship, then walked up and hugged him and kissed him. At first he tried to pull away, but then he acquiesced, though he seemed embarrassed as they parted.

"Have you missed me, darling?"

"Yes, Roxanne, of course, but you were supposed to be gone another three weeks."

"Oh, but I took another ship back. I'm dreadfully tired of Europe. I barely survived the dreadful food in Italy, and the men were dreadfully forward. But I've been ghastly by pushing my way in here, especially when you have a guest," she said, looking a little suspiciously at Priscilla.

"Oh, I'm sorry, Roxanne. I should have introduced you. This is Miss Avery. She is our newest employee. Miss Avery, this is Miss Saville."

"Pleased to meet you, Miss Saville," Priscilla said as she shook her hand.

"Likewise, my dear. Oh, Herbert, you simply must not hire such pretty women when I'm away. You'll make me dreadfully jealous!" she said, smiling at Priscilla.

Priscilla felt as if her heart fell into her stomach. She thought of how her face must look, and did not want it to give her away, so she turned away for a moment and looked towards the door. It had never occurred to her that Blankenship might have a girlfriend, but Roxanne had to be his girlfriend, she reasoned. She tried to recover, and once she thought she had victory over her face, she turned back towards them and smiled. "Well, I really must get back to work," she said, and turned away. Walking back to her office, she closed the door slowly and then sat down on the guest chair in front of her desk. She felt tears come involuntarily from her eyes, and then there was a knock on the door.

"Yes, who is it?" she asked, wiping away her tears.

"Mrs. Ross?"

"Oh, yes, just a moment." She looked in the mirror and used a handkerchief to dry her eyes. Then she took the seat at her desk, picked up a file, and tried to look preoccupied with it. "Yes, please come in."

Mrs. Ross walked in slowly, her face pensive. It was clear that she was not certain what to say, and she hesitated before she spoke. "I'm sorry, Miss Avery…. I think that I should have told you… I didn't realize…"

"Didn't realize what, Mrs. Ross?"

"That you didn't know…. I could tell by the way you looked that…"

"The way I looked? Didn't know what? I don't know what you are talking about."

Mrs. Ross looked at her for a moment. She didn't quite believe

Priscilla, but Priscilla was doing a convincing job of covering up her true feelings. Mrs. Ross was confused and embarrassed for coming into her office.

"I was just going to tell you that Roxanne is Mr. Blankenship's girlfriend."

"Yes, I assumed that."

"They've known each other for years and years, and I think I should have told you about her."

"No, there was no reason. That's his personal business. It has nothing to do with me."

"Oh, I thought maybe you... Well, I'm out of line, Miss Avery. I apologize."

Priscilla smiled. "All is well, Mrs. Ross. I see the misunderstanding. It was a nice thing to come into my office, but I have no designs on Mr. Blankenship."

"Oh, well, I never thought you did, I just..."

"It's quite all right, Mrs. Ross." Priscilla smiled again.

"You are very gracious, Miss Avery."

Esther knocked on Priscilla's door, but she got no answer. She knocked again and was about to walk away when she heard Priscilla's voice. The door opened and Priscilla walked out, and Esther could tell that she had been crying.

"The cook wants to know if she should leave the food out or refrigerate it."

"Don't leave it out, I'm not hungry."

"He's not worth being upset over. Remember, he's a hothead."

Priscilla looked at her sister for a moment and then turned away and walked back into her bedroom without saying anything. Esther followed her and sat down on the red velvet couch that was in the center of the large room. Priscilla walked to her four-poster bed and collapsed on it. Esther looked over at her, a little exasperated. "Can we talk about it?"

"Why?"

"Because you need to, that's why. All you said was that he had a girlfriend and then you went straight to bed. Come on, Prissy—it's me. You can talk to me."

Priscilla got out of bed and sat down on the couch next to her sister. "There isn't much to say. His girlfriend came into the office, and that's about it."

"What does she look like?" Esther asked.

"Pretty—very pretty."

"Well you are, too."

"I think she's prettier…maybe. I can't tell. She had a lot of makeup on, but I think so."

"What was she like?"

"Well, I didn't talk to her much, but…she seemed like the typical debutante—I take it she's quite wealthy since she's been gallivanting all over Europe where she said the men were "dreadfully forward.""

"She sounds like a young Mrs. Ingersoll or something."

"That's a good comparison. But I'm not mad at her, I was mad at him. But now I'm not sure what happened."

"What do you mean?"

"I mean I don't know if he was leading me on or not. I thought he was showing that he liked me. He took me out to lunch, and…oh, I guess it was all business. I'm the business gal, right? Not the type anyone would want to marry."

"No, he came on with you, and it was unfair. From the high heel to the almost kiss…he led you on."

"The heel who pulls out high heels. And I've put so much into that job."

"But you didn't do it just for him, did you?"

"No, I would have anyway, but it's just…"

"Do you want my opinion?"

"Yes, of course."

"Whatever he did, just write this off and start over. Don't give him another thought. I think he's trouble for you, anyway."

"I'm trying. But aren't they all trouble?"

"You have a point. But he sounds like more trouble than most."

"Maybe, but I could have dealt with it. He also has so much charm."

Esther took her hand and patted it. "I would try to forget him—you might be able to get a job somewhere else."

Priscilla looked at her, slightly surprised at the suggestion. "No, I'm staying. I want to continue with the experiment. I need the experience of working for someone else, and it would be very hard to find a job like this one again."

"But do you really want to be around him after this?"

"I'll be all right. I'm getting over it already," Priscilla said, taking a handkerchief and dabbing her eyes. "It's not like he ever said he loved me or anything—I mean we never even had a relationship."

Esther put her arm around her sister and the phone rang. They ignored it and sat together, and then heard a knock and looked around towards the open door. Mr. Standish stood outside in the hallway and smiled as they looked at him.

"Mr. Holt is on the telephone for you, Miss Esther."

Esther looked at Priscilla and didn't move.

"You must answer, Esther," Priscilla said.

"Oh, I'm going to." Esther walked towards the phone. "Can I take it in here?"

"Of course, silly, I'll just take a walk...."

"No, stay, there are no secrets," Esther said as she picked up the phone.

"Hello, dear," she said.

"Esther?"

"Yes, it's me, but wait a minute until the butler hangs up the extension," she said, hearing a click a few seconds later.

"Esther, I have to tell you something," David's voice trailed off.

"Are you okay, David? What's wrong?"

"I'm not okay, and everything is wrong, and I have to tell you something, but I'm not man enough to say it in person."

"What do you have to say, what is it?"

"Esther, I know I'm a cad to do this, but I must call off our engagement."

"Call off our engagement? Are you serious?"

"Yes, I'm afraid I am, and I know you'll never forgive me, but..." his voice trailed off.

"Have you been drinking?"

"No, you know I don't drink. You know that I—"

"Why, David? What have I done?"

"Nothing. You've done nothing—you've been perfect."

"Then tell me why!" Esther said, her voice rising. Priscilla looked at her a little shocked because her sister was normally so composed.

"Esther, I can't...not now."

They were both quiet for a moment, and Esther seemed to become calmer. "I think I know why," she said in such a low tone that David didn't hear her.

"Good night," David said.

She hung the phone up and stared ahead with a stoic look of unbelief. Priscilla stood up and looked at her for a moment with a questioning look in her eyes. "Did what I think just happen, actually happen?" she asked incredulously. Esther continued staring out but not at Priscilla, and she slowly nodded her head.

"On the telephone? No, no, no, he couldn't have done this on the telephone. Who would do such a thing? How could he? Oh, Esther, I'm so sorry," she said, kneeling down in front of her sister and putting her head in her lap. "I'm so sorry for you."

"I am too," Esther said, as tears fell from her eyes. "I am too."

22

Perry Adler sat at his large teakwood desk in his office that was paneled with cedar. He was a stockbroker, but he never bought a stock himself—he made his money by buying and selling for other people, and he constantly kept his "ear to the ground" for tips on stocks and information about companies. He had saved many of his clients—the ones who would listen to him—millions of dollars by telling them to sell out before the big crash. Although he was only thirty-five years old, he had already built a solid reputation on Wall Street. But his sedentary lifestyle was also taking its toll on his health, and his doctor had advised him to exercise regularly. As he sat analyzing information about various companies, his wife called to remind him about what the doctor had said.

"It's just that I care about you, Perry—I'm not trying to be a nag," she said.

"I understand. I'm going over to join a health club today. There may be some good business contacts there, also."

"Well don't let that stop you from the exercise," she said.

"Don't worry, I plan to put in at least thirty minutes a day. Goodbye now," he said.

After joining the Yale Club, Perry walked back to his new locker and inserted the key. He had a bag with him with his workout clothing, and he was about to put it in the locker when he noticed a letter at the back of it. He picked it up and looked at the addressee's name, which was David Holt. He then walked towards the front desk area with the intention of giving the letter to the clerk, but turned it over several times as he walked, and his curiosity got the better of him and he stopped and sat down and opened the letter instead. He read it carefully several times, his eyes widening as he read, and then quickly signed out of the club and hurried back to his office.

Once there, he dialed quickly and asked to speak to a Mr. Farb. When the man answered, he spoke in an excited voice. "Sell all your Strickland stock—now," Perry said.

"Slow down, Perry. Strickland is solid and they have no debt."

"That's what you think. I found out they leveraged to buy other stocks and they are broke now."

"How could they leverage and I wouldn't know about it?" Mr. Farb asked.

"Because the letter says they have French and English lenders."

"Are you sure about this, Perry? How do you know?"

"I can't tell you everything, but I saw a letter that was sent privately to David Holt—it came to me coincidentally. And the person who wrote it made it very clear that the letter was a confidential letter that no one was supposed to see. It warns Holt that he is marrying into a bankrupt family."

"So who warned him?"

"I don't know, it was just signed 'A friend.'"

"Are you sure about this? I've followed Strickland for a long time and he's always been very careful with his money."

"Yeah, and that's what they said about—"

"Okay, I know, don't go on—I know how they lie about things," Mr. Farb said.

"Look, I just happened to get the letter. It was left somewhere by mistake, and there is no way anyone would know that I would find it. It was by chance."

"Well, we know Holt's broke, so if he figured he'd marry to get the Strickland fortune, it makes sense that a friend might warn him. Okay, I'll unload now—and I need to call some other people. I hope you are right about this."

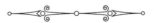

"I thought we would dine at LaRue's tonight, if you are in the mood for French food," Joseph Strickland said into the telephone.

"That would be wonderful, darling," Betty answered.

"Good, then I'll send a car for you around six—or is that too early?"

"No, not at all."

Joseph opened his desk drawer and took out a beautifully carved cherry wood jewelry box. He opened it and looked at the large diamond ring inside, which had belonged to his first wife. He picked the ring up and moved it in several directions, and it sparkled under the sunlight that was filtering in through a large window in his office. Then he put the ring back into the case and slowly closed the lid. "Not yet," he said out loud to himself. "I have to be certain. Lord, show me if she is the one."

Joseph was already seated at his table at LaRue's, located on Park Avenue, when Betty walked into the restaurant. She was escorted by the maître d' to Joseph's table, and he stood up as he saw her enter the room. She wore a low-cut white satin dress with an emerald green trim and matching emerald green shoes and purse which were made of shiny patent leather. A white mink stole was loosely draped around her shoulders, and she slowly took it off as she walked towards him. The dress was lower cut than Joseph thought was proper, but he was also having a difficult time keeping his eyes off her. She sensed that, and smiled demurely at him as she put the stole on a chair next to the one she was about to sit in.

"May I take this, madam?" the maître d' asked, but she put her hand on the stole and shook her head no.

"You know, there might be a chill," she said, as she stroked the stole slowly and made certain it was secure on the back of the chair. "I did not have much time to get ready," she said defensively.

"You look absolutely radiant—stunning," Joseph said, and she smiled at his response.

"How have things been for you today?" she asked in a confidential tone as she gently touched Joseph's hand.

"It's been a good day, except for..." Joseph stopped speaking as he noticed her attention shifting from him to a man who had just walked in. The man was about sixty years old and had an entourage of three other men with him, and a younger woman at his side.

"Isn't that Richard Chandler?" Betty asked.

"Yes," Joseph said.

"Do you know him?"

"Oh yes, we have had some business dealings in the past," Joseph said, and by his tone it was clear that his dealings were not pleasant.

"I think he made his millions during the war, didn't he?" Betty asked. "I think he's very rich."

"Yes, he's made a lot of money," Joseph said, and as he spoke, Chandler turned and noticed him and walked towards their table, but he seemed to be more interested in Betty than Joseph, and he stared at her for a moment.

"Good to see you, Joe—limping along, are you?" he said with a gruff tone.

"Hello, Dick. Yes, we are getting by," Joseph said modestly.

"Well, I'm glad you can still afford to eat here. But who is this vision of loveliness?" he asked, smiling at Betty.

"Betty Ingersoll. Betty, this is Dick Chandler."

"It is my great pleasure to meet you," Chandler said, bowing slightly as he stared at her low-cut dress.

"Mine also, Mr. Chandler."

As he walked away, Betty looked at Joseph questioningly. "You don't like him, do you?" she said.

"No, I don't. He was a profiteer in the Great War, and... You know, Betty, I'd rather not talk about him."

"But what did he mean about you being able to afford to eat here?"

"Oh, I don't know. I guess it's just his snide sense of humor. But that was an off-the-wall remark. Not certain what he meant, but I don't care. Let's just enjoy our evening."

"Yes, of course, darling," Betty said, and she smiled at Joseph and leaned over, revealing more cleavage as she did. "You don't think that my dress is too daring, do you?"

Joseph hesitated before answering. "It's a...a beautiful dress," he said, avoiding the question.

23

"Mrs. Ross, would you ask the chief engineer, Mr. Dulins, if I could speak to him for a few minutes when he gets a chance?" Priscilla asked.

"Yes, I'll ask him to come to your office," Mrs. Ross answered, and Priscilla smiled and went into her office.

Mr. Dulins, an Irish man of about fifty years old with an accent, was dressed in a tweed jacket, and he walked in a few minutes later, looking perplexed. He had a thick head of hair, long sideburns, and a mustache, and was smoking a pipe when he entered. "Did you want to speak to me, Miss Avery?"

"Yes, I keep seeing an expense for a certain part over and over again, and I was wondering why it was wearing out so quickly. I have the record here," she said as she walked over to a file cabinet. Pulling out the file, she passed it to him.

"Yes, there is a coating on this part to keep the high voltage from going through it, and when that wears off, we have to replace it. It's made of coated tin because it needs to be flexible. That's why we have to replace it so often."

"Oh, so that's the reason. I see."

"Is that all you wanted me for?" Mr. Dulins asked.

"Yes, but I wonder if something else could be used so the part would not have to be replaced so often."

Mr. Dulins scratched his head and looked at her for a moment. "Aren't you the bookkeeper?" he finally asked.

"Yes, I am," she answered.

"So do you do engineering, also?"

"Well, I just thought that if I could improve something…"

"There's no way to do that, and it doesn't really matter, because this part is very cheap—it costs very little."

"Yes, I see that, but the cost of the part was not my concern. It is the cost of shutting down the line for forty-five minutes to change it out."

"Well, we shut down the line for longer than that for other things," Mr. Dulins said, a little defensively. "So, if that's everything, I'll be getting back to my work."

"Mr. Dulins, I've calculated the amount of time lost for shut-downs, and I'm trying to find ways to minimize them."

"You are trying? I thought you were the bookkeeper? Are you now going to be an engineer, also?"

Priscilla looked at him for a moment, not certain how to answer. With her father's company, of course no one questioned anything she suggested, and she could analyze anything in any operation. But she realized that she was upsetting this man and decided not to discuss it further. "No, I'm not going to be an engineer, Mr. Dulins. Thank you for your time."

"Don't mention it, but leave the engineering to me, and I'll stay out of the bookkeeping," he said, smiling, and then he walked out.

She was trying to stay away from Mr. Blankenship as much as possible, but she realized that she would have to speak to him to get her idea implemented. As she was thinking about this, he knocked on her door and she asked him to come in. He was in a glum mood when he entered her office.

"These profits are not good—did you do a projection?" he asked, as he stood above her desk, going through some papers she had given him.

"It's not as bad as it looks. We had startup costs for the Strick-land pumps which we won't get paid for until we finish them. But they will probably increase their orders after they get the first batch, so I think your future is bright."

"That's good news, but what were you bothering Dulins about?"

Priscilla hesitated for a moment before answering. She realized he often said provoking things without thinking about them, and she wondered how much more she wanted to take from him. "I am very sorry I bothered him. I need to get some fresh air," she said, rising from her seat.

"Okay, I apologize for that. But I am interested in what you said to him—would you mind telling me?"

"Mr. Blankenship, Mr. Dulins is an engineer, so what could I possibly know about that would be of any benefit to him or you? I'm simply a bookkeeper."

Mr. Blankenship smiled for a moment and was quiet. "I generally don't continue to underestimate a person when they have benefited the company the way you have. So I'm sorry again about saying you bothered him—but you are very young and, being a woman, it's hard for some people to believe you have anything…well, let's just say you are full of surprises. Let's just leave it at that. But I know that if you have a suggestion, it is something I should listen to. So I'm all ears."

"Okay, you keep ordering a part that is coated in Bakelite to stop the conduction of electricity through the part, but the Bakelite is brittle and it often cracks and the whole part needs to be replaced. So I thought maybe you could have the part coated in PVC because it's softer."

"PVC—what is that?"

"Polyvinyl chloride—it's also called vinyl, and it's pliable, but it won't conduct electricity."

"Why haven't I heard of it?"

"Maybe because it was just invented by Walter Semon three years ago and not many people know about it."

"Then why do you know about it?"

"I don't know, I just read things. I sometimes read engineering journals and things like that."

"For fun?"

"Sort of."

"And what will it save us? The part is cheap, isn't it?"

"As I told Dulins, it is, but the down time is not cheap. In fact, I calculated the savings for the approximate extended life of the part if we change to PVC…" Priscilla handed him a notebook. He read it over, and as he did, his glum mood seemed to fade and he looked up at her, smiling.

"I'll see if we can get this Semon fellow on the phone and find out how hard it would be to coat the part in this stuff. Now, we haven't had lunch for a while—why don't we go today?"

"Mr. Blankenship, I would prefer to keep this a business-only relationship."

"Well, I would like it to be more than that, Miss Avery."

"How can you say that when your girlfriend came in right in front of me? Are you some kind of Casanova or something?"

"Oh, you mean Roxanne."

"Yes, that is exactly who I mean."

"Well, there is nothing between us."

"That's not how it sounded or looked."

"Okay, I see now. But you have to understand that our families have wanted us to marry since we were young because we…well, because it would keep the money balanced. But she is no more than a friend—it would be a loveless marriage."

"Does she know that?"

"I think she must have figured it out by now. She's the type of woman who— Well, all she can think about is her hair and her clothing and her makeup. She's frivolous—not my type at all."

"I'm not certain she knows that, and you are not being a gentleman by leading her on. She walked in here like she owned the place and you also."

"Deep down she knows."

"Well, Mr. Blankenship, she might be just a little too shallow to get that deep down, so you owe it to her to tell her the truth."

"I suppose you are right."

"I am certain I am right."

"If I promise to tell her, will you eat lunch with me? Because I need to talk to you about something very important."

"Would that be the union, or the bookkeeping, or the vinyl?"

"It would be none of those things—it would be about your plans for the future."

"My plans for the future—whatever could you be referring to?"

"You have to go to lunch to find out."

Priscilla looked at him for a moment and then smiled. "I don't know if I should, but I'm going to give you the benefit of the doubt."

"Does that mean yes?"

"It does, but if I slip again, please don't catch me—that was very embarrassing last time—in front of everyone."

"Okay, I'll let you fall and crack your skull—if that's what you want. But then I'd still have to pick you up to take you to the hospital, wouldn't I? So you would still end up in my dreadful arms!"

"Let's just hope, if that happens, it will be Jekyll and not Hyde."

"Yes, I think that Jekyll would be a particularly good choice, because I think he was a doctor, wasn't he? Unfortunately, Miss Avery, you get the whole package—a swirling, incomprehensible mix of Hyde and Jekyll to always keep you on your toes. Jekyll to love, and Hyde to fight—and I think some women rather fancy a little Hyde in there somewhere."

"Well I don't, so keep your Hyde hidden."

"I wish I could, but every so often he rears his ugly head—sometimes when least expected—that dastardly fellow! But a girl like you could probably stand up to Hyde and subjugate him."

Priscilla looked at him for a moment and then smiled and shook her head. Then she changed the subject. "Can we eat somewhere less fancy this time?"

"Of course. I was trying to impress you last time, but I guess it didn't work."

"Well, I have simple tastes."

"Really?" he said, studying her face. "Somehow I doubt that, but we can eat at the greasy spoon this time, if it makes you happy."

"Actually there is an Italian restaurant not far from here—and we could walk."

"Your wish, madam, is my command."

As Priscilla walked into the restaurant, she regretted the choice because she realized that some of the waiters there knew who she was. How could I have been so stupid? she thought, as the maître d' smiled at her. He was a newer employee, and she hoped he did not remember her name. He must not have, because he ushered them to a table and said nothing. She buried her face in the menu and held it up for a long time so she would not be seen. Eventually, Blankenship noticed.

"I would think you are reading a suspenseful novel rather than a menu," he commented.

"Oh, ah...I thought I'd try something new—I just can't seem to make up my mind." Their waiter approached, and she felt relieved since it was not one who knew her. She was so concerned about being recognized that she hardly heard Blankenship as he ordered, and had to be prompted when it was her turn. After ordering, she slowly put down the menu. He looked over at her and spoke with a light-hearted tone.

"Ah, I can finally be dazzled by your beauteous face," he said.

Suddenly she saw the owner of the restaurant coming towards them, and she put the menu up to her face again.

"Was it something I said—or are hunger pangs driving you?"

"I just wanted to see what there was for dessert," she said sheepishly.

"Well, there is a tray there." He pointed to the desserts as another waiter pushed them on a cart. "I think they will bring them over after we eat."

"Oh, yes, they look delicious," she said. "Do you see one you like?"

"Yes, I think I like them all," he said, still bemused and a little confused by the way she was acting.

"Which one will you order, then?"

"Well, nothing. Actually, I'm trying to quit—they ruin my girlish figure." As he finished talking, the owner walked up and greeted Priscilla. He had a very thick Italian accent and it was hard to understand him, and as he said "Miss Strickland," Priscilla started coughing loudly and the owner picked up her glass of water and handed it to her.

"Grazie, grazie," Priscilla said, and she looked up at the owner. After a moment he walked away and Blankenship sat gazing at her with a questioning look.

"Are you okay?"

"Yes—yes, I'm fine," she said.

"You must come here a lot—he was very happy to see you."

"Oh, I've been here a few times."

"You know, I thought I heard him say Strickland."

"Oh...well, he might have. I've been here before with the company—on company business when I worked for them—their subsidiary, I mean...That's how I know about this place."

"I see. Are you feeling all right now?"

"Yes, of course."

"And which one do you want?"

"Which what?"

"Dessert...which dessert do you like?"

"Oh, I don't want dessert, but thank you anyway." Priscilla had completely forgotten about the dessert after her interaction with the owner, but she remembered right after she spoke.

"Okay. You don't change your mind a lot, do you?" he asked, with a perplexed look on his face.

Priscilla smiled at him. "Lady's prerogative, is it not?"

"Evidently."

Priscilla kept her head down a little, still hoping no one would recognize her. Herbert watched her curiously, and she looked up and smiled at him.

"Is your mind on something else, today?" he asked.

"Oh, no. I'm altogether here. Now what did you want to talk

about?"

"I would like you to meet my mother."

"Your mother—why?"

"Because I promised her that I would introduce her first to any girl I might be serious about."

"Mr. Blankenship, you have never even asked to see me...never asked me on a date. What makes you think that I would want to meet your mother?"

"Well, would you...please? And call me Herbert."

Priscilla looked around the restaurant for the first time—she no longer cared who recognized her. She was confounded at his question and did not know how to answer.

"What makes you think that I have any interest in you beyond working at your company?"

"Okay, let me think. When you slipped that day and I caught you and looked into your eyes...I thought you looked interested. And then when Roxanne showed up it seemed that you might be jealous."

"That is ridiculous. I was not jealous, and I never said anything..."

"It was your eyes."

"My eyes. So now you can read minds by looking into someone's eyes?"

"No, I can't—not everyone, but I thought..."

"Well, you thought wrong. And if I was interested, I would not want a man whose first request was that I meet his mother."

Herbert looked at her and as she watched him she could tell she had hurt him—it was the first time she had seen him look vulnerable. Then his face seemed to firm up, as if he had accepted the answer, and he nodded in agreement. "Okay, I get the message. Are you sure you don't want dessert?"

She looked up slowly from her food, realizing that not only had she offended him, but that she was turning him down when she really liked him.

"I'm sorry—I didn't really mean that, but don't you think meeting your mother is a little...different?"

"Well, the Bible says honor your father and mother, and my mother asked me if I ever met anyone other than Roxanne would I please introduce her before anything got started. I also thought it would be fair to you, so you would know that my intentions towards you are completely honorable."

"Well, when you put it that way, it sounds okay."

"Very good. Then I'll pick you up on Saturday afternoon and we will drive to my mother's estate and have a late lunch. Just write down your address," he said, passing her a piece of paper and taking a pen from his pocket.

She looked at him for a moment and did not take the pen as he offered it. Not only was she surprised at how quickly he recovered from her first reaction about seeing his mother, her mind was also racing to figure out a way to avoid having him picking her up. "Mr. Blankenship…"

"Please, just Herbert—at least while we are alone."

"Herbert, I had really planned on some shopping this Saturday…"

"Well, if you can't make it…"

"No, I can, but would you pick me up at Bloomingdale's?"

"Bloomingdale's?…of course—just give me a clue where you will be in the store so we don't miss each other."

"No, I don't feel that way, I am so happy for you," Esther said as she combed Priscilla's hair. "Just because things aren't working out for me… Well, it makes me happy inside that they are for you. Wouldn't it be terrible if we were both sad?"

"You're the best—really the best," Priscilla said, and she held her arm to her face for a moment, and then she looked into the mirror. "I may never be as pretty as Roxanne, but—"

"Priscilla, that is a ridiculous thought. If he only wants you for your looks, then you may as well give it up now. He likes you. He has seen your abilities and he knows your personality."

"Thank you, again. I needed that."

"And it's not like you aren't pretty, by the way."

"Well, she is prettier, I think. In fact, I know she is."

"And he doesn't want her."

"Well, I'm not certain he…that he doesn't like her more than he is letting on. The way they smooched when she came in that day was—"

"If you keep thinking about her, you'll never have peace. Now either he is the one or he's not, and you'll know soon enough."

"You are right. Now, I know you would have told me, but have you heard from David at all?"

146

"No, but even if I thought he would call me, he's got other prob-lems—his grandfather just died, and he was close to him. I am con-cerned for him because he took it so hard when his mother died, and somehow…"

"What, Esther—what were you going to say?"

"I know it sounds like I'm denying reality, but somehow I think he still loves me. I don't know why I think that—it's probably just wishful thinking. But maybe he loves me, but he just loves my money more?"

24

David watched from his car as his father drove up in his Packard touring sedan and walked into the church where the funeral for his grandfather was being held. He waited until he thought his father had found a seat, and then he left his own car and walked towards the church. It was a large, somewhat ornate church, but it was not the one that his grandparents usually attended. He had wondered why the funeral was held there, but now realized it was because there were so many people in attendance—the regular church was too small for all of them. He saw his grandparents' pastor and then he saw his grandmother sitting with other relatives and with his father. He walked over to her and hugged her, and found himself more emotional than he thought he would be. Tears came to his eyes, and when they separated, she looked at him, smiling.

"He loved you so much, David. He talked about you right before the heart attack. He was so proud of you," she said. "But cheer up, because he's in a far better place."

"I'm more sorry for you, Gran."

"No, don't be. He suffered so much with the heart ailment. I'm glad it's over for him. He's so happy now, and he's just waiting for me to join him."

"Oh, don't say that…I don't know how much more I can take."

"Oh, my dear—God won't allow you to be tested beyond what you can endure."

"Yes, I know the Scripture…I've read it many times," David said, turning away from his grandmother for a moment.

"But you still don't believe it?" she asked, trying to look into his eyes.

"No, no, I do," David said reluctantly as he avoided her gaze.

Turning his head, he noticed his father sitting a few seats down, and he frowned and quickly turned back to his grandmother, who was watching his reaction.

"We can make room for you," she said.

"No, no, Gran. I'll just sit close by. It will be fine," he said.

"Okay, David, but please come to my house on Tuesday at two o'clock. Can you make it?"

"Yes, Gran—I'll be there." He walked away, and avoided looking in his father's direction and took a seat several aisles away, in back of them. His grandmother looked back at him as he sat down, then she turned to the front again, in thought.

It was a bright and sunny Tuesday when he visited his grandmother as she requested. The house was a beautiful old home in Scarsdale, and it was constructed with a rock veneer of various colors. The outside walls were partially covered with ivy, and the garden was filled with various colors of roses and other flowers. As he rang the doorbell, David remembered getting thorns from some of those roses when he played there as a child. She answered and seemed happy and excited to see him as she kissed him on the cheek and said, "Hello, David."

"You look very good, Gran. Especially considering what you've been through."

"Oh, it's not all that bad—my time here isn't much more. I'm just trying to make the best use of it. Follow me in the kitchen."

He followed her through the living room, which had a beautifully inlaid wood floor that had the pattern of a cross in the middle. The cross was in Brazilian cherry wood and he remembered that she had it installed when they remodeled the house when he was in elementary school. They reached the kitchen, and she went to the refrigerator and took out some milk and poured it into a glass. David noticed that it was a new model.

"When did you get the new refrigerator?" he asked.

"Just this year. It works on something called Freon."

"Wow, what did that cost?"

"I think it was about seven hundred dollars," she answered.

"That's a lot more than some cars."

"Yes, but it's worth it. Keeps everything cold and also has a deep freeze on top," she said, opening it up for him to look at.

She then put the milk down on the table along with a plate of cookies.

He looked at her questioningly. "Are these for me?"

"Yes. Remember how I always had freshly baked cookies for you when you visited?" she said sweetly.

"Of course, Gran," he said, taking a cookie to please her, even though he wasn't very hungry. "You were always the perfect grandmother."

She was quiet for a while and he began to wonder if she was getting senile or something because she watched him eat his cookie without saying anything. But, in fact, she was thinking about what to say.

"So, did you invite me over just for cookies?" he asked.

"No, dear, not at all. I invited you over because your father is very distraught and you are making things worse."

"I'm making things worse for him! He is the one who lost all our money. All I did was work myself to death to please him while he lied to me and wasted the company and ruined my life," David said, and as he spoke he realized that he was almost shouting. "I'm sorry, Gran, I over-reacted...I'm sorry."

"I understand why you are upset. I saw all this coming with him and I saw it coming with you," she said.

"What do you mean, you saw it coming? I don't understand. Did you know the market was going to crash in '29 and then crash again after it came back?"

"No, I don't know anything about the stock market. But I know about the souls of those I pray for every day. Your father was a wonderful boy when he was growing up. He was generous and caring, but when he went to college things changed. He started associating with those non-believers from rich families, who cared about nothing except getting richer no matter what it took. I tried to reason with him. I told him the love of money was the root of all evil. Your grandfather was always wealthy but he did not love money."

"I know, Gran. I understand. You've told me before."

"I told him the Bible says, in First Timothy 6:9, 'But they that will be rich fall into temptation and a snare, and into many foolish and hurtful lusts, which drown men in destruction and perdition.'"

"Yes, I know that one, also, Gran."

"I know you know, because I told you also. But you wouldn't listen either. It happened to both of you at the university. So I knew this would happen to both of you because I prayed it would happen."

"You prayed it would happen?" David asked incredulously.

"Not specifically, but that both of you had to be broken of this disease of covetousness and greed. So if you want to get angry at someone, get angry at me. I'm the reason the money and the business was lost. It's all my fault that you say your life is ruined."

David looked at her in wonderment for a while. "No, it's not your fault. You didn't make him gamble the company away. He did that himself. He had free will. You can't make someone do something like that."

"David, you must forgive him. No matter what he did you must forgive him. Jesus gave us the parable of the servant who was forgiven so much and then he would not forgive someone who owed him just a little. It's essential for your salvation."

"Gran, I want to forgive him, but I just can't seem to get past the anger. I don't know how he could have lied to me all those years and used me. He promised me the company if I worked hard, and I did work hard. I worked so hard that I started losing sleep. I stayed up at night and worked when others were having fun. I gave it everything I had."

"I know. And you shouldn't have. It became an idol in your life and you gave it more than you gave God."

"Gran, could you just quit preaching at me for a moment—could you!" he said angrily, his eyes flashing. As soon as he had spoken he regretted it.

"Yes, dear, I will quit preaching."

"Oh, I'm sorry, I didn't mean it that way. I think the world of you—you have always been so loving and kind. I'm sorry."

She walked over and put her arm around him and he hugged her. "I just don't know what to do. Everything has fallen apart. My life is in ruins and everything is bleak."

"At least you don't have to blame yourself."

"What do you mean by that?"

"I mean how much worse you would feel if you were responsible for all of it. That's what your father has to deal with. It is his fault. Think of how awful he must feel, especially with you so angry at him."

"You're right, Gran. You're always right. I need to make my peace with him."

"What about Esther Strickland? I understand the engagement is off."

"Yes, well, that didn't work out, either. She wouldn't want me now."

"Why? Did she turn you down because of the business loss? She didn't seem like that type to me."

"No, she didn't turn me down."

"Then what happened?"

"I don't want to talk about it. I have to see Father and make things right."

"You won't tell me what happened with Esther?"

David looked at her for a moment and relented. "I called it off— I couldn't go through with it after everything went sour. I didn't want to embarrass her. She wouldn't have turned me down, but how could I have dragged her through all of that? I didn't want her to be ashamed, and I didn't want to get charity from her family. Believe me, it's better this way."

"Do you still love her?"

David hesitated for a moment before he answered. "Sometimes it is better to give up someone you love rather than cause them pain."

"I see."

"Well, I'd better see Father now. Do you know where he is?"

"He was at the office this morning, so I suppose he is still there."

David drove to the office building and noticed that there were only a few cars in the parking lot. His father's was one of them, so he knew he was there. The building was eerily quiet as he walked towards the elevator. It was open and he walked in, but there was no elevator operator in sight. He looked at the controls and tried to run it himself, and then realized that the electric power to it had been turned off. A bit disgusted, he walked to the stairway and began climbing the stairs until he had reached his father's office, which was twenty-two flights up.

He walked into the reception area and there was no one there. Then he walked over to his father's office and knocked on the door, but no one answered. He knocked again and waited a few minutes, then he turned the handle of the door, but it was locked. He was about to walk away when he thought he heard a voice in the office, so he put his ear to the door, but was not certain if he heard anything or not. He walked to the receptionist's desk and looked in all the drawers until he found the last one locked. There was a screwdriver in one of the open drawers, and he used it to jimmy open the locked drawer, and it had keys to the offices in it. He took the ring of keys over to the locked door and began trying them until one of them opened the door.

As he walked into the office, pieces of paper were flying through the air and several hit him in the face, and he was unable to see because of the wind that was blowing through the four large windows, which were all open. He pulled a piece of paper from his face and walked over to the first window and closed it, and then he closed a second window, but he turned around because he thought he heard a voice.

"Father, is that you?" he said, and he looked around the large office and walked around the overstuffed chairs and a couch that was positioned in front of his father's long ebony wood desk, but no one was there. He walked away from the window towards a closet in the office, and he opened the door, but it was empty. So he returned to the windows and began to close the third one when he was certain he heard a man's voice. He looked around, and then he heard a man cough. Not seeing anyone else in the office, he leaned out the window and saw his father on the ledge. He was shocked and dumbfounded for a moment as he tried to think of what to say.

"What are you doing? Are you trying to kill yourself?"

His father looked over at him, startled to see him. He looked down towards the street below and spoke slowly. "I'm trying to solve one of the world's problems. I can't solve many problems, but I can solve this one."

"Father, what are you talking about—what problem?"

"I am the problem, soon to be solved and no longer a burden," he said, looking up and then down again. David also looked down and was thankful that no one on the street had seen him.

"Don't do this...please don't."

"Everyone will be happier and I will be happier when it's all over."

David began to crawl out of the window, and his father's tone changed and became harsh. "Don't come any closer—I'm warning you!"

David sat on the windowsill but did not climb out onto the ledge. He thought for a moment before he spoke.

"No one will be happier, least of all you."

"Yes I will, I'll be in heaven. I'm forgiven. I asked Jesus into my heart when I was a little boy."

"Father, it's murder. It's against the law!"

Gerald Holt then started laughing. "Then they can arrest me when I get to the bottom!" he said sarcastically. "But I don't have anything to worry about—I repented."

David began to move off the sill towards him.

"I said don't come closer!" his father shouted. "Can you at least obey me in this? Come closer and I'll jump right now."

"That's the last thing I want you to do," David said softly as he backed up. "I just don't want you to end up in hell."

"This life is like hell to me now, anyway. The people I thought were friends sneer at me now and mock me. I've ruined everyone's life including my own because I was greedy and stupid. There, I said it so you don't have to. But I won't go to hell, because I repented."

"Father, to repent means to turn from your sin. You can't repent and then sin and get forgiven ahead of time."

"What are you, a preacher now? I think I'll go to heaven."

"Are you sure you'll be forgiven for premeditated murder? Are you willing to bet your eternity on it?" David's father said nothing for a moment, and then he answered gruffly.

"It's really none of your business. Anyway, I didn't know you were an expert on forgiveness—in fact, I thought you had a problem in that area."

"I did. That's why I'm here—to ask you to forgive me."

"Me forgive you? Isn't it the other way around? I'm the one who destroyed your life."

"You already apologized to me, but I didn't accept it then. The way I acted was very wrong and I'm sorry. I am really sorry and I don't want you to jump. Please don't jump. Please, father, I acted abominably. There is no excuse for the way I acted, and I love you."

Gerald Holt looked over at his son, then down to the street again but said nothing.

"Please, Father, will you forgive me, and can we start over?"

David's father looked over at him for a moment and then back to the street, and he began moving towards the window. When he got to it, David grabbed him and helped him back into the office. Once they got in, David hugged him and as he did his father started crying and was shaking. After they hugged for a while, David walked him over to the large couch and helped him sit down. Then he closed the other two windows.

"You've never seen me cry before and I'm ashamed," Gerald said, tears still falling from his eyes.

"I'm glad I saw you cry. I like you better this way," David said.

Gerald looked at his son, in thought for a moment. "I guess I've

155

been too rough on you—always pushing you to do more. Never showing much emotion—but I had it in my heart—I did. In fact, I was so sorry for you after what I did…"

"Don't worry about it…I know, I see it now. And pushing me also helped me. I did a lot of things I wouldn't have. It gave me confidence."

They were silent for a moment, both feeling that this was the start of a new relationship between them. David finally broke the silence.

"Where is everyone? I thought they were going to keep the company intact."

"That's what they said, but they fired them all and moved the headquarters to St. Paul. It's their building now, so that's the end of it."

"That's not the end, I know the locations we had which are underserved, and we can start over again and open some new stores to compete. We ran this profitably, and if we get another chance we can make a new company work."

His father shook his head and smiled. "That would be true, but we're broke, and we can't get credit after this mess. It's all over."

25

"Well, they say you can get just about everything at Bloomingdale's!" Herbert said, as he opened the door of a 1931 Chrysler Imperial custom roadster for Priscilla. She smiled at his joke as he got into the sports car.

"This is a very nice car. Is it new?"

"Just bought it to pick you up in," he said, in such a way that she was not certain if he was teasing her or not.

"Well, it's very nice."

"Definitely the cat's meow. Will the top down spoil your hair?"

"No, it's okay, just let me pin my hat on a little tighter," she said, attempting to do so as he raced off with a burst of acceleration that threw her head back into the seat.

"That didn't seem to bother you," he said, watching her as she fumbled with her hat.

"Oh, my father likes fast cars, he likes his Duesenberg Model J because—"

Herbert laughed a little and interrupted her. "You don't have to tell me why. Everyone likes a Duesy, but no one can afford one, except Alfonso the Eighth the King of Spain and a few others…wait a minute, did you say `his model J'?"

Priscilla was flustered and angry at herself, and her mind was spinning trying to answer. "Yes…he has a model of the Model J…on his mantel," Priscilla said, happy that she could also tell the truth, because her father had both.

"I've seen those models—they are quite nice. Very exquisite replicas of the real car. Good for dreaming about, I think."

"Yes, well this is an expensive car, also," Priscilla said as she touched the dashboard of the Chrysler. "It's beautiful."

"Thank you. I hoped you'd like it. You see I bought this green color to match your eyes," he said, again making her wonder if he was jesting or serious. They drove for a while in silence, and then he looked over at her for a moment. "Mother may make you feel a little like you are under a microscope, so please do not hold that against her. It's just that she's planned for me to marry Roxanne for many years, and it will take some getting used to for her to accept someone different...I mean someone else."

"Different...do you mean poor instead of rich? Is that what you mean?"

"I will be candid, Priscilla. Mother was hoping I would marry someone who was equal in...wealth."

"So is that what this meeting is about, to see if I measure up... and I better really be something special if I don't have money?" she said, sounding a little testy.

"It's not like that, but I'm just trying to be honest in that it might disappoint her—she's often hard to read and I'm not certain how she thinks, and I don't want to upset her."

"Well, at your age, I'm surprised this would be such an issue."

"It's not that, but she does have some power. She still receives a lot of income from the business, and she also has money that she lends the business, which has recently become a real benefit, after the embezzlement and loss of business from the crash."

"So, what you are saying is that you have to make certain that Mother approves of me, a poor girl, because if she doesn't, you want nothing to do with me because she might cut you off from the funds you need for your business. So if that's it, why don't you just take me back to Bloomingdale's, Mr. Blankenship!"

"Oh, now you're offended. But you need to understand how... how people like her think."

"I understand very well, even for a wretched poor girl. You don't want me unless your Mum approves. And in my book, that means you aren't man enough for a woman like me. So turn the car around!"

Herbert pulled over and stopped the car. "Now wait a minute. I did not say that I would kowtow to my mother or that I would not choose you because she did not approve. Please try to understand. I am trying to keep peace with her and have her blessing for a relationship with you, not only for my sake and the company's sake but also for yours. Because if we get serious about each other you will have to deal with her, and it is better if you meet her first so there are no surprises for anyone. But let me tell you emphatically that if we want a relationship, I will not let my mother, or Herbert Hoover, or anyone else stand in the way. She does not tell me what to do, but I am trying to keep peace in my family. Okay?"

Priscilla looked at him for a moment and smiled. "Okay. I'm sorry. I didn't mean to insult you."

"And I didn't mean to insult you. And I would be happy to meet with your father and any other relatives, and they can question me in a dark room with a bright bare light in my eyes and ask anything they want to! Now can I keep driving?"

Priscilla laughed a little. "All right, Herbert, to Mother's we go. But by the way, I don't think you need to worry about her money anymore with the Strickland account. I'm sure you have heard from Mr. Marcus that they are very pleased with the products so far, so I think they will order more."

"If they stay in business."

"What? Why would you say that?"

"Priscilla, this is very, very confidential because very few people know about it, but Strickland is going bankrupt. I only found out the other day. So I wouldn't count on sales from them or any of their subsidiaries."

"Where did you hear such a thing?"

"I can't tell you, I promised not to reveal the source, and if I did not trust you implicitly I would not have told you, because my source made it very clear that this should not be spread around."

"Okay…I see."

"Well, here we are—Somerset," he said, and Priscilla saw the name engraved in the stone wall that surrounded the home. Herbert opened the gate, and they drove into the circular driveway of a large and beautiful stone English Tudor style home with the well-manicured hedges that are characteristic of English gardens. The estate, which was on ten acres, reminded her of some places she had visited many years before when her family had visited England. As she stepped out of the car, Herbert walked around and took her hand.

"Did you bring that back with you from Eton?" she asked.

"Well, Mother is British, as you will find out shortly, and this was father's gift to her to make her feel at home."

"I think he succeeded. This is a charming place, and I feel like I'm in England," Priscilla said, as they walked to the front door.

"This may be as close as you can get," Herbert said as the butler opened it and greeted them with an English accent. They walked into a large living room with white shiny marble floors and expensive pastel-colored Persian rugs. The room had twenty-foot-high ceilings, and one wall was mostly windows, and it looked out at the beautiful garden, which had a variety of flowers of various hues. As they sat down, Priscilla also noticed a huge fireplace that was screened off for the summer. On an adjacent wall there were paintings of men and women whom she presumed were relatives. And as she sat down on a couch with plush golden-colored fabric, she noticed several photographs on an end table next to her. One of them was of Herbert with a strikingly pretty girl.

"Please tell Mother we are here, Duncan," he said to the butler as he took a seat next to Priscilla. "Do you like that picture?"

"Yes, it's very nice. Is this another one of your admirers?"

"Absolutely. I love her dearly."

"And where is she now—not on a European odyssey, I assume?" Priscilla said, acting as if she was superficially jesting but in reality bothered that this could be someone he liked.

"No, she's in the upstairs bedroom at the moment."

"The bedroom?"

"Yes, that's my little sister, Charlotte.... I guess she's not so little anymore, at twenty-one years old. She'll be down in a few minutes, I suspect."

Priscilla was relieved, but she did not let on. She heard a sound and turned around to see Herbert's mother enter the room with the butler following. Mrs. Blankenship was dressed in a lavender dress with gold brocade which flowed around her ankles as she walked in a very erect and precise manner. She was not very tall, but her thin frame and manner made her seem taller. Herbert stood up, and Priscilla did also, somewhat instinctively, and Mrs. Blankenship smiled and they sat down together. Charlotte appeared just as they sat, and she walked over and sat on the couch next to Priscilla, rather than next to her mother, who was sitting on a small divan opposite the couch. There was an ornate coffee table between them, and a silver tray was set with cups.

"Miss Avery, from what Herbert says, you are a quite remarkable young lady," Mrs. Blankenship said in a way that Priscilla thought was somewhat challenging—as if she were saying it questioningly and that she wanted it proven to her. The statement was not what she expected and she struggled for a moment to figure out how to answer.

"Well, Herbert is quite remarkable too, I think—when he's relaxed...."

"You mean when he's not blustering?" Charlotte said, smiling, but causing her mother to wince. Herbert took it in stride, and nodded in agreement. Mrs. Blankenship ignored her comment and kept talking.

"So, I understand that your father is…multi-talented?" she asked.

"Yes, he is—quite so," Priscilla said in a manner that suggested that she did not want to pursue the subject.

"And your education—where did you learn so much so quickly? Did you go to college?"

Priscilla looked at Herbert and then back at his mother. She had not put her education on the employment application. "Yes, I did. I have a degree," Priscilla said.

"Well, that is quite an accomplishment for a young lady," Mrs. Blankenship said.

"Thank you."

"So what do you see in your future? Do you want to continue in the bookkeeping work, or…"

"Mother, Priscilla is much more than a bookkeeper," Herbert said.

"Yes, I know. You've told me so much about her I felt that I already knew her before we met. Do you think you have a family in your future?"

"Mother, what a question—we just walked in and you're already…" Herbert said, but Priscilla answered.

"Well, I like children, but I'm happy with what I'm doing now. I look forward to having a family one day, but I'm single now and I enjoy working."

"So once you get this out of your system, you might become more traditional?" Mrs. Blankenship said, but she regretted her words because she realized that they may have sounded as if she were meddling. Priscilla was a little irritated, but she did not react that way, as she thought about the reason behind the question. Mrs. Blankenship evidently wanted grandchildren, and this was an interview with a potential daughter-in-law. She couldn't blame her for asking, but thought she was getting personal a little too early. Nevertheless, she liked the fact that Mrs. Blankenship was straightforward, and she did seem kind, even if her manner was a bit condescending. Having been around many older women who were wealthy, Priscilla realized that she was probably unaware of the way she seemed. The butler came in with two pots as she was thinking about these things, and Charlotte smiled at

Priscilla.

"Would you like tea or coffee?" she asked.

"Oh, tea, please," Priscilla said, and the butler served them their drinks and also put a variety of pastries on the table.

"Mother, if someone wants to do something in life because they have gifts, should tradition stop them?" Charlotte asked.

"Oh, it was not a good question, I know. Forgive me, Miss Avery."

Priscilla smiled as she bit into the delicious pastry. How could she say that she thought she was the perfect match for Herbert because she did understand business and could help him with his decisions even if she was taking care of children at the same time? They were not even engaged, even though everyone there knew what this discussion was about. And if she spoke too bluntly, she would not only seem presumptuous about an engagement, she would also appear to want to marry this man who had not even proposed. For a moment she was angry that she had accepted the invitation, but then she heard herself answer, without thinking about what she would say.

"It's quite all right, Mrs. Blankenship. Perhaps we could discuss these things if we get to know each other better."

"Yes, I would like to get to know you better," Mrs. Blankenship said, smiling.

"So would I," Herbert said with a tone which seemed earnest and sardonic at the same time.

"You have the most beautiful gardens, here," Priscilla said as she looked out the picture windows and attempted to change the subject.

"Yes, we do, and you simply must take a walk with me in the garden," Charlotte said, and she stood up and took Priscilla's hand.

"I'd love to, but—" Priscilla began to say.

"Yes, have a nice walk. We can chat later," Mrs. Blankenship said.

Herbert stood up as Priscilla did, but Charlotte pushed him to his seat. "We will have some girl talk," Charlotte said playfully.

"Well, don't tell her what I'm really like," Herbert said.

"It's okay, I already know and I still came," Priscilla said as Charlotte pulled her towards a large wooden door with many panes of glass.

The fragrance of the flowers was delightful as they walked along a cobblestone path together. "You must forgive Mother, Miss Avery. She truly means well, but she is so protective of Herbert, especially since Father died."

"Oh no, she was fine—I understand her. But call me Priscilla."

"Of course, and call me Charlotte. I love working out here in this garden. It bothers Mother sometimes because she says the gardeners should do it, but it's a special place for me."

"I can see why, it is extraordinarily beautiful."

"Oh, you like flowers then?"

"Yes, I love them."

They approached a short bridge that went over a narrow stream, and Charlotte sat down on a stone bench that was on one side of it, and Priscilla joined her. "When I was a little girl I used to sit here and wonder about what I would do when I grew up. I was concerned about it, because I did not like playing with dolls much, but I liked some of the things the boys liked. And science was my favorite subject in school."

"That's interesting—I was the same way."

"Yes, I know a lot about you. Herbert has talked about little else since you came to work there, and I couldn't wait to meet you."

"He talks about me a lot?"

"Oh, yes, incessantly. But you thought differently, because he's lost his temper with you?"

"Well, I have wondered about him. I've told him he reminds me of Jekyll and Hyde."

"Yes, I see why you say that—that's one side. But I can also tell you that he respects women more than any man I have ever known, and he can be very kind. He is very honest and principled in everything he does. He may have his problems, but if he commits to you, he will be loyal and true to you always, and you can always count on him."

"I'm happy to hear that from you. That's rare in a man these days."

"Yes, I think so. I would like to meet a man like my brother—even with his faults. Father was always too busy for me, but Herbert has always been my friend and protector. If he thought anyone had dishonorable intentions towards me, he always said so. When I was in high school there was a boy named Alex that he told me to watch out for. Alex went to our church and he was so handsome that I was blinded to what he was like. One day I was on a church hay ride and he tried to take advantage of me. Herbert was with Roxanne and he heard me protest. Alex was bigger than Herbert, but the next thing I knew he had Alex in a headlock, and he threw him off the hay carriage."

"So was he ever in love with Roxanne?"

"No, I don't think so, but my parents were always pushing them together."

"Does Roxanne love him, though?"

"You know, I'm not sure about the way she feels because she's never even talked to me—not like we are talking now. It may sound funny, but I think she feels I'm competition for her, even though I'm his sister. Father was best friends with her father, and he had his heart set on their marrying."

"When did your father die?"

"Two years ago. That's when Herbert took over the company, and he's done a brilliant job—even in this bad economy we've been profitable. Mother thought he was too young, and she wanted to hire a more experienced person, but I told her I was certain that Herbert could do it if she would just give him a chance. And he's done better than we ever imagined. But how did you ever learn all the things you know? Herbert has given us such good reports."

"Well, I worked for another company."

"You worked for Strickland, didn't you?"

"Yes."

"I wondered why anyone would leave Strickland to work for our small company, but I'm glad you did."

"Well, I wanted to get other experience."

"I see. Now, may I ask a favor of you?"

"Of course. What would that be?"

"I want to work at the factory myself. Not for my whole life or anything, but business fascinates me and I want to learn about it, but Herbert is not keen on the idea."

"He wants you to be more traditional, I take it?"

"Not so much that, it is rather that I say what is on my mind, and it gets him angry, so I think he is afraid that I might want to control things. You see, I own an equal share. Mother owns most of it, but she is not interested in the business and is happy to leave it to him."

"How can I help you? I'm just an employee."

"Well, I thought if you see a job open up that I might do, you could recommend me. I am willing to do any job—I'd just like to be involved. And I won't challenge him about the business. I only say something to him when he acts up."

"Well, you are a brave sister then, aren't you?"

"No braver than you," Charlotte said, giggling.

Herbert opened the door and looked out at them and shouted, "Can I have my date back now?"

"Well, we better go back…do you love him?"

Priscilla was shocked at the question and was not certain how to answer. "Well, I…"

"Oh, I'm sorry. I should not have asked. But I'm so certain he loves you, and I hope you are the one. I've always wished I had a sister and I would love to have you as a sister in law—it would be such fun."

26

"That was a good sermon. I liked the way he spoke about our responsibility to help the poor—and I need to do more," Bart said as Anna got up to walk out of the church.

"Yes, I'm glad I found this church," Anna said. They walked towards the door, and the pastor was there shaking hands with the parishioners.

"What a lovely couple you two make," the pastor said as he shook Bart's hand.

"Thank you, Pastor. I was just saying how good your sermon was."

"Well, I'm glad you enjoyed it, Mr....?"

"Lewis, Bart Lewis. I can't say I enjoyed it, but I needed to hear it. I really have to do more for the poor."

"Well, come to the mission tomorrow night and help serve if you want to help."

"Okay, I'll see about that."

They walked into the foyer of the church and Bart smiled at Anna. "See, Lucy, even the pastor says we make a great couple."

"So, are you going to serve at the mission?"

"Yes, I think I am, will you come also?"

"Well, that's my only night off, but I will come if you do. I want to see you with your sleeves rolled up for a change."

"Then you will come! When can I pick you up?"

"I'll get there myself. Besides, I don't think that fancy car you had at the restaurant will go over very well there—you might want to park down the street or something."

"I tell you what, I'll even ride the bus if you go with me."

"I'll meet you there, Bart. I am not ready for a date with you—

even to the mission."

They walked out of the church, and the bright sunshine stopped them both for a moment and they waited for their eyes to adjust. "Can I at least give you a ride home?"

"No thanks, it's a beautiful day to walk."

"Can I walk with you, then?"

"Bart, you are incorrigible."

"No, I'm not, I'm just hopelessly in love with you, Lucy. I've never met a girl like you before. Not only are you beautiful, but you are also a woman of God. How much more could I ask for?"

Anna looked into his blue eyes and almost felt like giving in. He was, as they said, a real dreamboat, but something inside said she should wait a while longer. She also did not want him to know that she lived in the hotel, because the cost of one night's stay was more than she made in two weeks at the restaurant. "Thanks for the offer, but not today. I'll see you at the mission tomorrow—if you make it."

"Oh, I'll be there—I'd go anywhere to be with you, Lucy, the love of my life."

When Anna got back to the hotel room, Lucy was just waking up. She knocked on the door that separated them when she heard Anna come in.

"Anna, where have you been?"

"At church, of course—and you should go too."

"You shouldn't push religion."

"And you shouldn't talk to me that way. I don't mean the religion—I mean that you are supposed to accompany me. That's what you are here for."

"Well, you should have woken me up and I would have gone."

"I tried. You were three sheets to the wind."

"What does that mean?"

"It means you were still drunk."

"So what does that have to do with sheets?"

"Sheets were what they called ropes in England, and a ship would lurch like a drunken sailor when the sheets were not tied down but blowing in the wind. That's where the expression comes from."

"Oh, and you were ashamed to go with me, is that it?"

"That's part of it. The other part is I couldn't get you up in time. Now from now on, I want you home at eleven o'clock."

"What, are you giving me a curfew?"

"I am."

"You can't do that."

"Lucy, you are working for me and my family and are getting paid quite well for it. And you get to come down here for a free vacation. Now either do as I say, or I will inform my father."

"And I'll tell him what you've done, stealing my identity."

"Well, you can tell him what you want to, and the identity thing is just about over, but I want you home by eleven!"

"Okay, I'll be home by eleven—I'll do exactly what you tell me," Lucy said, speaking very slowly as she tried to control her anger.

Priscilla waited for her father to call her into his office. Finally the door opened and a well-dressed man walked out. She came in and sat down. "Thank you for your analysis of the oil operations," Mr. Strickland said.

"I'm sorry I forgot to do the steel report," Priscilla said.

"Yes, and you also forgot to monitor the expenses on the new mill in Ohio," Mr. Strickland said in a low tone.

"I guess I'm forgetting a lot of things, Father. I am truly sorry."

"I'm wondering why you think the oil prices will go down."

"Well, they dropped from a dollar a barrel after the big East Texas discovery, but since the Depression is continuing in Europe, and the U.S. produces two-thirds of the world's oil, I think that exports will diminish and prices will decrease."

"Yes, but Governor Murray is shutting down production in Oklahoma, and he's even using the National Guard to enforce quotas on non-complying oil fields. And Texas and California are also trying to curtail production under the guise of conservation, but everyone knows what they are doing. And Hoover just addressed Congress and told them that he wants to stop what he called destructive competition in oil, coal, and lumber."

"I know, and I may be wrong, but exports are also limited by the Smoot-Hawley tariff bill. Our tariffs on foreign goods caused other countries to impose them, making U.S. oil too expensive, which means more oversupply. And in the producing states they are still selling black-market oil beyond the quotas."

"Well, if the price gets much lower, our refineries are going to be losing money and we may have to shut a few down. But there's so much going on with Congress that I don't want to make any decisions yet. And if Roosevelt gets in, there's no telling what he might impose.

Some say he'll make it illegal to own gold, of all things."

"That can't be true—it must just be a rumor."

"I hope so. In the meantime, call David Silverstein and ask him to give you the profits from the refineries before and after the drop in prices, and the costs to restart them so we can determine if it makes sense to shut them down. They're very expensive to start up again, so I need you to analyze that."

The intercom buzzed and Mr. Strickland held up his hand, motioning to Priscilla to stay while he answered it. "It's Mrs. Ingersoll for you, Mr. Strickland."

Mr. Strickland pressed the button to receive the call. "Hello, Betty, did you get your shopping done? Good, I've booked dinner reservations for tonight at… Oh, you can't. I see. Well, I'm sorry to hear that you have a headache. Shall we make it tomorrow then? Well then, let's wait and see if you get better. Okay, good-bye." After hanging the phone up, he looked at Priscilla, trying to hide his disappointment.

"Father, what is it with her—is she avoiding you?"

"I think she wants to end the relationship. This is the second time we were to have dinner together that she's canceled. I wish she would just come out and say it if she wants to stop seeing me. The last time we had dinner she mentioned that our stock was going down. She owns some of it, and she was very troubled about that, and wanted to know if she should sell it."

"What did you tell her?"

"I told her the truth. I told her I had no idea why it was down, and that our earnings were solid, but somehow I don't think she believed me. The rumor about us being bankrupt is spreading, and she's heard it."

The intercom buzzed again. "Mr. Strickland, Dave Samuels is here to see you."

"I'll see him in a moment, Mrs. Wickland." He turned to his daughter. "I shouldn't keep him waiting, but I need to talk to you about something, and I've got reservations at LaRue's, so why don't you go with me?"

"I'd love to."

The valet parked the Duesenberg, and Mr. Strickland and his daughter walked into the LaRue's, which was quite busy with scurrying waiters and a maître d' who was trying to keep up with the customers. He nodded to them and went to seat a customer and then hurried back to seat them.

"Do you wish to visit the lounge first, or just have dinner, Mr. Strickland?"

"Just dinner, please, Martinique."

"Yes, a table is being prepared for you and your lovely companion at this moment. I am sorry for the wait, but as you see we are very busy."

"That's fine. But just in case a rumor might start, this is my daughter."

"And a beautiful young lady she is," Martinique said, smiling at Priscilla. "My pleasure, Miss Strickland."

"Father, you're keeping me in suspense by not telling me what you want to talk about."

"Let's wait until we are seated." As he finished speaking, Martinique came back and led them to their table. As they sat looking at their menus, Betty Ingersoll walked out of the lounge on the arm of Richard Chandler, whom Joseph had introduced her to when they were last at the restaurant. The lounge served only sodas, but everyone knew that customers would bring their own bottle into the lounge and pour it in to make an alcoholic drink. Joseph looked up, startled to see her. She tried to avoid looking at him, but Chandler, who appeared somewhat drunk, was reveling in his victory and smiled at Joseph.

"Joseph, it's good to see you. Why don't you and your young date join us for dinner?"

"This is my daughter, Dick. But we have business to discuss so I'm afraid I'll have to decline. Betty, I thought you had a headache."

"Well, I got better," Betty answered, very embarrassed, and wanting to get away, and turning to Chandler. "I'll just powder my nose and meet you at the table."

When she had left, Chandler stood, swaying over their table. "You know, the only headache she had was you. She told me she didn't want to support you. See, Joe, everyone knows you're broke—no sense in hiding it anymore. All this holier than thou Christian stuff when you've been lying all this time about your business."

"Dick, can we please have dinner in peace?"

"Sure, but you're not a man of honor. You told Betty that I was a war profiteer."

"You were."

"And you and your old man didn't make money on the Great War? Can you say that the increases in oil and steel and copper and the

171

rest didn't make you a bundle?"

"Yes, Dick—we made money. But we didn't buy up war materiel and hoard commodities to drive up the price so the military would have to pay more for them."

"That's because you're a fool and you don't know how to do business. And that's why…"

As he spoke, Betty walked up and smiled at Joseph.

"That's why you're all washed up and I'm still in the chips. Come on, Betty, let's find our table."

"I'll be there in a moment," Betty said, and he walked away. After he was gone, Betty leaned over the table and said softly, "I'm sorry, Joseph."

"I am too, Betty. Enjoy your dinner."

The waiter came up to their table just as Betty left. "Are you ready to order, sir?"

"Yes, I am. Are you, Priscilla?"

"Yes, I'll have the rack of lamb and iced tea."

"And I'll have the trout almandine and ginger ale."

"Very good, sir."

"How could she like him over you—he's…he's repelling."

"I think it's the money, not the man."

"As if she doesn't have enough of her own."

"Well, some people can never have enough," Mr. Strickland said. Then he added, "The irony is she's in for a big surprise."

"What do you mean? I've heard he is very rich."

"Oh, he has money, and he spends it like there's no tomorrow. Has to have the biggest estate and all the rest, and he's in debt up to his eyeballs."

"And she doesn't know it?"

"She must not, unless it's true love. He looks good until you scratch the surface, and he's into some risky investments."

"How bad could it be? Could he lose a lot?"

"From what I hear, yes. The market came back after the first crash in '29, and he is betting it's going to come back even stronger."

"And if it doesn't, and she marries him, she might be supporting him?" Priscilla asked.

"Well, I imagine he has enough stashed away that she wouldn't have to do that, but she may turn out to be richer than him. And if I know Dick, he'll get it out of her."

"How would he do that?"

"Simple. Just tell her that some investment is the greatest thing since sliced bread, and she'd probably give it to him, not knowing he's in trouble. That's what he did with his first wife."

"Well, if that happens, it serves her right—I'm angry at the way she treated you."

"I'm not. I'm glad she treated me this way, and I'm even glad for the stock rumor, because it made her show her true colors. I've always believed that all things work together for the good, and it's been confirmed. But you girls had an inkling, didn't you…didn't you?"

"We all thought she might be a gold digger, but we weren't certain so we couldn't say anything to you. None of us liked her."

"Yes, well, I figured the last part out. I should have asked you—somehow I didn't see it, but I will be more careful next time, if there is a next time. But let's talk about you for a moment. I don't think you have your heart in the company anymore. Your work just isn't the same as it used to be."

"I know, but I'll do better."

"But I don't know if you should try. I think Mr. Blankenship has stolen your heart, and I think it's difficult to work for two companies at the same time—sort of like having two masters, don't you think?"

"What are you saying, Father? Do you want me to quit?"

"Do I want you to quit? No, I want you to stay and be full time again. That's what I want. But I am thinking about what is best for you. Esther told me that he asked you to visit his mother, and I think you might be serious about this young man. Is that the case?"

"Yes."

"And I don't want to come between you two. As much as I want you here, I am giving you your liberty if you want it, and you may work there full time, if you wish."

"I don't know what to say. I want to stay here also, but you are correct, it is hard to do both jobs."

"Well, you think about it and any decision you make is fine."

"Father, I think it's wonderful that you have this attitude. I admire you for it."

"That's nice to say, but there is one thing you need to be careful about."

"What's that?"

"I hate to say it, but after Betty and Alice Jamison, are you sure about this young man? His company has already gained a lot of business from his association with you—are you sure his motives are pure?"

"Oh, he's not after my money—that much I am certain of. He has his own money," Priscilla answered.

"So does Betty. But if you're certain..."

"I am, Father, I'm absolutely positive."

27

Lucy would not come, so Anna took a cab to the mission. At the front of the building people were lining up for the food inside, but the door was not yet open. She was told to go around the back, so she did, and when she walked in some people were setting up tables. One of them directed her to the kitchen, where the pastor from her church was talking with some other men. He stopped speaking and smiled at her. "I'm delighted you could come—you're Lucy, is that right?"

"Yes," Anna said.

"This is Pastor Roberts, and Pastor Mills."

Anna greeted them both, and then she looked around and saw Bart walk in. He also greeted the men. There were several women preparing food in the kitchen, and one of them called for Pastor Roberts and talked to him, after which he turned around and spoke to the rest of them. "The food is ready to be put on the serving tables," he said. Bart moved quickly and began picking up bowls of food and putting them on the tables. The other men also helped, as did Anna, but Bart worked faster than they did.

"A man with a mission at the mission," Anna commented.

"Yes, you could say that," Bart said, smiling.

"Well, I'm glad you could come," Anna said.

"I want to do my part. I've been very blessed, so this is the least I can do for those less fortunate."

"Let's get in place to serve; we're opening up now," Pastor Roberts said, and they all moved to the serving tables. The doors opened and people rushed in as the workers tried to slow them down and keep order.

As Anna served a woman, she noticed that she tried to put some of the food into a bag she had, but one of the women who had cooked told her she could not take it home. "But I have children to feed at home," the woman protested.

"I'm sorry, but you must bring them. Food cannot be taken out, that is the rule, or we would not have enough for everyone who comes in to get it."

"Then what can I do for my children?" she asked.

"Here," Bart said, and he took a twenty-dollar bill from his wallet and gave it to her.

"Thank you, sir. May God bless you."

"And may He bless you," Bart said, as she moved down the line.

Another woman walked up and she had an open wound on her face. "What happened?" Anna asked, as she served her some corn on the cob. The woman said nothing but moved after getting her food to Bart, who was next to Anna. Bart gave the woman some bread, and she took it and began to move again when he stopped her.

"You need to go to the hospital and have that looked at—it may get infected," he said, with a caring tone. But the woman said nothing and moved down the line. Bart put down the tongs he was serving with and moved past the other servers towards her. "That may be serious. You need a doctor."

"Do I look like I can afford one?" the woman finally said.

"Well, you can now," Bart said, handing the woman some money. Anna could not see how much it was, but the woman, who had been frowning the whole time, smiled at him. "You are very kind. Thank you."

Bart moved back to his serving position, and an old man hobbled through the line and stopped for his bread. He had an old stick he was using as a cane, and it was wobbly. "Here, sir, buy a proper cane," Bart said as he gave him ten dollars. The man smiled and nodded in appreciation.

After they had served the last of the food, Anna and some of the others walked back to the kitchen and sat down at a table there to rest. Bart followed and sat next to Anna.

"You are truly amazing," Anna said.

"Who, me? What do you mean?"

"I mean you treated all of those people with respect, and you must have given out hundreds of dollars tonight."

"Oh, it's nothing. I can afford it."

"Well, lots of people can, but they don't care enough."

"Thank you, Lucy. I think that's the first compliment you've ever given me."

"It's the first time I've seen you help anyone. Before you were always drinking...soda."

Bart laughed. "Well, you know it wasn't just soda, don't you? But I've stopped all that also. I know everyone is complaining about Prohibition, but I'm starting to realize how bad liquor is for society. It's a wonder how Jesus can change your thinking."

"Yes, it certainly is."

"Well, I know you're not ready for a date with me, but I'm having some friends over for lunch and I told them we're going to talk about the Bible and how I've been saved, and I do wish you could come. I'm so new at this I don't know if I could answer their questions, but I think you could."

He looked intently into her eyes as he spoke, and she could not stop thinking of how remarkably handsome he was. She blinked and realized she had not heard everything he had said. "So did you say this would be in the daytime?"

"Yes, we'll have some lunch on my yacht about twelve noon."

Anna looked at him for a moment and said nothing. He smiled and put his head down, looking a little rejected. "I understand you may not want to come—maybe some other time."

"I didn't say that—who will be there?"

"Tony and Mike and their girlfriends. You've met them—they used to go to the restaurant with me."

Anna thought about the men she had seen him with, and she remembered that they seemed a bit rough. "You mean they are interested in the Bible?"

"Well, they weren't, but I keep praying for them, and they agreed to talk to me about it. Seems they've noticed a change in me."

"Can I bring a friend?"

Bart hesitated for just a moment before answering. "Sure, as long as it's not a boyfriend," he said, smiling.

"No, it's a girl—a woman I know—if I can get her to come. She's not a Christian either. But I can't stay too long; I have to be at work at three."

"That's swell, Anna. Can I pick you up and give you a ride?"

"No, that's okay. I assume it's at the harbor. Just give me directions."

28

Herbert was seated in front of Priscilla's desk as they debated. "The employee broke the rules and he needs to be fired. Smoking a cigarette in the men's room when you are supposed to be working and then lying about it is…"

"Punishable by death?" Priscilla asked, jokingly.

"No—not yet, anyway, but I might see about getting the law changed. But just what is your reason for not wanting him fired? I suppose he has eighteen children and really loves his poor old mother who is in a wheelchair or something."

"I have no idea even who he is—I've never met him. But he is a very skilled and hard-working machinist. There are very few who can make the parts he makes, and he produces a lot when he's…"

"Not smoking in the restroom?"

"Yes. This is going to hurt us more than him. With his skills, he'll find another job, but how many machinists can make precision parts as fast as he does?" Priscilla asked, passing him a list of the parts that the man had made. "At least wait until we can get a replacement." Herbert looked over it and nodded his head.

"You're right—it's not worth it. He'll be reprimanded. Now, where do you want to eat lunch today?"

"How about a Chinese restaurant?" Priscilla asked, thinking that it would be safe since she rarely ate Chinese food.

"Chinese—well, that would be different. Yes, that sounds good, and there is one within walking distance."

"Marvelous—then I don't have to get a whiplash to go there."

They walked out of the building and passed a jewelry store on their way to the restaurant. Herbert stopped in front of it for a moment and looked in the window at some watches. Priscilla had kept walking and so she stopped and walked back. "Are you looking for a watch?" she asked.

"Just window shopping," he said, and he moved a few feet until he was in front of some wedding rings. "What do you think about that wedding ring over there?" he asked, pointing to the one with the largest diamond. "Would a woman think that was ostentatious?"

Priscilla hesitated before answering, surprised that he would be asking such a question. "Oh, I think that a smaller one would do nicely for a woman who was really in love with the man and not his money."

"My, that is refreshing. Well, let's get a move on, I'm looking forward to something sweet and sour."

"I think I already have something sweet and sour—could that become your new nickname?"

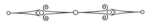

The doorbell rang at the Strickland home and as Mr. Standish answered it, his eyes lit up. "Master Paul, what a wonderful surprise! You weren't expected for another week."

"Good to see you, Mr. Standish," Paul said, and he attempted to give him a hug, but Mr. Standish resisted at first. "Oh come now, don't be so proper. You've been with us so long; you're like part of the family." Standish gave in and smiled as they hugged. At that moment, Esther came into the foyer. Standish pulled away quickly, feeling guilty for showing such sentiment. Esther smiled at the scene and ran to Paul, who not only hugged her but picked her up and twirled her around. "My, that was easier to do when you were a little girl," he said as they laughed together.

"Oh, it's so good to see you, but how did you get here so soon?"

"The university is running low on funds, so they curtailed the dig. I would have paid myself, but there were others who could not afford it, so I didn't want to cause problems. Anyway, I'm happy to be home early. Where are Anna and Priscilla?"

"They are both working. Come sit down with me and I'll tell you all about it."

Joseph Strickland sat in his office, watching a ticker that was spewing out paper with stock quotes. He shook his head as he read the latest figures, which showed that his stock was still declining. The intercom buzzed and he pressed down the button.

"Mr. Strickland, there is a call for you from a Miles Van Galen."

"Miles Van Galen? He's a neighborhood boy—I don't know why he would be calling me. Tell him to call me at home tonight—he has our number."

"Yes sir."

The intercom buzzed again and Joseph answered it, a little annoyed this time. "Yes?"

"I'm sorry, Mr. Strickland, but the young man says that this call is urgent. He says he needs to speak to you right now. It's about your daughter, Anna."

"Anna? Okay, put him on."

"Mr. Strickland, I had a dream about Anna and I think it's important," Miles said.

"Miles, what are you talking about?"

"Well, sir, I fell asleep a little while ago. I took a nap, which I normally never take."

"So?"

"Well, have you ever had a dream that seemed so real that you thought it was happening?"

"Yes, of course, Miles. Please get to the point."

"Okay. In the dream I saw Anna and she was working at a restaurant."

"Working at a restaurant? Doing what?"

"Well, at first she was working as a waitress, but then she seemed to be doing something else, but I'm not certain what it was."

"Miles…"

"Please let me finish, Mr. Strickland. There was a white cloud with a bright shining light that was following Anna, and then it turned into a black cloud—something demonic, and it was trying to overwhelm Anna. I was certain it was a prophetic dream and that she was in some kind of danger, and then the scene changed and she was—."

"Miles, how could you possibly think that dream could be prophetic when you saw her working as a waitress and you know she would never be doing that?" Mr. Strickland interrupted.

"Yes, that does seem unusual. But the dream was so real and powerful that I just thought I had to call you—just in case."

"Okay, Miles, thanks for calling. I know you think the world of Anna and I appreciate your concern. Tell your parents I said hello."

"But, Mr. Strickland, some more things happened in the dream. A lot more. Can I tell you about them?"

"Perhaps another time, Miles—I'm quite busy right now, but we can talk at another time. Good-bye now."

Joseph hung up before Miles could say anything else and went back to the ticker. Then he stopped, staring in thought and then turned back to the telephone and buzzed his secretary. "Mrs. Wickland, please call the long-distance operator and call Anna's hotel for me—you should have the room number there. Then buzz me when she's on the line."

"Yes sir."

A few minutes later the intercom buzzed and he picked up the phone. "Hello, Father."

"Anna, it's so nice to hear your voice. Are things okay there?"

"Oh yes, I'm having a wonderful time. Thank you for letting me come."

"Well, as you know, I had my reservations. Are you feeling well, and does it seem safe there?"

"Oh yes. Everything is fine. The weather is very warm, but the beach is beautiful, and the hotel is very nice."

"Is Lucy enjoying it also?"

"Yes, I think she is."

"Are you still upset that I made you take her with you?"

"Oh no—I think it was a good idea."

"You do? Well, that's good. Now, you have enough money with you, don't you?"

"Oh yes, more than enough—you have been very generous."

"Well, I have a meeting in five minutes, so I need to go. Be careful and have a good time."

"I will, Father, and thanks so much for calling. I love you."

"I love you too, honey."

29

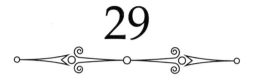

Herbert and Priscilla returned from lunch and walked to their offices. "Mr. Blankenship, your mother just called and she is still on the line," Mrs. Ross said to him as he walked by.

"Thank you, Mrs. Ross. I'll pick it up in my office."

"Did you have a nice lunch, dear?" Herbert's mother asked on the phone.

"Yes, Mother, it was fine."

"I understand that you went with Miss Avery."

"Yes, I did. Now, with all due respect, Mother, you know I have to get back to work. Was there something you wanted?"

"Yes, something is bothering me—about Priscilla."

"And what would that be. You don't like her?"

"Oh no, I like her immensely. I think she is a wonderful girl and don't think you could do better. But doesn't it seem a little unusual that you have never been to her home, and have never met any of her relatives—even the handyman—I mean her father?"

"Mother, please don't be condescending about her father. And I think you are suspicious by nature."

"I don't think so, Herbert. I think you need to know more about her. How could she afford to go to college if her family is poor?"

"I didn't say they were poor. I don't know anything about them...."

"My point, exactly. I am only thinking of you. We need to meet her family and get to know them before you make any commitments."

Herbert hesitated for a moment, but he did realize that the request was reasonable. "Okay, Mother. I will see to it that we meet her relatives. Shall we invite them to Somerset, then?"

"Yes, that would be nice, dear—perhaps this Sunday, after

church?"

"I'll talk to her about it. Good-bye now." Herbert looked around his office in thought. Was it unusual that he had not met her relatives? He had never asked, and so there was nothing out of the ordinary, he thought. But he did wonder why he'd had to pick her up at Bloomingdale's—well, she was shopping there, perhaps that was all there was to it. He got up and walked to her office and knocked on her door and entered.

"Priscilla, Mother asked if you would be kind enough to bring your relatives to Somerset on Sunday. Is there more than just your father?"

Priscilla was shocked for a moment at the invitation. She thought that perhaps she should just tell him everything, but she had made a vow to herself that she would not disclose her true identity until he proposed. "Well, this is sort of short notice—perhaps we could make it in about two weeks?"

"Okay, I'll tell Mother. Now, do you have more relatives than just your father?"

"Well, yes…I mean no—I mean not that would visit. They are a little scattered, I mean."

"So do you have sisters and brothers or aunts and uncles and…"

"Oh yes, I do have them."

"Them—which do you have?"

"Herbert, I'm not sure who could come. I need to talk to them."

"But do you have sisters and brothers? You have never talked about your family."

"Yes, I do have them. I have two sisters and a brother. But one sister and my brother are out of town, so it will be my father and my sister who will come. But I have to make certain they don't have other plans. Now, could we talk about this on Monday? Because I know you want this report finished before I leave today, and it's Friday."

"It's not that important."

"Well, it is to me. I take my work seriously."

"Okay, Priscilla," Herbert said, letting out a long breath. "Let me know who's coming, and we'll set it up for… what? The weekend after next?"

"Yes, I think that will work. I'll let you know."

After Herbert walked out of her office, Priscilla sank into her chair, trying to figure out how she was going to handle the visit. She realized that she would have to tell him the truth before anyone could visit, but she had hoped that he would propose marriage first.

Paul was sitting with Esther and she was bringing him up to date. "I got a letter from Priscilla about her working for a…a pump company, is that it?" he said.

"Yes, and she's been a big help to them. She was hired as a book-keeper, but she does a lot more than that," Esther said.

"I believe it. She has always been smart with business. And I bet Father has missed her."

"Well, she has been working part time for each company. I know he wasn't happy about it, but he understood that she wanted to experience working somewhere else. But he wouldn't let her take the subway—thought it was too dangerous."

"So how does she get to work?"

"One of the chauffeurs drives her—usually it's Ben."

"Well, that must be a sight. All the workers come out of the building and her chauffeur is waiting."

"Paul, she doesn't let them pick her up where anyone else can see. She meets the limousine around the block or something. Ben's picking her up today."

"Well, then I have a great idea! I'll ride with Ben and I'll jump out of the car just when she's about to get in."

"That's a swell idea, Paul—that would be a wonderful sur-prise," Esther said.

Herbert wondered about the way Priscilla reacted to his request to meet her relatives. She had agreed, but he thought she seemed a little apprehensive about it. His mother had been suspicious, and now he was becoming the same way. He looked at the clock and noticed that it was twenty minutes until five. He knew she would not leave early—she was always punctual about getting to work and about leaving. She would leave her office at precisely five o'clock, he thought, and he de-cided that he would follow her this time. So he walked out of his office and towards the restroom, and then he walked out of the building. He had seen her walk north on the sidewalk, so he decided to wait be-tween the two buildings until she walked by. There was a large truck parked in the alley between the buildings that led into the main street where she normally exited, and he hid there and waited. At about five minutes after five, she appeared, and he watched as she walked swiftly to the end of the block, then turned left and was out of sight.

He scurried to get to the end of the block, and when he turned the corner, he saw her walking up to the limousine. Moving back so he could not be seen, he watched as Paul got out of the car and walked towards her. Paul hugged his sister and then picked her up—sweeping her off her feet. The embrace lasted a few seconds and Herbert let out an audible gasp as he watched in disbelief. He stood stunned for a moment without moving, and then he decided to follow her as she got into the limousine. He ran towards his building and into the parking lot, and he fumbled as he tried to get his car keys out of his pocket. The Chrysler roared to life, and he raced out of the parking lot, hoping that he would not lose the limousine, but there was no problem finding it because it was driving past him as he moved his car into the street.

The traffic was heavy and the limousine virtually stopped only a few cars ahead of him. Eventually they were out of the city, and Herbert followed until the limousine drove up the driveway of the Strickland mansion, Eagle's Rest. He followed as long as he could, and then he parked his car on the side of the long driveway and walked on the lawn, using the trees and bushes to hide as he moved towards the entrance, and watched as she got out of the car. Paul hugged her again from the side, and she put her arm around his waist as they entered the house, and Herbert sat down on the grass, dumbfounded and angry.

He continued to sit there as the sun went down and more lights in the house came on. He walked back to his car and saw the name on the mailbox, Strickland. He grimaced and shook his head, then got into his car and started it and drove up the driveway towards the house until he could see the front door and a few windows of the house, and then he turned the motor off, determined to hold a vigil until he found out when she would leave the house. Finally the sun went down and it became darker and darker. Still and somber, he watched until lights went out, but no one came out of the Strickland home, and after a few hours he fell asleep in his car. When he awoke it was four in the morning, and he started his car and drove home.

30

"Lucy, it's time to get up. We have a Bible study to go to. Bart Lewis is having it and his friends will be there—Tony and some others."

Lucy turned her head towards Anna and opened her bleary eyes. "I can't go, I'm sick."

"Sick because you got drunk again last night?"

"What does it matter? If I'm sick, I'm sick, and I can't go."

"I really wanted you to go to this. I think you'll like it. We'll have lunch on a yacht and then the study. Plus you get to be a Strickland again when you go, and you like playing the role."

"I'll come later—as soon as I wake up."

"The address is on your chest of drawers, but don't come too late, because I have to be at work at three o'clock, so I will be back before then."

"Okay. If I don't see you there, I'll see you downstairs when you go to work."

"Lucy, don't bother."

"I'm sorry," Lucy said, and she closed her eyes and rolled over again.

Anna looked at her for a moment and then turned away in disgust.

"Lucy, you are truly a disappointment!" she said to herself, but Lucy couldn't hear, because she had already fallen back to sleep.

Anna left the hotel and got a cab to take her to the harbor where Bart's yacht was. She was surprised to see how large it was—she had heard he was wealthy, but the yacht was about eighty feet long, and its polished, shiny white hull gleamed in the sun as she approached it. He walked out dressed as the perfect yachtsman—light blue shorts, a cream-colored short-sleeved shirt, and navy blue deck shoes. He didn't see her at first, but when he did, he greeted her with enthusiasm. "You did come—it's so nice to see you!" he exclaimed.

"I said I would be here."

"I know, but I thought you may have had second thoughts." He walked over and tried to take her hand to help her onto the gangplank, but she politely pulled her hand away.

"I'm fine, thank you. My, you looked dressed for a voyage." She noticed that he seemed annoyed that she did not take his hand. However, he smiled and seemed to overcome it quickly.

"Yes, well, this is a spiritual voyage, isn't it?" he asked rhetorically.

"So where are your friends?" she asked, looking up and down the yacht.

"Mike chickened out, but Tony should be coming… Oh, there he is." Bart looked out as Tony drove up in a black Chevrolet. He parked in front of the gangplank. As he got out of the car the girl he was with opened the door herself. Anna was surprised that he didn't open the door for her, and as the woman walked up she noticed how cheap she looked. She had dyed blond hair with black roots, and she wore a low-cut blouse and tight pants. Her lipstick was bright red and it was imperfectly applied, and her eye makeup was heavy. Bart watched Anna and spoke in a low voice as they approached.

"I know what you are thinking, but didn't Jesus come to save people just like this? Wasn't Mary Magdalene a prostitute or something?"

Before Anna could answer, both Tony and the girl were walking on the yacht, and Bart introduced them. "I want you both to meet the prettiest waitress in Florida—Lucy Jenkins. Lucy, you've met Tony and this is Sally."

"Pleased to make your acquaintance," Anna said to Sally, and they exchanged greetings. On the deck there was a dining table with a large umbrella to keep the sun out and a bowl with red fruit punch on it. They walked with Bart over to it and he poured each of them a glass of punch.

"It's not spiked, is it Bart?" Tony said with a little snicker.

"No, just several fruit juices," Bart said in a disapproving tone. But Anna sensed that there was something amiss in the way he answered Tony because he kept staring at him with slight anger. She wondered why he would act that way if he was trying to teach him about God. She took a sip of her punch, but she did not like the way it tasted.

She tried it a second time, and decided not to drink anymore. It was a large glass, and she did not want to seem impolite, so she walked towards the side of the boat and quickly poured the punch into the water when no one was looking. Then she walked back towards them. Bart looked at her a little quizzically as she moved back towards the table.

"Where did you go?" he asked.

"Just looking at your boat—it's beautiful," she said.

"Thank you."

"Yeah, only the best for Bart—right, Sally?" Tony said in a rough voice.

"Yeah, a dreamboat for a dreamboat," Sally said flirtatiously in her deep Southern drawl as she smiled at Bart.

Anna was a little irritated as she watched Sally move closer to Bart. But he did nothing to encourage her and seemed a little embarrassed by her coquettishness. He moved away from her and changed the subject.

"Well, let's have some food—I had this catered, and it's in the galley. Would you help me bring it up, Lucy?"

"Of course," Anna said, suddenly feeling like she had a slight headache.

Bart noticed her empty glass as they moved towards the galley. "You've finished already?"

"Yes, I was very thirsty—it's a hot day."

"Would you like some more?"

"No, that was enough, thank you."

As Anna followed him to the galley she had to take several steps down, and suddenly she felt faint and started to slip a little. She held onto the rail, and Bart took her arm. "Are you all right?" he asked, his voice sounding very sincere.

"Yes, I think so. But I...maybe I need to rest for a moment."

"Do you know what's wrong?"

"No, I just feel a little woozy."

As she spoke, Tony and Sally walked up, and they noticed she was still at the steps and there was a problem.

"Are you okay, honey?" Sally asked, showing genuine concern.

"Yes, I...well, could I sit down for a moment, please?"

"Of course," Bart said. "Let's go below deck and you can rest there." He led her downstairs and Sally followed. Anna sat down on a couch and then she tilted against one side and closed her eyes. She felt the boat slightly listing from side to side. She wanted to open her eyes, but she couldn't seem to.

"I think she may need a doctor," she heard Sally say in a motherly tone.

"Yes, you may be right," Bart said. "But I'll let her rest first and see if she comes out of it. Lucy, you rest a while. If you're hungry, I'll bring you some food."

Anna could not make herself speak, and Bart sounded in a hurry to get his guests back to the deck. "Why don't we eat and I'll check on her later. Let's bring the food up," he said, handing some food to Sally, who proceeded up the stairs topside.

"Can I help you with the dish?" Tony asked, emphasizing the word "dish" and smirking as he watched Anna on the couch.

"Yeah, grab some sandwiches and I'll get the appetizers," Bart said, ignoring his comment. They went upstairs and put down the food.

"I can stay with your friend," Sally offered.

"Oh, she'll be all right. When she wakes up I'll give her some food and take her home," Bart said.

Tony looked at Bart for a moment as Sally walked downstairs to get the rest of the food. "She's a nice kid, Bart—take it easy on her, will you?"

"Of course, I will. I'll take care of her," Bart said.

"Yeah, that's what I'm afraid of," Tony said.

Anna remembered that information in her purse would identify her, and she struggled to take it and push it in a drawer under the bed she was lying on. Then she fell into a deep sleep.

31

"Were you able to actually play the instruments?" Esther asked Paul as they sat at the dinner table with the rest of the family.

"I don't know if you could say 'play,' but they did make a sound."

"Perhaps they were a little out of tune after forty-five hundred years," Mr. Strickland added, jokingly. "Aren't those the oldest stringed instruments ever discovered?"

"Yes, and they were well-preserved because they were buried in the royal cemetery—it's called the Royal Cemetery of Ur."

"So where exactly is that, and how many instruments were there?" Esther asked.

"It's in Persia—they are trying to change the name to Iran now. Before that part of it was called Mesopotamia. There were three lyres and one harp."

"A lyre—isn't that what King David played in the Bible?" Priscilla asked.

"Well, we're not certain it's exactly the same, but we think so."

"How remarkable—I wish I could have been there to see those instruments," Esther said. "Can you ever take others along on these digs?"

"Yes, that can be done. Max Mallowan's girlfriend even came, and that was okay with Leonard Woolley. She's a woman named Agatha Christie who's quite famous as a writer in England, I understand. Her first husband jilted her, and Max is marrying her."

"Well, I'd like to go on the next one—what about you, Priscilla, would you come with me if I went?"

"I'd like to, but I don't know if I'll ever have the time. I'm already trying to serve two masters," Priscilla said, smiling at her father.

"Yes, I don't know if I can share her anymore or the whole business might go down the drain…especially with the beating our stocks are taking," Mr. Strickland added with a more serious tone.

"I noticed that, but I can't understand why. The big drop already happened, and then the rebound and the second drop, but that affected all stocks. Why would ours be falling now, especially since profits are up for us?" Paul asked.

Priscilla and Esther looked at each other, and Esther involuntarily gulped but then smiled and turned to Paul again.

"So, when can we go? Do you have another excavation planned yet? I'd love to go, and it would take my mind off some of the things that have been happening here."

"Well, I was going to wait to mention this, but I guess this is as good a time as any. I won't be going on more digs, and I won't be going back to Oxford."

"What? You worked so hard for the PhD—now that you finally have it, why would you give up archeology now?" Priscilla asked.

"Because in visiting all these different countries, and seeing how the people live, and how many don't know who Jesus is, I have a burden to help them."

"Do you mean you're going to be a missionary?" Esther asked.

"No, I mean I'm going to work with Father, if he'll have me. I'm not cut out to be a missionary, but if I can help the business, then we can support those who are."

"Of course I'll have you—I'd love to have you. But are you certain of this, Paul? You've given so much to archeology."

"Yes, and I think I've given enough. I don't think it was an accident that I was born into this family, and it's important for me to make my contribution here."

"Paul, this is such a blessing for me—I never would have asked you, but since you've made this decision I am so pleased," Mr. Strickland said, and he got up and walked over to his son's chair and put his arm around him and hugged him. "It will also free Priscilla up." After Paul hugged him back, Mr. Strickland walked back to his chair.

"Well, I'm sure there is a lot she can teach me," Paul said, and then he looked around the table for a moment before speaking again. "Another reason for this decision is that a lot of the things we dig up… well, to many it's exciting to dig up the ruins of Nanna, the Sumerian moon god, and find the Great Ziggurat where his shrine is, but what you don't hear about is what their artifacts show about their society.

The things depicted in their artifacts are often disgusting, and I wish I'd never seen them."

"Paul, I don't think your timing could be better. Father will now have his right-hand man, and..." Priscilla began.

"And you can work for your young man without guilt," Mr. Strickland said, finishing her sentence for her.

"Well, why don't we call Anna and tell her about this?" Paul said. "I wish she could have been here."

"Yes, let's do so after dessert," Mr. Strickland said as the kitchen help walked in and began clearing the dishes from their entrée. "I'm a little concerned about her, because that neighbor boy called me the other day—what's his name—Miles."

"Miles called you? What did he say?" Priscilla asked.

"He said he had a dream about Anna—thought it was prophetic. You know he's always been the poetic dreamer, hasn't he? But I called her and she was all right—I called her right away."

"What do you mean, Father—what was the dream about?" Esther asked.

"Some nonsense—he thought she might be in trouble or something. I know it was hogwash because in the dream he said he saw her working as a waitress of all things. I told him how can this dream be from God when you know Anna would never be working as a waitress?"

Esther and Priscilla looked at each other, stunned, and were silent for a moment. Finally, Priscilla looked at her father, unable to speak for a moment. He looked back at her, with a perplexed look. "Do you want to say something?" he asked.

"Father, Anna is working as a waitress," she said.

"What? What are you talking about?"

"Well, it's a long story, but she had a good reason for it."

"A good reason for what?"

"For switching identities with Lucy. She's pretending to be Lucy, and that's why she's working as a waitress."

"I still have no idea what you are talking about, but if she is working as one, Miles may have been right," Mr. Strickland said, and he got up and walked to the telephone. "I need the number—Priscilla, do you have it?"

"Yes, I do," Priscilla said, and she put down her bite of dessert and ran from the table, racing upstairs to her room. When she found the number, she called it out to him from the upstairs balcony.

Mr. Strickland asked for the operator and placed the long-distance call. Lucy answered and he asked for Anna.

"She's not here, Mr. Strickland," Lucy said.

"Do you know where she is?"

"Yes, she's at a Bible study."

"Is she all right then? Has anything happened to her?"

"She's fine, everything is fine."

"Why aren't you with her? Didn't I tell you to accompany her wherever she went? Wasn't that what I told you?"

"Yes sir, but she...well, I offered to go but she wanted to go by herself. There was this man she liked there, and I think I would have been in the way."

"When is she supposed to be back—did she give you a time?"

"Yes, she has to—"

"Lucy, I know about the switch. I know she's working as a waitress. Now this is Saturday. Is she working today?"

"Yes sir. She's goes to work at three, and it's....it's two-thirty now, so she should be back any minute. All she has to do is change and then walk down to the restaurant."

"You mean she's working at Roney Plaza—at the hotel?"

"Yes sir."

"Well, tell her to call me at the house the minute she comes in. I mean as soon as she walks through the door. Do you understand?"

"Yes sir. I will have her call just as soon as she gets here."

"All right, I'll be waiting," Mr. Strickland said, and he hung up the phone and walked back to the dining room table. "Now what is this all about? I want the truth and I want it now without any nonsense mixed in. Do you understand me, Priscilla?"

"Yes, Father. I'll do my best to explain it."

"Please do. I'm waiting."

"Okay, you remember how Alice came over that day, and how her husband said he only married her for her money?"

"Yes, of course I remember."

"Well, because of that, we decided—I mean Anna and Esther and I decided that we would pretend we weren't rich so if we met someone we would be certain that they didn't like us just for our money. So I decided to go by Mother's maiden name, and I went to work for the pump company, and Anna switched identities with Lucy when they went to Florida."

"And what about Esther?"

"Well, we had to do something different for her. Something I should have told you about a long time ago. And I almost did tell you, but I was afraid."

"Who did she pretend to be?"

"No one, it wouldn't work for her because she was already seeing David, so we had to think of something else."

"So are you going to tell me before I go loony?" Mr. Strickland said, his voice getting louder and his face getting red.

"Yes, Father, I'm trying, but you're shouting."

"No, my dear, I'm not shouting yet. When I get to shouting you will know it. Now tell me!"

"Father, it's my fault," Esther said. "David was acting funny about things and Priscilla thought of a way to test him—so we could see if he was really in love with me, and I guess he wasn't."

"You guess he wasn't. And why do you guess that? Just what in the world did you do to test him, pray tell?"

"Well, I sent him a letter telling him something bad about our business."

"You did what!"

"Father, it was only to make certain…"

"What did you tell him!"

"That we were bankrupt."

"You told him we were bankrupt! You started that rumor that made our stock tumble, and made people sneer at me! It came from my own daughter!"

"Father, you really are shouting now," Esther said.

Mr. Strickland took a deep breath and then fell into his chair. "Yes, I was shouting," he said in a low voice. "I can't believe all this."

"I'm really sorry, Father, I did it with good intentions, and it just got out of hand," Priscilla said.

"I'm sorry too. We shouldn't have—it was completely wrong," Esther said. "Please forgive us."

"Haven't you both been taught since you were young, 'Oh what a tangled web we weave when first we practice to deceive?' Didn't your mother and I tell you that over and over again? Well, didn't we? And haven't we always taught you the ends don't always justify the means, and that just because something works, it doesn't mean it's right to do it?"

"Yes, Father, and I'm truly sorry—I apologize and ask for your forgiveness. Please forgive us as the father did with the prodigal son,"

Priscilla said, crying.

"Okay, okay. I forgive you—well I'm working on it, anyway—I'm still angry."

"Thank you, Father," Priscilla said.

"So now I know why Betty dropped me. And I thought an enemy spread it, but it was my own daughter. How did you do it?"

"I sent an anonymous letter warning David that our companies were bankrupt but it was not known yet, and it was put in David's locker at the gym. Just after that he broke it off with Esther and he gave no explanation."

"So David not only dropped Esther, but he also spread it all over town. Why would he be so vindictive? That does not seem characteristic of the young man I talked to who asked for your hand in marriage."

"We don't understand everything, Father, but that is what happened, and I'm so sorry about the stock. I never thought he would spread it."

"It's not all bad."

"You mean because you found out about Betty because of it?"

"Well, yes, that's true, but we have also been buying our stock back at a very low price, although I wouldn't have bought it back if I knew the rumor came from my own family."

"Oh, I wish we hadn't done it," Esther said, also starting to cry. "I knew it was wrong—deep down I knew."

"It was all my idea—I'm responsible," Priscilla said.

"No, we are all responsible for what we do, I can't blame you," Esther said through tears.

"Oh, you're both guilty as sin, so would you stop it!" Mr. Strickland said. Then he calmed down and looked over at Priscilla. "So—that is why you think that your young man—Blankenship—is on the level. He thinks you have no money and he still wants to marry you, is that right?"

"Yes—but it has become a problem because his mother is planning on him marrying a rich girl."

"So, do you think she will give in?"

"I think she likes me. I just met her. But if she doesn't, Herbert said visiting her was just a courtesy, and he'll do what he wants to do. But he hasn't actually proposed yet."

"How ironic that is. Don't you think you ought to tell him now?"

196

"Actually I must, because he wants to meet the family, but I was waiting to find out what his mother thought of me. I'm interested to see the look on his face when I tell him."

"We need to talk to Miles. I just remembered that he had more to say," Mr. Strickland said, and he picked up the phone. The butler answered and soon Miles was on the phone. Esther and Priscilla had picked up an extension across the large living room, and were sharing the phone.

"Miles, this is Mr. Strickland, and the first thing I want to say is that I apologize for not taking you seriously. But I must ask, did Anna tell you she was going to switch places with Lucy before she left?"

"Switch places with Lucy? No sir—oh, that may be why I saw that in the dream about her."

"Can we come over and talk to you about this, or can you come over?"

"I'll be right over, Mr. Strickland," Miles said and he hung up the phone.

"Father, we had an agreement not to tell anyone," Esther said. "Miles wouldn't have known because Anna would not have told him—she keeps her word."

"I never should have let her go," Mr. Strickland said, and he picked up the phone again and placed a long-distance call to Lucy.

"Hello?" Lucy said.

"Did she come home yet?"

"No sir. I will call you as soon as she does. I promise you."

"Yes, make certain you do—we have reason to believe she is in trouble."

The doorbell rang and Paul ran to answer it in front of Mr. Standish, who backed up in surprise to make way for him. Miles came in and he was sweating a little. "I rolled over as fast as I could," he said.

"Thank you, Miles," Esther said.

"So what else was in the dream? You said there was more but I cut you off last time we spoke," Mr. Strickland said.

"Well, I saw her waiting tables, and then she seemed to be doing something else at the restaurant and then—"

"She started to help the chef—that's the last thing she told us," Priscilla said, excited that Miles had such an accurate dream, but her father looked over disapprovingly because he wanted to hear what Miles was saying.

"Yes, by all means go on, young man," Mr. Strickland said.

"Well, it got sort of fuzzy after that. The first part was very clear—just like it was happening it was so real. But then the restaurant turned into the sea and she was in the middle of it."

"So what do you think that means?" Priscilla asked.

"I don't know, but in the Bible often the sea represents masses of people, so it may not literally mean the water."

"What was she doing in the water—was she doing something?" Paul asked.

"She was swimming, and the feeling was that she was in distress. That's why I was so concerned. There was this foreboding about the whole situation. I told you about the bright cloud that became dark, and that it was trying to overtake her."

"Yes, I remember. But she is near the ocean, so it could also be the literal water," Mr. Strickland said.

"If God was trying to show you something it might be a warning, so we need to tell her," Esther added.

Mr. Strickland nodded. "Yes, I'm calling again." He picked up the phone and got the operator to make a long-distance call. "Hello, Lucy. Is she back yet?"

"No, Mr. Strickland, and she usually does come back sooner to get ready for work. I should have gone with her, sir."

"Yes, you should have, but I need to know who she went to see and the address of the house where the Bible study is being held."

"It's not a house, it's a yacht."

"A what!" Mr. Strickland exclaimed, trying to calm down. "Did you say a yacht?"

"Yes, it belongs to Bart Lewis. He's very rich, and she said he just became a Christian."

"Lucy, I want you to call us as soon as she comes home. It is very important. Do not fail me in this, and do not leave your hotel room."

"Yes sir—you have told me several times now."

"I know...I know. We'll be waiting."

Mr. Strickland hung up the phone and looked around at everyone. "She went to a Bible study on a yacht owned by someone named Bart Lewis, and, Miles, you saw her in trouble in the sea. So I think there's a problem, and we need to go down there. Priscilla, call the police chief in Miami on my private line and find out if anyone knows anything about Lewis. Lucy says he's rich. If you can't get anything there, call a private investigator in Miami. Paul, use the business line and see when the next flights are to Miami. If you can't get one, see if we can charter a flight. I want the home phone line left open for Lucy or Anna to call. Please, no one use that phone line. She may just be running late, so we will wait two hours before we leave, just in case."

"There's one other thing I think we should do," Miles said.

"Yes?" Mr. Strickland said.

"Pray."

"Yes, of course—that's the most important thing, isn't it? Let's hold hands and I'll start it."

They formed a circle in the living room, and Mr. Strickland took a deep breath and sighed. "Oh, God, I have failed you. I allowed my daughter to go somewhere that I felt she should not. You were trying to tell me, but I was trying to please her and not You. This is my fault— have mercy on me, a sinner. I repent for letting her go, I repent for not listening to Miles, and now I pray for your mercy for Anna. You said the angel of the Lord encamps around those who fear Him—please encamp around Anna and protect her, in Christ's name, Amen."

Miles left, and the phone calls were made. Paul hung up the phone and turned to his father.

"There are no flights that leave tonight or tomorrow," Paul said.

"What about if we get a plane and I fly it?" Mr. Strickland asked.

"But you haven't flown since the Great War," Paul said.

"So are you afraid to fly with me?"

"I don't think we can even find a plane with enough range to get there any faster than driving," Paul said.

"Especially with Father driving," Priscilla added.

"But you sidestepped my question. Are you afraid to fly with me—do you think I'm rusty?"

"Yes, I am afraid to fly with you, and, yes, I think you are rusty," Paul answered.

"Well, you're probably right, but how long will it take if we drive?"

"I figure if we maintain seventy-five in the Duesenberg and switch off driving, we could be there in seventeen to twenty hours."

"It would be easier if you had three people to drive," Esther said.

Mr. Strickland looked at Paul and then at Esther. "Dear, you have rarely driven the Duesenberg—and we're talking about maintaining a high speed."

"Once we're on the highway I'm fine. I'm just a little slow shifting."

"Are you sure? This will not be a comfortable trip," Mr. Strickland said.

"Father, I'm very sure. I want to be there to help Anna, and three heads are better than one."

"Okay, but no complaining—we're driving straight through and if we stop to eat it will be in the car."

"I'd like to go too, but I've never driven the Duesenberg, so I wouldn't be able to help with that," Priscilla said.

"That's fine, Priscilla, I need you here in case Anna tries to call the house. I know you're supposed to go to work, so ask Standish to call you if you are there when she calls."

"Okay, Father, you're right. One girl on this trip is probably enough, anyway. I'll be praying for you."

The phone rang and Mr. Standish answered it and told Priscilla it was for her. She picked it up and listened, her face turning ashen as she did. "Yes, I understand. Thank you, Mr. Miller." She was quiet for a moment, as if in shock.

"Well, who was that, and what did he say?" Mr. Strickland asked.

"It was one of the private detectives I called—the only one who's called back. He says he can't help us but he does know about Bart Lewis. He said he's a major bootlegger. He has several large yachts and he uses them to bring the liquor in from Cuba."

Mr. Strickland shook his head and Esther looked as if she were going to cry, but Paul sat stoically. "This is terrible," Mr. Strickland said.

"It's worse than that. Miller said Lewis has mob connections, and we won't be able to find a P.I. to help us—they are all afraid of him, and so is he. That's why he won't take the case."

Mr. Strickland took a deep breath and stood up, and Paul did also. "Esther, tell Mr. Standish to throw some clothes into a suitcase for me, and Priscilla can help you pack some things. If Ben is still here, have him pull the Duesenberg to the front. Paul—let's go down to the game room."

As they walked down the stairs, Paul turned to his father. "Are we going down here for the reason I think?"

"Yes, but I didn't want to upset your sisters," Mr. Strickland said as they entered the lower room. He unlocked a large, walk-in safe, then opened a box in the safe that had money in it and took a large quantity of bills and put them in a briefcase. He also took out a .38

pistol and loaded it, then put it in his pocket. "I don't think we'll need this, but I'm not certain. Let's get a move on."

32

On Monday Priscilla went to work, but Herbert was out of the office most of the morning. When he finally came into the office, he barely said a word to her as he passed her in the hallway, mumbling "hello" and then disappearing into his office. She thought he was acting strangely, but knowing he was moody, she thought he would come out of it. They were regularly eating lunch together, but this time he did not buzz her intercom or come to her office as the noon hour came. She finally walked out of her office and slowly walked by his, but the door was closed. She said hello to Mrs. Ross, and then went back to her office.

Generally he would come into her office to discuss production figures and other business, but as the morning wore on, she still did not see him. She made a point of busying herself with a variety of issues—she was now helping with personnel problems as well as manufacturing issues in addition to her accounting duties. The time passed quickly and soon she noticed that it was about one o'clock, which was the normal time for Herbert to eat lunch. He hated the crowds so he tried to eat a little later to miss the lunch rush hour. Her eyes were tired from reading reports, so she stood up and stretched and walked out of her office and slowly walked by his, but his door was closed. She started chatting with Mrs. Ross, and as she finished, Herbert walked out, looked at her, and then looked back at Mrs. Ross. "I'm going to lunch now, Mrs. Ross. Should be back by two-thirty." He then hurriedly left the office without saying a word to Priscilla.

"Well, that was a little rude," Mrs. Ross said as she saw Priscilla's countenance had fallen. Priscilla felt insulted and humiliated, but she tried to hide her true feelings.

"Maybe he's just in a hurry about something. Would you like to go to lunch, Mrs. Ross?"

"Oh, I'd love to, but I brought my lunch today."

Priscilla decided to go to the same restaurant she had last gone to with Herbert because it was within walking distance. They had both thought the food was very good, and it was also inexpensive. As she walked there, she passed the jewelry store where they had window shopped and she winced. Something deep inside her could not get over the way Herbert had acted that morning, even though it was just one incident. After she reached the restaurant she walked into the ladies' room before being seated. As she came out, she saw Roxanne walk in and talk to the maître d', who then guided her to a table. Priscilla slowly moved so that she could watch where Roxanne was going without being seen by her. She almost let out a gasp when she saw that Herbert was seated at the table that Roxanne was led to.

She hurriedly left the restaurant and walked out into the street feeling disoriented and confused. She realized that she had to take control of her thoughts and emotions and try to analyze the situation objectively. She understood that her emotions could color things in a way that might result in coming to the wrong conclusion, for she had worked through that many times when making recommendations about employees. Often she felt one way due to her compassion for an employee that had to be terminated, but she had to temper that with her responsibility to advise her father or Herbert objectively. She knew now she had to compose herself and she tried to shake off her confusion and discern the true nature of Herbert's disposition.

First, he had ignored her, and she could understand that if he was under some pressure with the company, even though he had never acted that way before. But then, to eat lunch with Roxanne, after all he had said about not wanting to marry her? But was she over-reacting? She knew he was still friends with Roxanne, so was it really a problem? Priscilla knew Herbert had not yet formally proposed to her, but he had certainly insinuated that they would be engaged from the way he acted when they walked by the jewelry store. So was she wrong to be disturbed about Roxanne, she wondered. She felt butterflies in her stomach that would not settle down, and realizing she had now lost her appetite, she decided to go back to work.

When she got back to Superior Pumps, she had to walk past Mrs. Ross to get into her office, and Mrs. Ross was sitting at her desk typing. Priscilla smiled as best she could and walked straight into her office, and shut the door. She had work to do, but could not seem to concentrate—all she could think about was her relationship with Herbert. She concluded that the only way to know if there was a problem between them was to be bold and talk to him when he returned. She left her office door open because she could normally hear Mrs. Ross's voice when she greeted Herbert. Although her mind kept wandering, she did what she could—menial work—she had a number of files that needed to be put back, so she spent her time filing until Herbert returned from lunch.

"Did you have a good lunch, Mr. Blankenship?" she heard Mrs. Ross say about an hour later. As soon as she heard it, she stood up from her chair and walked quickly to the outer office just as Herbert was walking into his office. He was about to close his door when he saw her.

"Do you have a minute?" she asked. He was hesitant, and it seemed that he was about to say no, but he relented and walked in and motioned for her to come into his office. They both sat down and she noticed that his face looked strained and uncomfortable. Priscilla knew she had to tell him who she really was—the charade could go on no longer. "There is something that I have to tell you—it's about meeting my relatives. I want you to meet them but you need to know something—" she began.

"I think I need to tell you something first," he interrupted. "I would like to keep our relationship as a professional one only."

"What?" she said, her stomach now feeling even more distressed. She felt disoriented and for a moment her stomach was so queasy she thought she might faint. Had she heard him correctly?

"I just think that we should return the relationship to what it used to be—for now, Miss Avery."

Priscilla was stunned and did not know what to say. She wanted to ask why, but her pride stopped her. "That's fine, Mr. Blankenship. This will be my last day."

"I'm sorry to hear that."

"I doubt that," Priscilla said and walked out of his office, resisting the desire to slam the door. She felt involuntary tears falling from her eyes as she walked down the hallway to her office. She closed the door and locked it, wondering how he could talk to her that way. How could he be so cruel? What kind of man was he really? Why hadn't she seen what he was really like? The only explanation for this was that his mother was against the marriage, and he wasn't man enough to stand up to her. Yes, she knew that Herbert's mother held the purse strings, and it was obvious that Herbert had sold out. Was he now considering marrying Roxanne, even after he'd said he didn't love her? But couldn't he have been nicer? On second thought, she realized that tact was not his strong point and that he probably didn't realize how much he had hurt her by talking the way he did. What did it matter? she thought as she checked the office drawers for personal belongings.

She found a paper bag and put her things in it. She remembered how he had praised her for finishing her work when she left before. Well, she didn't care—not with his attitude. Let him figure it out, she thought, as she closed the ledger book. She couldn't work there a moment longer, so she picked up the phone and asked Mr. Standish to tell Ben to pick her up. She wanted to explain to Mrs. Ross why she was leaving, but she also figured that Mrs. Ross had probably already figured it out, since she probably handled the phone call from Roxanne and had heard how he had spoken that morning. She knew that her eyes were red from crying and she did not want to see anyone.

With the bag and her purse, she looked down the hallway and saw no one there, so she left the office and closed her door. She hurriedly walked past Mrs. Ross and was almost out of the building as Mr. Markowitz, the sales manager, was walking in.

"It's nice to see you. You've seen how the Strickland sales have increased—I think they saved the company," he said.

"That's very good news, Mr. Markowitz," she said, her voice cracking as she held her face down. He looked down to see her eyes and appeared concerned and somewhat fatherly.

"What is the matter, Miss Avery? Is there anything I can do to help—anything at all?"

Priscilla attempted to smile, but it was weak. "No, but thank you for offering."

"Well, if you think of something, please let me know. If there is anyone here that I owe a debt of gratitude to, it's you."

Priscilla walked down the street to the place where Ben was to pick her up. When he showed up, she rushed into the car and he closed the door. "My, are you leaving early today, Miss Priscilla?"

"Yes, Ben. And this is the last time you'll drive me—I've quit this job."

33

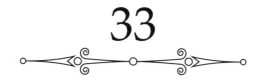

Anna was in a deep sleep, and she was dreaming that she was floating in the air—drifting through the clouds as she rocked back and forth. Suddenly she felt pressure on her chest, and it seemed that one of the clouds was pressing down on her. She knew that a cloud was damp air and that it could not press on her, but the pressure continued, and she woke up to find Bart Lewis on top of her. He saw her eyes open and he tried to kiss her, but she turned her head. "What are you doing!" she screamed.

"Just what you've always wanted. I'm going to make love to you."

"No you're not, get off me, you're smothering me."

"No one can hear you, we are out at sea," he said, slurring his words, and she realized that he was drunk.

"Get off me! I can't breathe! I'm suffocating."

"Okay, okay, take a breath," he said, and he took his weight off her long enough for her to sit up. As she did, she looked out the window and saw only water.

"Where are we?"

"We're almost to Cuba now. It's a nice cruise," he said smiling.

"What have you done, take me back!"

"Oh, I think you'll enjoy it here. It's still legal to drink in Cuba, you know."

"I don't drink, now take me back," Anna said, looking anxiously around the cabin.

"There's nowhere to go, so relax," he said, moving closer to her and trying to kiss her.

"Stop it!" Anna said, trying to get off the couch. At first he held her in place, but then he let her get up.

"I said there's nowhere to go, so just lie back and enjoy it. I know you like me—I've seen the way you look at me."

"You'd better take me back or you'll regret it. My real name is Anna Strickland, and my father is very rich and when he finds out, you'll be in big trouble."

"Oh, so you're Anna Strickland—that's why you're working as a waitress. And that's why I met Anna Strickland at Roney Plaza—no, you'll have to do better than that," he said, moving closer to her again, and grabbing her arm as she tried to move from the couch. "No, you're just a two-bit little waitress who makes up lies. Didn't they teach you in church not to lie? Isn't there a commandment or something, thou shalt not lie—there should be one like that," he said, drunkenly, as he tried to pin her down. She stopped struggling, realizing that he was much too strong for her, and she tried to think of a strategy to get free from him.

"I know you want me—quit pretending. All women want me," he said, moving on top of her and trying to kiss her. At first she resisted, but then she stopped, and put her hand through his hair.

"Now that's more like it," he said, kissing her on the neck.

Anna's eyes showed her terror at what was happening, but Bart wasn't looking at her face and she controlled her voice as she spoke. "Okay, Bart, you're right. I do like you—you know you're very handsome." She stroked his hair a little more. "But let a girl breathe a little."

"Oh, I'm sorry," Bart said, taking some of his weight off her.

"Bart, honey, I think I will enjoy this and I won't fight you, but I need to go to the ladies' room—I really have to go badly," she said, smiling at him. Bart said nothing for a moment but then agreed reluctantly.

"Okay. The head is through there," he said, pointing down the hallway. "I'll be waiting, and, remember, there's nowhere to go—water, water, everywhere."

Anna went in the bathroom and fell to her knees and prayed. "God, please get me out of here. I've played the fool, but please forgive me. Get me away from him, somehow." Her prayer was interrupted by his voice shouting out.

"Have a little drink and it will be more fun."

She opened the door slowly and saw that the kitchen was in the opposite direction of the room they were in. She took a deep breath and ran into the kitchen and opened a drawer looking for a knife. "Are you finished yet—you're not going to make me come after you, are you?" he said, hearing her in the kitchen.

"No, darling, you are much too handsome to keep waiting," she said, trying to sound calm as she opened another drawer and found a large, sharp butcher knife which she was about to grab when he suddenly appeared, smoking a cigarette. He had walked up another way, because there were two stairways that led into the galley area.

"Where are you going, Lucy? There is nowhere to go, remember?"

"I just wanted to get a drink," she said, taking a bottle of vodka from the kitchen and pouring it in a large glass that was on the counter, which she filled.

"That's a big drink," he said, laughing. "Can a girl like you hold her liquor?"

"Sure I can. But can I have a cigarette first?"

"Oh, you smoke, too? Well, I guess all that Christian stuff must be a smokescreen," he said, laughing a little at his small joke and sliding a pack of Lucky Strikes over to her. She took one from the pack, trying to steady her shaking hands. "You know it's going to be like heaven for both of us—I promise," he said.

"I need a light," she said, and he slid his lighter over to her. She lit the cigarette, but she didn't inhale. Instead, she moved away from the counter, the lighter still burning. She took a deep breath and threw the glass down on the floor between them and lit it with the lighter, and a small fire started. He stood for a moment completely disoriented and not certain what to do. She threw the bottle down on the fire and it broke and the flames flared up. Then she grabbed the butcher knife from the drawer and ran up the stairs to the deck.

"You'd better get back down here," he shouted threateningly, as he grabbed a towel and beat the flames out. He then got water from the sink and threw it on the fire. It was getting dark now, and she looked around the boat frantically, trying to find a life preserver. She finally saw one near the front of the boat, and as she raced towards it, he came up the stairs, his face contorted with anger. She tried to get the life preserver free but it was tied to the rail. Using the knife, she cut at the rope. At first, due to his drunken state, Bart did not seem to understand what she was doing as he watched from a distance. But as he realized it, he moved towards her. "Get back here, you little tramp—you're gonna pay for what you did down there!" he said as he moved. But when he reached her, she slashed the air with the knife, threatening him.

"Now, you wouldn't use that on me, would you?" he said, moving closer.

"Get back," she shouted, but he moved even closer and she swung out with the large butcher knife and cut his arm. He looked at her incredulously and the shock of the cut began to sober him up completely.

"You cut me, you little…"

"And I'll cut you again if you don't stay back!" Anna said, her voice going higher in pitch with fear. Bart realized she meant it, and he was cautious about coming at her again—he watched as she feverishly cut on the rope—sizing up the situation and looking for a chance to overpower her without getting hurt himself. Finally he decided to charge at her, but she had the life preserver free by then, and ran to the side of the boat to jump. He grabbed her dress and she slashed at it to get free, and it ripped the rest of the way as she jumped in the water.

As she splashed in the water, she let go of the knife so she could hold on to the preserver. He watched her, shaking his head. "I'll pull you back up," he shouted, throwing a rope to her, but she refused it. "You don't want to drown out here, do you?" She began to paddle away with her arms while she held the life preserver under her chest for buoyancy. He looked down at her again and spit in her direction. Then he shrugged and turned away. "Win some, lose some," he said as he walked back towards the center of the yacht, holding his bleeding arm. The cut was only a surface one, but the bleeding had not yet stopped. "Okay, she deserves to drown after that," he said, looking at the cut.

"Are you tired of driving, Esther?" Mr. Strickland asked.

"No, Father, you keep asking me that, but I'm fine."

"It's just that you've been driving now for over five hours, and Paul and I can take over anytime."

"I think I'm next," Paul said, his eyes opening as he lay in the back seat.

"Did you get any sleep back there?" Mr. Strickland asked.

"Yeah, a little, I think," Paul said, sitting up and looking around. "Where are we now?"

"We've got about three hundred more miles," Esther answered, as Paul moved up in his seat and looked at the speedometer.

"Eighty-five miles an hour! You must have it floored—that's faster than I was driving."

"Esther's become fearless," Mr. Strickland said.

"We need to get there for Anna," Esther explained. "But I am pulling over at the next town because we need gas, and then someone else can drive, because all of a sudden I do feel tired."

"We're coming into one now, it's called St. Augustine. I imagine there's a filling station there."

After pulling over for gasoline, Paul took the wheel and drove the last part of the journey as Mr. Strickland tried to sleep in the back seat, without success. At about five in the morning they drove into Roney Plaza and parked the car in the driveway in the front. Mr. Strickland sat up and rubbed his eyes. "I can't believe we're finally here. But I don't think we can do anything since it's so early on Sunday morning, so we may as well check in and try to get some sleep. I imagine the police department will have someone there around eight or so." He got out of the car and went to the front door, but it was closed, so he rang the bell. It took a while, but the night porter finally answered and they checked in.

34

Priscilla woke up early on Sunday morning with tears in her eyes. She just couldn't understand how Herbert could act the way he did, and was perplexed and astounded at how the relationship had ended so suddenly. One week she had thought they would be married, and the next week the thought of marriage was not only off, he was not even kind to her. What had happened? she wondered as she looked at the clock on the table next to her bed? Moving slowly, she got up and went to the telephone and called Alice Jamison, who was surprised to get a call on Sunday morning. "I'm sorry to call you so early, but I just needed someone to talk to," Priscilla said apologetically.

"You have no reason to be sorry—all of you are like sisters to me, and I'll be right over," Alice said. "Esther told me about Anna, and I've been praying. Let me just tell Roger first. Maybe we can go to church together."

"I'm sorry, I don't feel like going this morning. My eyes are red from crying and…"

"Say no more. I'm coming."

This time Alice smiled when Mr. Standish opened the door. As soon as she walked in, Priscilla came into the living room and they hugged. When they sat down on the couch together, Alice held her friend while she cried softly. Finally, Priscilla dried her eyes and sat up. "I always thought of myself as being strong…what's the Scripture, if you've run with the footmen and they've wearied you?"

"No one is strong all the time—that's why we need each other. That's what real friends are for."

"I have always been…strong…mostly, anyway. But this week— this is the worst week of my life. Anna may be in serious trouble.

There's a man she met and she thought he was a Christian, but he's a bootlegger and maybe a mobster and we don't know where she is. She never came home after meeting with him."

"Yes, Esther told me. But you mean you still haven't heard anything?"

"Anna never called and never came home. And…and as sorry as I feel for her, I also feel sorry for myself because the man…the one I thought I would marry has jilted me because he thinks I'm poor and he wants to marry for money."

"That's the one running the company you were working for, right?"

"Yes, and he had me meet his mother, and he told me that she might not like it if he didn't marry a rich girl."

"Well, if that's the reason, you can tell him who you are now—can't you? Oh, but you don't want to do that."

"No, if he doesn't want me because he thinks I'm poor, then I don't want him. I was just about to tell him I was a Strickland when he told me he only wanted a business relationship."

"But Esther told me that he said it didn't matter—even if his mother didn't like you, he would do what he wanted. Did that change?"

"I think so, but he never explained anything, so I think he turned out to be more of a mama's boy than I thought. I mean, sometimes I know how you felt when you came over. Once you realize they love money more than you, it's a terrible feeling. Esther has been jilted, and even Father has been. Everything is just so depressing!"

Alice took Priscilla's hand and held it. "Don't lose hope, Prissy. Things always change. There will be joy in the morning. Even Roger is acting much better now. I think he is sorry for what he said."

"Did he apologize?"

"No, he rarely does that. He just starts acting better—that's sort of the way he says he's sorry. And although there are some words you can't take back, I'm making the best of it, because I've forgiven him and it has set me free." Priscilla was quiet for a while, and was looking down. Alice looked down also, until she could make eye contact with her. "Have you forgiven Herbert?"

"I don't know," Priscilla said, sulking.

"Then you haven't. And have you forgiven Mrs. Ingersoll and David?"

"Yes, but I'm still working through it with Herbert. It was just such a shock. And I did so much for him. I caught his embezzler—and it would have gotten worse if I hadn't. I stopped his employees from turning against him, and I probably saved his company from bankruptcy. And what do I get in return? He doesn't even have the class to sit down with me and tell me the reason, even though I know it. He's not man enough to do that, and he's too selfish. So I guess I'm glad I found out before I married him."

"I know it's hard, but when you think about him, try to just feel sorry for him, because he passed up the best woman he could have married. Not only would you have been a wonderful wife, but you would have helped him in his business, and he threw all that away. He's the one who lost."

"Thank you, Alice. I feel better now, but I also feel guilty for even thinking about myself. There is no telling what trouble Anna is in, and it's my fault—I instigated the whole thing."

"Well, you didn't instigate her going to Florida—that was her choice and she argued with everyone about it."

"We thought that with Lucy going she'd be safe, but Lucy didn't go with her that day. And I've been worried sick about her, but I'm also feeling sorry for myself. How pitiful and weak I am. She's probably in real trouble, and I'm still concerned about my small letdown."

"Don't be so hard on yourself—you just happened to be traumatized at the same time this happened to Anna."

"I know, but when you see these things in yourself…"

35

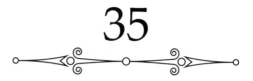

At eight-thirty in the morning they arrived at the harbor with Paul driving. Esther was reading from some notes that Priscilla had written down, and Paul stopped the car in front of a small office at the entrance to the yacht club. "Where do I go now?"

"The investigator told Priscilla that his slip is 47D, and the first one over there is A, so I think we should keep driving," Esther said. Paul drove along as they looked for the slip. When they finally found it, it was empty.

"He's gone. Let's ask around and try to find out when he left," Mr. Strickland said. They got out of the car and began walking towards a yacht on the south side of his slip, but then Esther stopped and motioned for them to come closer to her.

"I think it's better I inquire—they won't suspect anything if a woman walks up, but we might scare someone if we all walk up."

Mr. Strickland and Paul looked at each other for a moment. "She's right," Paul said, and his father nodded. "But don't seem too sophisticated," Paul said.

"I can play the part," Esther said, and she walked towards the boat as her father and brother got back into the car and watched her. They saw her walk up to the yacht south of his slip, but no one was there so she went to the one on the north side. She talked to the people in the second yacht for a long time before coming back to the car. "They say he left some time on Sunday. They said he was having some kind of party there on Sunday afternoon when they left to go into town for the evening. They got back around two in the morning and he was gone. They know him and they said he always goes to Cuba. I think they buy liquor from him the way they were talking."

"Why do you think that?" Paul asked.

"Well, I pretended to be one of his girlfriends and they offered me some champagne, and they said Bart would have plenty of good cheer when he came back."

"Let's go to the hotel and find out what we can," Mr. Strickland said.

Around nine in the morning, they knocked on the door of Lucy's room, but at first she didn't answer. Paul then knocked harder and they waited for a long time before she finally opened the door. She was dressed in an expensive silk nightgown that belonged to Anna. Bleary-eyed and irritable, she was obviously hung over. "What do ya want?" she rudely blurted out before she realized who it was. Slowly her eyes focused on them and she changed her attitude. "Oh, hello, Mr. Strickland," she said.

"Hello, Lucy. We need to talk about Anna," Mr. Strickland said. "Why don't you get dressed and meet us down at the restaurant."

"You mean right now?" Lucy asked.

"Yes, right now. This is very serious, we have to find Anna."

"Okay," Lucy said with a little sigh. "But I don't know if I can be of any help."

"Right now," Mr. Strickland said firmly. "You have ten minutes to get to the restaurant," he added and turned away from the door.

About fifteen minutes later she came down to the restaurant. Her hair was disheveled and she wore bright red lipstick that was unevenly applied. She was, in fact, still somewhat drunk from the night before, and everyone noticed but politely greeted her.

As soon as she sat down at the table, Mr. Strickland started asking her questions. "What does Bart Lewis look like?"

Lucy had to think for a moment to understand the question. "Well, he's very handsome," she said.

"So we've all heard. But describe him," Esther said. As she spoke, the waitress came to their table to take their order and heard what they said.

"If you want to know what Bart Lewis looks like, his picture is on the wall over there," the waitress said, pointing to a corner of the restaurant where there were photos of celebrities and regular customers pinned on the wall.

"Over there?" Paul asked, pointing as they all got up.

"Yes, I'll show you." They followed her over to it, and she pointed to a picture of him and a friend together. "Go ahead and take it," she suggested, and Paul took it from the wall.

"So who is this with him?" Mr. Strickland asked. The waitress looked a little flustered.

"Well, I don't know if I should say any more...."

Mr. Strickland took out a five-dollar bill and handed it to her, and held another in his hand, as if he were offering it. She reached towards it, but he pulled it back. "This is very important, please help us. We will not say a word to anyone, I assure you." The waitress looked down at the money and then back at him.

"Well, that's Tony," she said.

Lucy also gazed at the photo. "Yeah, that's the guy that I've seen with Bart," she confirmed.

"So you know him?" Paul asked.

"No, but I've seen him," Lucy said.

"Yes, they often come in together," the waitress said.

"Do you know where we can find Tony?" Mr. Strickland asked.

"Well...I went out with him a few times, but I don't remember..."

Mr. Strickland put the other five in her hand, and took ten dollars more from his pocket, and she looked at the bill.

"Well, I think it's the Sea Breeze Apartments. He has a real nice apartment with an ocean view."

"Do you remember the number?" Paul asked.

"No, but it's at the top—it's the first one on the right when you go to the second floor, as you face the building."

Mr. Strickland put the ten-dollar bill in her hand.

"So, do you want to order now?" the waitress asked.

Mr. Strickland looked at Paul and then at Esther. "No, I think we need to get going."

"Just give us a minute, please," Paul said, and he smiled at her.

After she walked away, Paul turned to his father. "Father, you didn't eat the whole trip down here, and we've had very little sleep, and you've eaten less than any of us, and I think we need to be strong now."

"I agree with Paul, Father. I'm feeling faint myself," Esther added.

"Okay, okay, I know when I'm outnumbered. Let's eat and then see if we can find Tony, and then the police."

It did not take long for them to find the Sea Breeze luxury apartments, and when they found a parking space, Esther sat up in her seat in the back and touched her father on the shoulder. "Let me go in by myself."

"No, Esther, it might be dangerous. These people are thugs."

"I'll be all right. But he may not answer the door for you."

"She's right, and we can be very close," Paul said.

"Oh, I don't know."

"Yes, it will be fine," Esther said as she took some lipstick out of her purse and applied a heavy coating. Then she pulled out her blouse from her dress and tied it underneath her bra, showing her stomach. Her father looked at her disapprovingly.

"What are you doing?"

"Baiting the hook—we want to find Anna, don't we?"

"Yes, but I don't know if I like this," Mr. Strickland said.

"We'll stand in the hallway," Paul said, but his father was worried and he frowned.

The hallways were open to the outdoors on the sides, and Esther could see the swimming pool as she approached the apartment. Paul and his father stood with their bodies flat against the wall about ten feet down the hallway on both sides and waited as she knocked on the door. There was a window near the door, and soon someone moved the curtain slightly, and then the door opened. Tony looked at Esther appreciatively. His eyes went up and down her body, making her feel repulsed, but she smiled at him in spite of it.

"Yes, darling, what can I do for you?" he asked.

"Oh, I'm looking for Bart, and someone said he might be here. I went to the harbor, but his boat was missing."

"He's made a run to Cuba. Why don't you come in and we'll talk about it?"

"But I feel bad. I was supposed to go to a little party he had on the boat on Sunday with Lucy, and I missed it."

"You didn't miss anything—come on in."

Esther looked around, acting as if she were making a decision. "But did he miss me? Were you at the party?"

"Yeah, I was at the party. It wasn't anything special. But come in and I'll fix you a nice soda mixed with something delicious," Tony said.

"Oh, that sounds good. You mean like the stuff that Bart has?"

"Yes... I have plenty of that for you, darling," Tony said as Paul signaled her to step out of the way. She moved, and Paul and his father rushed through the door and pushed Tony back into his apartment.

"What is this, what are you doing!"

"We want to know where Lucy is," Mr. Strickland said.

"I don't know any Lucy," Tony protested. "Now get out of my apartment before I call the police," he added, as he got his balance and pulled away.

"You were at the party, you saw her—we just heard you say so. Now she's been kidnapped, and you will be an accessory to that crime if you don't tell us where she is."

"I haven't done nothing, and I wasn't at the party—I just said that."

"Okay, we'll go to the police."

"Yeah, go ahead. Bart knows them all real well—and who do you think you are?"

"I'm Joseph J. Strickland. Maybe you've heard of my companies."

"Yeah, and I'm John D. Rockefeller."

Mr. Strickland pulled out his wallet and showed Tony his driver's license and a business card with his name on it. Tony looked at it and then he seemed to get afraid.

"Why do you care about this waitress?"

"She's my daughter—her real name is Anna Strickland and she was pretending to be Lucy—that's our maid."

"Well, I had nothing to do with anything," Tony said. "And that's the truth."

"Kidnapping gets the death penalty—maybe an accessory to kidnapping can also get it," Paul said.

"Yeah, who are you?"

"I'm her brother. Now if you did nothing wrong, you've got a chance to come clean about that party and help us find her."

"I said I wasn't there."

"Well, when we find the people who were there, and we will, and if they tell us you were there and you lied, then you have become an accomplice. You'll be guilty of kidnapping also."

Tony looked at them for a moment and took a deep breath. "Okay, okay. I was there, but I didn't do nothing."

"Well, what did Bart do?"

"I don't know. She started feeling sick at the party and she went down to rest—she was sleepy and she fell asleep and we ate lunch. That's all I know—we left after that."

"And why would she be sleepy?" Mr. Strickland asked.

"I don't know—she just was."

"Don't give me that—someone must have given her some-thing."

"Okay, I'll tell you this—she got tired fast like she had a Mickey Finn or something, but that's all I know—I swear that's the truth—the whole truth."

"Did she ever leave the boat?" Esther asked.

"I don't know. She was sleeping and my date told Bart she needed a doctor, but he said she'd probably be all right. Then we ate lunch and everyone left. She was still there sleeping down in the cabin when we all left. She's a nice girl—I told Bart to leave her alone. But you don't argue with Bart."

"So he's in Cuba now. How do you know?"

"He said he was going, you have probably figured out why."

"Yes, I know the reason. I know he's a bootlegger. But where does he dock there?"

"In Havana—but I don't know which dock in Havana."

"What's the name of his boat?"

"Lady Luck—it's a big one—about eighty feet. And I really hope you find your daughter, Mr. Strickland. I know you probably think... very little of me, but I mean that."

"Okay, thank you for the information."

36

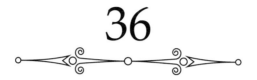

Herbert finished his breakfast, and his mother walked out of the dining room, leaving him with his sister. She had not said much to him, but now she was tired of restraining herself. "Do you think that you and Priscilla could work out whatever problems you are having?"

"No, I don't think so," Herbert said, as the cook walked in and served him more coffee. Charlotte waited until the cook walked out of the room before speaking again.

"I don't understand you—she may not have money but she's not a phony like most of the society debutantes that are after you. I know they have listed you as one of the most eligible bachelors in New York, but don't let that go to your head—you're not easy to get along with. But she knows what you are like and still wants you. Can't you see she's special?"

"I don't want to talk about it."

"Well, I do."

"Charlotte, it's my life and it's none of your business," Herbert said, raising his voice.

"Okay, you don't have to shout."

"I'm not shouting!"

"Yes, you are, and you don't even realize it."

"Okay, I'm sorry."

"Well, I'm sorry too—sorry to see you stop seeing the first girl you ever dated that I liked."

"I never dated her; we just went to lunch together a few times."

"Oh, you are impossible. So you don't think bringing her over here to meet us… I mean, were you just leading her on? How could you do that?"

"I wasn't leading her on."

"Oh, you just changed your mind suddenly, is that it?"

"Yes, that's it."

"And why did you do that?"

"I said I don't want to talk about it."

"Why not?"

"Because it's personal."

"Herbert—I'm your sister. I love you, and I pray for you, and I've been praying that you would find the right woman. And Priscilla is perfect for you. Not only is she very attractive, but she has an incredible ability in business—you said that yourself."

"Yes, I know."

"And she also can stand up to you, which is very difficult."

"Yes, I know that too."

"Oh, so that's it. You don't like a woman who could hold her own with you. You want a mouse you can boss around, is that it?"

Herbert began to speak, but then decided to stay silent.

"Then you are a fool, because you need someone like her. You need someone who will tell you when you are being unreasonable and bombastic. I can't do it forever because I'm your sister…. Are you listening to me?"

"Yes."

"You just don't know what you are giving up. You don't realize how much you need Priscilla."

Herbert took a deep breath and he shook his head. "Don't you think I know all of this? Do you think I wanted to break it off?"

"You didn't want to?"

"No, I didn't."

"Then why did you?"

"I told you, it's personal."

"Herbert, I'm not the gardener or the cook, or one of your employees. I'm your sister and I have a right to know, because this does not make any sense at all!"

"I can't tell you."

"You mean you won't tell me."

"I've got some things to do. I don't want to talk about this anymore."

"Herbert, please tell me. I can't stand this. I really like Priscilla and I haven't been able to sleep over this."

"No, I have to go."

"Are you going to just leave after I told you how much this is troubling me? Do you care so little about my feelings?"

"Charlotte, you know I care about you."

"Then tell me, Herbert. Let me put this thing to rest. I must know...."

"She's seeing someone else!" Herbert shouted.

"What? I can't believe that."

"Remember how she helped us get the Strickland account?"

"Yes, of course. It's your best account now."

"Well, I followed her after work—she's always been secretive about her life. And a limousine stopped and Paul Strickland got out and they hugged and kissed and everything. At first I didn't recognize him, but then I remembered him from when he played polo on one of the teams. He was always the richest kid."

"So she has another boyfriend. Maybe she was going to break up with him for you."

"It's worse than that. I followed them, and she went to his house and stayed there...she stayed there all night—or at least until four in the morning because that's when I left."

Charlotte looked over at Herbert and then walked over and took his hand. "Maybe nothing happened—maybe there is another explanation."

"Well, even if nothing happened, what kind of woman would spend the night?"

"I just have a hard time believing that the girl I met here and talked to is..."

"Is a floozy?"

"Herbert, don't say such a thing about her."

"Why not—the truth is the truth. Maybe she's just a gold digger, and if she is, then she's found more gold than she'd ever have gotten from me."

Charlotte shook her head and walked towards Herbert, and he took her hand. "I'm sorry to hear this. I really am."

"I am too, but I didn't want to tell anyone about it, and I don't want to ruin her reputation. I know you won't repeat it."

"Of course I won't. In fact, I still don't believe it."

"I understand...I didn't want to believe it, either."

"But I didn't say I don't want to, I said I don't believe it."

"Suit yourself. I know what I saw."

37

The Miami police station smelled of perspiration and cigarette smoke. The building was old and the paint inside was cracked and peeling, and the walls, once white, were stained brown from nicotine. The windows were open and fans were blowing, but the heat overpowered everything. The Stricklands had been waiting for the chief of police for about ten minutes, but he had not come to the counter. "I think we should skip this and go to Cuba," Paul said.

Joseph Strickland looked at his watch. "Okay, we will give him just two more minutes..." As he spoke, a somber policeman came to the counter and motioned for them to walk through a little gate and then into the police chief's office. He was a big man with a large belly and a large Cuban cigar. When he pulled it from his mouth to speak, it dripped with saliva.

"Yeah, Mister—I'm Chief Haskell—what can I do for you?" he asked.

"My daughter has been kidnapped, and I would like help finding her."

"Well, you told the sergeant that you think that Bart Lewis kidnapped her—is that right?"

"Yes sir."

"And why do you think that?" Chief Haskell asked challengingly.

"Because she was on his yacht, and she fell asleep and then he took off with her."

"Okay, okay," Haskell began—"you think that Bart Lewis kidnapped your daughter and took her to Cuba—is that it?"

"Yes, that's it."

"Well, I'm sorry to tell you that we have no jurisdiction in Cuba.

So we can't help you with this one."

"We think he might be in Cuba—we're not certain. But the crime was committed here, so you can at least question the people on the yacht."

"Mister, you come down here looking for your daughter and expect us to help you when there ain't a shred of evidence of a crime. But if he did take off with her, maybe she wanted to go."

"Do you know who Bart Lewis is?" Paul asked.

"I don't see what that has to do with it."

"I just asked if you knew him—I understand he's a very wealthy man and well-known in this city."

The chief looked at Paul for a moment, as if he were weighing how to answer. "Yes, we know who he is. And he's an upstanding citizen—I've never had a complaint about him."

"So is that why you won't even make a report?"

"Mister, there is nothing to report. Your daughter is of age, and if she ran off with this man, then what is there to investigate?"

"You need to investigate because there has been an allegation of a crime—that's your job, and my sister may be in trouble," Esther said, getting angry.

"Well, little lady, if she's in trouble, it might just be that she started it. Half the women in Miami are after Bart Lewis, and most of them wouldn't complain if he took them for a little test ride on his yacht," Haskell said, slowly saying the words "test ride."

Paul's face became red with anger and he walked closer to him and spoke in a quiet but threatening tone. "Mister, you'd better watch out what you insinuate about my sister."

"Are you threatening me? I'm insinuating nothing—don't even know her. But calm down—unless you want to go in the lockup for disturbing the peace."

"Let's get out of here," Mr. Strickland said.

As they walked out of the station, Esther stared at her father. "Why didn't you tell him who you were? He obviously didn't know or he wouldn't have acted like that."

"Because I don't think it would have helped, and there was more of a chance he'd warn Lewis if he knew. The whole bunch is probably getting paid off for bootlegging. In 1923 President Harding even admitted there was widespread corruption in law enforcement because of bootlegging—lots of people getting paid off to look the other way. Let's get a boat and go to Cuba—we'll stop at the hotel first."

"Why, Mr. Strickland, it's a pleasure and honor to meet you!" Newton Roney said as he held out his hand to Joseph. Joseph shook his hand as they stood in the lobby. "I understand you need some help with something—how can I be of service?"

"Mr. Roney, my daughter worked here as a waitress, but now it seems she has been kidnapped."

"Kidnapped!—why, that is terrible. But I don't think she worked here."

"She wanted to pretend she was not rich, so she used the name Lucy Jenkins, who is our maid, and she worked under that name."

"Oh, Lucy—yes, I know who you mean. A lovely young lady. So who has done this thing—do you know?"

"Well, we're not certain yet. But I need to rent a boat to go to Cuba, because I think she's there. And I would like to ask your front desk to take calls for me so we can communicate with the police and others. I could use our company in New York, but the connection from here is not very clear, and I may need to call from Cuba."

"Why yes, of course. I will tell all the front desk staff. We will keep a notepad of messages for you by the phone. But you don't need to rent a boat—my yacht is at the harbor and I will have my captain, Lorenzo, take you to Cuba. He speaks Spanish and can help you once you get there."

"Well, that's very kind, and I will pay you to use it."

"Just pay for the fuel. I am sorry that this happened to your daughter. Now, you look tired, so I will have the boat fueled up and stock it with food, and meanwhile come into the restaurant and our chef will prepare anything you want."

"Well, we do need to get moving," Paul said.

"Yes, but it will take an hour to prepare the boat, so you may as well eat some of Chef Mercier's famous cuisine—now follow me."

Mr. Roney walked to the restaurant and Chef Mercier soon came out from the kitchen, and he seemed excited. "So Lucy, this sweet girl, is really your daughter?"

"Yes, she is."

"I will pray for her—so sorry to hear about this. She is a very nice girl and with a talent for cooking, no? And so I cook something very fast for you, so you can find her. Perhaps a French omelet with special Gruyere cheese?"

"Can I make a phone call after we order?" Mr. Strickland asked.

"We can bring you one now. It has a long cord."

The chef went into the kitchen and soon a worker brought the phone to their table, and Joseph dialed the operator and told her that he wanted a number in Washington, D.C.

"Joseph J. Strickland," Joseph said, as he waited with the phone next to his ear.

"Father, who are you calling?" Esther asked, but he didn't answer.

"Yes, hello, Lou.... Well, it's very good to hear from you, also.... Yes, I pray for him every day—I know it must be very difficult.... Yes, of course, thank you.... Well, it's good to hear your voice also, sir. And I wouldn't bother you, but I've got a predicament—well, I need your help.... Thank you, sir. Okay, Herbert, then.... My daughter has been kidnapped and taken to Cuba and I'm in Miami. The police here are corrupt and they won't help because the man is a notorious bootlegger and they are thick with him.... Okay...the Roney Hotel, Room seventeen-twelve, but they are also taking messages for me at the front desk.... Yes, U.S. marshals and the coast guard. Okay, we're going to Havana—that's where she may be.... Yes, I know we have no jurisdiction there. Thank you, sir."

"You said 'Lou' and then 'Herbert'—was that who I think it was?" Paul asked.

"Yes, it was, and now we have the coast guard and the navy on our side and two U.S. marshals are coming, and a Bureau of Investigation man will be coming later. But none of them can help us in Cuba, so let's get moving."

38

Anna had been in the water many hours, and it had been pitch dark. Paddling was a waste of time because she did not know which way to go. She prayed and cried out to God to help her, but nothing happened, and often she felt like giving up. But then she thought of how she would have been dead from hypothermia by now if she had been in the cold Atlantic Ocean, and she thanked God that the water was warm in the Gulf of Mexico. Now that the light was getting brighter she noticed that her hands were shriveled from the water more than they had ever been before. She thought she could see land as she bobbed up and down, but she was not certain. As the sun had risen, she remembered that it always rose in the east and set in the west, and she knew that Cuba was to the south, and that was where she thought she saw land, so she hoped she was drifting towards land.

As the sun became brighter, she saw several fishing boats, and she waved her hands towards them. She was surprised at how little energy she had, for after she had waved she felt exhausted. A man in one of the boats saw her and began moving towards her. As it got closer, she saw that there were about five men on the boat, which was about thirty feet long. The men were dirty and they looked rough, but she was only concentrating on trying to get closer to the rope ladder they let down. It was difficult for her to reach it because the water was not smooth. The waves drove the boat from side to side and impeded her progress as she tried to get close enough to grab it.

She finally got one hand on it and then the other, and she began to climb up. But after a second thought, she grabbed the life preserver and put it over her head so she could climb with it. When she got near the railing, several of the men helped pull her into the boat, and she noticed all of them seemed to touch her, and it made her uncomfortable. When she finally got her balance on the deck, she saw that they were all looking at her lecherously. "Bonita Senorita," one of them kept saying, and she looked down and realized that not only was her dress missing on one side, which exposed her leg high up on the thigh, but since the dress was wet, it was clinging to her body, showing the outline of her figure. She began to move slowly away from the men, and they followed at the same pace. One of them had been cleaning a fish and he had a knife in his hand. He licked his lips as his eyes ran up and down her body, and she felt her stomach turn with fear. Then one of them moved even closer and said something in Spanish, as he tried to touch her leg.

Anna froze for a moment. Then she smiled at the man, which seemed to catch him off guard. Looking over the rail, she moved towards it, and he followed, this time reaching out to grab her. But she kicked at him, and as he moved to avoid her kick, she threw herself back over the rail, holding onto the life preserver as she fell into the water. From a distance, a much smaller fishing boat had gotten closer. There were two men in it and a boy of about fourteen. The men in the first boat kept looking at Anna, trying to figure out a way to get her back in their boat. They took a long pole with a hook and held it down towards her, but she refused it and tried to swim away from it.

As they reached Havana, Lorenzo, a short, pleasant man of about thirty-five years of age, looked through a telescope for Bart's yacht. "Do you see anything?" Paul asked.

"Not yet. But I know what his boat looks like. If you want to look, just tell me if you see anything big—it's a big one."

"Okay," Paul said, taking the telescope.

"Are you sure it will be in Havana? Could it be somewhere else?" Mr. Strickland asked.

"If he's a bootlegger, they all fill up in Havana," Lorenzo answered.

"Lorenzo, do you know who Bart Lewis is—have you seen him?" Esther asked.

"Yes, I have. And we will find him, of this I am certain."

"Thank you, Lorenzo—you are a Godsend."

"Oh, that makes me very happy, Mr. Strickland, for you to say that."

"Well, it's true...."

"I see a big yacht in the harbor," Paul said, passing the telescope to Lorenzo.

Lorenzo looked through the telescope. "We are too far away, but that could be it."

"If she's on it, he must be keeping her as a prisoner. It just makes me sick thinking about it," Esther said, breaking down in tears. Her father moved closer to her and put his arm around her.

"Now, let's have faith, let's believe God for his protection for her. Let's stay strong for Him and for her."

"Father, I am trying, but…"

"I think that's it! It says Lady…something." Lorenzo passed the telescope to Paul. "Take a look."

"Yes, I can read the Lady part, but aren't there a lot of boats with a name like that?"

"Probably not that large," Lorenzo said, pressing their boat to go as fast as it could. The boat started bumping against the water as it sped up. "I hope this doesn't bother anyone.…"

"No, no, no, full speed ahead," Mr. Strickland said.

As they got closer, Paul kept looking through the telescope. "Lady Luck…that's it. We've found it very fast."

"Because it's so big," Lorenzo said.

"Let's pull into the dock far enough so he doesn't notice us," Mr. Strickland said.

When they reached the dock, Paul jumped out of the boat and tied it up with the bow rope. Lorenzo got out last and tied it in two more places. They walked down the dock to a narrow road that ran in front of it and then towards Bart's yacht. As they approached the yacht, they stopped so that Bart would not see them if he walked out or was looking through the windows. "Could we call the Cuban police and tell them about Anna?" Mr. Strickland asked Lorenzo.

"No sir, I do not think that is a good idea. They are paid off very well by the bootleggers to keep quiet about everything here, so I think it would be us who would end up in jail. And I think the boat is loaded with liquor."

"Why do you think so?" Paul asked.

"Look how low it is in the water. It's carrying a heavy load, and I don't think it's cigars."

"Oh, I see. It does look lower than the yachts we saw in Miami," Paul said.

"I'll go up there and knock on the door," Esther said.

"Hold your horses—let us think this out—this man's a gangster, and if he's got an illegal load of liquor he'll be even more dangerous," Mr. Strickland said.

"The longer we wait, the more danger she might be in," Esther said. "I'll go up and see if she's there."

"Esther, please wait a minute!" Mr. Strickland said, getting irritated at her anxiousness. "We'll be back in a moment." He took Paul by the arm and beckoned Lorenzo, and they walked away until they were out of earshot.

"Do you think he'll be armed, Lorenzo?" Mr. Strickland asked.

"Oh yes, he will be," Lorenzo said.

Esther waited impatiently, and she finally walked over to them. "What are you discussing? This is not a time for secrets."

Mr. Strickland looked at Paul and then back at her. "I didn't want to upset you, but I'm armed."

"That doesn't upset me, it's a relief. Now let me walk up there," Esther said.

"It's better if Paul walks up."

"No, I need to go. He probably won't open the door for Paul, he'll be just like Tony. Anyway, what would you say if he did?"

"What will you say?" Paul asked. "I don't think he'll tell you anything."

"Maybe not, but I might hear her voice or something. I'll just ask him where a good restaurant is. Maybe I can get him to leave with me and you can search the boat for Anna."

"I've already allowed one of my girls to get into trouble and I don't want it to happen to another one," Mr. Strickland said.

"Father, we need to find her, and I am aware he is dangerous. Please let me go, time is passing."

"Okay, but scream at the top of your lungs if he tries anything, and do not go inside that yacht."

Esther smiled because they finally gave in, and she walked up to the yacht with them nervously waiting across the street. They walked around the corner of an industrial building and watched her from there. She knocked and knocked but no one answered, so she finally walked back and they walked out to meet her.

"I wonder where he is," Paul said.

"There are many nice clubs and restaurants in town where Americans go," Lorenzo said.

"Let's go into town and look for him," Paul said.

39

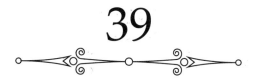

Anna paddled away from the hook, but the men kept trying to follow her in their boat, holding out the hook and telling her to take hold of it. No matter how hard she paddled, she could not get away from the first boat, and her arms were getting weary. One of the men threw down the rope ladder and began to descend on it. She watched with fear mounting as she tried to figure out how she could get away from him when he got to the water. The man shouted something in Spanish to her as he got closer, but then a man from the second boat shouted at him, saying in Spanish for them to leave her alone. He said he would call the police on them if they didn't. Although Anna did not know exactly what he was saying, she could tell by the tone of his voice that he was admonishing them. The men in the first boat were disappointed but decided to give up, and they moved their boat away from Anna as the second boat moved closer.

She was afraid to get near the boat, but the men were saying something to her in Spanish. Extremely exhausted now, she was trying to paddle away as one of the men said something to the boy. The boy then shouted in broken English. "It is okay, Senorita. We bueno—good men. We help you. We no hurt you." Anna turned towards the boat and looked up at the boy. She partially heard him, and was not certain about it, and then he spoke again. "We good men—good men," he said again. Anna saw that they were smiling at her, and their faces looked peaceful, and the teenage boy looked sweet and not rough.

She decided to take a chance and paddled towards the boat. When she reached it, they threw out a large net that fell against the side of the boat, and she tried to climb up, keeping the life preserver over her head. This boat was smaller than the first boat, making the climb up shorter, but she was so tired she couldn't seem to find the strength to finish the climb, so she waited for a moment. The boy then descended down the rope ladder until he reached her, and he took her hand. He pulled her up as he climbed, and she was able to get up the ladder with his help. When she finally got into the boat, she collapsed on the deck. One of the men went into the shabby-looking cabin as the other one and the boy helped her up. When the other man returned, he had a blanket which he held out for her to cover herself. She smiled and put the blanket on.

"Muchas gracias," Anna said, which was about the extent of her Spanish. The boy smiled at her and said, "You are welcome. My father says we are good men and we take you to village. Then we must go again to sell catch in another village, because that is how he pay for family. So mi madre will take care of you."

"Tell your father I'm very grateful to him, and I will make it up to him for any fish he has lost because of me. But can you tell me where we are?"

"Ten miles from Cuba. We live in little village Puerto Escondido, and I am Ernesto."

"I am Anna," Anna said.

The boy's father began to talk to him in Spanish and afterwards the boy turned to Anna again. "My father says that you go into the cabin. We stay out while you rest. When get home, we will tell you. There is some dress that my madre—mother—has in cabin. You wear it." Anna closed the beat-up old door on the cabin and looked around for a moment, then she took off her wet clothes and put on the dry ones that belonged to Ernesto's mother. She lay down on a cot that smelled like fish, but she didn't care. She thanked God she was safe and quickly fell asleep.

She awoke with Ernesto gently moving the cot. He smiled at her as her eyes opened and she looked around, at first forgetting where she was. After a moment she remembered and smiled back at him.

"We are here now, Senorita. I will take you to our casa, where my mother is. My father will leave now."

"But can he do without you?"

"He will have to, because you need me to speak English for you."

Ernesto's father smiled at Anna, and she smiled back. "Muchas gracias. Please tell your father I am very grateful for the help, and I will repay the kindness."

Ernesto spoke Spanish to his father, and then his father answered back. "My father says you no repay anything—we happy to help you, and he wishes you Dios de velocidad—ah…Godspeed in getting home."

Anna looked back at the rickety old boat and wondered how it even floated. Then she followed Ernesto from the old, broken-down dock onto a dirt road that ran in front of it. After they walked on it for a few minutes, he took her up a path that went to a two-room shanty that was their house. His mother came out and he spoke to her in Spanish, and she took Anna's arm and guided her to a bed in the other room. Anna smiled, but shook her head. "I need to get to a telephone—is there one near here?" she asked.

"No, but is telegraph office in the village," Ernesto said.

"Oh, good. Can we walk there?"

"Yes, let me tell mi madre—mother," Ernesto said, and as he turned, his mother walked back with some eggs she had cooked for Anna, and she spoke in Spanish to her son.

"My mother says to eat—because you very weak."

"Yes, I am famished," Anna said. Then she ate the scrambled eggs and a tortilla that the woman had prepared. When she was finished, she smiled warmly at the woman. "That was delicious. You have been so nice to me, but I need to get to the telegraph office now."

Ernesto translated for his mother, and she smiled and waved for Anna to go. They walked together into the center of the village and Anna saw the telegraph wires and knew that it had to be the office. This was also the post office, and a man was sorting mail as she walked up. Ernesto told the man in Spanish that she had to send a telegraph, and he answered back how many pesos it would cost.

"I don't have any money, but I promise to pay as soon as my family picks me up. I'm sure they are looking for me. And you can keep this until they get here," Anna said, taking a gold ring she still had on her finger and passing it to the man.

Ernesto translated, but the man waved off the ring and went to the telegraph machine and looked at Ernesto for the message. Anna began, "Am okay…stop…in village in Cuba, Puerto Escondido…stop… Please come now…stop."

40

"Lorenzo, where do you think he would be?" Paul asked, as they walked from the dock road to Avenida Washington, to get a taxicab.

"Probably at one of the expensive restaurants or bars that Americans like."

"Here is a picture..." Paul took out Bart's photograph and showed it to Lorenzo.

"Yes, we can use that," Lorenzo said, and he hailed a cab, which stopped in front of them. Then he told the driver in Spanish to go to Mission Square. Once there, Lorenzo led the others into a large, expensive restaurant. He then motioned to Paul and asked for the picture of Bart, which he showed to the maître d'. The maître d' said something to him, and Lorenzo turned to Mr. Strickland. "May I have a dollar?" Mr. Strickland reached into his pocket and gave it to him, and he gave it to the man, who said something in Spanish.

"What did he say?" Esther asked impatiently.

"He said he has seen him many times, but not today. He said he also goes to a bar down the street—another favorite for Americans. We can go there now."

Again they followed Lorenzo. The bar was not very full and they were able to look around, but they saw no one. Lorenzo walked out of the bar and they walked a few blocks to another restaurant. There, the manager came out and Lorenzo asked Mr. Strickland for five dollars, which he gave to the man, and he showed him Bart's picture. The man nodded yes, and talked to Lorenzo for a long time. Finally, Lorenzo turned away from him.

"He says he was in earlier and ate here."

"Maybe he is back at the yacht now," Paul said.

"He thinks he is at...a..."

"A what, Lorenzo?" Mr. Strickland asked.

Lorenzo turned away from Esther and spoke in a low voice. "A brothel."

"Well, let's go there," Paul said.

"It will be hard to...there will be several strong men on guard there," Lorenzo said.

"Well, we need to think this out. But let's call home first and see if there is any word," Mr. Strickland said.

"Yes, there is a quiet one at the restaurant we just visited," Lorenzo said, and they followed him there. After they reached it, he talked to the operator and asked her to dial their phone number in New York. Then he passed the phone to Mr. Strickland.

"Hello," Mr. Strickland said, and then he talked louder. "Hello, hello."

"Hello, this is Priscilla."

"Priscilla, have you heard anything yet?"

"Yes, I was hoping you'd call. Anna is safe. She's in a village called Puerto Escondido near Havana."

"Oh, thank God. But what was the name of the city again? The connection is very bad."

"Puerto Escondido," Priscilla almost shouted into the phone so she could be heard.

"Okay, we will go there now."

"She's safe," Mr. Strickland said, as he hung up the phone. "She is in a place called Puerto Escondido."

Esther closed her eyes in relief and Paul smiled.

"That's very close—maybe thirty miles down the coast. We can go back to the boat and get there very quickly," Lorenzo said.

<hr />

After landing in Puerto Escondido, Lorenzo led them from the small harbor, which only had a few broken-down docks, into the village.

"How will we find her?" Esther asked.

"The telegraph man will tell us. It is a very small village and everyone knows everyone," Lorenzo said, as they neared the shack where Anna had sent the telegram.

"This village looks so poor compared to Havana, which is so modern," Esther said, as she wiped her brow from the heat and humidity.

"Yes, that is the problem with Cuba. It is rich and poor and hardly anything in the middle," Lorenzo said.

The houses were painted in festive colors of bright yellow, blue, and chartreuse green. The people smiled at them and small children walked up to them and looked curiously at them. "Very few Americans would come to this village—so you are interesting," Lorenzo explained.

After getting directions, they walked together up the path to the fisherman's old but homey house. Ernesto's father was back by then, and as they walked in, Anna ran to her father and hugged him and then hugged Paul and Esther. She clung to Esther for a long time, and they both cried tears of joy. Mr. Strickland asked Lorenzo to thank the family for helping Anna, and after Anna finally separated from Esther, she turned her attention to the family and then to her father.

"Father, I will tell you the whole story later, but not only did they pull me out of the water, this man and his son and another fisherman stopped some other men in a boat from attacking me. They did much more than they had to. They probably saved my life."

"So what can we do for him—do you have any ideas?"

"Well, the boat is very old and dilapidated."

Mr. Strickland looked at the man and smiled, then turned to Lorenzo. "Would you translate for me, please?"

"Of course."

"Do you know his name, Anna?"

"Yes, it's Mr. Garcia."

"Mr. Garcia—thank you very much for what you have done for my daughter."

"It was my pleasure to help," Mr. Garcia said.

"Mr. Garcia, this is my son, Paul. He likes to fish, so if I were to set my son up to fish here, how much would a good fishing boat—a very good boat and all the rigging—cost to fish like you do?"

Mr. Garcia looked at Paul and then back at Mr. Strickland. "You want a very good boat for your son, so I think it would cost, maybe twenty thousand pesos. But I don't think they let Americans fish here—you have to be Cuban, I think."

Lorenzo translated, and Mr. Strickland smiled at Mr. Garcia. "Well, then, since he can't fish here, we will just have to get the boat for you."

As Lorenzo stopped speaking, Mr. Garcia sat with his mouth open, speechless for a moment. Then he shook his head and held his head down, not looking at Mr. Strickland. "No, I did not help her for a reward. I just believe in treating others the way I would like to be treated—that's what the Bible says."

"You did much more than that—you helped her at risk to yourself. You protected her from other men. Now I also have to treat you the way I would want to be treated—you would not deny me the opportunity to do that, would you?"

Mr. Garcia listened carefully to Lorenzo's translation and looked up, in thought about what Mr. Strickland had said, and appearing a little confused for a moment as he tried to figure it out.

"You wouldn't make me disobedient to God, now would you?" Mr. Strickland added.

"No, I should not do that," Mr. Garcia said, and then he smiled.

"Very good then, that's settled. Lorenzo, what is the exchange rate, please?"

Lorenzo told Mr. Strickland and he counted out some money and gave it to Mr. Garcia.

"Father, will they take dollars here?" Esther asked.

"My dear, they will take an American dollar anywhere in the world, but especially in Cuba. Havana thrives on dollars—isn't that right, Lorenzo?"

Lorenzo nodded, and Mr. Garcia reluctantly took the money, but then he protested, saying something in Spanish to Lorenzo.

"What's the problem?" Mr. Strickland asked.

"He says you gave him too much—this will not only buy the best boat, but there is more than that."

"Please take this gift," Mr. Strickland said. "You can give to others what you don't need. But may I suggest that you tell no one in the village about this until you have your new boat?"

Mr. Garcia smiled again. "Thank you so very much. I will do as you have said, and go to Havana to buy the boat first, then I will help others."

The two men shook hands. "I appreciate what you have done for my sister," Paul said, and he also shook the fisherman's hand, and Anna hugged his wife. When they looked over at Lorenzo, they saw tears in his eyes.

"This is a wonderful day, sir. You are doing a great thing for this family," Lorenzo said, choking up.

41

"Oh, it's so good to hear your voice!" Priscilla said into the phone, as Anna sat on a chair in the hotel room. "I figured you were all right when I got the telegram, but now I can relax and rejoice."

"I can't wait to get home. Please tell Miles I'm safe."

"I will, but I want to know what happened."

"Well, there is so much, but let me call you back because we have to meet with some U.S. marshals and other people in a minute, so I have to go now."

"Good-bye, Sister. I am so happy you are safe."

"Good-bye, Priscilla."

The Stricklands sat in a small conference room at the hotel with two U.S. marshals and the Miami district attorney. One of the marshals nodded as Anna finished telling them what had happened.

"I was in the water a long time before some Cuban fisherman picked me up."

"You're a very brave young lady," the first marshal said admiringly. "We've got the coast guard waiting for Lewis to come back to Miami, and we even have a couple of navy ships. We know he's left Cuba, so he should be caught pretty soon. You must have friends in high places, Mr. Strickland."

"Yes, yes, I do. But what will happen when he's arrested for bootlegging, Mr. Pearson?" Mr. Strickland asked, turning to the district attorney.

Mr. Pearson, a bespectacled man of about forty years of age who often had a wry smile, thought for a moment before answering. "Well, as you know they increased the penalties a year ago, so now he might get up to five years. They used to only get six months, and even now he might get that if he was just caught with a flask. But since he's a major smuggler, I think we might put him away for five years."

"But what about kidnapping and attempted rape—the punishment has to be more for that!" Anna blurted out, her voice rising.

"I understand why you are upset, Miss Strickland, but I don't think you want to press charges on him for those things."

"Why not?" Esther asked.

"Because it will just be your word against his, and being from a well-known family, you might be believed, but there would also be a lot of damage."

"What do you mean by damage?" Paul asked.

"Well, you would have to testify, and the courtroom would become a three-ring circus with reporters and all of that. This story would follow you the rest of your life, and you have to decide if it's worth it."

"If it stops another girl from going through what I have, it is."

"But it may not stop it—there just isn't enough evidence to be certain of a conviction—and you'd be risking your own reputation. You told me you pretended to be your maid, and I don't mean to be offensive, but with his money he will have a very sharp lawyer. And I'm sure they will try to destroy your credibility with the jury by saying if you lied about who you were, you might be lying about this, also."

"But there is a big difference. I can explain why I traded identities with Lucy," Anna said. "What do you think, Father?"

"I'm sorry, Anna, but I think he's right. I think you will be put under a microscope for a long time if this goes to court, and I don't know if it's worth it. I've been able to keep the press out of this, but of course I can't if it goes to a public courtroom. And you mustn't think the reporting will be fair; there will be no end to the stories and lies that are made up about you, and a lot of them may not be pretty."

"But if I want to press charges, would you stand behind me?"

"Yes, I would, but just be sure of your decision. And remember, he will be judged eventually for everything—in the next world if not in this one."

Mr. Pearson, obviously not a believer in what Mr. Strickland said, looked away with a mocking smile.

"Well, I want to press charges, and I want to testify. I will not be silent for my own reputation. How long could he get if we do win?"

Mr. Pearson thought for a moment. "Kidnappers have at the most gotten life in prison—it can also mean the death sentence, but in this case that's unlikely. I'd bet he might get at least fifteen years."

"That's a lot more than five. And I want to see him in court—I want to see him and tell the world what he did, even if we don't win. I want the truth about this…this person to be out."

Mr. Pearson turned to Mr. Strickland and smiled. "Well, sir, your daughter certainly does have spirit. I think she'll be a good witness in court. But I would still think about it, Miss—you don't have to decide until we arrest him. And he should be bringing the contraband in soon."

"What about the IRS? I heard Capone would get more time for not paying his taxes than for bootlegging," Mr. Strickland asked.

"Yes, that's right. It can be ten years, I think. But that's not too easy to prove, unless he was stupid enough to put the money into the bank. If he did that, we can audit his accounts and the IRS could have a pretty good case."

"So that might add to it, Anna," Mr. Strickland said.

"No, I want to press charges. I'm certain, and I will not change my mind, and I don't want anyone to try to get me to change my mind. I want justice, and I will not be the person who stops it from happening because I'm a coward."

"I agree with you," Esther said.

"What about you, Paul?"

"I'm sorry, Anna. I just don't know. I want him punished, but I'm concerned about the effect this will have on you. He's already terrorized you."

"And that's why I want to press charges. Let's do it now. Is there some paperwork or something?"

Mr. Pearson smiled slightly because she was so strident. "Yes, we can write the complaint in my office—it's getting late, so let's make it first thing in the morning. I understand you didn't exactly hit it off with the chief?"

"It's pretty clear he's protecting Lewis, but we can discuss that later," Mr. Strickland said.

"Oh, don't be so suspicious, Mr. Strickland. The chief is a good guy when you get to know him."

The second U.S. marshal stood up and spoke. "Mr. Strickland, if you and your daughter could stay around the hotel, we'll call you when we arrest Lewis. We'll need Miss Strickland to make a positive I.D. if she's going to press charges."

"We'll either be in the restaurant or in our rooms," Mr. Strickland said, and he got up and headed for the door as the rest of the family followed. When they got into the hallway and Mr. Pearson had left,

Anna turned to her father.

"Do you think he's in cahoots with the chief? Is that why he doesn't want me to press charges?"

Mr. Strickland looked around to make certain no one but the family members could hear him. "There's a good chance of that, but everything he said to you also made sense."

"Father, you're beginning to sound like you're on his side."

"No, Anna, I'm on your side. I just want you to make a decision you can live with years from now."

"I can live with it—I will live with it."

"I know you think so, but you're young now. Things may look a little different later," Mr. Strickland said.

They reached the restaurant and it was still early and most of the tables were empty. Jeremy had just come to work, and he walked over to them. "May I seat you?"

"Yes, may we have a table with an ocean view?" Mr. Strickland asked.

"Oh, yes sir. There are many tables available."

As they neared the table, Jeremy talked to Anna in a low tone. "Everyone in the place is so happy you are safe."

"Thank you, Jeremy," Anna said.

"But now I know why you were sticking up for the aristocracy," he added.

Paul heard him and stared at him. "I think that will be all, maître d'. Thank you." Jeremy looked at him, his feathers a little ruffled, and then he walked away.

"One of your fellow workers?" Paul asked.

"Yes, and he hates rich people," Anna added.

"Well, I don't know why he's working here, then," Paul said.

"That's what I told him."

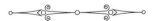

Bart Lewis sat comfortably in the cockpit of his yacht, tilted back on his captain's chair, drinking a martini with one hand and steering with the other. He was a little drunk from the martinis and from the party he had been to the night before in Havana, and his eyes were closing and opening as he got closer to Miami. He was falling asleep when a large wave jolted his yacht, and startled him. He looked towards to Miami and realized he was very close to the shore, but there were also many more boats than he expected to see. He sat bolt upright, and he stared

246

again towards the Miami coastline and grabbed his telescope. "What the…?" he said to himself as he noticed that most of the boats were coast guard vessels. Then he turned around and searched the waters southward and saw that there were two navy ships and a couple of other boats closing in on him. He put the telescope down and rushed downstairs into the cabin and found a rifle and some ammunition. Then he bent down and opened another drawer and reached into it but was surprised to find Anna's purse. He looked at it for a moment and then dug deeper and retrieved a pistol and some ammunition for it. He loaded both guns, put the pistol in his waistband, then grabbed her purse and went back to the cockpit.

When he reached it, he put the rifle down and picked up the telescope again and surveyed the boats around him. Then he looked out at the water, his face showing how serious he knew the situation to be. He thought of the purse and opened it and saw Anna's driver's license and other identification. "So that's what this is about. She is Strickland's daughter and now everyone is after me—the whole armada. She never seemed like a waitress—I should have listened to her," he said to himself.

Looking through the telescope again, he shook his head, took the pistol out of his waistband, and put it down. "No chance with them," he said to himself as he stepped out of the cockpit and walked over to the railing, wobbling a little from drinking so much. He untied a life preserver and jumped off the boat, but in his somewhat drunken condition he slipped as he jumped and his foot caught in the railing, causing him to bang his head against the side of the boat and knocking him unconscious as he fell into the water. The life preserver dropped from his hands and he went under the water.

After they had finished their early dinner, Lucy came down to the dining room. When she saw the Strickland family at the table, she came over and gave Anna an apologetic look. "Oh, I'm glad you're safe," she said.

"Sit down, Lucy," Mr. Strickland said. He waited for her to sit before speaking again. "Lucy, you will go back to New York tonight on the bus and leave all of Anna's clothes here. She has put yours in your room."

"Yes sir, I saw them when I woke up this morning."

"When you get back to the house, collect your things, and Priscilla will give you your two weeks' wages. You can stay in your maid's quarters the night you arrive, and then you must leave."

"You mean you're firing me?" Lucy said, angrily.

"That's exactly what I mean."

"But I only made that one mistake."

"And that mistake may have cost Anna her life."

"But it's so hard to get a job these days."

"Here is the money for the trip back. The bus leaves at six. You have plenty of time to pack and get to the station if you start now."

Lucy stared for a moment and then turned away in a huff. As she walked away, the first U.S. marshal walked into the restaurant and walked up to their table.

"Miss Strickland, you won't have to identify Mr. Lewis."

"Why not? I said I wanted to file charges."

"Because Mr. Lewis is dead."

"What? How did that happen?"

"When he saw we had him surrounded, he jumped off the boat, but his foot tripped on the railing and it threw his head into the side of the boat, which knocked him unconscious. One of our men saw it through a telescope, but by the time they got to him, he had drowned."

Anna was quiet for a moment, and then she started crying a little. "This is so strange, it's like a terrible nightmare."

"Why did he try to leave the boat? Didn't he know you'd pick him up?" Paul asked.

"He knew that if we caught him on the boat he'd be charged, but if he got away from it, he could say someone else took his boat and he might get off. Bootleggers know that, so they always try to get away from the contraband. He was close enough to the shore to swim in, if he hadn't hit his head."

"Well, at least you don't have to testify against him," Esther said, putting her arm around Anna. But Anna pushed away.

"Thank you, Marshal. I guess we can all go back to New York now?" Mr. Strickland asked.

"Yes sir. Have a good trip."

He walked away and Paul looked over at Anna. "Are you crying for him? I thought you wanted to see justice, and he evidently got it from God."

"I know, but...I can't explain it. He was so rotten, but to be dead so quickly. It's just a shock." Anna reached out to Esther and touched her arm, and Esther took her hand and smiled back at her.

42

Priscilla ran out to the driveway when she saw the Duesenberg drive up. As soon as the car stopped, she opened the door and hugged Anna, tears flowing from her eyes. "Oh, I'm so happy to see you. I don't know what I'd do if something had happened to you."

"I can't tell you how wonderful it is to be home," Anna said as she also began to cry. They walked into the house with Paul and their father following. Mr. Standish beamed at Anna as she walked through the door.

"It's so glorious to have you safely back, Miss Anna," he said, and Anna hugged him, causing him to blush.

"Thank you," she said, and Standish walked towards the car.

"Don't move those bags yourself, Standish—have the gardener do it."

"Yes sir—I'll just take the light ones, then."

"As you please," Mr. Strickland said.

As they entered the house, Esther turned to her father. "Can we take Anna upstairs now—we don't want to be rude, but we want to talk to her."

"Of course," Mr. Strickland said, but Anna turned to her father and hugged him for a moment and then hugged Paul. "You were both so wonderful, and brave, and Esther too. You could have just sent someone but you came yourselves. Driving all night and…no one could have done more. I am so grateful."

They walked upstairs together and then went into Esther's bedroom and Anna collapsed on the bed while the other two sat on the sofa. Anna looked up at the ornate canopy and smiled with relief.

"So how are you feeling?" Priscilla asked.

"I'm not sure yet. It all seems surreal. I keep thinking it's a bad dream and I'll wake up."

"At least it's over—no courtroom and no press to deal with," Esther said.

"Yes, I have been spared all of that. Now I have to get things back to normal—somehow."

"You have been through so much," Priscilla said, and she moved to the bed and sat down next to Anna. "I'm so sorry I started all of this—it was a big mistake, and I dragged all of you into it."

"It was our decision," Esther said. "It's not your fault."

"So we set out to find men who wouldn't marry us for our money, and it didn't work for anyone but Prissy," Anna said.

"It didn't work for me, either," Priscilla said.

"What do you mean—I thought he proposed—didn't he? When I left everything was fine," Esther said.

"He broke it off while you were gone. I guess I can't say he really broke it off because he never really asked. He told me he only wants a business relationship now, so I quit."

"Oh, Prissy, I'm so sorry," Anna said, and she reached over and hugged her sister.

"You're sorry for me? I've been through nothing compared to you."

"Tell us more about what happened. Why would he call it off so quickly?" Esther asked.

"Well, I think it may have been his mother— But I want to hear everything that happened to Anna. I only got some of it on the phone."

"I'll fill you in. I don't think Anna wants to talk about it anymore, do you?" Esther said.

"No, you tell Prissy about it. I'm looking forward to getting some sleep in my own bed for a change."

Anna slept for over twelve hours. When she slowly awoke, she stretched as she looked around her sun-drenched room and through the window panes of the tall French doors that went out to the patio. She could see flowers blooming around the periphery of the tiled walkway adjacent to the patio. Her sisters liked roses, and there were roses of many colors—red, yellow, pink, and white—but she was partial to the simple daisies, and she loved the fragrance from the honeysuckle vine that ran along the patio doors. The coolness of the morning had left, and she opened the door to breathe in that fragrance, and realized that she had never been so grateful for what she had. She knew that if she had been the waitress she pretended to be, Bart Lewis might have gone free. She thought about what Jeremy had said about rich people getting justice when poor people might not, and she knew there was some truth to that, and wondered what she might do to help other women that had been in her position. The thought left her mind as their white Persian cat, Summer, walked in when she opened the doors. She purred and wanted to be petted and rubbed against Anna's legs, showing how much she missed her. "You didn't forget about me, did you?" she said to the cat.

She thought of how much she missed talking to Miles—what a comfort he had always been to her. She wondered how he could have known about where she was and so been such a big part of her rescue, and she decided to visit him. Dressing in a loose-fitting white summer dress with small pastel flowers on it, she put her hair back in a quick pony tail and put on a floppy hat to keep the sun out of her eyes. Then she walked to the garage and found her bicycle and rode to his house. It was very close, but she felt like riding the bike, and as she peddled up his driveway, she saw the family doctor coming out of the house. She put the bike down and ran up to the door before the butler had closed it.

"Is everything all right? Is Miles all right?" she inquired.

"Yes, madam, Miles is fine, but his father had a shortness of breath. He's quite all right now."

As the butler finished speaking, Miles came to the foyer, and Anna ran over to him, and hugged him and kissed him on the neck. "Oh, Miles, how can I thank you for what you did? You rescued me."

"No, God did—He just used me."

"I know but… Oh, but how is your father—is he okay?"

"He'll be all right. He hardly ever exercises, and then he got it into his head to lift some of my weights. He tried to lift one that was too heavy and it got to him. But he's okay now."

"Oh, I'm so glad. So how have you been while I've been gone?"

"I've been…very concerned. It's just so good to see you again. I know you went through a lot—Priscilla told me all about it."

"So, do you have any new poetry?"

"Not really, but—follow me, and let's get out of the dark part of the house," Miles said, and rolled his chair into the sunny drawing room. Anna noticed that there were newspapers from many other cities and even other countries in the room.

"My, you are becoming international."

"Oh—those are… Well, Father uses this room too—sometimes."

Anna noticed his hesitancy as he mentioned the room and wondered why he was so concerned with this answer. "It doesn't matter, silly. I was just teasing a little. So tell me, do you have any new poetry?"

"Not really. But I am curious about how the identity switch started."

"First you must show me your latest, `Not really' means that you have something—don't you?"

"Well, it's very short—not much at all."

"Let me be the judge of that. It doesn't have to be long to be good."

Miles nodded and then quoted the poem from memory.

"Time whispering to me—this is the treasure, don't you see?
Eyes clear and seeing bright things—the song summer sings;
Soul reaching and considering every day—move forward this way;
Heart trying for truth that only God shows—only He knows;
Life precious but hard and unknown—seeds are sown;
Some things tangle but some straighten—my spirit has grown."

"Miles, that's another great poem you've written—very deep though. I need to read it to grasp all of it. You must have it written down somewhere, didn't you?"

"Yes, but it's just a silly—"

Anna walked over and put her finger over his lips. "You mustn't say such things. It's not silly. It is very good. You are talented and you must send these poems to a publisher."

"I don't think many people are reading poetry these days—now they want sultry novels and such."

"Well, I read poetry. And I want to send this poem and the other one in to some places. May I have your permission?"

"Do what you must," Miles said, smiling.

"Do you have any others?"

Miles hesitated. "Not really."

"So how many do you have?"

"Really, Anna, some of them are personal and some aren't finished. I think only the two that you have read might be suitable for the public."

"Okay, we'll start with those. And when I go back to school, I'll also give them to my English Literature professor—he's very interested in poetry. Did you finally make up your mind where you are going this fall?"

"Not yet."

"Well, you should—you can't stay in this...gloomy house all of the time."

"I get out quite a bit, but..."

"But what?"

"Well, it's very difficult to get around at a university, and I was so tired of asking people to help me in high school. It's humiliating. I decided to build up my arms to get stronger before I try school."

"Yes, I noticed—you're starting to look like Hercules. But I could also help you. If you went to Columbia I could transfer to Barnard from Sarah Lawrence. Barnard is so close to Columbia that I could help you when you need it."

"But you miss the point—I don't want to be reliant on anyone. But I appreciate the offer. Now tell me about what happened."

Anna took a breath and then stood up and stretched. "We devised this plan—Esther and Priscilla and I devised it. It was Priscilla's idea to begin with. I told you about Alice's husband, do you remember?"

"Yes, he told her he only married her for her money—is that what you mean?"

"Yes, and we decided that we needed to pretend that we didn't have money so when we met someone we could be certain he wouldn't want us just for that."

"So you switched with Lucy?"

"Yes, she pretended to be me, and I went to work as a waitress."

"Weren't you concerned about Lucy hurting your reputation—don't you know that she comes off as very low class?"

"That came up later—that did bother me."

"So that guy who tried to assault you thought you were poor?"

"Yes—that may be why he thought he could get away with it."

"I wish you had told me about this before you left. Remember, I said something was leading me to tell you to be careful."

Anna was starting to get irritated at Miles's attitude and she stopped speaking for a moment, then answered slowly. "Miles, we all decided we would not tell anyone. In fact, I wanted to tell you, but I had promised my sisters."

"But to say you are someone else is a lie—it's wrong. Can't you just trust God to find you a husband who doesn't care about your money?"

"You make it sound like it was some terrible thing we did. It was just an innocent scheme to find out about someone's true character."

"No—it was a deliberate deception. And if you had met the man of your dreams, would he not have questioned your character knowing that the first thing you said to him was a lie? How could he trust you again—knowing that?"

"Miles, I don't want to hear any more of this!" Anna said, sobbing with tears of frustration. "I don't like your judgmental tone. Now I need to go."

She turned and ran from the house, almost colliding with the butler as she reached the front door. Miles tried to follow in his wheelchair, and cried out to her, but she did not hear him. "Anna, I'm sorry. I just tried to be…honest." He looked down at his legs and then backed up and shook his head, closing his eyes. "Miles, you fool!"

Anna ran in the house and up to her room, and Esther watched as she went by, noticing her eyes were red and she was upset. She followed Anna up to the bedroom where she found her sister collapsed on the bed.

"What's wrong—what happened?"

Anna spoke her words slowly, choked up with tears. "Miles said I'm a liar and a deceiver. He's become Mister Holier Than Thou. I can't stand him anymore! I never want to see him again."

Esther walked over to her and stroked her hair for a moment, then spoke consolingly. "But he's been such a good friend. Don't write him off so quickly—we all make mistakes. You know he cares about you, and he was the one God chose to show us where you were…. Was he talking about the identity switch?"

"Yes, he acted like I was a terrible person because of what we did," Anna said, her voice still cracking as she began to regain her composure. "He said if I had met someone while I was pretending to be Lucy, the man could never trust me again because I began the relationship with a lie."

"That is harsh, Anna, but remember that Miles has a prophetic edge, so he speaks his mind very clearly and that can hurt. But I have to say he's right to some extent. I felt a twinge in my heart when I agreed to have David tested, and the trouble you had in Florida was all because of it."

"Not you, too! How much more can I take? Especially after all I've been through!" Anna said, starting to cry again.

"Okay, I'm sorry."

"Just leave me alone."

"Yes, I will," Esther said, and she stood up and walked quietly to the door, closing it gently.

43

At the New York Press Club, Mr. Strickland got up to speak and Priscilla and Paul watched him make his way to the podium. Flashbulbs from many cameras lit up the room as he took his place in front of the crowd and spoke into the large microphone.

"Good morning," he said. "I want to make a statement on behalf of the Strickland companies and subsidiaries, and then you can ask questions."

"Is it true that you only have about six months left before it all crashes?" one reporter yelled at him.

"Why did you lie about your debt? Don't you care about your stockholders?" someone else shouted.

Joseph waited for the crowd to quiet down, and then he spoke again. "I have not personally, nor have any of my companies, borrowed any money, and we are not in debt at all, and the public companies we own will open their books to confirm this. We don't open the books of our private companies, but I am here to state that they are not in debt either."

"But your stock has gone down—you can't deny that," one reporter said.

"Of course it's gone down—it went down with all the rest in '29 and then bounced back and went down again—it's followed the cycle of many companies."

"But it just dropped more than ever before—it's near the bottom now."

"It went down because people think we are bankrupt, but we are not."

"Then why does everyone say you are?" a reporter asked.

"Because of a rumor that is false and not true."

"Mr. Strickland, do you know who started the rumor?"

Priscilla and Paul were tense as they waited for their father to answer. They knew how he felt about lying, and the question was posed very clearly. Priscilla found it hard to breathe as she waited for him to answer.

"Yes, I do…it was started by someone who made up a story that wasn't true and it got spread by other people until everyone believed it. But it is not true. Our company has not borrowed any money, nor do we plan to."

"Didn't you lose money when the banks closed?"

"Yes, we lost some from the bank collapse in '29 like everyone else, but not everything, and we are not in debt, and have not borrowed one cent from anyone, and we are profitable. Any more questions?"

"Who do you think would do this to you—who would spread a rumor like this?"

Priscilla looked at her father for a moment, her stomach churning. Joseph hesitated for a moment before answering. "Well, since we have now rectified the situation, I would prefer not to belabor the discussion on how it started. That is irrelevant at this point."

"Mr. Strickland, there was a rumor about your daughter having some trouble in Miami…"

"Be careful about printing rumors—you don't want to repeat your mistakes. You've seen how this one about our companies hoodwinked the press. Now I believe I've answered enough questions. I came to assure everyone that our companies are solvent, and not in debt, and as a matter of fact, I do not buy the stock of other companies and have never speculated in the stock market, even when it was at its peak. I only invest in my own businesses. Thank you, ladies and gentlemen."

Joseph walked to his table, and Priscilla smiled at him. "You did a great job."

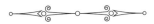

The living room was littered with dirty plates, old food cans, newspapers, and magazines that were strewn across the floor. They seemed incongruous in this stylish apartment that overlooked Central Park, and they were even more inconsistent with David Holt's personality, which was always known for neatness and order. But these days he was living from the money he had saved and knew that he would be moving out soon because of the exorbitant rent. He had looked for a job, but it was a terrible time to find one, made worse by the fact that he had just left an organization that had been on the brink of bankruptcy before it was turned over to its creditors.

He lay in bed. It was eleven in the morning, but he didn't care. There seemed no reason to get up anymore. He'd reconciled with his father, but that was the only good thing that had happened since the business fell apart. None of his Wall Street friends wanted to see him anymore. He wondered about that, since he'd been available to help some of them when they were at low points. But there was no one for him. He thought of Esther from time to time, but he would never want her to see him in his condition. He watched the ceiling fan spin around. It was another hot day, and he thought about what he might do. There were some jobs out there, but no one wanted to hire him. The unpleasant realization that he might just have to move back in with his father dawned on him—imagine having to live at home again at his age. Well, at least they were getting along now, he thought as the phone rang. He was going to ignore it, but it rang and rang and rang, so he got up to answer it, but then it stopped. He breathed heavily, happy that it was no longer an intrusion, when it rang again.

"Hello," he said slowly.

"Hello, David."

"Hi, Gran—how are you—are things well with you?"

"Yes, but are they well with you?"

"Um, well, I guess so. I guess they are okay. I made peace with Father."

"Yes, I know that. He told me. I am very pleased about that and proud of you. You were finally able to forgive him."

"Well, he meant well—he just got off track at the wrong time. You and him are about all I've got now, and I don't want to lose either of you."

"Can you come over today?"

"Oh, I don't know Gran...I'm pretty busy."

"It's exceedingly important."

"Are you sure you're okay?"

"Yes, it's not about my health—it's not about me, it's about... well, you just need to come. Please visit your old Gran, I do have something very important to talk to you about."

"Okay. How about...what about two o'clock, would that be a good time?"

"Yes, dear, I will look forward to it."

David had not shaved for many days, and when he looked into the mirror, he winced. "Now that's no way to look for your grandmother," he said to himself as he reached for the razor. He also showered and put on fresh clothing, and was soon at his grandmother's house. She smiled widely when she saw him and gave him a hug.

"How are you getting along?" she asked.

"Oh, I'm surviving."

"Well, I think that you will survive a lot better after we have this talk. Would you like some cookies and milk?"

"No thanks, Gran," David said, wondering if her age was finally getting to her mind as he thought that was an offer that should be made to children. It also made him wonder what the "very important" meeting was about. He expected it might be a sermon to him about something, but he was determined not to react in a way that might disturb his grandmother.

"Well, sit down, dear," she said, and both of them found a place on her large sofa. "What would you do if you had a large sum of money right now?"

David was taken by surprise with the question, and he looked at her for a moment, studying her face for some understanding of the reason for the question. "Why would you want to know that, Gran?"

"Just answer the question, David," she said in her schoolteacher voice.

"Okay, Gran. If there was enough money, I'd open a-five-and dime in one of the underserved areas of the country. We were always looking for new locations, and I'd take the best one and begin with that. Even with the Depression people are buying five-and-dime, but you have to know what products they will buy, and you have to know how to make the right deals with the manufacturers to make it work. And I do."

"I believe you."

"The profits are thin now, so it takes a very experienced person to know how to stock the stores correctly."

"And you know how to do that, also, I suppose."

"Yes, Gran. Also, the real estate is dirt cheap right now, but it won't stay that way forever, so it makes sense to buy and not lease. Now what was it you really wanted to talk to me about?"

"David, I have money you don't know about and I want to invest it. I was waiting for you to reconcile with your father, and now that

260

you've forgiven him, I'm ready to help you."

"What? Are you serious, Gran? I knew you had enough for yourself, but you also have more than that?"

"Yes, my dear," she said, passing him a bankbook which she had opened to a certain page. He looked at it and whistled, and shook his head in disbelief.

"And you want to invest this with me?"

"Yes, I'm going to let you use the money interest-free."

"How much of it?"

"All of it."

David looked at her, a bit stunned. "I could open ten stores with this much money. Oh, but I don't know, Gran. Times are strange and I don't want to make a mistake and cause you to lose your money."

"I have faith in you. But if you do lose it, you lose it. Just promise me that you'll be wise in using it, and you won't borrow any other money. Just use this. Are you willing to do that?"

"Well, of course I would promise you that—I don't want to borrow and get overextended—that's what has sunk a lot of people. I was never for that—Father did it, but I didn't know about it. But this is so much money—I thought you'd given everything to Father when Grandfather gave him the business."

"David, I love your father dearly, but I held back because I was concerned about the way he handled money. He was always taking risks that were too great and it finally caught up with him. But you are not that way. That is why I'm giving it to you and not him."

"This would be a fresh start—I will be very careful—I'll only open one store at a time and wait until it's profitable before I open another one. Yes, I think I can make a good profit for you, Gran."

"But I don't want a profit—just repay what you use when you can—I want no profit or interest. So will you take it, then?"

"Yes, I will, and how can I thank you?"

"Well, you could have some milk and cookies," Gran said, smiling.

David smiled back. "Yes, I think we should celebrate with milk and cookies, and yours are the best in New York!"

His grandmother got up and brought the cookies over to the coffee table. Then she poured two glasses of milk and sat down next to him. David held his glass up and they toasted. "To this new venture," David said.

"One more thing, dear. Would you mind letting your father

work with you if he wants to?"

"Of course, Gran. He knows the business inside and out, so I'll ask him."

"Any chance of you still marrying that Strickland girl? Is that completely over now?"

"Yes, I think it is, but I still…"

"You still love her, don't you? It's your pride that has stopped that from happening the way it should have."

"I don't know if it would work out now—it's probably too late, and I never explained myself—I was ashamed to."

"You don't know until you try. Girls like Esther are hard to find. Here—I put this account in your name," she said as she handed him the bankbook.

"Thank you Gran and thank you God," David said, as he hugged his grandmother. "This is hard to believe—it's like a gift from heaven."

44

"Well, the stock is up again," Priscilla said, as she reclined on the red velvet sofa in Anna's large bedroom, and read the paper.

"Oh, I'm so glad—Father has suffered so much for what we did," Esther said, as she combed Anna's long auburn hair.

"You should have seen him at the press conference—the questions were so pointed I thought he would have to tell them that it was all my doing. But he was able to maneuver around them without lying—he was like an artist with words."

"Well, it did get Mrs. Marry the Richest Man I Can Find off his back. I still can't understand how he missed what she was really like," Esther said as she put the comb away and walked over to Anna's bed and sat down.

"She's a very beautiful woman—that has blinded many a good man, I think. Now I just want to find one that I can blind long enough to marry me," Priscilla added.

"You mean before he finds out what you're really like?" Anna said mischievously.

"Before he finds out I can beat him up with just a pillow," Priscilla said, hitting Anna with a pillow from her bed. "Seriously, though, I think it's so easy to be deceived by looks. Father and Ingersoll, and you and Bart Lewis—and I read Herbert wrong also. It's scary!"

"Don't forget that I read David wrong. Just where are there men who we can trust? How do we know who the person really is until it's too late? And I'm not just talking about gold diggers—look at Bart, gangster in disguise," Esther said.

"Oh, please don't talk about him anymore," Anna said.

"I'm sorry. But we have all learned a lot of lessons if nothing else—haven't we?" Esther asked.

"I guess so, but I'm still trying to figure out exactly what they are. I guess if I'd never pretended to be someone else, I wouldn't have met Herbert and that would have saved me a lot of heartache, and Anna wouldn't have had her ordeal. But it helped Father and you, didn't it?" Priscilla asked as she looked at Esther.

"I honestly don't know—maybe I would have figured it out anyway, and Father is not stupid, and we were praying for him to see it," Esther said.

"We should have just trusted God—that's what Miles said," Anna added.

"Miles said that, did he?" Priscilla said.

"Yes, and when you think about it, that's about the only way we can know who to marry and who to avoid. We need to give God a chance to show us."

"Well, we're all starting over again now—fresh start. Let's not get discouraged," Esther said, and they heard the phone ring. A few moments later Mr. Standish knocked on the door and Priscilla opened the door.

"Mr. David Holt for Miss Esther," he announced.

Esther looked surprised and then she pursed her lips. "Please tell him I'm busy—I am busy talking to my sisters, so that is true."

"Yes, Miss Esther."

"Are you sure you don't want to just talk to him a little—don't you want to know why he's calling?" Anna asked as Mr. Standish closed the door.

"I don't know and I don't care, but I think I can figure it out. It seems interesting that he calls just after the press conference and after the stock is back up. I mean, when he got the letter saying we were bankrupt he dropped me right away, and now, just like clockwork, he's calling again. You think he would at least be more subtle."

"Priscilla sat next to her sister and put her arm around her. I'm sorry, Esther, I…"

Esther started crying and Anna also came over and hugged her. "I don't want you two to see me like this."

"It's okay—anyone would feel that way," Anna said.

"Yes, you have a right to be angry," Priscilla said.

"But you don't understand. I'm not angry—I still have mixed feelings about him. That's what's bothering me. I can't stand to see what he has become and what a perfect fool I was."

"We've all been perfect fools, including Father—but at least that's better than being an imperfect fool," Priscilla said.

"A gangster, two gold diggers, and a stuck-up momma's boy—we really hit the jackpot!" Anna said, smiling.

Esther smiled also although she was crying, and she picked up the pillow and threw it at Anna, but she ducked and it hit Priscilla. "Oh, well, both of you deserved it," she said, and they all started laughing but stopped when the phone rang again. Soon Mr. Standish was at the door again.

"It's Mr. Holt again, Miss. He says he wants to talk to you, but if you are busy, he wants to know when you will be available."

Esther dried her eyes from her tears, not certain which ones were from sadness and which were from laughter. "Tell Mr. Holt I won't be available until…until about 1960," Esther said, and they began laughing again. Mr. Standish tried not to show it, but his face betrayed some slight amusement as he waited patiently for a proper answer. "Oh, I'm sorry, please just tell him that I am not available and I would prefer that he did not call again."

"As you wish, Miss Esther," Mr. Standish said.

"And Mr. Standish—I regret you are in the middle of this."

"Please do not concern yourself, miss—I understand and I am pleased to be of service."

Mr. Standish left and Anna fell back on her bed and stared at her teak-wood canopy, which was draped at the top with red velvet that matched her sofa. "You were wondering where the men are we can trust—but I trust Father, and Paul, and I trust Miles—but those are the only three."

"I think they're one in a thousand, or a million," Esther said.

"Well, there must be some men like that we just haven't met yet—they can't all be greedy and selfish," Priscilla said.

"Are you sure of that?" Esther said, and then she threw a pillow at Priscilla and giggled.

"No, but if we're going to regress to childhood, then I want a real pillow fight," Priscilla said, grabbing two pillows and throwing them at Esther and Anna at the same time. Her sisters picked up some others and the feathers started flying amidst the laughter.

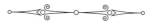

The butler knocked on Miles's bedroom door. "Master Miles, Miss Anna Strickland is in the foyer," he announced. Miles was lying in bed and was almost asleep.

"I wonder why she didn't call," he said.

"She did not say. Would you like me to tell her you are unable to see her now?"

"No, I want to see her. She can wait in the drawing room and I'll be in there shortly."

The butler ushered her in, and Anna looked around the room and noticed that there were about five newspapers on the desk where Miles sat. She walked over and picked up the New York Times and glanced at it. Then she picked up the Los Angeles Times. She noticed that the business sections were out of the papers and were stacked on one side of the desk. Then she saw other newspapers on a bookshelf on one side of the room. She walked over and noticed the London Times, a newspaper from India, and other domestic papers like the Denver Post. Life magazine and other magazines were also stacked up. She wondered why Miles seemed defensive when she had asked about the papers—and he did say they were his father's, she remembered.

She walked over to his desk and noticed some writing on a large pad, which she recognized as Miles's. There were many numbers under the headings of Steel, Oil, Copper, Gold, Silver, and Other Commodities. A freehand graph that was next to the pad on a loose sheet of paper appeared to track the price of several commodities over the past three years. She picked up the graph and noticed a small pad under it. She looked around for a moment, and then she opened the pad, and saw that it was a collection of poems, evidently written by Miles. She began to read the first one.

Anna—her smile like the sunshine on a summer day;
A darting glance, but there's no chance, I would ever get to say
The way I feel, when she looks at me, and I must turn away.
Anna—her eyes are soft and sweet—the kindest I've ever seen;
I must not look—she takes my breath away,
Her face is so serene;
I cannot tell her, our friendship would end,
For me she's just a dream.

Anna—she moves so effortlessly,
As she walks in and sits near me;
I swallow hard, I try to smile, my heart she must not see;
This is a love that I must hide; it's a love that cannot be.
Anna—she's like a beautiful flower,

With a fragrance that's so rare;
When I see her face, my spirit soars, and I feel I've not a care;
But when she leaves, joy leaves too,
And there's nothing but despair.

Miles entered the room as she was reading, and she looked up guiltily.

"What are you reading?" he asked in a demanding tone.

"The most beautiful poem I've ever read," she said, almost in tears over the poem. She smiled at him and began reading it to him, but he became angry and interrupted her.

"You aren't supposed to read that—you're snooping, and I did not think you would do such a thing!" He turned away angrily and left the room, but she followed after him.

"But I love this poem—can we talk about it?" Anna said as he rolled down the hallway.

"No, leave me alone—it is just a poem, and I thought you would misunderstand if you saw it."

"Misunderstand what? What are you talking about? Isn't it about me?"

"Absolutely not. It's not about you. Now you barged in here and didn't even call...."

"Because I wanted to ask you to forgive me for last time. You were right about everything you said, and I was taking a walk, and I didn't think you'd mind if I just came over.... You've always been happy to see me before."

"Well, I do mind."

"Oh, I thought we were friends. I thought I could drop in on you and tell you anything and it would be all right. I thought you were that kind of friend. Was I wrong?"

"Anna, I really don't want to discuss this right now. Can we talk about this some other time?" Miles said, and he rolled to his bedroom and used a wooden device to close the door. Anna looked around and then walked back to the drawing room and opened the book again. She found a pencil and a piece of paper and copied the poem, and then she walked towards the foyer, where the butler saw her.

"Hello, Miss Strickland. Very nice to see you again," he said, and she nodded as he opened the door for her to exit.

Anna went home and stayed quiet about the encounter with Miles, but she opened up the paper with the poem on it several times and read it to herself. After dinner, Esther and Priscilla sat in the living room and Esther played several classical pieces on the piano and ended with Für Elise. When she sat down on the sofa, Anna applauded. Then she said, "What is true love, really? I mean I know there is the attraction we have to someone, but that can't be it, because we can be attracted to lots of people."

"Yes, that's lust, not love, I think," Esther said.

"Then what makes it different from love? You see someone and like the way he looks—that's usually the first thing, isn't it? And then if you get to know him, and like him, you keep seeing him—but how do you know if you love him?"

"I think you just know. You have that special feeling for the person," Priscilla said.

"But what makes that special feeling—what characterizes it? Isn't it just that you want to spend time with the person? That when he's gone, you miss him?"

"Yes, I suppose so," Esther said.

"But how is that different from having a friend? I mean, if you have a male friend that you like to spend time with, does that mean you love him?" Anna continued.

"Perhaps it depends on how much time you want to spend with him. I might like talking to someone about something for an hour or so—that might be informative, particularly if the man has knowledge in an area I'm interested in, but that doesn't mean I love him. I'd have to say that it would be a person that you would like to be around all of the time. That you wouldn't get tired of," Esther answered.

"And maybe someone who you get jealous about if he's around someone else," Priscilla added.

"But it also has to be someone that you feel comfortable being intimate with. I don't think I could marry someone that didn't interest me at all that way. Call it lust if you want to, but it's part of the equation. But on the other hand, if that's all there is, it can't last. Remember that everyone handsome today will be old and gray tomorrow, so if you can't deal with that, don't get involved," Esther said.

"I think it has to be something that touches your heart about the person. Something special—not in a physical way, but that you just care about them, and you think about them. That's why it's hard to deal with if they fail you—you have to get them out of your mind."

"Yes, I know what that's like," Priscilla said.

"Herbert is still bothering you, then?" Anna asked.

"Yes, but I don't know why. He was such a pill sometimes, and he shouts when he gets angry. I don't like the idea of living with that so I guess it worked for the best. Still, there is something about him—something about his personality, as flawed as it was, that I'm having a hard time getting over. And he didn't do things the way others do them. At first I didn't like that, but in some ways that unpredictability had a charm about it, and when he was charming, well…he was very charming."

45

Anna called Miles, but he did not return her call, so she made a point of looking for him at church after the service was over, but the church was large, and she never saw him. She thought he might not have come, but then she remembered that his driver normally parked the special car that they used to transport him in his wheelchair in the back of the church, so she walked in that direction, through a hallway, when suddenly he turned a corner and was in front of her. She ran to catch up with him, which was difficult because he was moving so fast.

"Miles...Miles, slow down, please," she called out. He turned and saw her, and hesitantly slowed down for her to catch up. "I want to talk to you about the poem."

"It means nothing—it's not about you, it's about someone else."

"Who could it be about if it's not about me?"

"You know the Tolstoy novel, Anna Karenina? I wrote it about her."

Anna pursed her lips in unbelief. "Really?"

"Yes, really, but I thought you would misunderstand, and that is why I was embarrassed."

"I see. She is an interesting character—but I didn't know you were in love with a fictional woman. Especially one as sordid as her, with adultery and all."

"Are you really so daft! I wrote the poem from the perspective of Count Vronsky, who was at first hopelessly in love with her. That's why he says it's a love that cannot be...you've read the novel—you must understand."

"Well, I thought that they ended up together...."

"It was before that, when he first met her. And since she was married, he thought it wouldn't happen. Do you understand now?"

Anna looked at him for a long time before answering. "Yes, I think I understand, Miles. I just hope our friendship will continue."

"Yes, of course—but maybe in a different way. I'm sorry I called you daft. Please forgive me. But now you know what the misunderstanding was about. The poem was not about you," Miles said, and he briskly wheeled his chair down the hallway, and she stood and watched. When he reached the door, he hit it very hard with his right arm, which threw it open wide enough for him to get through it.

Later that day, Anna sat in the living room while the radio played, but she was staring in the opposite direction and not paying attention to it. Esther walked in and turned it off, and she did not respond. "A penny for your thoughts?" she asked.

"They're not worth a penny. I'm very confused."

"Over what?"

"Well, this for starts—here," Anna said, passing the poem to Esther. Esther read it and looked up and smiled.

"Did you write this to yourself?"

Anna looked over at her and answered a bit sharply. "Of course not."

"Well, it's your handwriting," Esther countered.

"Oh, I'm sorry, Esther. Miles wrote it."

"Then he's in love with you—is that it?"

"He didn't show it to me, I found it in his house, and he says it's a poem based on Anna Karenina—it's supposed to be Count Vronsky writing to her."

"But you don't believe it?"

"Well, it seems…well, what do you think? You've read the book, haven't you?"

"Yes, but it's been a long time. But I remember that Vronsky told her he loved her and then later he left his wife—I think he was married, but he left his wife and he and Anna got together, but I think she never married again. That's actually a pretty dismal story."

"And why would he be writing a poem about something like that?" Anna said.

"What did he say when you found it?"

"He was very defensive and later he said I was daft because I thought it was about me."

"So you asked him?"

"Yes, and he denied it. I went over there to apologize about getting angry for his rebuke about the identity switch, and we just end-ed up having another argument. Then I asked him at church and he rushed out."

"He was probably embarrassed."

"Because I confronted him about it?"

"No, silly, because he wrote the poem for you. Why else would he get upset about you seeing it?"

"Well, he said it was a misunderstanding, and that's what both-ered him. But when I asked in church if our friendship would continue, he said yes, but maybe in a different way, and I don't know what he was talking about."

"Maybe you don't want to know what he was talking about. Maybe you should just let sleeping dogs lie."

"What do you mean?"

"I mean, if he did write the poem for you, and he is in love with you, then it's better that you don't talk to him as much anymore, espe-cially about the poem. Just leave it alone so you don't have to let him down."

"Oh, yes, I see now. It's just that I've been so used to telling him everything. He's been such a good friend and I missed talking to him the whole time I was in Florida."

"Anna, I'm afraid he is right—the relationship has to be differ-ent now."

"Yes, I see that. He also told me it would change when I got married, because my husband would not want me talking to him."

"He was right. Having a male friend who is as close to you as he is and also having a husband won't work. Your husband will be jeal-ous—maybe not because he's worried about anything improper hap-pening between you two, but because he would not want you sharing your life with another man."

"Well, I don't think that should be a problem."

"Believe me, it would be. Think of it this way. Pretend you meet a man and he has a girlfriend who he talks to all of the time. Once he marries you, I don't think you would want him to continue with that relationship—even if she was in a wheelchair."

"Okay—you're right again. And Miles, as usual, was miles ahead of me and had already figured that out. But tell me your honest opinion—do you think the poem was written for me?"

Esther looked at the poem again and read it before she an-swered. "I think there is a ninety-eight percent chance it was written for you, so tread lightly. I'm sure Miles has enough of a cross to bear being in that wheelchair. Don't press the issue with him, and you can probably keep him as a friend—but with a little more distance."

"You know, I always just thought of him as a younger kid, but he really looks like a man, now."

"Yes, it's too bad he had that accident—that is so tragic," Esther added, and then she looked at her watch. "Oh, I've got to get ready to meet Alice—we're going to the museum. Would you like to come?" she asked, as she stood up.

"No, but have you asked Priscilla?"

"Yes, she's busy going over reports for Father. Even though she had the day off, she can't seem to let it go."

"I wish I had something I was that interested in," Anna said, looking a little morose.

"Oh, you will—one day," Esther said and she walked upstairs, leaving Anna to stare in thought. Priscilla walked out from the study and sat on the sofa next to Anna.

"My eyes are hurting from reading those ledgers—they ought to test the bookkeepers for handwriting before they hire them," Priscilla said, and then she noticed that Anna was not paying attention.

"What planet are you on, little sister?"

"What? Oh, were you speaking to me?"

"Yes, I was—there is no one else in the room."

"Sorry, I was preoccupied. Can I ask you a question—I mean one about Herbert. Or will that upset you?"

"What's the question?"

"What is the thing you miss most about him—or the thing you miss most doing with him? Was it when you were helping him with the business or something like that?"

Priscilla thought for a moment. "No, I think the lunches were the best times we had. Once we got away from the company he seemed more relaxed, and he was witty and funny. It was like the tension left him and we could talk about other things besides work."

"So it was just spending that time with him—at lunch?"

"Yes, that was it. Seems simple, doesn't it?"

"Yes, but that is it, isn't it? It's like we said before—that's what it distills down to. It's that you miss the person when they are not around. It's not really anything else, because if you're going to spend the rest of your life with someone you have to really like his company. It can't just be looks or other attributes—it has to be his personality."

"Yes, well, Herbert was also Jekyll and Hyde, like I told you."

"But it was worth putting up with Hyde for the moments with Jekyll—is that it?"

"Yes, maybe, but I've already put him in the sour grapes department, and I don't want to change that," Priscilla said.

"Oh, I'm sorry I brought it up," Anna said.

"No, that's fine. You're trying to figure some things out, and if I can help, that's what a big sister is for."

"Yes, thank you, Prissy."

46

"It's been a very difficult time for all of you girls," Mr. Strickland said as Mr. Standish and a kitchen helper served a prime rib roast at dinner time. "So I would like to arrange a trip for all three of you—and I thought Paul might like to go, also. I thought it would be refreshing for you to get away. I thought perhaps somewhere in Europe—is there a place you would like to visit?"

Priscilla looked at Esther and then back at her father. "Well, we've actually talked among ourselves about going to Paris someday. Only Esther has ever been there, but we've all taken French. And yes, I'd like to have Paul come—I would prefer to have a man with us."

Paul looked surprised at the question. "Okay, I'll go if you want me to. If you are certain it won't spoil your vacation if your big brother tags along."

"Oh no, it would not be like that at all," Anna said. "We'd love to have you. But my French isn't very good, so I'll be counting on the rest of you."

"What do you think, Esther?" Priscilla asked.

"I'd love to go, I like Paris, and we can go to the Musée de Louvre. And I want Paul to go also."

"Then I can beat back those Frenchmen when they bother you—is that it?"

Esther laughed a little. "I don't think we would have to worry about that. But I'd like to tour the Louvre again. It would be lovely to go with my sisters—and my brother. The Eiffel Tower is also fun to see, and it's the tallest building in the world."

"Not any more. The new Chrysler building right here in New York is now taller," Paul said.

"Oh, I thought your specialty was the Middle East. Now you're stretching to Europe, huh?" Esther said.

"I wrote a paper on it in college. It was built in 1889 for the world's fair and the Parisians hated it at first and called it an eyesore. It was supposed to be torn down after the fair."

"So what stopped them?" Anna asked.

"Well, it started growing on people, and the military started using it for communications. In 1914 it was used to jam German radio communications. The French author Guy De Maupassant said he hated it, but he ate lunch there every day. When they asked him why, he said it was the only place in Paris where he couldn't see it."

"Now I know why you have a PhD," Esther said teasingly.

"Is it settled that everyone wants to go, then?" Mr. Strickland asked.

"Father, what about you—you never take a real vacation. Can't you come with us?" Priscilla asked.

"Not this time. I need to watch the store."

"I'll watch it, and you can go," Priscilla said. "I'll send you a telegram for every major decision. I promise I will keep you up to date."

"I appreciate the gesture, but I want my daughters to have this trip together. Now we have to get the dates fixed, because Anna has to go back to college in the fall, so we don't have much time left. Let's figure it out and have the travel advisor book the passage."

"Father, I may transfer to Barnard—I'm still thinking about it, but I don't know when their classes start."

"Why would you want to go there?" Mr. Strickland asked.

"Well, if Miles goes to Columbia, then I would be near to help him if he needs it. But right now he's angry at me, so I don't know if he will want my help."

"Have you asked him if he wants you to transfer?" Priscilla asked.

"We talked about it and he said he would prefer to be on his own, but I thought that he could use the help."

"Well, I would assume the starting dates are the same for both, so it shouldn't matter. But that reminds me that we do need to invite Miles and his family for dinner—we need to formally thank him for all he did for us. So when you see him next, ask him when he would like to come."

"Anna, you can't follow him around his whole life and try to help him—he might become dependent on you, and it will interfere with your own life," Esther said.

"But he may not even go to college unless he has someone to help, and what a waste that would be," Anna said.

"We should talk about this later," Priscilla interceded. "Thank you, Father, for thinking of us—I'm sure it will be a wonderful vacation."

After dinner, Anna walked past Esther in the hallway but did not speak to her. Esther knocked on Priscilla's door and she said, "Come in."

"She's mad at me again," Esther said. "She can't take any advice from me anymore."

"I think I understand why—you need to be more subtle, and you said that in front of Father and it embarrassed her. You should wait until you are alone with her."

"So everyone thinks I'm wrong now, is that it?" Esther said, flustered.

"No, now don't exaggerate. You played the mother part for a long time even though you're her sister, and she has to go through the separation from that. And I'm sure she's still smarting over the fact that you didn't want her to go to Florida and all that trouble she got into."

"I guess you're right. I just think she's trying too hard to help Miles...."

"I know what you think and I agree. But maybe she will have to learn on her own."

As they were talking, Anna knocked on the door and walked in after Esther opened it.

"Are you two talking about me?"

"As a matter of fact, we are."

"Behind my back?"

"Anna, that carries an unpleasant connotation. Now I'm sure you and Esther have talked about me when I was not present, but there was nothing insidious about it," Priscilla said.

"So you think I should forget about Miles, and leave him to himself? Is that it?"

"Anna—why are you so extreme in your thinking about Miles? Can't you be his friend without worrying about his life? You didn't put him in that wheelchair and you are not responsible for him just because he has a crush on you."

"No, but I am a little, because we've been friends so long. I need to consider his life, also. He's been my closest friend, even though he's a boy...I mean a man. And I feel guilty because I like to talk to him and be around him, and yet someday that will all end—just like he says. And I worry about that."

"Well, there's enough trouble in one day without worrying about the future. Just let it go."

"Oh, you don't understand," Anna said, and she left the room and went into her own bedroom and lay down on the bed in frustration. But she left the door open and Esther followed her in.

"It's true, I don't understand. Can we talk about it some more?"

"No, because I don't understand it, either."

"I think that's just because you know he likes you and you feel sorry for him. The relationship has gotten messed up that way. It's too bad you saw that poem."

"It was because I was snooping—it was wrong. But I wasn't really snooping—it was just there on his desk under a paper. And I haven't meant to lead him on—I didn't know he felt that way about me until I read the poem."

"Oh, Anna, quit condemning yourself. You just can't have the same relationship that you had with him before now that you know how he feels, but it's good that you found out now."

"It is good—but I liked it better before—I think."

"Yes, it's always good when truth comes out, because now you understand each other and can act accordingly. But I don't think it's so unusual for him to want you—you're very attractive and a lot of men would. He's just reacting in a normal way."

"So you think he's interested in me just because of my looks, is that it?"

"I didn't say that. Don't twist my words."

"But you said, because I'm attractive. Is that all I have to offer? Is that all he sees?"

"Well, not according to his poem—it seems there is a deeper attraction. So, okay, he likes you just for yourself—for who you are. That's wonderful, and that's why you've been friends all these years. But things change as we get older."

"Yes, I guess they do. Esther, thank you for talking to me, especially when I've been so horrible. I'm just so upset about this whole thing, because he's been such a good friend and I hate to see that end—especially after God gave him the vision about where I was. That was so unusual."

"I understand," Esther said, and she put her arm around Anna.

"Well, I might as well call him and get the dinner over with," Anna said, and she got up and walked towards the telephone as Esther left.

"May I speak with Miles?... This is Anna Strickland...he's not available?...okay, please have him call me back. Thank you." Anna hung the phone up and sat down on her couch and picked up a novel she was reading. After about an hour, she called again but got the same response. Miles had always come right to the phone before, and now she began to realize that he was avoiding her. She went back to her book and waited for about another hour and then called again. "May I speak with Miles? This is Anna again.... Oh, he's still not available... okay, but before you hang up, tell Miles that I will keep calling until he's man enough to answer the phone himself. Please tell him that while I hold."

Anna waited for a long time before she finally heard Miles's reluctant voice answer. "Yes, Anna?"

"My father asked me to invite you and your family over for dinner," she said briskly. "Thanks for finally answering."

"I don't think that's a good idea right now...we're really busy. Can we take a rain check?"

"Miles, why are you avoiding me...why won't you talk to me?"

"Anna, I really have to go now. Good-bye."

Anna stared at the phone after he hung up, exasperated. "Miles...how could you!" she shouted into the phone, and then she went to the bed and pounded on her pillow in frustration. "I just can't bear the idea of us not seeing each other like it used to be," she said to herself. "Yes, that's it, isn't it? I don't want it to end this way." She went back to the phone and called again, but the butler said Miles was unavailable. She shook her head and then she looked outside and noticed there was a full moon. She changed into a simple housedress and walked out of the house onto the veranda and then to the street. When she reached Miles's house, she went to the front door and rang the doorbell. After a minute or two, the butler answered.

"I'm here to see Miles," she said.

"I will see if he is available," the butler said politely. He walked away and came back rather quickly. "I'm sorry, madam, but he is not available at this time."

"Oh, he's not, huh. Okay, I see," Anna said, and the butler closed the door. She walked away from the house, frustrated, and then she went to her room and closed the door. She got into bed and stared at the ceiling, then closed her eyes and tried to sleep. A knock on the door woke her up, and she groggily opened her eyes.

"Who is it?"

"It's me—Priscilla."

"Okay, come in."

"It's dinnertime and we have been wondering where you were. Will you come down to eat?"

"No, I'm not hungry."

"What's wrong, are you sick? Should we call Dr. Katz?"

"No, I think I'll be all right. I just want to sleep some more."

"Anna, is there anything I can do to help?"

"No, I just need to be alone for a while. I'll be all right. It's just that I don't think I can trust men anymore after what Bart tried to do to me."

"Well, you're still probably a little in shock. No one could go through what you did without needing some time to recover."

"I don't know—maybe that's it."

Priscilla was quiet for a moment, then she spoke. "It's something else isn't it? Is this about Miles—are you still worried about him?"

"Prissy, please let me sleep," Anna said as she pulled the covers over her head.

"Okay, I'm sorry I bothered you."

Anna fell back to sleep, and she began dreaming. In her dream, Miles was there, and he was walking. He smiled at her as they walked together through a park somewhere. She remembered asking him how he was able to walk, and he answered, "I'm the same person I've always been—nothing has changed." She was confused by the answer, but in her dreamlike state was unable to concentrate on it. As they walked some more, she began to talk to him.

"Miles, I can't see you again, I'm getting married."

The smile faded from Miles' face. "Well, I knew this day would come. I hope you are very happy with him. But who is he?"

"Well, he's..." Anna kept trying to think in her dream of who she was going to marry, but she could not think of anyone. Every time she tried to answer him, she came up blank—no name, no face, nothing about the person she was supposed to marry. Finally Miles spoke.

"I understand—anyone but me. I hope you are happy, my dear friend." Then he started walking away, and although she tried to follow she could not keep her eyes on him and soon he was gone and she looked around at the trees, and felt empty. Then she shouted for him.

"Miles, I don't want you to go. I don't care who else there is, I don't want you to go." But he didn't answer. She started to run in the park, feverishly looking for him, but she couldn't find him. Then she saw a man that she thought was him, and she went up to him, but when he turned around it was not Miles. The same thing happened several times, but every time the man would turn around it was someone else. "Miles, where are you? I need you. Miles!" she screamed in frustration, and then she woke up suddenly, and she was out of breath and her heart was racing and she was perspiring.

She sat up in bed, relieved that it was just a dream, and tried to calm down. After a few minutes, she closed her eyes again and fell back to sleep. A few hours later, the morning light filtered through the windows of the French doors in her room and she woke up with the dream fresh in her mind. Normally she forgot her dreams as she was waking up, but she remembered all of this one, and she thought about it as she lay there. Then she got out of bed and dressed and walked over to Miles's house and knocked on the door. The butler answered and she detected a slight grimace when he realized it was her. "Yes, Miss Strickland, may I help you?"

"I'm here to see Miles again."

"Yes, I will see if he is available."

Anna waited for what seemed like a long time, until the butler finally returned. "I'm sorry, Miss Strickland, Master Miles is not taking company at the present time."

"Okay, thank you."

Anna began walking away from the house. Then she stopped and walked back to the house and then around the side until she reached a basement area where there were several windows and an old door. To the left of the door was a large rock, and she struggled to move it, turning and rolling it at the same time. She smiled when she saw that there was a key there, and she picked it up and used it to open the basement door. Then she walked into the basement and up the stairs where the lights were on. No one saw her as she made her way to a room adjacent to the drawing room. Then she stuck her head out of that room enough to see into the drawing room, and she saw Miles reading quickly through various papers.

She watched him for a moment, wondering why he was flipping through so many newspapers, but as she stepped backwards, the floor creaked and he immediately looked up, startled. "Who is it?" he demanded. Then he put down the paper he had in his hand and moved towards the fireplace and retrieved a heavy metal poker. "I know someone is there—show yourself—now!" he said. Slowly, she walked out of the room and he put the poker down in disbelief. "What are you doing here?"

"Well, I thought I'd invite myself since you wouldn't talk to me."

"How did you get in?"

"Remember when we were kids and you showed me where the key was to the basement door?"

"Yes, I do remember. So you broke in. Very resourceful—now why in the world did you come?"

"Because I wanted to see you to ask you a question."

"Oh, Anna, please let me get on with my life. I'm just not in the mood to talk to you right now."

"Okay, Miles, I promise to leave if you answer one—no, two questions."

Miles took a breath and shook his head, but then relented. "What are they?"

"First, did you write that poem for me? Now before you answer, remember how you rebuked me about lying when I switched with Lucy. I don't mean to be judgmental, but you know what the Bible says about liars. Was it for me or not?"

"Yes, Anna. The poem was for you, but it is not fair, because you were not supposed to see it. Yes, it was for you. Are you satisfied now?"

"Yes, I'm satisfied—almost. So do you love me?"

"Anna, I really don't want to go into this...."

"Do you love me, Miles?"

Miles hesitated before answering. "Of course I love you, Anna. You're a good friend and I love all my friends."

Anna looked at Miles and squinted her eyes with anger. "Miles, there are different ways to lie and deceive, and I want the truth. Now you know what I'm talking about. I don't mean love me like a friend."

"Anna, why are you trying to humiliate me?"

"Miles, tell the truth."

"Yes, Anna, I love you, now please leave me alone," he said and he turned and tried to roll away from her, but she walked in front of his chair and put her foot in the way.

"What in the world are you doing? Are you going to bully me?"

"No, silly, I'm going to marry you."

"Marry me? Are you jesting?"

"No, I am perfectly serious. You are the man I want to spend my life with."

"No...no, this can't be. There are thousands of men out there that would like to marry you and they can walk."

"And I don't want any of them—I only want you."

Miles looked at her incredulously. "No, it would never work. You would always resent me. Later, you would regret it. If we had children, I can't even walk in the park with them, I couldn't play catch with them....You'd spend your whole life looking after a cripple."

"You wrote a poem for me, and I've got one for you. Roses are red, violets are blue, I don't care if you're crippled, I still love you." She then reached over and kissed him on the lips, and when she pulled her head back, there were tears rolling down his cheeks. "I mean, you do love me, don't you?"

"Oh, Anna, you know I love you," Miles said, trying to control his emotions.

47

Anna ran home, smiling. She raced in the front door, and startled Mr. Standish, as she ran past him and up the stairs to Esther's room. The door was open and she was talking to Priscilla, but they both stopped when Anna stood at the door, breathless for a moment. "Guess what—I'm getting married!"

"You're getting married?" Priscilla asked with a puzzled look on her face. "To who?"

"I believe that's 'to whom,'" Anna said.

"Okay, to whom, then?"

"To Miles."

"Miles?" Esther asked.

"Yes."

"Are you sure?"

"Yes, yes, a thousand times yes. It was Miles all the time."

"So, I take it the poem was for you?" Esther asked.

"Yes again." Anna took a breath. "You know how I've been leery of men since I came home—I told you that I had a hard time trusting them. But I trust Miles implicitly, and I know everything about him. I've known him for so long, and I know he's honest and loving and dependable—all the things you want in a man but are so hard to find. And I've missed him the whole time I've been gone."

"And you know he's not after your money," Priscilla added.

"Yes, of course not. I know he loves me for who I am, and I love him. Even if he was poor it would make no difference. I know his heart—it came out in his poetry."

"So when did you realize you loved him?" Esther asked.

"It started after he said that our relationship would need to change and we couldn't see each other as much. Both of you saw that, too, and while I was away I kept thinking of how I missed talking to him. I knew he was right—another man would not stand for our close relationship, but I couldn't imagine meeting anyone that I'd rather spend time with."

"I remember we talked about that—and we came to the conclusion that it comes down to if you want someone's company all of the time," Priscilla said.

"Yes, and then when I read the poem, and realized he was in love with me, I knew I'd have to make a decision, and the more I thought about being married to him the happier I got."

"So he was avoiding you because you figured out he loved you?"

"Yes, he didn't think I would love him because of his handicap. He is still bothered at the idea that I will have to take care of him. But I want to."

"As long as you love him and he loves you, nothing else matters," Esther said, getting up and hugging her sister. "Congratulations. I know Miles is a fine boy—sorry, I mean man. I've always liked him."

Priscilla hugged Anna also. "I'm so happy for you, Anna. It's sort of ironic—you're the youngest, but you're getting married first. Life is full of surprises."

"Oh, but I want the same for both of you—I believe it will happen—it really will."

"Why don't we go downstairs and tell Father?" Esther suggested.

"For some reason, I'm afraid to. But I must tell him before Miles formally asks him to marry me, or he'll be very surprised."

Anna went downstairs with her sisters in tow and knocked on the door of her father's study.

Mr. Strickland listened diligently, expressionless to all she had to say, and then he finally smiled after she finished. "Congratulations, I think that Miles is an outstanding boy."

"You mean man?" Esther asked.

"Yes, of course—I need to start thinking of him that way now."

"Oh, thank you, Father. Now I must run to my room and call him and tell him that everyone knows, and he can come and ask you when he's ready."

Anna ran out of the study, and Esther and Priscilla looked at each other and then at their father.

"Father, you seem a little unhappy about this. I hope Anna didn't notice," Esther said. "You know how she craves your approval."

"Sorry, it was a shock, but I'm getting used to it now," Mr. Strickland said. "And yes, I am a little bothered about this, but don't say anything to Anna."

"Why aren't you happy, Father? I like Miles. I know him being crippled will be difficult for Anna, but if she loves him, what does it really matter?" Esther said.

"It's not that he's crippled—any one of us could be crippled tomorrow. If she's willing to bear that burden, it's fine with me. And I know his character is the highest. What bothers me is that he's unmotivated. What are they going to do for the rest of their lives? Will they just read poetry to each other and talk about classical literature every day?"

"Actually, that sounds quite nice to me," Esther said.

"Father, I think you are being too hard on him. He is in a wheelchair, so you can't expect that he could do that much. And if they like life that way, what's the harm? Besides, Anna will help him find out what he can do. She's a hard worker and her influence will be good," Priscilla said.

"Yes, you're right. I do like the boy, and he is very stable. I just never thought of him as a son-in-law, but I think he'll be a good husband to Anna. Perhaps some people are born to be romantics. So if that's how he wants to spend his time, it's good he's got a large inheritance coming."

"I think he'll find something to do; he's always seemed energetic to me," Priscilla added.

"Well, we need to invite them for dinner, so talk to Anna and schedule it. We will want something special prepared—perhaps some filet mignon. The cook may have some suggestions. But come to think of it, find out what his parents like to eat first, if you can. Miles will know."

"Mr. and Mrs. Van Galen—what a pleasure it is to see you," Mr. Strickland said as the butler led them into the living room and the men shook hands. "And, of course, it's always good to see my future son-in-law," he added, shaking hands with Miles. "Please take a seat and be comfortable—dinner will be served shortly."

"Mr. Strickland, I just want to say what a wonderful girl we think Anna is—we just couldn't be more pleased," Mrs. Van Galen said.

"Oh, please call me Joseph. We are soon to be family."

"Well, make that Mildred and Stanley," Mr. Van Galen said as one of the kitchen help served hors d'oeuvres and the daughters entered the room and greeted the Van Galens.

"Now, I understand that your mother is in poor health, Mildred. We are sorry to hear that and have been praying for her," Joseph said.

"Well, it's to be expected, since she's in her eighties, but I've been trying to give her the care she needs even though we've had to hire a nurse as well. I just hope I haven't been neglecting Miles too much."

"Oh, it's fine, Mother," Miles said, a little embarrassed.

"So are you going to the charity gala?" Esther asked.

"Yes, I think we are. But if we can't make it, we'll make a donation and send it in," Stanley said.

As he finished speaking, Mr. Standish announced that dinner was ready, and they moved from the living room into the dining room.

"Would you say grace for us, Miles?" Joseph asked, and Miles prayed over the food and they began to eat.

"We are so glad that Anna is safe now," Mildred said. "I've never seen Miles so upset about anything. Isn't that right, Miles?"

Miles was embarrassed again, but he nodded as he ate his salad.

"We were also disturbed over that yellow journalism about your company, Joseph—it must have been so unpleasant for you."

"Yes, it was," Joseph said.

"I wonder how that rumor got started. Perhaps someone was trying to sabotage your companies. You know the press came to me and asked me questions about you, and I told them that you'd been my neighbor for over thirty years and that you had nothing but an impeccable reputation. They didn't like hearing that, so they didn't print it. But I knew what they were saying couldn't be true, because whenever we've talked, you told me you never even buy stocks."

"Stanley—I think that's enough about that," Mildred said in almost a whisper to him.

"Oh, yes, well, I'm sorry to bring up a sore subject. Please forgive me."

"That's fine—it's all over now. By the way, you've made some shrewd moves with your stocks, haven't you? You avoided the big crash by selling out just in time—my compliments."

"Well, I'd like to take that compliment, Joseph, but it wasn't me who made the right decisions. I just had good investment council—the best."

"Really? That's interesting," Joseph said.

"Yes, my analyst studies the markets every day, and he predicted the crash. Like most people, I had been shifting my money into stocks from the mining company, and I think eighty percent of it was in the market, and I told him there was no way I was going to pull out of the market—it was skyrocketing, and we'd made millions and I told him there were millions more to be made. But he kept at me. He said I would definitely lose everything I had made in the market if I didn't get out. But he was so young and inexperienced that at first I didn't believe he could be correct. But then he showed me his research—all the stocks he'd been tracking, and the reductions in orders and profits, and how the stocks were trading at multiples that were ridiculously high."

"What is a multiple?" Anna asked.

"It's the stock price compared to the profits a company makes—sometimes called the price earnings ratio. In other words, the stocks were selling for so much more than their earnings—such a high multiple—that I started to agree that there was a bubble that had to burst. Especially after my analyst showed me how many of the companies we had stock in had declining profits while stock prices were still escalating. It made sense after I thought about it. We also sold our own stock while it was still high. I hated to do that—it sort of felt like we were selling out our own company, but every day my analyst came to me and argued with me, insisting that we were going to lose really big if we didn't sell out. So I finally gave in. That was six months before the crash, and after we sold, many of them continued climbing and I wasn't very nice to him—in fact, I lambasted him over it, but he took it pretty well. Then on Black Monday everything he said would happen came true, and I'm so glad I listened to him."

"Okay, Stanley, I can't stand any more, will you share his name, or is it a family secret?" Joseph asked.

"It's no secret, but it is family—he's sitting next to you."

Esther was sitting on Joseph's left and Miles was on his right, and Joseph looked over at Miles incredulously.

"You mean Miles?"

"Yes, you may be losing a daughter, but you just got the best business analyst I know."

"But I thought you were…interested in poetry…. You are apparently a remarkable young man. First you get a dream about Anna and then this. When did you get interested in business?"

"I started helping Father after the accident. I tried being in the plant after school and weekends, but it was hard to get around, and I didn't feel comfortable there. So I picked up the Wall Street Journal one afternoon and I haven't missed a day since."

"He makes long-distance calls all over the world to research industries—you ought to see my phone bill. But it's paid off handsomely. Since the crash we've made some incredible buys."

So that's what all those newspapers were about. But you never told me, and we've talked so many times," Anna said.

"Well, I thought you'd find it boring—you said it was not interesting when your Father talked about business…oh, I'm sorry, Mr. Strickland."

Joseph chuckled and smiled at Stanley. "So can we share him after this?"

"You bet—just pay half the phone bill!" Stanley said, but his wife frowned at him. "Oh, I'm just joking."

"Of course," Joseph said, smiling.

After the Van Galens left, Mr. Strickland looked at his children and smiled. "I think that went well. I've always liked Stanley."

"He does seem to put his foot in his mouth a bit," Paul said.

"Oh, I know, but actually that's one of the things I like about him—makes things a little colorful. But we do need to talk about the charity gala—it's only a week away. And I'd like all of you to go, if you don't mind."

"It seems more like a social event than for charity. I think that may be the only reason some of the people go, so they can say they can afford the plate price and rub shoulders with other rich people," Priscilla said.

"Yes, I know it's quite pretentious," Mr. Strickland said. "But we do raise a lot of money for the poor this way, and if we all attend, it will help to attract more people. There are many citizens in breadlines across this country, and the money goes directly to feeding them. We have everything we could ask for, and I think this is the least we can do for them."

"Of course I'll go, Father, but won't it be embarrassing for you with Mrs. Ingersoll there—I mean she is on the board, isn't she?" Esther said.

"Well, I don't want to see her, but I have no choice. So will all of you attend?"

"I'll go," Paul said, and Anna and Priscilla agreed.

48

The evening of the gala came soon, and Esther and Anna were almost ready, but Priscilla found it difficult to figure out what to wear. She tried on several dresses, walking into Esther's room to model them for her sisters as they sat on the sofa and gave their opinions. "I like that green chiffon a lot," Esther said, as Priscilla looked at herself in the green chiffon in Esther's full-length dressing mirror. "Why don't you just wear that?"

"I don't know, nothing seems to look right to me," Priscilla said, and she rushed out of the room and changed into another dress, a white silk with cream-colored lace.

"What about this one?"

"Oh, Prissy, you're wearing us out. Everything you've put on looks good to me," Esther said.

"Well, I like this one the best," Anna said. "Why do the men have it so easy with these formal events? They just wear a tuxedo, and that's it. Not many choices to make there."

"I should wear a tuxedo myself and shock them all," Priscilla said.

"Do you have one of those, too? I knew you had just about everything in the wardrobe but I didn't know you had a tux," Esther said teasingly.

"Very funny. Looks like we're running out of time, and I need to figure out which dress is the right one."

Esther and Anna looked at each other and smiled as Priscilla re-examined herself in the mirror. "That's the one," Esther said. "I agree with Anna. There is nothing better than that dress. So that settles it."

"Oh, I don't know. There will be many important people there and…"

"You mean some important young men, don't you?" Esther said, laughing a little.

"Well, don't tell me that's not on your mind, too," Priscilla said.

"Of course. But you have to get ready now because there is no more time to change again."

"Okay, white silk it is—it's a couple of years old but I don't think it's out of fashion, do you?"

"No, Prissy. It's beautiful. In fact, I like it so much that if you don't wear it, I will," Anna said, looking over at Esther and smiling, because she was using this as a ploy to get Priscilla to choose the dress.

"No, I'm wearing it, I'm wearing it," Priscilla said, looking in the mirror again. "Yes, I think this is it."

"Oh, hallelujah!" Esther said. "Let's get downstairs before Father sends Standish for us and Priscilla changes her mind again."

The grand ballroom where the gala was being held had long tables set up where the banquet would be eaten. Someone in the press had complained the previous year about the expensive dishes being served, so this year the menu would be simpler—with an entrée of roast beef with various vegetables and salads, and fewer fancy desserts than last time. Hundreds of people were mingling before the dinner was to begin, and many who had found out about the engagement were congratulating Anna and Miles. Joseph was greeting and talking to many of the attendees, but one pretty young woman, named Amanda Parker, whom he vaguely remembered as an acquaintance of Esther's, seemed to be fluttering around him. She finally walked up to him and said hello, and he greeted her and then turned to greet others.

Priscilla and Esther were talking to some of their girlfriends, but they saw Amanda hovering around their father, and Esther made a face to Priscilla showing her displeasure. Paul did not like crowds, and he walked around until he saw an outdoor balcony and then stepped out into it for some fresh air. To his surprise, a very attractive young lady was sitting on a stone bench and he stopped as he saw her. "Oh, I'm sorry, I did not mean to disturb you," he said.

She looked up at him and smiled. "Oh, you're not disturbing me. It's certainly big enough for two. I just wanted to get away from the crowd for a little while."

"That's how I feel. I've been out of the country quite a bit, and these social engagements take getting used to."

"Really? Where have you been?"

"Well, I was most recently in Persia, and before that I was in Palestine."

"That sounds very interesting. Why were you there?"

"I'm an archaeologist, or I was, anyway."

"Why did you stop?—that sounds like a fascinating profession."

"I thought it was time to help my father with his business. I love archeology, but I also have other responsibilities. What about you? What do you like to do?"

"Well, I like gardening and I am also interested in business. My brother is running our business because Father died recently, and I'd like to help him."

"So why don't you?"

The young woman smiled. "You don't know my brother—he's not the easiest person to convince, but I'm working on it. Part of the company belongs to me and my mother, so I should have a chance to be involved, wouldn't you say so?"

"Why yes, I would. And it turns out that my sister is working with my father and doing very well—she's been interested in the business since she was very young."

"You must have an interesting family. By the way, my name is Charlotte Blankenship."

"I'm pleased to meet you, Miss Blankenship. I'm Paul Strickland."

"Did you say Paul Strickland—like Strickland Oil and Gas, and Strickland Steel and those companies?"

"That's the one."

Charlotte got up quickly and began to walk away. "Where are you going?" Paul asked.

"I have to leave now."

Paul got up and walked after her. "But can I see you again?"

"Absolutely not," Charlotte said, and she walked even faster to get away from him. He stopped and took a breath and shook his head, perplexed.

"Well, I guess there's something about the Strickland name that she doesn't like. Maybe she still thinks we're bankrupt," Paul said to himself as he walked slowly back to the ballroom. He saw Priscilla and Esther, and he walked over to join them.

"There are some pretty heiresses here, Paul. Why don't you

strike up a conversation with someone?" Esther asked.

"I tried that already, and when I said I was a Strickland, she walked out on me so fast, you'd think I was Dracula."

"Well, maybe I can introduce you to some of my old acquaintances. Oh no! Hide me! That's David's grandmother."

"Too late, she already saw you."

Mrs. Holt walked up to Esther and smiled sweetly. "It's nice to see you, dear."

"Thank you, Mrs. Holt, nice to see you also," Esther said, and she began to walk away.

"Can I have a word with you, dear?"

Esther hesitated, but she couldn't say no without being rude. "Of course, Mrs. Holt."

"Then follow me away from this noise so we can chat for a moment," Mrs. Holt said, and Esther followed her to a side room that was quieter. There were some chairs there, and Mrs. Holt gestured for her to sit down. Esther reluctantly sat but looked petulant. "You're such a fine young lady, and I am so sorry to see you break up with David."

Esther was quiet, but she nodded her head in agreement, not knowing what to say but wanting to get away. "It was his pride that ruined it, you know. When he found out the money was gone, he wouldn't go through with the marriage—how pathetic his pride is. But I thought you would give him a second chance."

"Mrs. Holt, you are right about David's pride, but his other problem is greed. He dropped me when he thought we had lost our money, and he only called back after he knew it was a rumor. I would have given him another chance if he hadn't shown me clearly that he was only interested in my money."

"My dear, David was not interested in your money—he was too proud to marry you when his business failed."

"What do you mean?"

"When his father lost all of their money in the stock market, he broke off the engagement because he said he didn't want to embarrass you and he didn't want charity from your family."

Esther looked at Mrs. Holt for a moment. "Then why did he call me back just after my father went to the press and said we were not in financial trouble if he wasn't after our money? What other reason would he have to change his mind about the marriage?"

"Miss Strickland, David called you back because he had just gotten a large sum of money again—my money, which I gave to him for a fresh start. After he had that, he felt he could still marry you, and that's what I'm talking about when I say he had foolish pride. You see, he had no idea I had held back so much from his father, but I did it because I knew his father played too fast and loose with it, and I thought he might lose it. It was only when David found out that he had a chance to start a new business that he thought he could ask you to marry him again. He told me that he loved you, but he wanted you to be proud of him, and he thought if he had nothing you would never be pleased with him."

"Well, that is foolish pride. I never cared about what he had at all. But I do remember how he misunderstood the discussion he had with my father. He thought Father was concerned about how much money he made, when it was quite the opposite."

"Oh, dear Esther—if I may call you that. David has many problems, but I assure you he was not marrying you for your money, even if it seemed that way. Remember this—there is so much opposition to love in the world. The enemy confused him and made him proud to try to destroy a chance for you to love each other."

"Is he here tonight?"

"No, he's busy rebuilding the drugstore empire, but he's been quite depressed because you turned him down. Can I ask him to call you, then?"

"Yes, that would be all right," Esther said.

"Thank you, my dear, I will."

As Joseph Strickland greeted people, he had noticed Betty Ingersoll looking at him several times. But every time she got close to him, he was able to get away and greet someone else. However, now he saw her coming towards him and there was no one around to speak with except Amanda Parker, and he did not want to talk to her again. Betty approached and he managed to smile at her.

"Oh, Joseph, you look so nice in that tuxedo," Betty said as she approached him. "You are such a distinguished man." Joseph looked at her for a moment. Her diamond earrings and matching necklace shimmered in the lights above her, and she was dressed in a beautiful maroon gown, with a white mink stole draped around her shoulders. Her physical beauty was very tempting, even now, but he took his eyes off her and looked out at the people passing by as he spoke.

"Thank you, Betty, you look very nice yourself."

"Well, I've missed you," Betty said sweetly.

"How are things going with Mr. Chandler?"

"Oh, what a horrid man. He talked me into investing in something and I never saw my money again. I actually hired a lawyer to try to get it back, but I'll never see it again. I'm just glad it wasn't that much."

"I'm sorry to hear that."

"Oh, Joseph, I know what I've seemed like. I know how terribly I've acted, but I truly do love you. Is there a chance that you still love me? I don't like to beg, but I am humbling myself and asking. Is there a chance?"

Joseph looked at her for a moment before answering. Her eyes were pleading, and she moved closer to him, and took his arm. He stood without moving, but he could smell her expensive perfume. "No, I'm sorry Betty, there is no chance."

"I understand, Joseph." As she finished speaking, a man and his wife approached Joseph to say hello. She managed a weak smile for them and then walked away. He watched her as she left, biting his lip. He still felt something of a loss as she walked away, but he knew he had to let her go, and he composed himself and turned to the man and his wife.

"Mr. Strickland, it's nice to finally meet you," the man said. "We need to talk about my steel factories and how we can work together."

"Yes, Mr. Collier, I'd like to, but let me find my daughter, because I know she also wants to meet you. In fact, she's the one you talked to on the phone."

"Oh, you mean Priscilla."

"Yes, but I don't see her around anywhere," Joseph said as he looked around. "When I find her, we'll get alone and talk for a few minutes."

Paul walked with Priscilla and Esther towards the back of the room where hors d'oeuvres were being served. As he stopped and took a stuffed olive, a friend of his from high school walked up.

"Hello Paul, when did you get back? I thought you were in the sands of the Sahara or in Timbuktu or somewhere. It's good to see you again."

"Yes, I have been gone, Ralph—and who is this?" Paul asked looking towards a younger girl with Ralph.

"Oh, this is my sister, April."

"I'm sorry, I didn't recognize you, April—you were so much

younger when I saw you before."

"Oh, that's okay," April said, evidently interested in Paul, although he was not in her. At that moment Charlotte Blankenship turned around and found herself facing Paul and Priscilla. She was with April and could not avoid an introduction. "Have you met Paul Strickland, Charlotte?"

"Yes, I have," Charlotte said coolly. "Hello again, Mr. Strickland." Paul nodded, still confused at her attitude.

"And this is his sister, Priscilla."

"His sister?" Charlotte said, confusion showing on her face as she looked at Priscilla. "I thought your name was Avery."

"That's my mother's maiden name. I'm Priscilla Strickland."

"So Paul is your brother, not your...boyfriend?"

"No, why would you think such a thing, Charlotte?" Priscilla said.

"Oh, wait right here, I've got to get Herbert," Charlotte said and she walked away.

"Well, that's a good reason not to wait here," Priscilla said, and she smiled and headed towards Esther, who was a long way across the room.

Herbert was talking to a friend of his when Charlotte walked up to him. She waited for a long time, but when he did not conclude his conversation, she finally interrupted him. "Herbert, I need to talk to you—now."

"Charlotte, can't it wait? Wayne and I are talking."

"It can't wait; I promise you it can't wait!" Charlotte said, seeming upset. Herbert looked at her and winced, and then he looked back at his friend and rolled his eyes. "Must be important—we will talk later."

Charlotte took him by the arm and moved him away so others could not hear. "Priscilla is here," she said.

"Yes, I saw her here with Strickland when they walked in. She definitely hit the jackpot with him—I can't compete with that."

"You don't have to, because Paul is her brother, not her boyfriend. She is Priscilla Strickland."

"What—how could that be?"

"I don't understand it, but when I mentioned her name was Avery she said that it was her mother's maiden name. So she must have been using that when she went to work for you."

"Well, why would she do that? But if Paul's her brother, that's why she hugged him and that's why she stayed at their mansion all night."

"Exactly—I told you she wasn't that kind of girl."

"Oh, Charlotte, this is great news. I've tried so hard to get her out of my mind, and nothing has worked. Now this changes everything. It's like my dream has been restored. I've been so depressed since it fell apart."

"Yes, Mum and I have noticed."

"Yeah, well, I'm sorry about that. But I need to talk to her. I need to straighten this out. Do you know where she is?"

"She was by a table with hors d'oeuvres, over there," Charlotte said, pointing. Herbert walked quickly in that direction, but when he got there he did not see Priscilla. So he hurried around the room, looking for her and when he spotted her, he walked straight towards her. She had her side to him and did not see him coming so when he walked up to her, she was startled, and then she tried to walk away.

"Wait, Priscilla. I want to talk to you."

"Sure you do, now that you know I'm a Strickland. I assume your sister just told you."

"No, that's not the reason."

"Yes it is. Before I was poor and not good enough for you and your mother, but now I'm a good catch—from a very rich family."

"Please, Priscilla, give me a few minutes," Herbert said, taking her arm.

She pulled away, indignant. "Keep your hands off me! I don't want to talk to you—you're the last man on earth I ever want to talk to," she said, but the emotion of the whole encounter was getting to her, and she started crying and ran away from him. She looked for an empty room and found one and sat down in a chair and tried to compose herself. "He shouldn't have that effect on me," she said to herself, and then she heard footsteps and saw him walk in.

"What are you doing! I told you no. It's no, no, no, I hate you and I never want to see you again."

"Fair enough. But just give me two minutes to speak, and I'll leave the party afterwards if you don't want to talk to me anymore so you won't have to see me. Just two minutes. Please, Priscilla."

Priscilla was embarrassed that she was crying and was trying to stop. Fighting back the tears, she swallowed hard. "Okay, two minutes, and keep your word."

"I thought everything was going wonderfully between us, but

then I saw the limousine pick you up. Paul got out and you hugged each other and he twirled you around, and my heart sank. I was so angry, thinking you had another man all along. So I followed the car to the Strickland mansion. I saw the chauffeur stop in front of the house and you went together. I sat in my car in your driveway until four in the morning, but you still never came out. So what was I supposed to think?"

"You mean your opinion of me was so low that you thought I would do something like that?"

"What was I supposed to think?"

"Is that why you told me you only wanted a business relationship? Saying that was very cruel, by the way."

"It is the only reason. You broke my heart that night."

"You could have told me."

"What was I supposed to say? 'I know you're a fallen woman and I want nothing to do with you?' I didn't know what to say."

"So instead you had lunch with Roxanne? I saw you meet her in the restaurant."

"Priscilla, I met her to tell her we would never be more than friends. Remember, I gave you my word I would tell her."

As they were speaking, Mr. Strickland, who was looking for Priscilla, heard her voice and was about to walk in, but then decided he should not interrupt them. He stood outside the door, waiting for them to finish.

"I still think you could have told me the truth, instead of just brushing me off."

"Well, look who's talking. You could have told me the truth instead of deceiving me. You could have said you were a Strickland and not lied and said your father was a handyman."

"I didn't say that—I only said he did a variety of things—you said he was a handyman, and I didn't correct you."

Still listening, Mr. Strickland smiled and whispered, "A handyman," to himself, chuckling. Then Amanda Parker showed up again. She smiled and looked sweetly at him. "You know, you are the most attractive older man here," she said, touching his arm as she spoke. Mr. Strickland was not certain what she wanted, but he moved away from the door so Priscilla and Herbert would not notice him.

"Why, thank you for the compliment," he said.

"Can I get you some punch, or hors d'oeuvres, or anything at all?"

"No thank you, Miss Parker. I promised to get back to Mr. Collier and his wife and they are waiting for me."

"Maybe I'll see you later then?"

"Yes, perhaps," Mr. Strickland said, and then he went to find the Colliers.

The conversation was beginning to get heated between Herbert and Priscilla. "And why in the world didn't you tell me who you really were, anyway? Why were you masquerading around as someone you weren't—what was the point?" Herbert asked.

"I was trying…trying to make certain that if I met a man, that he loved me for me and not for my money. But what about your mother? She didn't want you marrying some poor girl, did she?"

"She thought you were wonderful. She said you were, quote, a rare jewel. She was so disappointed when I stopped seeing you. And my sister liked you so much that she even hounded me about it until I told her the reason, and then she said that she couldn't believe it—that it must be some kind of mistake because she knew you were not that kind of girl. But I couldn't see how it could be—especially when I thought you stayed there all night."

"Yes, you said that already," Priscilla said.

"So we've cleared up this misunderstanding; now can we just start over?"

Priscilla sniffled a little and dabbed her eyes with a handkerchief and looked at him. "Okay, how do we do that?"

"Well, let's pick up where we left off. You can come back to work for me and we can get to know each other better and…"

Priscilla stood up, and her anger showed clearly in her eyes.

"You're asking me to come to work for you?"

"Well, I thought that was what you wanted."

"No, Mr. Blankenship—I'll never work for you again. Don't forget I'm a Strickland, and that means that you work for me. So those pumps better be perfect or we will find a new supplier and put your little business into a tailspin!"

"But Priscilla…" Herbert said.

"You have had your two minutes, sir. Now keep your word!" Priscilla said, and she stormed out of the room.

As she left, Charlotte saw her walk by and noticed how upset she looked, but Priscilla did not see Charlotte. Charlotte walked in the room they were in and saw her brother sitting there, looking unhappy.

"What's wrong—did you ask her?"

Herbert looked up slowly. "Yes, I asked her but she's pulling rank on me now."

"Pulling rank…what does that mean?"

"It means I asked her to come back to work for me, and she told me that I worked for her!"

"You mean you didn't ask her to marry you?"

"Well, I thought it was a little too soon for that."

"Oh, you did, did you? Herbert, you idiot! Of course she got angry at you. She wants to be your wife, not your employee. You just insulted her again."

"Well, maybe you're right."

"I know I'm right. Go and find her and apologize."

"I can't do that. I gave her my word that I would only talk to her for two minutes and that I'd leave the gala after that. So I need to keep my promise."

"Okay, but I'm staying." Charlotte walked back into the ballroom and saw Paul Strickland talking to several other people. He noticed her as she got nearer and smiled at her, and she made a point to give him a big smile back. Paul excused himself from the conversation and walked over to her.

"So are you still allergic to the Strickland name?"

"No, no, not at all. I apologize for the way I acted."

"So what is your name?"

"I'm Charlotte Blankenship, Herbert's sister. Your sister, Priscilla, worked for him for a while."

"Yes, I recall the name now."

"Well, let me explain why I avoided you at first, and what just happened between Priscilla and Herbert. Can we sit down somewhere?"

"Of course—let's find a quiet room," Paul suggested.

Priscilla walked past her father, and he stopped her, but she was not looking directly at him. "Mr. Collier is waiting to meet you—you know, about your idea that their mills could fill orders for ours and vice versa, so we could save the shipping expenses." Priscilla looked up and he could see that her eyes were red from crying and that she was upset. "Okay, I see—it's that young man. I'll tell Mr. Collier we'll meet another day."

"Thank you, Father. I'm going home now—I'll just take a cab," Priscilla said, as she hurried out of the gala.

49

The next day was Sunday, and the Stricklands normally had a large meal in the afternoon instead of in the evening on that day. After church, the girls were in Esther's room, talking.

"We already talked about this last night. I'm finished with him," Priscilla said. "He's a lout."

"But he must care about you—he wouldn't have tried to explain everything if he didn't," Esther said. "There's still a chance there, I think."

"No chance as far as I am concerned. I'd never work for him in a million years."

"Prissy, maybe he was getting around to asking you, but he was shy," Anna suggested.

"Herbert, shy? He's a lot of things but he's definitely not shy. He is exasperating and irritating, but not shy."

"Well, just don't write him off yet," Esther suggested.

"What else can I do? I think he just wants me back at his company because I helped him make it more profitable."

"It must be more than that," Anna said.

"Well, I need to cool down a little about the way he treated me," Priscilla said.

The door was open to the bedroom, and Paul stopped in front of it and they ceased talking and looked up at him. "I hope nobody minds, but I've invited a couple of guests for Sunday dinner," he said.

"Oh, that's nice—who are they?" Esther asked.

"People from the gala last night."

"Okay, thanks for letting us know—now we'll wear something nice for dinner."

About an hour later, the family was gathered in the dining

room when the doorbell rang, and Mr. Standish walked towards it, but Paul ran out in front of him. "I think I'd better answer this one—no announcements are needed," he said. He opened the door and greeted the guests, and they walked into the dining room with him.

Priscilla looked shocked as they walked in with Paul, because the guests were Charlotte and Herbert. She gave Paul a disdainful look, and she wanted to leave the room, but it would have been discourteous, so she stayed. Mr. Strickland had not entered the dining room yet, but the rest of the family was there. "I'll wait for Father for introductions," Paul said, and just as he finished speaking, his father walked in.

"Father, this is Charlotte Blankenship, and Herbert Blankenship."

"Nice to meet both of you. I think I've heard a bit about you, Mr. Blankenship."

"Yes, I'm afraid that you have," Herbert said.

"Well, I mean your products have fewer defects than our previous suppliers."

"Thank you, sir, we do try."

"Well, you know Priscilla, and this is Esther and Anna," Paul continued.

"I'm sure you've heard a bit about me, also," Herbert said.

"Oh yes, we have," Esther said, but Anna only smiled.

"Well, my sister was coming, so I thought I'd tag along."

"We are so glad you did, Mr. Blankenship," Mr. Strickland said. Then he turned to Mr. Standish. "Please serve the salad now."

There was awkward silence as the kitchen help came in and served the salad and offered condiments and poured glasses of lemonade. "So how is your business doing now, Mr. Blankenship?" Mr. Strickland asked, trying to break the silence.

"Quite well, sir. Thanks mostly to your company. I've got Priscilla to thank for that." He looked over at her, but she breathed huffily and turned her face away.

"It is good to see you again, Charlotte," Priscilla said, with an emphasis on "you ". Did you and Paul meet at the gala for the first time?"

"Yes, we had an interesting encounter," Paul said.

They began eating their salads and everyone was quiet again for a while, then Herbert dropped something on the floor. "Oh, I think I've lost a cufflink," he said, and he got down on his knees under the table to look for it. Priscilla looked over at him wondering what he was doing, and suddenly he appeared by her chair. "Now while I'm on my knees, I have a proposal to make," Herbert said to Priscilla.

"Herbert," she said. "What in the world are you doing?"

"I am asking you, Priscilla, to marry me."

After a stunned pause, Priscilla found her voice and spoke. "Herbert, my whole family is here and this is embarrassing."

"Priscilla, I want to tell the whole world that I want you to be my wife! You don't have to work for me—you can run my company if you want to, or you can work for your father, or you can stay home and have children. Anything you want, but I love you. I have loved you from the very beginning—I loved the way you looked when I first met you and I pulled the heel of your shoe out. I loved you for who you are right after you came to work for me. I've wanted to marry you since that time. I have never loved any other woman—you are the first and only one. And I bought this for you. I'm sorry, Priscilla, but it's the big, flashy diamond that you said you didn't need, but I wanted you to have it." He then opened the box and handed it to her. She looked at it and let out a little gasp, and a tear fell from her eye. Then she looked down at him, her expression switching to one of wonderment to that of being slightly annoyed.

"Oh, do get up, Herbert."

"Not until I get your answer. And by the way, think of how embarrassing it will be for me if you turn me down in front of your whole family and my sister! Priscilla Strickland...now, I have the name right, don't I? Will you marry me?"

"Herbert, you are at times exasperating, incorrigible, mercurial, comical, difficult to get along with, and also wonderful, and yes, I will marry you."

Herbert got up and smiled at her and kissed her on the cheek, and the family applauded. Herbert then turned to Mr. Strickland. "Can we have the talk some time, sir?"

"Yes, of course. I look forward to it," Mr. Strickland said.

The Blankenships had gone home, and the girls were in the living room with Paul.

"Okay, dear brother," Priscilla said, "did you put him up to this?"

"Not exactly. I wanted everyone to meet Charlotte, and she suggested that we bring Herbert, because she knew he messed it up when he spoke to you at the gala. Priscilla, she really likes you and looks up to you. She's very excited about getting to know you and Esther and Anna."

"And what about you—do you think she might want to get to know you, too?" Priscilla asked sardonically.

"Maybe a little bit," Paul said, smiling.

"She's a sweet girl, Paul. I think you're on the right track."

"Well, I certainly didn't think I'd meet anyone this quickly. But we're still getting to know each other. Anyway, she asked me if I thought you still wanted to marry Herbert."

"And what did you say?"

"I said, I didn't know, but if Herbert wanted to know, he should ask you. But I thought he'd talk to you privately."

"Well, Herbert has his own way of doing things," Priscilla said.

"He's so funny—I almost started laughing when he said, 'do I have the name right?'" Anna said.

"Yeah, I almost slapped him over that one."

"I think he's just right for you, Priscilla, and he's also got a most pleasing English accent," Esther said. "I'm very happy for you, Sister."

"So am I," Anna said. "Perhaps we can have a double wedding—that would be lots of fun. Or maybe a triple—isn't David supposed to call you, Esther?"

"He already did, and we're meeting Monday," Esther said unenthusiastically.

"You don't sound too happy about it," Priscilla said. "I thought his grandmother made it clear he didn't break up with you over money."

"But he did break up with me over money—that's the problem. It just wasn't over my money—it was over his, or his lack of it. At least that is what his grandmother said. I'll know more when we meet. But I don't know if I want to marry someone who is too proud to marry me because he is poor—or thinks that I care so much about money."

"Esther, you need to look at the whole man, not just the flaws. You don't get everything with anyone, but there are so many good things about him. Herbert has lots of problems, but I love him anyway—maybe even for his flaws also."

"In his mind, he may have been thinking only of you when he broke it off—he didn't want you to be embarrassed because of his financial problems," Paul said.

"Well, I didn't care at all about his money, and I thought I made that clear to him many times," Esther said.

"Give him a chance to explain himself—maybe you'll understand him better then," Anna said. "Miles wouldn't even ask me to marry him, and if I hadn't seen that poem, I don't know what would have happened."

"Okay, okay. I will speak to him with an open mind."

"We just want you to be happy, and David's always been so nice. We may even make it a triple," Priscilla said.

"Now, Prissy, don't get carried away," Esther said.

50

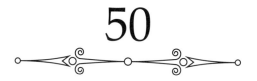

The next day Esther met David at a café in Manhattan. He was smiling when she saw him at the table, and when she sat down, he took her hand.

"The first thing I need to say is that I'm sorry," David said. "I was going through so much turmoil when Father said he'd lost all our money, that I...well, I guess I lost sight of what you meant to me."

"David, I told you I didn't even want the house—I never cared about that type of thing."

"I know, but I did."

"So you never got the letter saying that we were bankrupt?"

"No, what letter? I never got anything in the mail."

"It wasn't in the mail. It was dropped off at the athletic club."

"Then that's why I didn't get it. I had to quit because I couldn't afford the dues anymore. But who would have sent a letter like that and how would you know about it?"

"Priscilla sent it."

"Priscilla—why would she do something like that? She knew you weren't in financial trouble."

"Well, I'd rather not go into it."

"Okay, but I still want to marry you, and I won't change my mind if you will still have me."

"David, what if you lost your money again?"

"That won't happen. I know this business inside and out. If Father had never gambled it all on the stock market we would still be in excellent shape. In fact, five-and-dimes sell more in tough times—it's the department stores that lose. And before I do anything, I ask myself many hypothetical questions about what can happen, and I'm very confident that it will be a success."

"Okay, David—then consider this hypothetical question. If you lost everything tomorrow, would you still want to marry me, or would you feel the same way you did when you called it off last time? The answer is important to me."

"Esther, I would never back out again. I know now that it was foolish of me to back out the first time. But I was depressed and confused, and I didn't have my priorities right. Now I do."

"Are you sure? Because this money thing can be like a disease. It becomes more important than anything else in a person's life and then it drives every decision they make. I've seen it with my friends—especially the richest ones. They have so much, but then all they want is more and more and it makes no sense at all. They live just to show they have a bigger house or car than someone else, and they become so phony that you can't find a real person anymore—there is just a shell of a person."

"Yes, I know exactly what you mean, but I've been broken of that. Someone wanted me to fail so I could see it."

"Someone wanted you to fail? Who could that be?"

"My grandmother. She said she prayed for me to be delivered from the disease of covetousness and greed. She used the same word you did—disease."

"You never told me that."

"I just found out myself. She held money back for me just for this time. Her faith is very strong, but her ways may be a bit peculiar."

"Look, David. I know you don't think it can happen, but if for some reason you did lose your investment, and we had to live on my money, could you accept that?"

"I couldn't before, but I can now. Esther, I want you more than I care about business or money or anything else. Your love is more important to me than all the money in the world, and I mean that with all my heart. My father was about to commit suicide because he lost everything, and when that happened I realized our priorities were all wrong. He'd made it so important that when he lost it, he lost everything, and I promised myself then and there that I would never let money and success control me. As hard as it's been, I'm glad I went through what I did, because it's got me thinking the right way now."

"That's all I wanted to hear, David. I will marry you. But I have to tell you the truth about that letter. I don't want to keep any secret from you."

"Okay—you mean the one from Priscilla?"

"Yes. She sent it to test you. You started acting funny about money and she thought we should send it to see if you would still want to marry me. But it coincided with your financial loss. And then when the press reported that we were okay, you came back, but I thought it was because you were after my money. I'm sorry I thought wrongly of you, but I have to tell you the truth."

David looked at her for a long time. "It's okay, I understand. Anyway, maybe it's good that we both have to forgive each other— makes me feel a little better about things. It's a little too hard when you're perfect."

"I'm far from that."

"Not to me. You're imperfectly perfect for me," he said and squeezed her hand.

"As you are for me," Esther said.

51

"So we've gone from three broken hearts to three marriages, is that it?" Mr. Strickland asked as they sat in the living room.

"Yes, Father—that's it."

"Hmm…I wonder if I can get some wholesale prices on the weddings. What about you, Paul? Are you getting ready to tie the knot also?"

"No sir. I'm just getting to know Charlotte. It's much too early for that. And she's a lot younger than me, so I'm not sure how that will work out."

"Is she twenty years old?"

"No, she's twenty-one."

"And you're twenty-eight. That's only seven years. As you get older it won't seem like so much. You said you wouldn't get married until you got your PhD, and now you have it, so maybe it's time."

"Father, don't rush me."

"Okay, I won't, but she is a very lovely girl." Mr. Strickland looked up as Mr. Standish came in and served them. He poured tea into Mr. Strickland's cup, and Mr. Strickland looked up. "This is either very weak coffee or it's tea."

"It's tea, sir," Mr. Standish said.

"I asked for it, Father," Priscilla said. "Herbert always drinks it – you know his mother is English, so I'm getting used to it. Mr. Standish, do we have any coffee brewed?"

"No, the tea is fine—it's actually better. Coffee has too much caffeine. Thank you, Mr. Standish," Mr. Strickland said.

Mr. Standish left and Mr. Strickland took a sip of his tea, and then looked around the room at his children. "I just don't know what I'll do when everyone moves out of this house."

"We'll still visit, Father," Esther said.

"Do you know the Parker girl, Esther? Wasn't she a friend of yours?" Mr. Strickland asked.

"Not a friend—but I know her."

"It was the strangest thing—at the gala almost every time I turned around she was there. I wonder if she wants a job?"

"No father, she definitely does not want a job—she wants something else," Priscilla said.

"Oh, do you know her also?"

"About as well as Esther. And we both know she wants to get married very soon to someone with a lot of money."

"Well, she was in the right place then—all the up-and-coming wealthy young men were there."

"But she wasn't interested in any of them," Esther said.

"She was interested in you," Priscilla said.

"In me? What do you mean?"

"I mean she was interested in you as a husband," Priscilla said.

"Oh, that can't be. She must be half my age. Are you teasing me?"

"No, Father, she's not," Esther said. "Amanda is a little tart that has dollar signs in her eyes, and she wants to marry the richest man she can find. And the word is out that you and Betty are no longer an item."

"The word is out? Are there people monitoring me?"

"Oh yes, that's why so many widows and divorcees were talking to you—didn't you notice?"

"Well, yes, I did notice that—I know many of them are looking to remarry. But that girl is so young. What is the world coming to? She comes from a respectable family—would she just sell herself to an older man?"

"As a matter of fact, yes," Priscilla said. "And her family lost almost everything in the crash."

"Well, it sounds like there are many women hunting rich men."

"I think more than you realize."

"Well, I'm waking up—believe me, I am. But it makes me wonder if I'll ever know if someone wants me or my money. I understand more now why you went incognito."

"Father, I'm not saying you are not attractive—I hope I did not insult you."

"Not at all—think no more of it. But I do think that we ought to cancel the trip to France. I set it up because I thought you all needed a change of scenery, but I'm thinking that you would rather be here for your fiancés—isn't that right?"

"Well, we've talked about this, Father, and we'd like you to agree to what we are going to propose," Esther said.

"You want me to agree before I've heard it?"

"Okay, maybe that's not fair. But here it is. We still want to go to Europe, but we want you to go with us."

"Me…no, I couldn't do that. I need to be here."

"Paul said he would stay and handle things, and you have enough management in place for almost any problem that might arise," Priscilla said.

"I know I'm still learning, but if there is anything major I will wire you right away," Paul offered.

"But then you couldn't go," Mr. Strickland said.

"Father, I never really wanted to go. I've traveled abroad so much I'd like to just stay home and rest."

"And be around Charlotte, perhaps?" Mr. Strickland said, smiling.

"That did cross my mind," Paul said.

"And we are paying for the trip—it will be our present to you for all you've done for us. Now, I know it really is your money, but—" Priscilla said.

"But you need to get away—and we want to treat you," Esther interrupted.

"Well, I could go to Lyon and visit our factory there, if we went to France."

"No, you absolutely cannot. No business—this has to be a real vacation. No ticker tape, no business calls. We're paying for it, so you must do what we say," Esther said.

"Oh, I don't know…" Mr. Strickland said.

"It will be the one trip we take with just you before the weddings. Please say you'll go. We really want the time with you, and you need to get away—especially after going through all you have with Betty Ingersoll."

"Did you know she came up to me at the gala?"

"No, what did she say?" Priscilla asked.

"She wanted to know if I would give her another chance. Evidently Chandler swindled her out of some money. She said she knew she had treated me terribly and that she still loved me."

"I agree about the way she treated you," Anna said.

"So what did you tell her?" Esther asked.

"I said no. I've already played the fool once, and I don't want to go for a second time."

"Oh, Father, it must hurt," Esther said, and she walked over to his chair and put her arm around him.

"I think what hurts the most is that I was somehow blind to her scheming. Did all of you see what she was like? Come on, answer me."

"Yes, but it didn't seem our place to say anything, although we thought about it," Priscilla said.

"Then you must promise to tell me if you see this happening again. I knew she was a little artificial, and I doubt I would have married her. But it's so humbling that she was able to string me along like she did."

"Father, after what happened to me, I understand completely," Anna said.

"It's interesting how even with age and experience we can be susceptible to such things," Mr. Strickland said, shaking his head slowly. After a moment of reflection he turned his attention back to the girls. "Now, are you absolutely certain that you want to leave your beaus to go on a vacation with your old man?"

"Yes, I want you to go so much," Anna said.

"We want you to go with us," Esther said.

"Yes, we are looking forward to it. And we'll put you up in the finest hotels," Pricilla said.

"I certainly do hope so—but can you get reservations at palace of Versailles?" Mr. Strickland said jokingly. "Okay, I agree. We'll go on a carefree trip to Europe and I'll forget all my worries. But right now I need to go into the study and do some work." He got up and walked out of the room and the girls smiled at each other and at Paul.

"I think this will be his first real vacation," Esther said.

"Priscilla, you need to get me up to speed on the operations before you go," Paul said.

"We'll start tomorrow," Priscilla said.

"By the way, did you say that this whole identity switch thing happened because Alice Jamison said that Roger told her he only married her for her money?"

"Yes, that's exactly what she said. And he's never even said he's sorry. But she's getting by now," Esther said.

"You know I went to high school with Roger and we were pretty good friends. So could you invite him and Alice over tomorrow for dinner?"

"Yes, I'd like that, but what have you got in mind?"

"I'm not sure yet. I have to rummage through some old letters in the attic first. But I would like to see him—both of them. You girls can chat, and then maybe Roger and I can talk—I haven't seen him for years."

The next day, the Jamisons came over, and Paul and his sisters greeted them together as Mr. Standish ushered them into the living room.

"Paul, it's great to see you again," Roger said as he shook hands with him, but Paul moved closer and gave him a quick hug as well.

"Great to see you also, and your ever-beautiful wife. How are you, Alice?" Paul asked.

"I'm fine," Alice said, with reticence in her voice, as they walked into the sitting room. After sitting and chatting for a while, they went into the dining room and ate, and later they came back to the living room. As they walked in, Paul spoke loud enough for everyone to hear.

"If everyone would have a seat, I have a little surprise," Paul said, and he picked up a photo album that also had some letters in it. "I thought we could have a little fun reminiscing about the past. Here's a picture of Roger and me in eighth grade. I'm the handsome one," Paul joked, as he showed the picture around. "And here is one of us in high school, and another on a fishing trip."

"Oh, I remember that one. We were so embarrassed that we caught nothing that we went to the fish store and bought some there," Roger said.

"Yes, and Mother raved about what a great fisherman I was after that. But I got so guilty that I had to confess to her. I thought she'd be mad, but she laughed it off," Paul said. "And here is one in Dad's 1917 Lincoln L—I think it was the first V8 produced. I had just learned to drive."

"Oh, I remember that. My parents didn't want me to ride with you, but they finally let me."

"And then we got it stuck in the mud—remember how narrow those old wheels were? I drove right into that mud puddle and it sunk down so fast. That's when we had to get the horses to pull us out," Paul said.

"Oh, yeah, it was Mr. Johnson who did it, and then he lectured us about how automobiles would never replace horses, and this was one reason why."

"You think he still thinks that?" Paul said.

"I don't know, we ought to ask him, he still lives on Seminole Drive, but I have noticed that he has a couple cars now," Roger said, laughing.

Paul was quiet for a while, as he shuffled through the letters, then he looked up and spoke. "Now when I was at Harvard, Roger was at Yale, and he wanted to date Alice, but he was afraid to ask her. He wrote me a few letters during the year. Here is one of them: 'Dear Paul, I'll be home in June, and I'm trying to get up enough nerve to ask Alice out on a date. I just can't get her out of my mind, but I don't think she even knows who I am. Well, I mean she knows who I am, but I don't think she even thinks about me that way. It would be a dream to go out with her, so if you see her, put in a good word for me, okay? I think I fell in love with her in the twelfth grade, but she was younger and was seeing that football player, so I knew I didn't have a chance while he was around.'"

Alice turned her head towards Roger and appeared to be studying his face. He finally looked back at her, and her mouth opened and she began to say something, but then she decided not to. Paul picked up another letter.

"'Dear Paul, I am trying to get through finals, but I find myself daydreaming about Alice. Do you think that is what you do when you love someone? I know your sisters know her—maybe they could invite her over and I could be there too. That way I could sort of find out if she likes me at all. There are many girls here, but no one like her. Someone fixed me up on a date with a girl they thought I'd like, and she was very pretty, but she was so stuck-up. All I could think about was how sweet Alice is. Write and tell me if you can arrange it, okay?'"

"I remember when you asked me about that," Esther said.

"Paul, this is getting kind of personal," Roger protested, but Paul ignored him.

"Here is one after they met and he went back to college in September. 'Dear Paul, I think Alice may actually like me. Thanks for arranging that at your house. I hope your sisters didn't figure it out. Alice and I talked a lot, but I wasn't sure if she'd go out with me, and I don't want to get turned down, so I'm waiting. She's the only girl I've ever felt this way about....'"

"Paul, please—I didn't think you would read these letters in front of everyone," Roger said.

Alice looked at Esther and then at Paul. She hesitated, but then she spoke. "Well, I'm very pleased you read them, Paul. It's very kind of you to go to the trouble of finding them," and her face showed real joy for the first time since she had come into the house.

"Well, we will leave you to a little girl talk. Roger and I are going out in the garden for a while," Paul said. "Come on, Roger." Paul got up and Roger followed him, and when Paul closed the door, Roger spoke angrily. "What do you mean by reading those letters in front of everyone? I thought you were my friend."

"I am your friend and that's why I read them. My sisters told me that Alice came over here sad and sobbing some time ago because you told her that you only married her for her money."

Roger thought for a moment. "I never told her that—I don't think I told her that."

"Oh, you told her all right. She didn't make a mistake about that."

"Well, I might have. But you know what my family is like—you've heard them. They're always arguing and they say the worst things they can to each other when they're mad. But they don't really mean it. So I still do that, but I'm trying to stop. It wasn't a big deal."

"Roger, there are some things you can say to a person that don't go away. Some things stay and fester and destroy a relationship, even if you didn't mean it, and this was one of them."

"And so Alice is still upset about something I said—about marrying her for her money or something?"

"Yes, Genius—you've figured it out. She thinks you never loved her—that you only married her because she was rich. You and I know that isn't true but that's what she believes and it's ruining her life and your marriage. And it hasn't helped that your family lost so much in the crash."

"Yes, but we were rich when I married her—that came later, so it's not logical."

"It doesn't matter, you still said what you did and you've wounded her deeply."

"She has seemed depressed a lot lately, but she always says there's nothing wrong when I ask her."

"Don't you know her well enough by now to know she won't confront you with it? But that's why I read those letters—to help your marriage. So now, when you tell her how sorry you are that you said such a terrible thing to her, she will believe you, and forgive you—and you had better tell her."

Roger was quiet for a long time, and then he held out his hand to Paul and they shook, and this time Roger hugged him. "All this time what I said has been causing her this terrible pain, and I never realized it. Okay, I'll apologize as soon as we get home. You're a real friend, Paul. Not many people would have gone to this much trouble."

They walked back in, and Alice was laughing and giggling with Paul's sisters as they looked at other old photo albums.

"Honey, I think we have to get home," Roger said, smiling at his wife.

"Yes, it is getting late," Alice said, and they said their good-byes and the Stricklands walked the Jamisons to the door. As soon as Alice and Roger were out, Esther walked over to Paul. "Paul, that was great—that was exactly what she needed. When you walked out with Roger, she was so happy because it was clear to her that the letters proved that he really loved her."

"Well, I wasn't sure I could find them, and there were an awful lot of letters to go through, but God helped me."

"Oh, that was just wonderful," Priscilla said, and Anna nodded in agreement.

"There's more. Roger didn't even remember that he'd said that to her, but after we talked, he realized the damage he'd done, and he's probably apologizing right now. I knew he didn't marry her for her money, but the letters didn't come into my mind until last week."

"I'm so glad they did," Esther said.

52

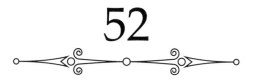

The Stricklands were enjoying their second day in Paris after spending seven days on the ocean voyage. They were finishing lunch in a cozy French restaurant on the Rue de Rivoli, and Priscilla looked up from her plate after eating her last bite. "Any more of this rich French food and Herbert might change his mind again when I get home," Priscilla said.

"Don't worry; you'll burn it all up walking through the Louvre. We've got about fifteen acres to cover," Esther said. "When I lived here for that year as a student, I only saw a little of it."

"Well, let's start at Cour Napoleon, and then go to Cour Carrée," Priscilla suggested, looking at a map. "Is that okay with you, Father?"

"Anything is fine, I'm just along for the ride," Mr. Strickland said.

"Is there something wrong, Father? You seem unhappy," Esther asked.

"No, everything is fine. Let's get a move on."

"You know there will be someone besides Betty," Priscilla said.

"There may not be, but that is something I have to accept," Mr. Strickland said.

As they walked across the Rue de Rivoli towards one of the entrances to the Louvre, Priscilla took Esther aside so their father could not hear. "When we get back, let's make a list of all the women we know and do a little matchmaking for Father."

"I've already tried to think of someone, but most of the wealthy ones are snobby society ladies that even I don't like," Esther said.

"Yes, I know. And the problem is the same for him as it was for us, but worse—he's too well known."

"Well, God made a way for us, let's keep believing He'll provide for Father," Esther said.

"That doesn't mean we can't help a little."

"You're right—let's brainstorm when we get home."

Mr. Strickland and Anna were ahead of them, and they looked back at the sisters. "Come on, girls," Mr. Strickland said. "We have a lot to see today."

Esther giggled as they walked briskly to catch up. "Just like Father—he even makes touring a museum like work."

"Let's go slow today, Father—a relaxing pace for a change?" Priscilla said.

"You're right—I'll slow down," Mr. Strickland said as the girls caught up. "We'll never see it all, anyway."

After reaching Napoleon Square and touring the exhibits, they walked out of the main building and were about to descend on the stairs that led to the road in front of it when Priscilla looked around and did not see Esther. "Where's Esther?" she asked.

Anna looked around. "I don't see her. She was quite taken with the antiquities' exhibit—I'll bet she's still there. Let's go back."

Priscilla turned to her father. "We'll find her. Why don't you wait here in case she shows up."

"Okay," Mr. Strickland said. The girls walked back into the museum, and he noticed an intricately sculpted lion at the bottom of the stairs. As he began to walk towards it, a very attractive woman of about forty years of age began to walk down the stairs at the same time. Someone had spilled some liquid on one of the stairs, and when her foot touched it, she slipped, and her purse went flying through the air and landed on the stairs and most of the contents fell out of it. Mr. Strickland caught her before she fell, and she looked up at him, startled.

"Merci, Monsieur," she said, trying to catch her breath.

"Vous etes...les beinvenus," Mr. Strickland said with hesitant French. "Oh, my French is so bad," he said under his breath, and he noticed how attractive the woman was and how kind her eyes seemed. She had light brown hair and light brown eyes, and high cheekbones which made her look like a model.

"Oh, you're an American," she said, in a charming Southern accent. "You seemed to come out of nowhere!"

"Are you all right?" he asked.

"Yes, but everything fell out of my purse."

"Let me get it for you," he said, and he helped her sit down on the stair and then rushed over and picked up her purse and began putting things back into it. One of the items was a small New Testament, which had fallen on one of the steps. It was open and he noticed that some of the passages were underlined as he put it back into her purse. Then he brought it back and handed it to her. "It looks like you are using that book quite a bit," he commented.

"Oh, yes. I'm a Sunday school teacher and I've got lessons to prepare for when I get back to South Carolina. Are you familiar with it?"

"Yes, I read it every day."

She smiled when he said that, and she began to stand up but was still a little shaky, and as he steadied her for a moment they looked into each other's eyes. "You are certainly a kind gentleman, sir," she said. As she finished talking, a couple walked out of the building and saw them together.

"Oh, there you are, Ann. We've got the taxi waiting," the man said.

"Looks like your husband has found you," Mr. Strickland said.

"No, that's my brother-in-law—my husband died from cancer a few years ago."

"I'm sorry to hear that—it's very difficult to go through—my wife also died from cancer."

She looked at him sweetly and hesitated before she spoke. "Then you do know what it's like—I'm sorry for your loss also," she said.

By that time her sister and brother-in-law had reached her. "Are you all right?" her sister asked.

"Yes—I almost fell on the stairs," she said, pointing to where the liquid was, "but this considerate gentleman grabbed my arm just in time."

"Well, we must run—the taxi will be leaving if we don't—it's waiting outside the other entrance," the man said.

"Yes, I must have walked to the wrong one," Ann said. She smiled at Mr. Strickland, and it was clear that she wanted to talk to him some more, but her brother-in-law took her arm, and she turned away and walked back into the building. The Strickland daughters were at the top of the stairs, and they had been watching. They walked down towards their father.

"What was that about?" Priscilla asked.

"That woman almost fell on the stairs, but I was able to catch her," Mr. Strickland said.

"She was quite beautiful," Anna said.

"Yes, she was…she definitely was. I'll be back in a minute." Mr. Strickland turned and walked back up the stairs and then looked for the other entrance, but he could not find it at first. When he finally did, the taxi had left and all he could see was the back of it driving down the road. A look of disappointment came over his face, and he turned around, and Esther was there. "I missed my chance—I should have asked who she was—they called her Ann but I don't know her last name."

"Let's go to the next exhibit, Father."

"Okay, I'm coming," Mr. Strickland said, with a last mournful glance towards the stairs of the second entrance. "I guess some things are not meant to be."

Mr. Strickland was slightly morose the rest of the day, and the next morning they all met for breakfast in the hotel restaurant. They were finishing their food when Esther spoke.

"I'd like to go to the Sully wing today if everyone agrees," Esther said.

"What is there?" Anna asked.

"It's the medieval part of the Louvre and there are the remains of a moat that was part of the original fortress that was there. I remember it from when I lived here, and I think everyone will like it."

"That sounds like fun," Anna said.

"Yes, it does," Priscilla said. "What do you think, Father?"

"I think I'll stay at the hotel today," Mr. Strickland said. "I'm a little tired."

"Oh, Father, you've been moping around ever since you saw that woman. Is that what's bothering you?" Priscilla asked.

Mr. Strickland didn't answer but looked down at his plate.

"Are you taking the fifth amendment?" Priscilla asked.

"Okay, that's true. I just don't know why I didn't get her name and…but things happened so fast. Oh, I'm going on like a teenager. It probably would have turned out to be nothing—I mean I only talked to her for a few minutes."

"Maybe you'll see her again," Anna said.

"I don't think the odds of that happening are very good," Mr. Strickland said glumly.

Esther coupled her hands on the table. "Let's pray—God, if

you want Father to meet that woman again, please arrange it, in Jesus' name, amen."

"Amen," everyone said.

"But you can't expect to find her if you stay in your hotel room, and you need to get your mind off it," Priscilla said.

"Okay, let's go," Mr. Strickland said.

53

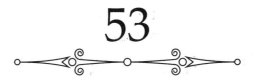

After spending the morning touring the medieval art and architectural remnants, they walked back towards the hotel, which was across the street. They were almost in the front door when Priscilla looked down an alley where there were many street vendors selling various items. She saw a satin royal blue dress and stopped for a moment. Everyone kept walking until they realized that she had stopped, and then they looked back at her. "Time for lunch," Esther said.

"You go ahead, I want to look at a dress," Priscilla said.

"I'll look too," Esther said, but Mr. Strickland looked a little chagrined, because he did not like shopping.

"Okay, we're coming too," Mr. Strickland said, and he and Anna joined them as they followed Priscilla to the open marketplace, where people were hawking their wares. When some of them discerned that they were Americans, they shouted in broken English to get them to buy their merchandise. Priscilla held up the dress to her body and looked in an old partially broken mirror that the vendor had propped up against a table.

"Esther, my French isn't as good as yours. Please ask this man if there is a place I can try this on."

"Priscilla—we are all getting hungry. Can we do this after lunch?" Anna asked, noticing that her father was fidgeting a little.

Priscilla was so interested in the dress that she apparently didn't hear Anna. The man led Priscilla to a tent that was about two feet square, and she walked in and secured the flap. A few minutes later she walked out with the dress on.

"That is really stunning," Anna said.

"Yes, it does look nice, but it needs to be taken in here and here," Esther noted, pointing to the waist and back areas. But I'm sure they have a tailor who can do it."

Esther asked in French about the price, and then told Priscilla. Esther assumed she would pay it, but Priscilla bargained with the man, and they went around and around until she was finally satisfied. Then she turned to Esther. "Now ask him where the tailor is, and how much that will cost—my French is good enough with money and numbers, but I can't remember the word for tailor."

Esther asked the man, and he told her that the tailor would not be back until the afternoon. In the meantime, Anna found a leather purse she liked, and Esther asked the price. Anna was about to pay it when Priscilla got involved and bargained the man down and got it for less.

Anna touched Priscilla's shoulder and spoke to her so her father could not hear. "Is it okay if I go with Father to the hotel, and we'll save you and Esther a seat in case you finish your shopping before we finish eating? You know how Father hates shopping, and this vacation is for him."

"Oh, you're right, of course. I've been selfish. We'll go now. I've got to return anyway for the tailor, so we'll come back after lunch," Priscilla said as her father approached.

"Well, the way they serve lunch around here, it will be hours before we finish anyway. They seem to make it an event or something," Anna said.

"Yes, to the French, food is very important, and they like to take their time with every meal and stretch it out," Esther explained. "Many of the men even love to cook and trade recipes."

"Well, I wish they were more interested in enforcing the Treaty of Versailles. The Germans never even downsized their army in 1920, which was part of the agreement, and they've kept breaking the treaty ever since. I'm beginning to think that the War to End All Wars will be repeated if they don't do something," Mr. Strickland commented.

"Oh, Father, it's a vacation. Let's think of happy things," Esther said.

"Yes, you're right, I'm sorry."

After lunch they walked back to the marketplace to get the alterations. The man selling the dress whistled, and a woman who was a tailor came over, and Priscilla tried it on again. This time Mr. Strickland bought an iced lemonade drink at a nearby stand and found a shady table to sit at, where he could still see his daughters. He had just begun to drink it when Anna hurriedly walked over to his table with an excited look on her face.

"I saw her…I think. The woman, you said her name was Ann? I think she is way over there," she said, pointing down the marketplace alley hundreds of feet in the distance. Mr. Strickland looked intently in that direction.

"Yes, I think that is her," Mr. Strickland said. "You wait here and I'll be back." He then started walking quickly in that direction and then started running. Esther and Priscilla watched in amazement as he passed by, and then they walked over to Anna.

"Did I see what I think I saw? I haven't seen Father move that fast even in a tennis match."

"Didn't he say something about acting like a teenager?" Esther asked, laughing.

"Well, it's good to see him excited about something besides business. Oh, it looks like he's catching up to her, and now he stopped running and is walking."

"Yes, I see—wants to play hard-to-get, I would assume," Priscilla said.

As Mr. Strickland caught up to Ann, he slowed down and walked past her slowly, then turned around as if he were surprised. "Well, hello again!" he said, a little out of breath but trying to hide it. Ann was standing by herself as her sister and brother-in-law were busy looking at some small clocks on a vendor's table.

"Oh, it's nice to see you again," Ann said. "You were so kind the other day…Mr…?"

"I'm Mr…ah…Mr. Strict," Joseph said.

"Well, I hope that's not as foreboding as it sounds," Ann said, smiling.

"No, not at all. I'm actually quite amiable."

"That's nice. I'm Mrs. Pennington."

"So what part of South Carolina do you live in?"

"Charleston. And yourself?"

"I'm from New York."

"But you don't sound like a New Yorker—you don't have the accent."

"No, I never picked that up, but you have a delightful southern accent."

"Oh, you like it—some Easterners think it sounds ignorant."

"I think it sounds melodious—even mellifluous."

"Well, that's nice of you to say, Mr. Strict," Ann said, smiling again.

Ann's sister looked over at her and then walked over to them. "So this is your knight in shining armor," she said. "Ann was hoping she would see you again." Ann made a little face at her, not wanting her to let on how much she had wanted to see Joseph.

"Yes, what a coincidence this is," Joseph said.

"This is my sister, Mrs. Paisley, and her husband…" Ann waited for him to walk up before introducing him. "Mr. Paisley, this is Mr. Strict."

"What a pleasure it is to meet both of you," Joseph said, shaking their hands.

"Yes, thank you so much for helping my sister-in-law yesterday," Mr. Paisley said.

"Oh, Ann, don't you think this is just the most beautiful little clock?" Jane asked, and she pointed to one on the table next to them. "And it's so cheap!"

"Yes, that is quite nice," Ann said, and then she turned back to Joseph.

"I love to shop like this," Ann said. "Do you enjoy it, Mr. Strict?"

"Oh, ah yes, I do," Joseph said, immediately feeling like a hypocrite, but the words were out of his mouth before he knew it. "Well, sometimes I like to shop," he added, trying to ameliorate his lie.

"My husband didn't like it at all. He could last about thirty minutes and then he became a bear. But he was so good about almost everything else."

"How long ago did he die?"

"It's only been a couple of years, and I still miss him so much. But one must get on with one's life and be productive. I've gone back to teaching school now, and I'm enjoying it."

"What subject do you teach?"

"English. I taught before we were married, and I stopped when we had children. But they are grown now. And what do you do, Mr. Strict?"

"Well, a little bit of everything—a variety of things."

"I understand. When the economy is bad, a person has to do everything they can to make a living. I am very blessed that my husband paid off the house before he died. I'm also glad I'm a teacher. I don't make a lot, but my job is safe."

"Yes, I think that would be a very secure profession."

"I would normally not have taken a trip this expensive, but my husband had some life insurance, and when my sister asked, I knew I probably would not get another chance. What about you—do you find it expensive?"

"Well, it would be, but my daughters are paying for it. They are all getting married when we get back, and they chipped in together to take me with them."

"Oh, how wonderful they must be to give you such a gift."

"Yes, it's very nice of them."

"Well, we don't have a lot to spend, but we shop the bargains—there are many here, I think, because of the Depression."

"Yes, but it's actually not as bad as the U.S. Our industrial output is down forty-six percent, but theirs is only down twenty-four percent," Joseph said, and then wished he hadn't spoken as Ann looked at him curiously for a moment.

"Really? Well, we have found some very reasonable restaurants where the food is good, but you have to get on the side streets to save money. And we found a very inexpensive hotel—but it's not the cleanest place."

Joseph looked back and saw his daughters walking towards him. Alarmed, he realized that his real last name might be discovered. "Mrs. Pennington, we like to be informal, so may I ask that you just use my first name, Joe, if that's all right with you?"

"Of course, Joe. And you can call me Ann. Are those your daughters coming now?" she asked.

"Yes—I'll be back in a moment," he said, and he walked back and met with them.

"Hello, Father, it looks like things are going swimmingly," Anna said.

"She looks like the cat's meow to me," Priscilla said.

While Joseph was talking to them, Jane took Ann aside. "That is one very distinguished looking man—he has a special presence, I think," Jane whispered to her sister. "I can see why you are interested in him."

"I never said I was," Ann said to her sister with a little protest in her voice.

"You didn't have to. I can tell by the way you look at him. Now, you haven't dated since Robert died, and you're not getting any younger. It's time to live again."

Meanwhile, Priscilla was talking to her father. "But, Father, we insist—we want to meet her." They began walking towards Ann, forcing their father to follow.

"Yes, remember you said you wanted our approval," Esther reminded him, with a slightly ironic tone in her voice.

"Okay, you've got me," Joseph said, and he walked faster to get in front of them. Soon they reached Ann.

"This is Ann Pennington," Joseph said, as they walked up. "Ann, these are my daughters, Esther, Priscilla, and Anna."

They all smiled at Ann, then Esther spoke. "It's a pleasure for us to meet you, Mrs. Pennington."

"Oh, just call me Ann. Joe said to be informal. What a delightful family you have, Joe."

"Are you staying in France long?" Priscilla asked.

"About four more days," Ann said, and then she realized that her sister and husband had moved ahead down the road. "Oh, I think I have to go, now." Jane and her husband waved to her when they saw her with Joseph and his daughters.

"I'll walk with you," Joseph said, and when Ann wasn't looking, he motioned for his daughters not to follow.

"Father, we will be in the market here—there's still more shopping to do," Anna said before he left them.

Joseph walked with Ann, trying to figure out how to get her contact information without seeming too forward. "I was hoping we could see each other again before you leave."

"That would be nice," Ann said.

"And you mentioned restaurants, so I wonder if you would join me for dinner tonight. Perhaps we can go to one of your discoveries," Joseph said, but he was concerned that she was going to turn him down, so he added, "And your sister and brother-in-law are also invited if you like."

"I will talk to them about that, but I would like to," Ann said. "Would you call me at the hotel about five o'clock and we can discuss it further? It's the Hotel Paul Henri, room 27."

"Okay then, I will get back to my daughters," Joseph said. "I can't tell you how nice this day has been with the blessing of meeting you again."

"I feel the same way, Joe," Ann said, and they both hesitated, but then pulled away, and Joseph walked back and rejoined his daughters.

"She is a very sweet woman, Father," Anna said. "I like her a lot—she's the opposite of Betty Ingersoll."

"Yes, there is something about her—something very attractive and I don't just mean her looks. But why did she call you Joe? You've never allowed anyone to call you that before," Priscilla asked.

Mr. Strickland looked around, then answered. "I guess she prefers the shortened version—and it's okay with me."

Ann caught up with her sister, and they stopped at another vendor selling jewelry. Jane moved away from her husband so he couldn't hear what they said. "So what happened?"

"Nothing, he just asked me to dinner tonight."

"Oh, I'm so excited for you."

"He also invited both of you, so we can all go together."

"No, we can't."

"Why not?"

"Because we're busy, so you'll have to go by yourself."

"But I hardly know the man."

"Dear sister, do you think he's dangerous?"

"Of course not."

"Then I don't think you need a chaperone. Anyway, Henry and I have something to do by ourselves—we need some time alone, you know."

"Okay, if you put it that way, I guess I'll have to go alone," Ann said, pouting a little.

"Oh, it won't be so bad. This is Paris, the city of love, and this just may be the man for you."

"Oh, you're so presumptuous, Jane. Would you quit trying to marry me off?"

"Ann, dear, you haven't even had dinner with a man since Robert died. And you've had plenty of offers, so there must be something special about this one."

"I don't know what it is about him—but he just seems exceptionally honorable."

54

"Would you like to order for us?" Joseph asked, as they sat together in the restaurant. "My French is poor, but yours is good."

Ann laughed. "It only sounds good to you. To a French person it sounds atrocious, I think."

"That's why I prefer not to try—they seem to laugh at me when I do."

"Well, the last laugh may be on them, because English is quickly replacing French as the international language. I also hear that the schools will be teaching Spanish more than French in the future."

"That makes sense to me—the Spanish-speaking countries are closer to us."

"So, are your daughters going to marry well? Is that how they were able to offer you this gift?"

"As a matter of fact, their fiancés are fairly well off."

"I'm sure many men would be attracted to them—they are all so sweet and pretty. But you never really told me what you do. You said you do a variety of things. So what does that mean?"

"Well, I ah…one of my daughters insinuated that I was a handyman."

"What? You seem very businesslike—much more like a senator or something."

"No, I'm not in politics."

"I understand. This Depression has caused a lot of people to have to work at jobs that they are overqualified for."

The food was served and they began to eat. "What kind of fish is this?" Joseph asked.

"It's sole. Is it all right?"

"It's very good, but the sauce is a little rich," Joseph said.

"Well, everyone always says French food is so wonderful, but I think they tend to use too much butter."

"It's not a problem for me—I just scrape it off. I'm okay with most French dishes except escargot."

"Oh, I know what you mean. My sister likes them, but I just can't get used to eating snails," Ann said.

"I think my gardeners—I mean U.S. gardeners—work hard to get rid of them. Perhaps they could send them to France for a new source of income."

"Ah, see? I said you seemed businesslike."

The sisters were sitting in Esther's lavish hotel room, which was similar to their own, but each had different color schemes. Esther's sitting room adjoined her bedroom, and it was decorated in a subtle pastel orange and cream motif, with twelve-foot windows which extended from the floor to the ceiling, from which there was an excellent view of the Seine River. The furniture had the same colors, and the couches were of modern art deco design. "We've finished dinner and he's still not home. I wonder what they're doing," Anna said.

"Probably just taking their time. The shops are all open late, and there is also the theater," Priscilla said.

"Father would never go to the theater here—it's generally bawdy in Paris," Esther said.

"Yes, I guess you're right," Priscilla said.

"He used to take us everywhere with him after Mother died—he was trying to make up for her being gone. And now being on this last trip with him, I'm realizing how much my life is going to change when I leave home. I'll only see him now and then, and both of you will be gone, too." Anna looked at her sisters and paused for a moment. "When I think about getting married and living somewhere else, it seems unreal to me."

"I know. I'll miss so many things about our home," Esther said.

"Yes, I feel the same way, and I doubt Herbert will want me to keep working for Father—but Father will have Paul now, and I'm so glad he decided to work in the business. It's nice how God worked that out—His perfect timing," Priscilla said.

"But I do hope Father gets married again, because I don't know what he'll do with thirty thousand square feet of house and only the butler and maids and cooks to keep him company. And I don't think Paul will want to stay at home at his age," Anna added.

"I don't think Paul really cares about those things, and he and Father get along very well," Priscilla said.

"That is, if he's not soon married to Charlotte," Esther said.

"Yes, they do seem like a good match," Priscilla said.

"Father hasn't said anything, but I think he will miss us a great deal," Anna said.

"Well, if I can convince David to move into one of the guest houses, I'll be close enough to look in on him," Esther said.

Joseph and Ann strolled down the Champs Elysees looking at the shops and chatting. "I really should be getting back—Jane has a full schedule for us tomorrow," Ann said.

"Will you be going to the Louvre again, or somewhere else?" Joseph asked.

"The Louvre."

"Let's get a cab and we'll go to your hotel," Joseph said.

"I can ride by myself—it would be cheaper that way," Ann said.

"No, I won't hear of it, I'll accompany you," Joseph said.

"Well, I still want to pay my share of the dinner. There is no reason for you to pay for everything; I told you I have money from the life insurance."

"Ann, you are so considerate—it's so refreshing to meet a woman like you. But I can afford to buy dinner for us. Please trust me on this." A cab stopped and they got in, and were soon at the hotel. Joseph asked the cab to wait, and Joseph walked out with her and into the lobby.

Ann looked at him for a moment. "I've had a wonderful time— it passed so quickly I can hardly believe I'm already going back to the hotel."

"Well, at the risk of being too forward, can we have dinner again tomorrow night? You only have a few more days here."

"Yes, I would like that. There's another restaurant I'd like to try, and it's less expensive."

"Even less expensive? Well, anywhere you would like to go would be fine—as long as I can be with you, I'm happy," Joseph said, and his tone became so earnest that she smiled at him, and they were both silent for a while. "I'll come to your hotel at the same time, if that's okay."

"Yes, that would be splendid."

At breakfast the next morning, the sisters were peppering their father with questions about his dinner with Ann. "So you said she is a school-teacher—an English teacher, is that right?" Esther asked.

"Yes, she taught when she was younger and then stopped when she had children, but now they are grown and she's teaching again."

"What did you do all that time?" Anna asked.

"We ate dinner and strolled down the Champs Elyseés and just took in the sights."

"Oh, that is so romantic, Father—in Paris, on one of the most famous boulevards," Anna said.

"Well, don't you think it's time for her to meet the family?" Priscilla asked, but her father was silent.

"Remember, you don't want another Betty," Esther added.

"Okay, enough of that. Let us be alone for a few more days and then I'll have her over to the hotel for dinner and you can give her the third degree. Now I wish I'd never said that about asking your opinions, because it's definitely coming back to haunt me."

"Well, I think I have already made up my mind about her—but I'd like to meet her and talk to her, since you are spending time together," Esther said.

The next evening, Joseph and Ann took a cab to the restaurant she wanted to try. As they entered, there was so much cigarette smoke that Ann started coughing. "I think we'd better try another place," Joseph said.

"Yes, you're right. There is no outside area to eat here, and I can't take all this smoke." They walked out and Ann took a deep breath. "Oh, I can breathe again!" she said, as they stopped for a moment on the sidewalk.

"It's a balmy night, so let's just walk down the boulevard and see if there are other restaurants," Joseph suggested.

"Yes, that's a good idea," Ann said, and they started walking.

"So what did you see today?"

"Well, we looked at many different artists, and I wanted to see a Monet or a Renoir because I like the impressionists. But they don't have any paintings by them. I wonder why?" Ann said.

"Well, Renoir died in 1919 and Monet died in 1926, so I think it's too early for them to be in the Louvre, and with money tight, it may be a while. But we have the same taste, because Monet is my favorite."

"So we have that in common. I think Monet and Renoir knew each other," Ann said.

"Yes, he studied with Renoir, Alfred Sisley, and Frederic Bazille in Paris under Charles Gleyre. They replicated the natural light when they painted outside—en plein air, as they called it."

"What else do you know about him?" Ann asked.

"Well, Monet's father wanted him to go into the family grocery business, but he declined. His mother was a singer, and he learned how to paint en plein air under Eugene Boudin. His wife, Camille Doncieux, was the model for Woman in the Green Dress and Woman in the Garden, which are two of his most famous paintings. But she died having her second child at the age of thirty-two of tuberculosis. Monet had a collection of botany books and he designed precise garden layouts of specific plants which he used for models in his garden paintings. His weeping willow tree paintings were a homage to the fallen French soldiers of the War to End all Wars...."

"Joe—that's all I can process for now," Ann said, interrupting but also smiling.

"Oh, okay. Sorry, I didn't mean to go on."

"You sound more like an art encyclopedia than a handyman," Ann said suspiciously.

"Well, I studied art a little bit," Joseph said, a little defensively.

"Yes, so it would seem."

"Oh, this looks like a nice place," Joseph said, and they stopped in front of a large, ornate restaurant that also had an outdoor area.

"It looks expensive."

"Well, let's take a look—they have the menu next to the door."

"These prices are sky-high," Ann said as she read the menu.

"It's okay, I'd like to splurge tonight."

"But it's three times what you spent last night, and I don't want your daughters to think you're spending all your hard-earned money on me. I don't want them to think that I would take advantage of you."

"I promise you they won't think that."

Ann thought for a moment and took a deep breath. "Okay, we'll eat here, if it makes you happy, Joe."

"It does—very much."

"I guess he won't be in until later again," Anna said, as she sat with her siblings at the hotel restaurant.

"He's probably having a wonderful time. I'm so glad he met her," Esther said.

"But we brought him to spend time with us," Anna complained.

"Oh, Anna, I think we brought him to meet Ann and we didn't even know it. Do you know she tried to pay for her own dinner last night?"

"No, did Father tell you that?" Anna asked.

"Yes, it came out, and then he acted as if he wished he hadn't said it. I'm not certain why."

"Well, he certainly is keeping us away from her, and I don't know why," Priscilla said.

"Would you want your kids around if you were him and you were trying to court a woman? Of course he doesn't want us with him," Esther said.

"I agree with Priscilla—he wasn't that way with Betty. I just wonder if there is some other reason," Anna said.

55

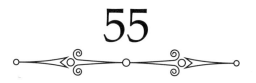

"That was a wonderful dinner, Joe," Ann said.

"Yes, I think it was worth every penny. And now it's time for dessert."

"No, I need a little walk before I can eat anymore. Look, my hotel is near, and we bought some croissants and some chocolate truffles today, so let's have those."

"Okay, if you're sure. There's a chocolate mousse that sounds very good," Joseph said, looking at the menu.

"Yes, and it costs more here than two dinners cost at most restaurants," Ann said.

Joseph paid the bill and they began walking again. "It's another wonderful night," Ann said, smiling at Joseph, as they approached a bridge on the Seine River.

"You mean the weather?" Joseph asked.

"No, that's not what I mean," Ann said, still smiling at him, and he took her hand and they held hands as they walked. They passed several young couples on their stroll. "I'm starting to feel like one of them again," Ann said.

"Yes, I have the same feeling, and I'm not looking forward to you leaving so soon. So I need to ask you now—can I see you when you go back to the U.S.?"

"Yes, Joe, you can see me. And I wanted to tell you that we have a small guest house on our property—you see we have five acres just outside of the city. My daughter used to stay there but she has recently married and she moved. So, if you want to, I'm inviting you to visit. The guest house is small but it's cozy, and it will save you a hotel bill."

"Ann…I'd love to visit, and I can't tell you what the last few days have meant to me—I'm afraid to because we've known each other such a short time."

"You don't have to say any more, Mr. Strict, because I feel the same way."

"Can I tell you, then, that I think I am falling in love with you?" Joseph said.

Ann was not certain how to respond, but they had reached the hotel, so she changed the subject.

"Well, here we are," she said. "Let's sit in the outdoor café and order some coffee and I'll go up to my room and get the desserts."

Ann returned and they sat together enjoying the evening. Then Joseph looked at his pocket watch, which he'd been careful to hide, because it was so expensive. "I need to get back, Ann. Can we do this again tomorrow night?"

"Yes, but not at a restaurant that costs so much, please."

"Okay, I'm going to visit the restroom and leave."

"But you have to pay if you use it down here," Ann said.

"That's okay."

"No, there's no reason. You can use the one in my room—at least we don't have to walk down the hall in this hotel."

"Are you sure? I don't want to defame you."

"I'm not worried about that, Joe. Come on up."

"Okay," Joseph said, and he walked up the stairs to her room and used the bathroom there, but while he was in it, his hotel key fell out of his pocket. After saying good-bye, he left and took a cab back to his own hotel. When he could not find the key, he went to the front desk and asked them for another one.

Early the next morning, Ann got out of bed and went into the bathroom to take a bath. As she put a towel next to the tub, she saw the key lying on the floor and picked it up. "Oh, I better get this back to him," she said to herself. After bathing and dressing she got a cab and asked the driver to take her to the Hotel Le Meurice, which was the name on the key. When the car pulled up to a magnificent building she looked at it, perplexed. "Is this the Hotel Le Meurice?" she asked in French.

"Yes, the finest five-star hotel in Paris," the driver said.

She got out of the cab and walked into the hotel and up to the front desk. One of the clerks came up to her. "May I help you?" he asked in French.

"Do you have a Mr. Strict staying in room ninety-four?" she

asked.

He looked at the register for a moment. "Well, we have a famous guest there, Joseph J. Strickland. That's the presidential suite."

Ann looked bewildered for a moment. "Does he have his family with him—that would be Esther and Anna and…I think Priscilla?"

"Yes, they have adjacent suites—would you like me to call them?"

Ann looked away from the clerk for a moment, trying to figure out what was happening. Finally she answered him. "Yes, please call Esther and tell her that Ann Pennington is here."

The clerk called and soon Esther and her sisters came down together and greeted Ann. "We were wondering if we would ever see you—Father has kept you away so much," Anna said.

"Well, we've enjoyed our time together, but can I come up to your room and talk for a moment?" Ann asked.

They took the elevator up to the top floor and then they all walked into Esther's room. "Please have a seat, Ann, and I will tell Father that you are here. He's in his room," Esther said.

"Can you wait just a minute before you do that? I'd like to talk to you about something first," Ann asked.

"Why, of course, please have a seat."

"What is your father's name?"

"Joseph J. Strickland," Esther said, surprised at the question.

"You mean the Joseph J. Strickland, the multimillionaire?"

"Yes, of course."

"So his name isn't Joe Strict?"

The girls looked at each other, smiling and beginning to realize what had happened. "No, that's not his name," Esther said.

"Well, I need to ask you a few more questions," Ann said.

Mr. Strickland answered the phone, and Esther told him that they were ready to go sight-seeing. He finished dressing and went to her door and knocked. She opened it quickly, and when he saw Ann, his mouth fell open and he tried to talk, but found himself momentarily speechless. However, his daughters weren't.

"Oh, what a tangled web we weave," Anna said.

"When first we practice," Priscilla said.

"To deceive," Esther said.

Joseph frowned for a moment, but Ann smiled at him and so he began to smile also. "I'm guilty—I'm sorry, Ann. I wasn't truthful and I apologize."

"It's all right—your daughters told me the whole story, so I know the reason. And although it was still wrong, at least I understand why you did it."

He walked over and sat down by her. "Does this mean we can eat dinner at a nice restaurant without you offering to pay?" Joseph asked.

"Yes, Joseph, I think it does," Ann said.